# The Winged Witch of Matches

## PART 1 OF 5

*Do enjoy!*
*Adrea Elizabeth.*
*315 323 0922.*

ADREA ELIZABETH

Copyright © 2025 Adrea Elizabeth
All rights reserved
First Edition

Fulton Books
Meadville, PA

Published by Fulton Books 2025

This is a work of fiction. All of the characters, names, businesses, events, and incidents/situations bear zero resemblance to an actual living and/or dead person, and any such cause is purely coincidental.

ISBN 979-8-89675-246-2 (paperback)
ISBN 979-8-89675-247-9 (digital)

Printed in the United States of America

# Book Reviews

*The Winged Witch of Matches* is a spellbinding fantasy novel that takes readers on a thrilling journey through a world of super and omnipotent beings. The book's intriguing premise of realm jumping adds a unique and exciting dimension to the story, as characters find themselves bound to different worlds, facing challenges and adventures they may or may not have chosen. At the heart of the story is Claura, a young woman born from one of the most powerful witches in existence. As she grapples with the weight of her lineage and the responsibilities it brings, she also finds herself dealing with personal struggles and matters of the heart. The author artfully weaves a complex tapestry of relationships, where love and desire intertwine with blurred lines, making it difficult for Claura to discern her true path. One of the novel's strengths lies in the development of its characters. Each member of this fantastical world comes alive with unique traits, emotions, and motivations. Claura's journey of self-discovery and growth is deeply relatable, making her a compelling protagonist to follow. The dynamics of the romantic relationships in the book add depth and complexity to the plot. Two men vying for one woman might seem like a typical scenario, but the author deftly defies expectations by introducing unexpected twists and turns, creating a love triangle that keeps readers on the edge of their seats. Highly recommended.

*The Winged Witch of Matches* continues the spellbinding journey of Claura, the powerful witch, in a new realm full of secrets and hidden motives. This installment picks up where the prior plot left off, offering readers a seamless transition into a fresh and intriguing narrative. In this next part, Claura finds herself in a realm she can't quite remember but feels a deep connection to. The author skillfully weaves a web of mystery, making readers eager to uncover the truth alongside the protagonist. The exploration of Claura's powers and her intuition adds an exciting element of discovery to the story as she navigates an inner battle influenced by her enigmatic past. As the plot unfolds, readers are kept on their toes, wondering who Claura can trust and who will stand by her side in this new realm. The author's well-crafted character dynamics keep the narrative engaging, with each individual playing a crucial role in the unfolding mystery. The author's world-building remains a strong aspect of the series, and in the next chapters, the new realm adds further depth and excitement. The attention to detail in describing the settings allows readers to immerse themselves fully in this fantastical world. The pacing of the novel is well-balanced, with a seamless blend of action, intrigue, and emotional moments. The story takes unexpected turns, maintaining the element of surprise and suspense throughout.

The author's writing style is immersive, and the pace of the narrative is brisk, making it an enthralling read from beginning to end. The Author has described everything so perfectly that the readers can literally imagine every character and every situation inside their heads. It was like watching a movie! One of the strengths of the book is the way it gradually builds tension and suspense throughout the whole story. The language used in the book is easy to understand, making it accessible to everyone. Overall, it was a fantastic read, and one must not miss this book. I highly recommend this book to everyone. This book is true to its genre and will leave you asking for more.

*The Winged Witch of Matches* is a spellbinding journey into a world of magic and powerful beings. The author's skillful storytelling and relatable characters make this book a delightful and enchanting read.

*The Winged Witch of Matches* is a captivating fantasy that explores themes of love and self-discovery. The author's imaginative storytelling and intricate plot make this book an enthralling and engaging adventure.

*The Winged Witch of Matches* is a beautifully written fantasy that captivates with its magical world and complex characters. The novel's exploration of love, fate, and self-discovery makes it a must-read for fans of enchanting and emotional stories.

*The Winged Witch of Matches* is a mesmerizing fantasy that weaves a tapestry of love, destiny, and self-discovery. With its immersive world-building and captivating characters, this book offers a thrilling and emotional reading experience.

## ADREA ELIZABETH

*The Winged Witch of Matches* invites readers into a captivating world filled with super and omnipotent beings, constantly embroiled in a thrilling saga of realm-jumping and entangled relationships. At the heart of this enchanting tale is Claura, born from one of the most powerful witches, who finds herself entangled in a web of love, destiny, and self-discovery. From the very beginning, the author immerses readers in a world of boundless possibilities, where the characters are bound by both choice and fate, weaving an intricate tapestry of emotions and connections. Claura's journey of self-discovery takes center stage as she grapples with her identity and seeks to uncover the truth about her origins. The characters in *The Winged Witch of Matches* are multi-dimensional and relatable, each facing their own trials and tribulations as they grapple with love, duty, and the allure of the unknown. Claura's journey of self-discovery is relatable and empowering, offering a strong and captivating protagonist to root for. In conclusion, *The Winged Witch of Matches* is an epic tale of love, adventure, and self-discovery that captivates from start to finish. The Author's imaginative world-building, skillful character development, and intricately woven plot make this book a must-read for fantasy enthusiasts seeking a thrilling and emotionally satisfying story.

*The Winged Witch of Matches* is a spellbinding fantasy novel that takes readers on a thrilling journey through a world of super and omnipotent beings. The book's intriguing premise of realm jumping adds a unique and exciting dimension to the story, as characters find themselves bound to different worlds, facing challenges and adventures they may or may not have chosen.

*The Winged Witch of Matches* is an epic tale of love, adventure, and self-discovery that captivates from start to finish. The author's imaginative world-building, skillful character development, and intricately woven plot make this book a must-read for fantasy enthusiasts seeking a thrilling and emotionally satisfying story.

The Author crafts a fantastical tale of love and destiny in *The Winged Witch of Matches*. The author's attention to detail and emotionally charged narrative create a compelling and immersive reading experience.

To myself, for coming up with every word and every plot twist all on my little own with zero help nor influence from a single other soul than my own. I did not expect my brain to take off into a whole series, my main goal was two hundred pages just to see if I could do it, with originally zero intention to publish it in any form or place.
Turns out...
I can do it.
And as well...
Am not afraid to publish it.
Everyone should write their own book. Seriously, get to it.

For all the author's stories.
Or use
https://www.amazon.com/stores/author/B0CB4N8652/allbooks

Claura/Adera

A witch's magic is only as strong as her intuition, and her intuition must come from three places.

Her heart.
Her mind.
Her soul.

Do enjoy.

# Chapter 1

# Off to ROMANia

It was her last doctors visit after everything. She couldn't believe that they trusted her to take care of herself again so soon. It just didn't seem like what should be the norm for someone in her situation. She was a grown adult, yes. She had her own job that maybe was going somewhere that would maintain stability, with enough time and effort, yes. Claura loved being a photographer, and the city gave her more work than she ever imagined she could have. She never expected to find herself feeling like a victim out of nowhere in a life that had been going so good for so long. She was stuck, and not a midlife crisis stuck. She feared her feet were in the deep mud for good kind of stuck—heartbroken, cold, relentless mud. The sound of the only voice she wanted to hear these days broke through her thoughts. There was just something about her doctor, his unique baritone, that added warmth to her entire now-chilly universe. As she came out of the fog, she slowly recalled his last words that she was paying attention to along the lines of depression and pills to help her sleep for a while. Her insides laughed at "awhile," as if now she would ever sleep the same again.

"They say with enough depression, fear goes away," his voice broke through. "And that's where suicide comes from, that lack of fear to do such a thing. The majority of people think that when a person commits suicide, they don't feel, and they are wrong. That's why people who commit suicide can still be crying and be emotional during—they still feel. It's just, the fear is…gone."

Very few people could make Claura feel even just seminormal again after everything that's so recently happened, even people she knew all her life. But her doctor, someone she had only known since just the beginning of her very recent pregnancy, did have an aura about him that just helped. His voice was always so honest and calm despite the slight intensity underneath his every word. Whether other people recognized that in his voice or not, she couldn't say. His caring eyes would make it easy to assume one imagined the undertone. But she liked it. It was another appealing thing about the man's company. Just being taken seriously was a comfort, and with him being a doctor, she secretly hoped she wasn't seeing him just for that, as all of them were supposed to be taking their patients seriously. His voice suddenly brought her back to reality—her ever-changing reality. Her main reason for her present illness and even being in his company in the first place.

"Claura, your postpartum is still going to be very real, and after what you've been through, possibly tenfold."

"Don't sugarcoat it, please."

"I won't." No humor. He was very serious, almost worrisome.

At his tone, a slight shiver went down her spine. She could have sworn a light growl emancipated from those two small words, making her reaction to look up at him seem in slow motion. The patience on his face when their eyes did collide helped her ease a little bit, and she couldn't help but have an instinct that he was doing it on purpose for her so she wouldn't feel threatened by his undertone. Despite how much of a bite to his words when he spoke facts, his eyes held a 180 almost too smoothly. He read her, read through her quite easily, and

Claura couldn't tell if it was due to his job to be so intuitive with people or if he was just that way with her.

"My dear, I expect to hear from you. In cases like yours, I prefer to keep an extra eye. I can have a female therapist provided for you immediately if you prefer. Either way, you need to reach out to me or someone close to me on my staff." His voice was so serious yet soft. In a way, a part of her was getting tired of him being so both ways and confusing to her a little, but just something about his voice…

"Claura?" He snapped his fingers in front of her. "Back to earth?" He watches her do a slight jolt in response, followed by a deep sigh.

"I would like to be anywhere but here. I feel like I don't even want to be a part of the human race anymore. I just feel so done. Depression speaking or not, I don't care."

"Good. Keep going." He clearly had patients like this before in his field, knowing any communication was good communication.

"I need you to know…Doctor, that I would never commit suicide. I would love to see…her"—tears started to swell up, her throat starting to clog—"to just know she's fine wherever the next…I don't know…realm is. That's all I'd be willing to do suicide for. See that she's okay, then come back." Staring at her open palms, seeing the salty tears land. Wondering why, with how she was feeling on the inside, there could be only four of those small clear puddles on her slim fingers on the outside. "Look at me. I can't even really get a good cry in. This whole thing makes me feel like I can't even help myself, no matter what you or I do or say."

"You're doing just fine right now, saying this."

"My throat feels like I've been screaming for days, and I haven't even started." She looked like she was about to break down but was too tired to do so. He thought for a long moment, really taking into consideration whether he should say what was truly lingering in his mind—only to decide that he would feel he would regret it, for some unknown reason, if he didn't. He decided to go with his gut.

"I have a recommendation for you," he finally said sternly, seeing her face of "here we go" as she glanced his way before looking around the room once again.

"I need time before I even see a therapist. I need some privacy. I don't want—"

"No therapist. I don't know how you are doing it, but you are already ten steps ahead of other women I see often in your shoes, which is why I'm hesitating to say this, just in case I am missing something, but I'm going to anyway."

"Nothing is going to harm me any more than what's happened. Your hesitation is actually a little silly."

He smiled, though hardly reaching his eyes. "Traveling."

"Traveling? I don't think even strangers at the airport would want to deal with me right now."

"It's funny how you already knew I was going to mention a place even requiring a plane to get there."

"Just hearing the word 'funny' seems like it's meant for someone completely else right now."

She shrugged off his initial indication of her just already knowing something. She just didn't have the energy to really dig deep right now. It was hard to get over something when you don't even have the stamina in any way, shape, or form to face it all in the first place. He clearly didn't miss a beat from the look in her eyes.

"You will laugh again. You will, Claura. And this place I am offering has plenty of privacy."

There was that serious undertone again.

"I'm curious as to where you think a person like me would belong."

He smiled, almost like a wolf. As if he already innately knew something about her that she didn't know about herself yet. The solidity of his voice in the way he answered her next made her breath catch, as if he was trying to hypnotize her into following his suggestion. "Romania."

"I know nothing about Romania. Really wish you would have mentioned Bali. It was my dream for a long time," she said with a half-smile. The wolf vibe subsided in him, his calmer demeanor appearing at just noticing her trying to smile a little. He clearly enjoyed the sight but was determined still to remain professional. Glancing at her facial features quickly before returning to her eyes.

"Do you know much of Bali?" Leaning forward toward her on his stool as if trying to prove a small point, she still fiddled with her salty semiwet hands on her lap, sitting on the edge of her very familiar exam table.

She actually laughed—just a little. And something in the small sound seemed like music to his ears, just a small part of it.

"Absolutely nothing."

"Exactly. Well...plenty of people speak English over in Romania. It's not so hard to get around, and I already have a spot that will be quiet for you." He started to push himself away from her and slid on his eerily silent stool over to his desk. He began writing quite quickly on a small notepad for someone with such a calm demeanor. She frowned, unsure of the need for speed all of a sudden. Maybe he was determined to get to his next patient.

"You are welcome to stay in this room as long as you need," he stated suddenly as if already knowing her thoughts. She decided to shrug off the coincidence.

"I'm cold. I'm so fucking cold," she said more to herself, knowing full well he would hear all the same. She started rubbing her hands up and down her own arms.

Knowing full well she meant not on just the outside, still, he quickly got up to grab a blanket from one of the cupboards to wrap around her shoulders, enclosing her in it. She rubbed up and down her arms, trying to warm her. He notices her instantly tense up even more, despite all they've been through in the last few months during her pregnancy journey.

"Breathe, Claura. You do that too often. You forget to breathe."

She takes a deep breath, shivering while doing so—more from nerves than temperature. Sensing already, for some strange reason, that it would be a while before she saw him again, she looked up into his face to accept the familiarity he so easily and openly offered. His eyes held such acceptance yet worry. She couldn't help but wonder if this was how a father was supposed to be looking at his daughter during such a time. It would have been nice to have such an experience. One of the nurses knocked on the door, breaking the moment, reminding her of all the times she got dirty looks from some of the female staff here, apparently jealous of the random connection she so obviously had with her doctor. It also confused her as to how they couldn't see that it was strictly platonic, that he simply felt like a family member to her that got lost from her somehow. It was a strange feeling, one she hadn't had time to really focus on, not with everything else that had happened in the past year. Her pregnancy had not been easy. In the third trimester, she was in the hospital just as much as she was out of it. Maybe it was just natural for her to lean toward a person like him after what her actual father did to her.

Claura had finally found her real father after being in foster care since she was pretty much born, only for him to just walk away from her. Literally just turned around and walked away with zero care when she mentioned who she was. Talk about a dent in the old heart. She decided maybe she shouldn't take the paperwork contents to heart anyway, for if he couldn't even have a chat with her, then how could she know he was her true father anyway? Then, only a month later, she found herself pregnant, causing her roommate to move out because she didn't want to live with a baby and refused to replace her spot first. Rent was hard enough, with someone actually helping to pay half of it. And now due to life being a jackass again… her baby.

"I will be out in a minute. Please do not come in," he said almost coldly, as if sensing on some strange level he was going to miss this particular patient while she followed his suggestion to go somewhere else to heal from all this. Knowing from digging a little at her background and some files that if anyone needed this from him, it was her. His voice jolted her from her thoughts, making her kind of blush at how she was just staring into space while looking into his eyes for a few moments, completely on another mental vacation again.

"I'm sorry. I keep doing that. I can't control it." She looked away, embarrassed and like she just needed to sleep for a month.

"Claura, don't ever say sorry to me. Even as common as it is, no mother should have to go through this sort of thing."

"Am I still able to own the 'mother' title?" she said half sarcastically.

"You owned it the minute your body started giving itself to making that baby inside of you. You are still a mother, Claura, and you always will be. Saying sorry just doesn't come close to this kind of loss."

Even through the numbness, she managed to feel something truly genuine from those words. "Thank you, Doctor."

"I know it's not professional, but for some reason, you have my complete permission to call me *anything* but 'doctor,' please."

He made it clear that he was truly tired of people seeing him as such a title rather than a normal person day after day in such a profession, trying to be humorous with her about it. She literally felt embarrassed that she didn't actually learn his full professional name this entire time. After seeing a few doctors before him, she just got tired of jumping from one to the other until they all blended into just the same title for her to see. Even the paperwork became a blur for her, whereas others had probably been taking photos of it all with their phone and categorizing it into little cell phone folders. Lying in the hospital bed so much recently gave her time to focus on just finally downloading a Google app, only for it to seem like a pain to try to learn. She accidentally deleted a few she'd never get back, pretty much giving up after that. She wanted to take a picture of her, but she also wanted the picture to be of her while she was.

He suddenly snaps his fingers before her face again.

"Wow. I really can't stop doing that, can I? Umm…okay, what do you want me to call you?"

"Roman."

"Like from Romania, maybe?" She puts her hands up slightly as if to say *really*, watching him slightly laugh.

"Yes. Fortunately and unfortunately. I am from there, hence having a quiet place for you to stay. Haven't been to my home there in many years now. It almost feels like I've abandoned it."

"Have you?"

"I suppose for certain reasons, yes."

"Reasons?"

He just stilled, as if a statue in deep thought suddenly. The look on his face made her freeze as well. Finally, after a few long moments, he caught himself not being the one breathing for a change and suddenly took a huge deep breath before speaking.

"The plane ticket will be provided. Just let me know when you want to come back, and I'll take care of it then too."

"How spoiled of me as a patient. I can't imagine for your own kids how nice things must be."

She attempted to look amused in her state, knowing she was failing.

"Kid."

He had a frozen look back, again—just as intense. She could tell he was trying to hide it.

"Just one? Well, me too."

Sudden sadness took over the entire room around them—a room too used to such a feeling within its walls from the same situation with other patients. There was a long pause between them. Only Roman was willing to make eye contact, reading her as she was clearly fighting inner demons again.

"Claura, you are young. And you don't really know what your future may hold. Despite how hard it is to feel that way right now, it is true. Your body will heal from this, and in your own way, you will learn to live through it all. I watch it all the time. I don't know how women do it, but they do. Your gender is truly more extraordinary than you give yourselves credit for. It is one of the main reasons why I became a doctor in this particular field."

She knew that just from the way he spoke to her that she could trust him to actually send her off to a safe place in a whole different country, and with the nurses waiting for him to get back to work with other patients right outside, she decided to wrap it up.

"When do I leave?" she asked quickly, suddenly looking ready to just get some fresh air, if anything.

She straightened her spine on the exam table, lightly slapping her thighs with her palms, her face looking ready to just do something—anything—because deep down, she just really needed some time alone.

"Today," he finally remarked after studying her for another moment.

"Wow." She rubbed her temple, looking surprised and now nervous.

"Yes, today before anything else happens to you here. Though you are the obvious one needing comfort after everything, there is just something about you taking advantage of my home in Romania that truly brings me comfort. I can't describe it. I am just happy you are willing to take me up on my offer, to be honest, Claura. It is not a common thing for me to offer to anyone."

"And it's an offer I was never expecting to receive"—she waved her hand toward the staff outside doing their duties—"despite what others may think." There was a slight disgust in her voice. "So thank you."

"Don't worry about what the nurses think. They are not like us."

Clearly, he'd noticed some jealousy in the workplace aimed toward her. And by the look of her alone, it did not surprise him. Claura was gorgeous. Her green eyes were a shade that was unique, like an emerald gem. Her cheeks held the perfect amount of freckles, barely noticeable unless one stood close. Her lips were just the perfect little amount of plump to them. And her figure…

Roman welcomed her voice as the much-needed intrusion to his thoughts with ease.

"Like us?" She couldn't help but think now that there was something he wasn't telling her. Roman looked stuck between a rock and a hard place all of a sudden, clearly trying to think fast of how to cover what he may have just given away.

"Smarter." He decided to keep it simple. Leave it at that.

For once, she was the one not shying away from eye contact as she watched him continue to jot down some notes at his desk. She really wanted to know what he was thinking, but she also didn't want to push someone who was being so kind to her. She kind of felt like she was half dreaming and would wake up soon to realize this trip was just a prank. But she really had no reason not to go. Her roommate had just moved out, and she hadn't been able to find a new one to fill the spot. Her job told her to take some time off after everything anyway, and she didn't have any close friends or family to see these days. She didn't really have anything to lose really.

*Not anymore.*

He did a deep sigh as if knowing her thoughts again and turned to his phone to tap on a few screens. Next, she heard his printer come to life. Roman stood up lazily as if he was tired of hearing the same sound from such a small important machine in his routine and walked over to grab the paper. Turning around to walk back over, he handed it to her. She could tell alone, by the way he was holding the paper, that he needed her to look at him and hear something first before she took it. Seeing a glimpse of the word *flight* and a specific time on it was all she needed to know to make it clear what he was holding out. Suddenly, it kicked in, the enormity of what she agreed to do—leaving everything she knew, her home, her belongings, just all of it, and with how she was feeling, to possibly never return to face any memories that she would much rather live without.

"Claura, look at me," Roman said gently, watching her face take a long time to look up from the papers and into his eyes.

"Hmmm?"

"When you first get there, I need you to go straight to this home and nowhere else first. Understand?"

*Odd request.* She tried her best to hide her frown and continue looking appreciative. "Yes, fine."

"Okay. I'll email you the rest of the information. Flight leaves in four hours. I believe this will be good for you. You need a different environment to heal that's separate from where the initial trauma happens."

"Doctor Psychology 101," she said, trying to smile.

"Yup." He gently smiled back. "I suggest you go do what you need to do, and don't miss your flight."

He gestured to her coat, looking at her like he did not like seeing her go but needed to all the same.

There was no hug and no more words—just an eerie comfort in the air between them as she set the blanket on the exam table, pushed her bottom off it, and reached for her hoodie on the hook by the door. She turned toward the doorknob with a feeling of regret, not knowing why, knowing she could have used a hug, but still knowing he was her professional doctor. Definitely knowing he full-on watched her leave long after the door closed behind her, for some reason, she felt like he could hear her say it under her breath from down the hall still anyway.

"Thank you, Roman."

# Chapter 2

# Drugs for Dreams

Claura couldn't remember the last time she was in an airport. The security was ridiculous. It all felt more annoying than useful. Clearly, it had been a while due to the fact that she seemed to be the only person in the place slightly disturbed over removing both shoes and even some clothing just to get to her gate.

*This is fucking ridiculous.*

As much as she loved dogs, and German shepherd being her favorite breed, she never came across one that was actually intimidating to her until now. As beautiful as the dog was, she felt like a piece of meat in its eyes. She couldn't help but wonder if a dog trained too well was just inhumane in a way. On some level, a dog deserved to still be just a damn dog. And from just those kinds of thoughts, she realized her vision of things has permanently changed drastically. She wasn't the same. Becoming a mom did something to her. Growing a baby and going through a pregnancy, it was just obvious something changed in her own genetic makeup. She couldn't help but wonder if she would have kept changing more and more as time went on with her.

"Stop it! Just fucking stop! Save it for the mystery home," she angrily whispered to herself while surrounded by way too many people.

In his first email, Roman mentioned that the airport might be the main hard thing until she arrived. She wasn't so sure. Maybe even with how great of a man he seemed, he just still didn't get it. Somehow, the stimulus and noise of the airport experience just added to the already noisy, dramatic pain inside of her. And she was truly afraid of this trip not helping at all.

*How embarrassing would that be, having to pretend this great free vacation actually helped, and I'm kind of healed now! Thanks, Mr. Roman!*

Deep down, she didn't want to lie to him, of all people. Yet also deeper down, she knew she wouldn't be able to, for whatever reason. He was just clearly one of those people that easily read you.

She noticed her gate number wasn't as packed as all the previous areas of the airport, the calm after the storm. It was almost relaxing, which surprised her. Checking her watch, thirty minutes until take-off, she decided to be cliché and grabbed an overpriced book and latte at the nearby little bookstore. Even at the Chicago airport, there was a book devoted to Romanian life.

"What the heck is up with this coincidence?" she said to herself in a low voice, trying to keep her small surprise to herself and be successful in avoiding drawing any attention from any other person around her.

She really was not in the mood to communicate with any other human being right now. In a way, she was proud of herself for being able to even be in an airport in the first place—no need to push it further.

She waited for the line to disperse before even bothering to pay. Unsure of whether this mystery home would have any books to her liking, she grabbed a couple more while practicing patience for strangers to just be out of the way already. Having that thought in the middle of an airport, she had to laugh at herself. She let a few minutes pass before walking over to the cashier, seeing her proudly observe her book choice as if from there herself. Claura was glad the lady just smiled and didn't say anything. She wasn't really sure how to even pretend to converse anymore. Every conversation just seemed so fake now after what happened. Her life had taken a full 180, and it wasn't fair. None of it was fair. Roman did mention a book about recovery just for her particular situation. She regretted not taking him seriously about it beforehand. Going on this journey for healing in the first place, it only seemed right to have the correct tools. With a deep sigh, she knew deep down her only therapy right now would be to finally be able to be alone. And for this opportunity, she really didn't think she'd ever get to thank Roman enough. On that thought, she decided to check her email again.

She saw three from Roman titled "Info for Flight," then an unread one, "Info for Rental Car," and lastly, also unread as yet a "Home Info." Oh, how it would be so nice to have a place to really own and call home. A part of her maybe thought this wouldn't be a good idea, that somehow this trip would only be a tease toward something she'd never be able to have and afford on her own.

*This fucking economy. This fucking life.*

Brushing away a runaway tear, her nervous system jolts at the overhead speaker. "Flight 39 will be boarding in ten minutes." It was loud and clear—too loud.

"Here we go."

Boarding the plane wasn't so hard other than the security guard looking like he was trying to hide any recognition when their eyes collided for a brief two seconds on her way to her seat. The takeoff wasn't so bad other than it made her nauseous as if on a roller-coaster ride when before she actually used to look forward to that feeling.

*Maybe my hormones now.*

The eleven-hour flight wasn't so bad. Claura was super relieved to find she was the only one taking a seat in her aisle. Only one of the flight attendants gave her special attention despite there being three of them total, and she was placed close to the bathroom.

*Coincidence there, Mr. Roman?*

She couldn't help but laugh at her reaction to her being on a plane now, as if it was her first time, due to all the updated changes. She was flattered, really not expecting it to be this nice. She really couldn't decipher if this was all from having a nice little doctor connection now or just how updated things are for everyone who travels via air these days. She did an inner shrug and decided not to think too much about it.

Reaching into her only bag, her backpack that sadly did fit everything she felt she really needed, she grabbed one of her medication bottles that started to feel like a new lucky charm. She opened the bottle with sleeping pills and decided on maybe more than one. "Two shouldn't kill me, unfortunately." She made besties with her $25 air pillow purchase, knowing she should have plenty of time to read through his emails later anyway. *I mean the flight is almost twelve damn hours...*

*****

## Eleven and a half hours later...

"Ma'am? Hello?" one of the flight attendants said.

"Is she okay? Her chest is barely moving," said the second flight attendant.

"She's fine! She's been dreaming up a storm," said the third flight attendant.

Claura could hear their voices from a distance. Deep down, she knew she really needed to wake up, but she was struggling. She could feel her body being pulled upright and the warmth of a light being shown in her eyes, suddenly a deeper voice broke in.

"Lady? We have arrived, and if you don't speak soon, the paramedics will have to arrive as well. Can you hear me?"

"Emm...it's...I'm fine...," was all she could manage before opening her eyes. "I'm sorry. I took prescription sleeping pills. I never expected them to work so well. Jesus..."

"Oh, thank God!" the first flight attendant said.

"I was about ready to splash cold water in her face! Jeez!" said the second flight attendant.

"No, you weren't 'cause then I'd have to clean it up!" added the third flight attendant.

Claura's laugh had to remain on the inside, at least until she could find some coffee. She decided to try her voice again, still not quite awake. "Are we really here already, in Romania? 'Cause holy shit."

"Ma'am, we've noticed you have a rental car waiting, but we think it's best if someone drives you to wherever you are staying for tonight, and the rental car company can deliver your wheels to you tomorrow. They have already been informed," said the man.

"You don't understand. I am literally trying to follow doctor's orders here. I don't want any stranger giving me a ride."

He continued, "It's fine. They are from the actual car company, no stranger."

She laughed. "That's cute. Umm…I'm from America."

All of them were literally in sync with "Ohh…"

The male pilot gave a nervous laugh but continued with the suggestion. Claura clearly read from the man's energy that he wasn't going to listen and was just trying to get her off his damn plane so he could continue on with his day—like she could blame him.

"I am going to just grab a coffee and maybe nap right here in the airport, and then I'll just drive. I'll be fine. Thank you."

"Okay then. They do hold any car reservation for only twelve hours normally at this particular airport, just so you know. Please just call security if you have any issues."

"Will do." She gave a lame thumbs-up and grabbed her stuff while standing with wobbly legs, and she walked zigzag to exit the plane.

She could totally hear the first flight attendant comment, "Are we sure she's not drunk?" and couldn't help but quietly laugh as she sauntered by the eerie security guard a second time. She sensed full well that he was watching her with more concern than he should be but decided to put that off as well.

*Just need to get to this mystery home, and I'll be fine.*

Claura strolled through the terminal, searching for any place that looked nonsuspicious for a nap. It was not like it was a strange thing. People waiting for flights slept in the airport often. Inwardly swearing at herself for taking more than one sleeping pill and wishing she could just get on with getting to a place of solitude, she ended up actually finding some random furniture in one terminal corner and made haste before some stranger claimed it. She plugged her phone in, realizing she should respond to Roman's emails out of some semblance of respect. Little did he know she wasn't really trying to avoid him. She thought for a minute, deciding not to go into too much detail to avoid any potential lectures on semioverdosing. Plus, she really didn't want him to think even in the slightest that she did it on purpose because, with his doctor brain, that may be one of his first thoughts exactly.

She decided to respond with a simple "Landed safely. In much need of sleep. Will respond more later."

Well, she wasn't lying—not really. Her heavy eyelids drooped down within seconds as she only needed confirmation. She could feel herself being swept into a dream right away, her subconscious intuition taking hold of her.

*****

Claura could feel his breath on her skin. The smell of him was unlike anything she'd ever experienced before, as if that alone could heighten all the rest of her other senses. With only the full and bright moonlight around them in the dark house, complete silence other than the tension ringing between them, she started to feel like her own nervous breathing was too loud. A whimper escaped her throat, more of exhaustion than fear. She felt as if she wanted to speak but was too intimidated to do so. An impatience to know more of this man before her took over her mind despite his actions seeming questionable at the moment. He gripped her chin with his fingers to study her features gently. She held her in front of him against the cold hallway wall gently. He took his time not to make any sudden movements so as to frighten her further, obviously. Something in her could sense already that he was simply fighting his nature, constantly trying to reel in something within him. In how she knew, she simply did not know.

When she went to speak, the look in his eyes that darted to her own made her stop, made her catch herself. She suddenly realized this person before she was something more than a mere man, unable to stop her thoughts from drifting to the book she found in the airport and that particular story about the Romanian Species of the Night. She couldn't help but wonder if any of it was actually correct simply due to this man's perception style alone. And right now, it was quite clear his only perception was of studying her…late at night.

In the darkness, Claura could tell when he was looking straight into her eyes, but only barely. There was not enough light to make out even a blue versus brown eye color, and for some reason, it seemed really important to her to know. She sensed he wanted to say something as well, but for some reason, she couldn't, as if not allowed by an outside force or simply had to choose his words extra wisely, which, on some level, really bummed her out when anyone in their right mind would be more focused on a lot of fear right now. Instead, she was mainly intrigued. But to care and be scared, you must care for your own safety, you must care about yourself, and she was too depressed to care…after "her." It was like her mind had a mind of its own, and she completely took the chance to grip onto something else to focus on for a change.

He caught the sudden extra weight of sadness around her from her thoughts and looked even deeper into her eyes, searching for an answer. She was surprised the action was even possible as he was already looking into her face so intently. His recognition of her mood was clear on his face.

"Yes, I am sad. I will not discuss why." Her voice was calm, slightly cracking from emotion.

He went as still as stone. The sound of her voice apparently had a shocking effect on him, and she had no idea why. The look in his eyes suddenly became startled, knowing, and territorial; loving yet determined; cold yet understanding; soft yet full of will. She loved the complexity really. It did not set her back. Instead, it forced her brain to focus as if her intuition held the real steering wheel here like a mental breath of fresh air, which shocked her, as her heart would take a while to feel the same…if ever.

She figured she'd try again. She wanted to hear his voice. For some reason, her soul itched for it.

"I need you to say something. Despite you saying a thousand things with your eyes, I need to hear you use words. Please."

To her shock, he did respond, as his aura clearly held some kind of natural authority that Qs were not normally asked of him. The energy between them was insane, and it was the only thing that started to let a little fear creep into the moment…for her anyway.

He cleared his throat. Acted beyond unrushed. Seeming to still enjoy just visually drinking her in. "Dragostea mea…aerul meu… casa mea. Te-am gasit."

Not English, figures. "Umm…" She laughed. "Forgive me for being from Chicago, I have just the one language."

He nodded in soft understanding as if displeased not in the slightest. He gestured to his mouth with his free hand. "Romanian." Then he did a swipe with it as if to say, "That's it."

"I see. If we can't communicate, I really am not sure what to do here." Her knees started to wobble, her body felt extra warm, and her entire aura felt more relaxed than it's ever been recently. All he said was one word, and yet the sound of his voice sent flames through her in areas she didn't even know she had. "Are you doing something to me to make me feel…?"

The bastard smirked—actually smirked. Claura hadn't been around enough men to just simply know better already than to leave that door wide open for him. He silently shook his head no and went straight back to serious mode with those eyes as if he could tell he offended her and did not like himself for it. She felt herself admiring him all over again. She felt herself sensing he was way more than the cliché man…again.

"Name? If you are okay with letting me know."

He smiled, the type of smile that held a deeper meaning than she expected—a meaning as if it was silly she didn't think she had a right to know. "Tronan."

"Tronan."

He sighed, a deep, manly sigh as if feeling pure pleasure and appreciation at his name coming off of her tongue, as if he'd waited so long to hear it. His eyes held a soft kind of passion as if savoring the moment, still so close to her, perceiving her. Reading her. For some strange reason, the dark experience was bringing her comfort when it should have realistically brought fear. He gestured gently, raising eyebrows as if to say, "And you?"

She swallowed hard, falling into the moment too easily in her own way as well, as if having to snap out of it to answer his Q.

"Claura."

The first-name basis seemed good enough for now. It sounded casual, tired, careless—mostly tired. He sensed that. Somehow, she knew he could sense that. Her lack of energy was starting to take ownership of the moment. Between the sheets at 4:00 a.m. was where she was heading in the first place before seeing him slowly walking toward her down the hall. In a way, she already thought she was dreaming and was just possibly having a nightmare. With no stamina to react, her entire being was still just emotionally drained from grieving the loss of…her.

He wasn't quick to be upon her, as if already recognizing she held no real threat. He didn't roughly force her to place her back up on the wall, merely guided her already self-directed actions in response to him simply wanting to see her up close. It was all over his face that he simply wanted to know who was roaming the house, as if he belonged there too.

Claura suddenly found herself being placed on the large bed as if a precious child was being put to bed for the night after falling asleep on the couch. She literally had no real recognition of the hallway to the mattress, which was beyond strange. He took a moment to just look into her eyes again, leaning over her on the mattress as she lay half curved looking back up at him, then stepped back and waved his hand in front of her face…and out like a night-light she went. Her last image was of him putting distance between them, yet somehow, she knew he wasn't leaving her to be alone again.

*****

Claura awoke to the increasing noise surrounding her. She checked her watch, realizing that airports do actually get busier in the early morning, just like so many other businesses. She lay back down with her eyes closed, in no rush to wake up. Suddenly, everything came back to her, and she remembered she only had so much time to get to her rental car before the rental status expired. She honestly had no idea how much time she had left to hold the keys in her hands before it was too late. She honestly had no idea how far Roman's place was if she had to walk or pay for a taxi. Only half the time was the taxi driver an actual good driver, from her experience anyway.

She sat up, gently slapped her knees as if to say, "Alright, let's go," and grabbed her bag to swing over her shoulder as she stood up. Following the signs until she saw one for car rentals, secretly appreciating how airports made it easy for even the most unwise of souls to get around, she put together that it would be a good twenty-minute walk to that part of the airport. She inwardly hoped she was not too late, wondering why it was such a big deal anyway. All she'd have to do was choose and pay herself for a different car.

"Chill, Claura, you've come this far. Breathe. Just breathe."

And just like that, he popped into her mind, as if she felt betrayed by her own body for taking forever to remember him from her dream. She actually felt mad at her own intellect if such a feeling was possible. The memories of the dream came rushing back, breaking through as clear as day, making her feet slow until they came to a complete stop. She stared into space in the middle of the airport, just as she stared into the depths of space in those eyes.

"Tronan."

The whisper of his name to herself, for no one else's ears, just felt so personal. She looked around, all worried, as if some part of her already knew no one was supposed to know his appellation. She took a few more deep breaths and decided to splash her face with some cold water quickly at the next sign of a bathroom, suddenly and completely nonchalant about being late for a silly rental car. As if on cue while drying her face, over the intercom was a rental car special, as if secretly urging her to get a move on. Within ten minutes, she was standing at the car rental window, saying Roman's name, only for them to ask her for the last name as well. She stuttered, looking embarrassed.

"We need a last name to make sure we have the correct vehicle on file for you. Do you have the information?"

"Just one sec, please…let me find it. One second." She pulled out her phone. Thinking about calling Roman directly, yet realizing he may be busy with work, she decided to hope in the emails he sent that his signature at the bottom of them held his full name. She fingered crossed. She opened the email app only to see a couple more unread emails already.

*Shit…he's worried, obviously.* Name…name…name… She scrolled to the bottom of the first email he sent that was already marked as read. "Okay! Thank God. It's Dr Roman Valdimir."

The lady in the window started typing. "Got it. It says to give you the option of a small, midsize, or large vehicle. Which do you prefer?"

"Umm, wow…okay"—nervous laugh, happy laugh—"larger car if you got one. Black preferably."

The lady gave her a look as if disapproving of the needed detail. But Claura didn't care. The window lady had no idea how good it felt to just be in control of a simple color and size decision after her entire life this past year. She inwardly decided she couldn't care less about anyone's opinion, especially on this trip. Deep down, she did want to enjoy it. She was just scared it wasn't going to be a full possibility. She still had some healing to do, and that healing may take the rest of her life. Roman told her she would laugh again, really laugh. So far, she figured as much as he tried to be of help, he could still have his full-of-shit moments like the rest of us.

The window lady broke her thoughts. "Going to fetch that for you. Need to return with a full tank. Sign here, and I will be right back." She genuinely smiled as she walked away. Five minutes later,

# THE WINGED WITCH OF MATCHES

Claura could just sense the next set of wheels she heard were hers, turned, and actually had half a second of pure joy jump inside her bones for a serious change.

"Just off the lot new pretty much, only 157 miles on her. Here is your Buick, ma'am."

She stepped out and tossed the keys, leaving the driver's door open for her. She did a light laugh at the look on Claura's face, did a friendly salute with her hand, and jetted back to her little work window.

"Roman, Roman, Roman…doctor of trouble and baby-delivering vaginas."

She suddenly felt slightly joyful. With a wide smile that she knew she deserved to have for a change, Claura swung into the car as if already familiar with it, steadfastly tossing her bag into the passenger seat as she did so. She took a minute to figure out the features, adjust the controls and mirrors, and a steady rev on the pedal to anticipate its getup level. Suddenly realizing she had been walking from place to place in the city too long, Claura made way for the nearest highway, despite being in the correct direction or not just yet, and floored it.

"Ticket Tuesday, shall we?"

# Chapter 3

# Child Psychic

The home was about a mile from any neighbor, which was great. The home was also mostly large fancy windows for walls, which was not so great. "So much for privacy," she whispered to herself, staring down the place from the car window, wondering if this would really be good for her. She wondered if being all alone here would be more scary than not, more lonely than expected, more quiet than needed. She figured she simply didn't need to stay any longer than she wanted to and was simply curious as to what the inside looked like anyway. She figured she'd get settled in and then finally actually call Roman to thank him personally over the phone. As much as she didn't want to talk to anybody, it was simply the least she could do.

She walked up to the front porch, and it was easy to see that it wrapped all the way around, which she loved. The front doors were taller than she'd seen on any houses lately, making them look kind of intimidating despite being only large chunks of wood. The main color of the whole exterior was a dark brown, making it blend in with the rest of the woods and landscape almost too well, as if intentionally built to be hidden. Only some of the edging and molding was a different color, and the porch furniture added some mild contrast to the entire structure. Unsure of where to find a key and completely forgetting to ask, she decided to attempt the handle—never know.

"Oh, good. Hate to come this far for nothing." She stepped inside. "Holy shit…" She opened the door to find one of the fanciest entrances in Pinterest history: high ceilings, beautiful flooring, and furniture that actually looked cozy and not just for looks in the nearby living room. "Definitely not nothing." Her heart felt relaxed at just the style of the fireplace in the living room. She had always wanted one. The only apartments with a fireplace were ones that were always out of her budget. She really never thought she'd get to enjoy one this nice. Seeing a switch right beside it, she decided to test it out. It lit up like it was just installed yesterday. Her lips finally really curved into an overdue smile. She stood lost in thought, staring at the fire. Everything was so quiet, not even the sound of a random little animal scurrying around outside, no wind, no city noises in the least.

*Tronan.*

Her memories of her dream suddenly took her over again, unblinking until her own eyes became dry from the all-encompassing stillness within her. She rubbed her face in a "snap out of it" kind of way, massaging her hands over her suddenly itchy eyes. She then noticed a fancy stairway to her right and decided to find a room to set her stuff down in before exploring more—hopefully, a room with an attached shower—as a sudden need to splash her face with cold water rushed back. It was anything to distract her from what should have been just a damn dream. As she turned the corner at the top of the stairs to head in the obvious direction of any bedroom, she looked up and noticed that the hallway looked exactly.

"Oh my god…is this…?"

The hallway was identical to the one in her dream. She stared at the exact spot where she had stood with him, wondering just how much of it may have been real. Knowing to think it was real meant she was losing her damn mind. A part of her brain blamed it immediately on the effect of those damn sleeping pills that were clearly meant for football players, not women recovering from a cesarean surgery followed by emotional and mental trauma. Perhaps motherly hormones made one this way? With increased intuition...or increased crazy? She couldn't help but think maybe it was all a part of this postpartum crap that women get blessed with. She walked past the spot slowly, as if cautious about it, and something might appear and jump out at her. She found what was clearly a master bedroom and decided to simply make use of it, knowing it was silly to feel weird about it. After all, Roman said he hadn't been here for a long time, and it was not like he was sleeping with her in here. The conflicted feelings at that thought got her feeling all antsy. She decided to simply call Roman later due to not wanting to come off as any level of awkward over the phone now, as she knew he would sense it. She decided to just send a quick updated email again, knowing full well the man deserved better, and took advantage of the ridiculously welcoming shower room, not stall, no tub, literally a small room turned into a huge shower. It was truly a doctor-level kind of design.

"Must be nice."

She laughed to herself as she swirled her fingers under the spraying water, waiting for it to come to temperature. She knew full well that the mirror was behind her above the luxurious sink counter topping of doctor's choice, being completely content in avoiding it. She was not ready to look at herself, not up close—naked, in someone else's shower room, in a whole different part of the world. A part of her still hadn't succumbed to the fact that she was even here, doing this, traveling, living out someone else's advice. It was not easy at all, despite how the other 95 percent of the population may see her situation as a vacation. She couldn't blame them. At that thought, and the sound of her rumbling stomach all of a sudden, she realized that she had forgotten to check the fridge, unsure if Roman had food here already or not. She was willing to be happy with a couple of slices of bread at the moment if it meant not having to seek out any grocery or corner store at this hour, thinking to herself that it's going to really suck if all she has to eat for now is her gum, her one granola bar, and leftover plane peanuts.

"Way to start off that nutritional post-baby diet I've been so wonderfully lectured about." She slowly scolded herself for feeling the hot water run down her entire body. Every part of her anatomy felt different now after her pregnancy. She didn't expect even just a shower to feel so different. She figured it simply must be the environment. Who wouldn't enjoy their shower more in one like this? Everything just felt more personal even though she was by herself, simply washing herself. Her thoughts wandered to how it would feel to shower with one's own baby. How sweet that would be—to play with them in the water, watch their little hands reach for things, and see them smile at the new sensations. There were so many books she read that gave her so many ideas, a simple shower with her child being one of them she held most dear. Now she would never get to hold…her.

Claura stood in the shower for a long time. Let her tears fall down the drain with the rest of the droplets. Her shaking hands covered her face for most of the time, the urge to punch the glass doors a constant battle to not give in to, the slight fear at still feeling her scar on her lower abdomen. She figured if she was ever going to let it out, now was the perfect time, and there was no one around to hear—at least she hoped not. If Roman had someone coming to check on her, she had no idea. Then again, she hadn't really taken the time to fully read through all his emails during her travels just to even get here. She figured she had done enough of "facing her feelings" for one day, as one therapist mentioned she truly needed to do to heal and decided to simply hit the sheets. Turning the knob off slowly, as if not really wanting to get out. Her pruney fingertips caught her eye as if a small reminder she should just already be in bed and not hanging out in someone else's shower for so damn long. No matter how nice this place was, it was not her home. The towel was literally warm from all the steam, as if it had just taken out of the dryer. She wrapped the navy terry cloth around her, letting her body remain mostly wet still as it simply just felt refreshing honestly. She let the beads of water from her hair tickle down her back as she walked back into the bedroom and aimed the TV remote in its direction and started flicking through the channels.

"Please, please, please...."

She wanted nothing but her favorite station, those old black-and-white movies, or those old game shows from the 1970s—just anything simple to fall asleep to. She couldn't stand half of the shit that was on actual television these days, news included. To her luck, she found *Match Game* and did a small inner thank-you to the gods—gods of smaller tasks, of course. Deciding she needed just one more thing before finally trying to pass out, she walked slowly toward the stairs to get some water in the downstairs kitchen. She felt her heart do a leap as she passed the particular spot in the hallway. There were absolutely no creaks and squeaks in the flooring, which she loved compared to her old apartment, where she felt loud, just trying to go to the bathroom at 1:00 a.m. sometimes. It was so annoying that she complained, but as usual with most landlords, all she got was that they'd add it to the list—of course, to never be fixed.

The entire downstairs was gorgeous in the light from the fire. She decided to just turn it down on the switch instead of completely off, needing to feel the warm glow in the place. It just helped it to feel more welcoming while she was all alone. She suddenly remembered that she didn't even have her knife anymore in case someone broke in, as airport security decided to claim it. Feeling like she should at least grab a kitchen knife or something, she walked over to the first counter to look for one and saw a note that no part of her was surprised about missing earlier while looking around.

You are safe.

She drummed her fingertips on the counter, biting her lip while reading it again. "Aww...how sweet am I, though?" She still found it hard to trust people again. Deciding to add this to the conversation topics with Roman later, she still grabbed a knife, just maybe not one as large as originally intended. She found the cupboard with some very nice glasses and was about to fill it up at the sink when she noticed a water dispenser by the fridge. "Must be nice." She made her way to the stairs to head back up and, on the first step, got a feeling—an intuition really—of someone. Looking around, of course, she didn't expect to see anybody. And she doesn't.

But her gut...

Claura decided to simply hurry back to bed. The sheets felt amazing. Her favorite show was playing, the place was gorgeous and all hers...for now. She took one sleeping pill and curled in further. She imagined to herself what it would sound like to hear little baby cries needing their mommy for something in the other room, knowing she would jump up in less than a heartbeat to see to their every need. She started crying, but not for long. The sleeping pill gave her a break from her troubles for the time being.

*****

Roman really couldn't wrap his head around her lack of words in her emails. Claura just didn't seem like the kind of person who would take this offered opportunity only to barely communicate with him at all once she landed. He considered his lack of perception that maybe she did need more time to herself than she led on. He tried to let it go, knowing that may be all it was—that he would simply hear more from her later. Sticking to emails, after all, did send a very platonic and "let's keep this professional" vibe between them when she had his own cell phone number and knew he had it on him at all times, even at work. There were no single text message notification, definitely not a missed call, and he was really starting to wonder if he misread things and made her uncomfortable.

Suddenly, he got an email notification on his cell phone. He read his screen and let out a sigh of relief, eyes not moving fast enough to see what she finally sent him.

> Just a quick update. Arrived and am in awe of this house. Must be so nice to have something like this to call your own. I thank you again, Roman. Talk soon.

As short as it was, he was just glad to hear from her. He checked his watch and knew that it must be about 10:00 p.m. where she was, and she was probably just simply going to bed and jet-lagged. The quick thought of what bedroom she chose made him go still in his office chair for two seconds. He quickly brushed the needless thought aside, wondering where it was coming from after all he had been through with her as her doctor after all she had been through since he'd known her as his patient. He shook his head, trying to rid his thoughts, and decided now was not the time to respond with an email for fear of coming off wrong. He cared about Claura but felt strange for doing so, like she, in a way, belonged to him yet also didn't.

Feeling how conflicted he was and the fact that his last patient had to cancel anyway, he decided to call it a day. He could finish the leftover paperwork at home, preferably anyway. While packing up his briefcase, he noticed her folder still in the pile, hesitated for just a moment, figuring what could it hurt, and tossed it in with the rest of his stuff. His phone suddenly ringing startled him enough to make him drop her folder, papers splaying everywhere on his office floor, as the ringtone was a significant one he never thought he'd hear again. His heart stopped while staring at the screen, deciding whether to answer or not. He did. Fuck it.

"Tronan." His tone completely possessed an intense question mark.

"You have a guest," someone said, completely unaffected by such tone.

"Yes." The voice was firm as stone as if daring to be questioned.

"The one you called for protection for her was…released," Tronan clarified.

Roman was not surprised at all by that. He already knew. It was simply a territorial thing for his kind to know who needed a bodyguard in the area, as was their charm, one could say, in the modern workforce. Sending her to his home first was for a very important reason so that others in the territory knew she was to be left alone ASAP. As much as many of their people looked down on Roman for leaving, there were just as many for still respecting his reasons.

He was very favored among his kind with his particular passion for medicine and healing. Many families who relied on him were not happy with his departure, clearly in need of his knowledge for their well-being. It was why he was, after all, still welcome to return. He just simply chose not to.

"I'll call for a replacement. Can you stay in the meantime?" There was a long pause. "Please?" He sounded as serious and forward as a man could.

To hear a "please" come out of Roman's mouth, he said everything about the value of this guest to him. Roman was not a "please" kind of man among their kind. Tronan took a few long moments to try to put the pieces together, only to realize saying yes was the only way to get a few pieces in the first place. He could hear Roman waiting on the other end. It was clear the man had no intention of asking twice.

Tronan noticed movement downstairs in the house suddenly. He could see slim feet trotting across to the kitchen, her looking startled while stopping and staring at a note, clearly seeing it for the first time. He put the phone down over his chest while he watched her face as she thought it over, not wanting to miss her reaction to those three little words. It was not the reaction he expected. It was clear she did not know what to think and did not trust what she read, as she was clearly very comfortable in the way she held the medium-sized blade in her hand while filling the glass with water with the other a very quick moment later. He smiled slightly. Something inside him was already proud of her.

He put the phone back up to his ear as he leisurely watched her go back up the stairs.

"I am the replacement." Firm. As. A. Brick.

"She doesn't know about us, Tronan. She doesn't need to. Having a bodyguard like you around may not be good for her. The man I already had intended for her, who was with her on the flight there as well, he was suitable."

"I will not harm her."

"You have enemies that don't need to know about her existence at all. I know you do! Not long ago, I was one—"

"Your tone suggests you still are Roman."

"Perhaps. Or perhaps that was foreplay compared to what will happen if anything happens to her."

Tronan's blood went hot at just the mention of something happening to Claura. It let Roman think he was only her bodyguard. That's all he deserved to know. Roman left his kind a long time ago, revoking his right to be unkempt with matters within the bloodline. The man was never going to come over here anyway, or was he? Tronan was not about to concern himself with the man. He had more important matters now—important matters, specifically. Tronan was trying to be clever in not giving himself away with what was happening, for he could sense Roman would visit in a heartbeat if he did. He knew Tronan's main gift, the Dreamer, as they called him. Some feared him for it. Others were jealous. Some simply stayed clear. Tronan already knew what this woman meant to him, so be it that their first meeting was within a dream. It was enough for him. He simply was trying to piece together how Roman was involved, as was his home she was residing in…unfortunately.

"No one will harm her." *Click.* Tronan needed to think before saying more.

Roman, on the other end, swore up and down, almost tossing his phone across the room. It was all coming back to him real fast as Tronan was always not just a man of few words but hardly into conversing at all. He was shocked to hear from him. He did not trust him, but it was for completely separate reasons alone that he felt that way toward him. He knew deep down he'd never really hurt Claura and that he truly was one of the best to hire for the job. If it hadn't been for their differences, he would have hired him first anyway. Tronan was one of the best in the territory. He was one of the longest-standing guards in his bloodline, going back a couple of centuries, at least in just one profession. The particular profession was obviously expanding in current times. It had made it harder to keep their kind a secret, but they found ways. The lack of cleverness that most humans had was ironically a bonus almost too suited to the needs of his species.

Taking a few deep breaths as he knew he still needed to pull himself together just to leave his office and get to his vehicle, he leaned down to grab her papers and place them back in the folder. Uncaring at all in the moment, if they were in order, he shuffled them together to fit, and his eye caught the words "child psychic" in her notes. They were from her only a couple of times. She did actually agree to meet with a therapist in an adjacent clinic. Feeling ashamed that it was obvious he hadn't actually looked through all her paperwork, he started to feel less uncanny about bringing her file home now.

He sighed deeply as if already defeated and unsure why, trying to brush off what that could mean for her around his kind over in Romania. A part of him hoped she didn't feel the need to stay long, as much as he enjoyed knowing she was in his home. He frowned at his own thoughts, unsure of how to stop the chronic conflict inside him when it came to her.

# Chapter 4

## Crown Royal and Postpartum

Claura woke to complete silence. There was not even the sound of the birds singing. It was creepy and comforting at the same time. She decided she'd simply have some groceries delivered if such a service was available out here. She assumed by the size of the city she drove through to get here that surely that was a modern option from at least a couple of places. She grabbed her phone, only to realize it was completely out of battery. She searched through her one bag to find it and carried it to the bathroom with her to plug it in. Realizing she had forgotten her toothbrush and paste, she decided to add that to the list she needed to start making. She figured he surely must have something to eat around here as she headed to the kitchen. Still feeling awkward for some reason while passing through the hallway, she laughed at herself, wondering if the feeling will ever go away.

"It was just a dream."

She could feel herself blushing and lightly smacked her cheeks as if to say stop it to her own body while rushing down the stairs. She felt a surprising perk in her step due to just finally being alone for a bit. She hadn't even realized until now how much noise and stimulus a hospital held, even if you were in a bed doing nothing while there. During the last couple of weeks, she didn't even hear the nurses come in. A few had even startled her to where she jumped as if an actual intruder had come into her room, making her react like she needed to defend herself and completely scaring the nurse. She figured they were happy to be rid of her, too, by now.

She reached the fridge and opens—nothing. "Damn." She thought to herself she would have to roast Roman for that one, making her come straight here while knowing she'd only have to go back out for food soon anyway. The thought reminded her of needing to call him, more so out of politeness. She figured he'd know some information about the area anyway, one thing being about any places that deliver food specifically.

She decided to just grab some more water to hold her stomach over, figuring if she had to, she'd just suck it up and find a drive-through place somewhere, at least. A reason to drive such a nice car again wasn't really all that much torture anyway. If she was really honest with herself, though, the car was dangerous. She knew suicidal feelings. She was very familiar with them. And the car was an easy way out. People died in accidents all the time. She knew her worst postpartum moments were coming, as she had experienced it with more than one girlfriend in her past many years ago, and figured just hanging out at the house was simply her safest bet for now.

She strolled back upstairs to grab her cell phone, seated herself on the bathroom counter to accommodate the outlet, and dialed his number prior to a few deep breaths. Of course, he picked up after just one ring, giving her hardly any moment to clear her throat at least and calm her nerves. She didn't know why she was so nervous calling him. He had been in her life for months now. She let him be her doctor, and during pregnancy, she did not inquire, just chatting about belly width and healthy body weight. The man knew her intimately in a professional manner.

"Claura, I'm glad you called."

"Ya, hi, Roman. I apologize I haven't actually read through your—"

"Don't apologize to me. I meant that the first time."

"Okay. Got it."

She started swirling her finger on the marble design, leaving it up to him to continue the conversation suddenly. Her mouth felt dry. She could hear him do a light laugh on the other end as if already knowing of her needless nervousness.

"Well, I did try to tell you ahead of time about needing to grab food for yourself if you had read the emails."

A part of him was still relieved that she went straight to his home as he asked. He felt humbled she had listened to him. But he knew he needed to keep up a human front as best he could, and humans needed food. He silently cursed himself for forgetting such an obvious detail. He didn't have to think of such things while living alone, and at work, it was easy to make it appear normal to just be too busy for a lunch break.

"About that, any places that deliver food around here?" she asked softly, feeling shy for some reason.

"Plenty. Are you looking for groceries or just a restaurant for now?"

"How about both…may as well while I have you on the phone."

"You can call me anytime, you know. I know you are alone out there"—Tronan, the bastard, suddenly popped into his head—"and it was my idea for you to go there, so you have a right to call me anytime you need, got it?"

"Ya. Thanks." Her tone was now leaning toward a slight depressive streak.

"Claura, what's wrong? You can talk to me."

"Isn't it obvious? Hasn't been that long yet."

With a deep sigh, he wiped his hand over his face, clearly taking a moment on the other end to find the right words without giving anything away about himself. "I am just trying to help, really help. And I am unsure what to say. For that, I am sorry." He cursed himself inwardly for knowing exactly what to say, just not wanting her to know so much about him—not yet, at least.

"At least you know what to feel."

At the comment, his heart broke a little for her, reminding him of the meds he prescribed to help until some time passed. "Have you tried the medication yet? Any of them?"

There was a long pause as if she was unsure. She should admit she kind of overdosed on the plane ride here.

"Well, the sleeping pills work wonders." She had a sarcastic laugh.

"How many did you take?"

The serious tone was back. In a way, it comforted her, the familiarity of it.

"Two."

"At one time?" He held the phone closer to his ear now.

"Umm…ya." She could feel the lecture coming on from over the damn phone. He started to say something, and she stopped him, really not wanting to feel like someone's kid these days after everything, a lecture being the last damn thing she needed. "I'm fine. I read the bottle too late. I'm fine."

"Claura…"

"The flight went by superfast. It was great. Who doesn't want to make that long of a flight be over asap?"

"I gave you strong ones for a reason. I felt I could trust you."

"Felt?" As in past tense? She could hear him pause, clearly stuck for words again with her hurt tone now. "Look, Roman, if anyone is going to mess up, trust it's someone in my shoes right now. And I haven't necessarily had the best of circumstances, nor amount of time, to prove any trust to you."

There was a long pause still on his end. He decided to risk it. Knowing even if she didn't like the idea, he had someone keeping an eye on her anyway. And that's all the bastard better be doing.

"Claura, would it be okay if I had someone check on you now and again? I still have some friends in the area I can trust."

The way he said that took her back as if there was a sad story behind having only a few left instead of many in the area anymore.

"How often would they visit?"

A part of her felt like an ass for asking. This was *his* home. She figured maybe they were people who already stopped in any way to simply check on the house while he was away.

He tried to steady his voice, not wanting to give away that someone was already keeping an eye on her around the clock. A part of him felt like a creep for it. A more important part knew it was necessary.

"How often would you feel comfortable?"

He knew he was just going to have to go along with telling her what she wanted to hear.

"Would it even help, really, Roman? I'm an adult. I have 911."

"Please. It will help me have that peace of mind."

Having the original bodyguard would have given him much more peace of mind.

"I guess once a week."

"Good. I'll call them this afternoon. Tell them to stop by in a couple of days."

He swore inwardly at having to lie so carelessly to her. But it was in honesty that he cared for her for doing this. He had to keep checking himself on boundaries, not wanting to risk pushing her away. He knew how sensitive a woman with postpartum could be on top of just already dealing with postpregnancy hormones in general.

"Them? As in more than one?" Making it clear her own company was all she really wanted, and she was just doing this for him.

"It simply depends on who has an open schedule, that's all."

*Liar.*

She took a deep breath, feeling her stomach roll again. "Okay. So which restaurant do you recommend? I fear no matter who I call, they won't deliver fast enough. I feel sick, to be honest."

"Don't take any more pills I've given you until you eat. There is an Italian place I recall that should still be open. Cantina Verde, I believe. And I think any of the local grocery stores deliver, any one of them should do."

"Thank you, Roman."

She clearly meant it on a deep level. Her tone suggested a thank-you for so much more than just a couple of food referrals.

"Please just relax and enjoy yourself, for me. Okay?"
"Yes, Doctor."

She gave a silent smile. For some strange reason, she could tell through the phone he could sense it as if standing right in front of her, seeing her eyes light up just a little. Her sad eyes were full of appreciation.

"Call me soon. Let me know how your meal went, if they are as good as they used to be."

"Yup."

She was quiet, shy, and unsure. She slowly lowered the phone as if she wanted to say something else but wasn't sure what words to put together, and she continued to choose the red button instead.

In the silence of the house, it was the loudest end-call click she ever heard. She stayed sitting there and staring at it until the screen went black on its own. A few seconds went by, and she got a text with a link to the restaurant and a grocery store. Another message came through right after reading, "To save you some time," as if she was in a hurry for anything.

She set the phone down, leaned forward on the counter, and stared at her toes while lost in thought. Feeling the cold counter underneath her palms, in a way, the coolness felt soothing. She took a deep breath while feeling the tears come on, as if her heart had a mind of its own, as if her heart needed to cry out of nowhere, as if her heart just needed some emotional release. She watched her teardrops fall to the cold floor below her, her vision becoming blurry, not caring to wipe one small puddle away. Her body was doing that involuntary response thing of taking a quick, deep breath into her lungs all on its own, making her slightly snap out of it. Her stomach rumbled again also helped her to jump out of her sad stupor.

She opened her text message thread with Roman and clicked on the link for the restaurant. Only three rings and a man answered, his accent sounding very warm and polite, taking her back for a moment after all her straying thoughts that were just taking up all her brain space again. She cleared her throat and asked for a simple fettuccine alfredo dish with a side soup and two drinks. He gave her the total and asked for the address after she said she needed delivery, making her pause. She didn't actually know the address off the top of her head. *Shit.*

"Umm, can you please hold for a moment? I have to ask a friend with a text quickly, as I'm staying in their house. Just a sec—"

"Well, we know a lot of people around here for the most part. We have a lot of regulars. We may already have it on file if you can give me the full name of the owner of the residence?"

"Sure. It's Roman Vladimir."

There was a long pause, long, long pause. There was literally no breathing on the other end of the phone anymore from what she could tell.

"Umm"—he cleared his throat quite loudly—"yes, we have that name on file. We can have that delivered for you in about forty minutes."

Damn. She was so hungry. She didn't want to wait that long. "Thank you so much."

There was a sudden click from their end. No goodbye. "Rude." She silently hoped to herself that the meal would make up for the awkwardness during that phone call over just wanting a damn meal.

"Roman, what is up with you? What the hell am I missing here?" she whispered to herself.

Suddenly feeling her ass grow a little too cold from the countertop, she slid off and decided to go curl up in front of the fireplace and wait for her warm meal.

*****

Claura felt so tired, but she knew it wasn't from the alcohol that was a miracle to find stashed in one of the fancy kitchen cupboards after her very awkwardly delivered dinner. She sat staring into the flames, curled up with a blanket and pillow, feeling like the solitude suddenly wasn't helping. The odd feeling of what Roman was to this place was starting to throw her off. She couldn't help but wonder if she was just thinking about it too much as she simply had the time to do so. It all was leading up to a bad feeling that was about to make its way to the surface like a demon waking up from its slumber. Something just surfaced and was ready to rage.

"Fucking postpartum. Here we go."

She half guessed herself. She was shaking her head back and forth, already sick of what was to come, hating that she had no control over the simmering emotions getting ready to boil over.

But she knew it was that and so much more. She was grieving.

She set the picture down on the table gently, as if no matter how mad she felt, she would never let any harm come to it. She started to wonder just how much Roman cared about this house, how much he'd be mad if she threw a few things against the walls as hard as she could, wondering what was sentimental to him and what wasn't. She started to feel so angry she laughed, twisting her suddenly sweaty and shaky fingers together like that crazy laugh one had when one couldn't believe what was happening—when one was about to lose it. She stood up and started pacing in circles, hands clasped behind her head, eyes closed, trying to breathe deeply to calm herself. She suddenly felt the pent-up anger building uncontrollably and heard herself screaming. Next, she grabbed the books off the living room table and tossed them against the wall, feeling suddenly even more angry that the crash they made wasn't good enough. It wasn't loud enough, damaging enough.

Suddenly uncaring of what Roman liked in his home, the man was never going to be feeling what she was feeling now. And she was so angry she couldn't help but think that maybe he shouldn't have invited someone like her to stay in his home anyway. I mean, the man didn't really know her. No matter what was going on between them, whatever this was, it had only been a few months, and he already hadn't really seen the best of her due to her circumstances. Roman didn't really know the happy version of her that existed not too long ago yet now felt like a lifetime ago—literally...a lifetime ago, according to the ridiculously unfair length that her baby girl's life had to be.

A part of him must have expected the unexpected.

She reached for the bottle that was nearly empty, crying hysterically, grabbed the neck of it, and tossed it with full fury at a shelf.

Meaning to hear everything on it came crashing down with it. Next, she turned to a vase, completely missing the small green light that appeared briefly among the broken bottle pieces on the floor, and watched as it hit the far wall and broke into pieces; next, a small but heavy and hard statue of a wolf; next, another heavy figurine that was completely minding its own business on a shelf in the corner. Her arms shook uncontrollably over her ears as she screamed as hard as she could until her throat closed on its own and her legs gave out. She leaned on her hands, her knees already feeling sore from the quick landing, her throat feeling raw already. She inwardly cursed her body for being such a weakling, feeling like she couldn't even vent the way she deserved without hurting already.

"Fucking human body!" She looked down at herself, at her anatomy, with disgust. "It's all my fault. I wasn't strong enough! I don't care what they tell me. I wasn't strong enough!"

She quickly stood up to find something else to destroy, a part of her feeling sorry for her beautiful surroundings, knowing full well she was not going to be able to be in control of herself. She briskly walked to the kitchen, full of aggression toward another bottle, any attempt to stop feeling. For if she got drunk enough to where it was difficult to even walk, then she figured she could stop herself from destroying this house. Sadly, alcohol was her only option in her situation. She had the sleeping pills but, deep down, knew that was a cowardly way to go. She was suddenly feeling more sympathy for drunks all over the world—an inner connection to them now more than any other kind of human being. She wasn't really feeling the human way of existing anymore. She was actually frightened for herself. She had no clue how far downhill she was going to go. She officially knew what it was like to not be in control of her future. She wasn't sure if she even cared anymore. No one missed her. No one would. Roman knew her for such a short amount of time that he'd grieve and move on in a fair amount of time. He'd be fine.

She grabbed the only other bottle, cursing at no option three if this one didn't do the trick. Turning too quickly, she slipped, and despite her semidrunk stupor, she, as clear as day, recognized the sharp corner of the island coming toward her temple, completely unable to stop it. Out of nowhere, a large hand is felt under her skull, moving her head away from the sharp edge and her body into a standing position. She looked up to see...

"I would miss you."

The shock on her face almost made his lips curl into a small smile, only for the look in her lost eyes, making it impossible to do so at the same time as he looked down at her. He had to admire her lack of fear, for he had no choice but to do what he did—to appear out of nowhere so quickly. He watched her go through whatever she was going through from not far outside absolutely broke his heart. Ever since she arrived, he was not far. He knew from his premonition dream with her that she was upset about something but was unsure as to exactly what. And in it, she had made it clear she would not discuss it. But now, after this, he needed to know. From what he just heard and witnessed, she clearly found something awful to be all her fault alone. And that's exactly how she looked, so alone.

"So you are real," she said, sounding relieved just as much as surprised.

She couldn't tell if it was relief that she wasn't as crazy as she may be assumed after her dream or because of how she felt about him despite never even really meeting him until now. He was looking at her so intensely that her head was spinning, and his eyes were looking into hers yet checking her head at the same time for signs of injury. She suddenly felt embarrassed, yet more sorry for him for obviously being so close that he was witnessing all of this.

"Or I am that drunk." She laughed, yet it held no real humor.

"My love, I fear for you."

"And you do speak English." She said it like she felt betrayed—the memory of being so unexpectedly disappointed that she couldn't understand his words during the dream, with the sound of his voice being so...well, dreamy.

"Yes."

"And you couldn't before? For me?"

"I simply did not want to risk saying the wrong thing. I was in slight shock."

"Shock?"

"That you exist."

She honestly wasn't sure how to reply to that. Right now, the last thing she felt she wanted to do was exist. She felt like such shit, and perfect timing, of course, with this man before her who looked like the best dream ever. She had to laugh to herself. He literally was in the best dream she ever had.

"How do I know you exist, Tronan? That this isn't just a dream sequel?" *Because I feel like I'm losing my damn mind.*

He smiled slightly, though clearly not reaching his eyes all the way, his concern for her still owning the majority of his expression. His fear of what almost just happened made the energy in the room still ridiculously intense between them.

"Sweetheart, I'm sure all the proof you need will be in your morning headache."

"I suppose we are both having a hard time believing that this is happening, aren't we?" she said simply, looking like she felt nothing but defeated.

"Please tell me what have you so upset. Now."

At his firm tone, she tilted her head and looked at him like he really didn't need, nor want, to go there. Not while she was in this mood. Of all the times to meet the most gorgeous man she'd ever seen, of course, it had to be when she was having a breakdown. He tried again, more politely.

"Claura, please."

Her name sounded brand new, coming from his mouth. She knew instinctively that if no one else in this world ever said it again other than him, she would be just fine with that. His entire scent was invading her space, reminding her of how it made all her other senses come alive the last time he was this close. Didn't matter whether it was a reality or not the first time. It felt real enough for her. She took a deep breath as if savoring it as if already instinctively knowing that his natural scent would calm her nerves down. It worked. She looked up at him with uneasy surprise. She clearly was trying to figure out the lure he had over her. Being untrusting of the sudden invisible connection between them was clearly written all over her face. He nodded his head forward toward her as if inquiring if she just said something.

Anything.

She didn't.

Instead, she reached for his hand while their eyes still held one another captive. Damn, he had nice eyes. She could stare at them for hours. She'd actually never seen eyes on a man that she cared to look at even twice, let alone want to have framed by her bedside. *Other than my friggin' doctor.* His hand felt warm, manly, big—the way a man's hand was supposed to feel. She could feel his gentleness in response, as if clearly just wanting to help her and make sense of what was going on.

She moved her clothing out of the way with her other hand, slightly lifting her T-shirt up and slowly lowering the top of her undies. Both were her only clothing at the moment as she wasn't expecting company—least of all him, despite thoughts of him still taking up so much of her mind after just one dream. Even if he was only in the back of her thoughts, he just remained there. It never went away. Like a comfort that was permanent, a part of her now at just knowing of his existence. Something about him was just feeling eerie and familiar.

A part of her still feared this was all a fucked up semi-nightmare with the most gorgeous guest of honor in the middle of it. She could see his eyes get more serious, yet more full of wonder the closer she moved his hand toward her lower abdomen. She moved his index finger forward and let the tip caress along her scar. She was moved at the realization in his eyes appearing so quickly. She admired how he still looked at her like his only concern was for her and not a drop for his own uncertainty at the moment. He looked at her like his heart broke for her at that moment. It suddenly felt so natural between them when his entire hand palmed over the spot now. It was numb around the scar, yet somehow, she could still feel butterflies.

"Hmm…the warmth from your hand feels really nice."

She lazily smiled up at him, such sadness in her eyes. He could tell she was already coming to terms with the best she could at losing her child. Her scene, which he had been watching through the window some distance across the yard, suddenly didn't seem so crazy. As if on cue…

"I am sorry you had to see me acting so insane. But I can't help it…" She looked away, down toward the floor, her face holding the torture of trying not to lose it again. He raised both hands to cup her face, making her look at him.

"Tell me what to do." His tone was gentle, soft, and completely calm.

"Give me a stronger body. So that this may never happen in the first place."

At her words, he was set back, as he knew damn well he could actually do such a thing with just a drop of his blood. What Roman told him suddenly came to mind, him stating that she did not need to know of their kind. He knew damn well already that it was just a matter of time. He'd have to be dead before he was able to let her go. He was even more at a loss now as to entering her life and courting her, getting to know her. Yet, at the same time, it didn't matter. He was here. And he wasn't leaving no matter what happened. She just didn't know it yet. The ties between them were already growing. He could feel it, and he sensed she could too. Behind her sadness, her depression, he could see it in her eyes. It was a distance away, but only due to her situation being upfront and foremost in her mind and heart right now, and rightfully so.

He sighed with a slight growl, internally angry that this was a pain he had no control of ridding. He held her face between his hands still, reading her. So close. Now was not the time to lose control, but he had to at least kiss her. The way she was looking at him, he truly felt he had no choice in the matter. And he did it so gently yet so possessively. His lips were surprisingly soft, hers salty from all her crying. They both took a deep breath together and shared it as if completely in sync with each other already. She leaned into him as he ended the kiss, uncaring if she could control her reaction. She's not. She simply didn't want to.

Didn't want to at all.

"Dragostea mea," he whispered inches from her face, wiping her tears away with his thumbs, still cradling her beautiful face in his palms.

A small part of him hated himself for being so lost in her features during such a serious moment. She had one of the most beautiful faces he had ever seen. He was still coming to terms with being the one for her, as he truly gave up hope a long time ago of ever finding his Match. Now that he was experiencing what it was all like, the term Match felt so shallow. It was nowhere near good enough.

"Can you tell me what that means in the morning, please."

She could feel her legs turn to rubber. Her eyes fight to stay open, her mind unable to remain focused the way she wanted to be able to when he was around. Her eyes held an obvious plea that he would still be here tomorrow. He looked saddened suddenly, and it worried her on a level she didn't know she had. Tronan wasn't like others of their species. He could actually come out during the day. It was simply around noontime. He had to remain in the shadows, at least. He feared the information would not settle with her so soon. He quickly decided it was best to make her sleep until he could return. She clearly could use it.

"May I lay you in your bed, Claura? See to it myself that you sleep?"

He knew that she didn't fully understand what he was asking. He wanted to send her to sleep using his ability to do so, being able to command when she closed her eyes and when she opened them again.

"Last time you sent me to sleep, I feared you were never going to be even just a dream for me again."

"You never have to fear that. I am right here in front of you. I am not going anywhere."

The affirmation held authority she never heard in a person's tone before. It actually sent a slight chill down her spine. As if even if she wanted to get rid of him, something about him simply wouldn't be able to allow it. The thought worried her yet warmed her. She inwardly laughed at the realization that, apparently, all men were capable of being so confusing in their own way. The next thing

Claura knew was the feeling of soft cool sheets underneath her skin, the coziness of the bed feeling like paradise. Her head was spinning, but she liked it. The feeling made her fall asleep easier. She snuggled into the pillow, facing toward the windows, facing away from him. She wanted to look at him just once more, but her body and eyelids clearly had other plans. She felt his lips on her forehead only seconds before she passed out. She was suddenly angry at the alcohol for taking away more time she could have had with this man, yet grateful it was what helped bring him here in the first place. Life was so damn strange.

"Tronan?"

"Yes?" He leaned over her, fists pressed into the mattress along her sides.

"I am sorry."

Her tone made it clear that even in her state, she was still feeling embarrassed. No one in their right mind would want to meet someone they clearly had a strong connection with during such an episode. It became obvious to her that grief held way more power than she ever realized it could. It consumed you and changed not just your personality but your very soul and right to the core. His scent coming closer helped her thoughts come back to the here and now. She could feel the heat from his body and knew some part of her had a right to be frightened of him. He was different. She still couldn't believe he was here to stay. That part definitely sounded too good to be true.

"You don't ever have to say sorry to me."

Her brain remembered another man saying those same words to her with the exact same tone and timing, and before she could wrap her head around any further thought, her body gave in.

First postpartum episode. Check.

Mr. Perfect saw me at my worst. Check.

Knowing I'll never drink Crown Royal again. Check.

# Chapter 5

## That Particular Cologne

The sheets felt cool compared to only a short while ago before she fell asleep. Her hand lingered as the smile on her face increased, reaching for his pillow. She was slowly awakening to pulling it close to her face and inhaling the scent. She remembered that particular cologne. It was one of her favorite things about him. It lingered even stronger in his pores during their lovemaking. She could feel it became her own as their sweat mixed while their bodies collided and pleasured one another. Memories of his hands and mouth being everywhere, a little rough sometimes, but she knew he would always take it only so far. She heard his footsteps come closer from down the hall, unhurried, full of male confidence. She turned to see him holding two cups of coffee, a grin on his face, as he came closer and set them on the nightstand. He then turned to wrap himself around her, on top of her, kissing her. His hands lingered into familiar territory again, clearly deciding that the coffee could wait. Claura laughed and started to push him off a little to reach for the cup. His hands pressed harder into her skin, forcing her back down, looking up at him in surprise. He had never startled her before despite their relationship being kind of new still, but the instant change on his face… she actually felt scared. His expression was of full-on possession, a need to control no matter the consequences, a way that he never looked at her before. She heard herself whispering, "Stop." He smiled and shook his head with a clear no, clearly meaning it. She looked around the room, remembering her knife in her jacket pocket by the door, recalling her phone on the kitchen counter…and was at a real loss as to how to help herself. Somehow, the plead in her eyes turned him on more, and deep down, she knew it was stupid to fight, but she couldn't help it. She could feel herself screaming his name and for him to stop, yet no words were coming out of her mouth, no matter how hard she tried. Her hits made him laugh, as if all the strength she had meant nothing—absolutely nothing. His hands were rough, as if he was meaning to leave bruises. She could feel tears start to swell up as he forced her knees apart.

*****

"Claura!" Tronan swore up and down, unable to get her to just open her eyes and look at him already. "Claura! You need to wake up."

She fought him with a fury he hadn't expected her to be capable of. He could tell she was fighting more out of pure fear than anger, the look on her face of full defeat that was making his insides turn cold toward whatever, or whoever, was doing this to her. Her voice finally broke through after acting like she was trying to dry scream in her sleep. Her screams seemed to echo off the walls as if her voice was literally her only weapon to save herself.

"Stop! Jayson! Stop!"

"Claura! Wake up *now*."

Tronan didn't even bother anymore to hide the growl in his voice, uncaring if it at all frightened her further when she finally came to. He was simply fed up with seeing her going through such torment.

She finally opened her eyes but took a few very long seconds to see it was Tronan attached to the hands holding her wrists in place and not anybody else's. The pain of him holding her wrists was suddenly not as horrible as what her mind was framing it to be, as the man before her looked nothing like the man in her nightmare. Suddenly, embarrassment welled up all over again. She was literally starting to feel pity for herself. She had so many damn issues she needed to work through. She was scared to even look him in the eyes right now…again. As expected, though, he did it for her, lifting her chin with one finger to make her look at him. She could see the worry in his eyes fade as she came back into reality more fully, only for them to do a 180—a 180 that made the air in the room suddenly feel cold. She noticed him take in a very deep breath before his perfect mouth began to move.

"Who is Jayson?"

The way he said the name had her literally afraid to move, and the manly growl in every syllable made her pause despite knowing the harm was not at all intended for her. She looked into his eyes, trying to block out the memories, trying to gain some control over what was just her past now—a past that she was still recovering from.

"My ex." She looked away for a second, needing the moment to think. "He was a boyfriend."

"Boyfriend?" he asked as if he clearly didn't understand the term, as if the word was actually very foreign to him.

"Unfortunately. Although near the end of our very short relationship, the last thing he became was a friend." Tronan's eyes went dark. She could tell he clearly wanted more information, but she wasn't sure what to say as she was simply trying to forget the man even existed.

"He hurt you." Retaliation was set as stone in his voice.

Deep breath. Shaking. Trying to hide the shaking. "Yes."

"What did he do?"

Apparently, blinking was not needed anymore from him. The sense of patience, yet firmness, that he had in waiting to know more came off as almost eerie.

"Some didn't believe me…"

"I will believe you."

"Since we were seen as already dating to everyone who knew us, despite me still getting to know him really, him raping me was not taken so seriously."

She looked back up into his eyes and jumped at the sound of something cracking into pieces all of a sudden, the noise coming from his other hand. She could see crumbles of wood fall to the floor from his tight fist. A large piece of the edge of the bed frame was clearly missing. She looked at him with a Q in her eyes…clearly wanting to know how he was crushing it with just his hand. He followed where her eyes led and then looked back to her with zero need to explain written all over his face. As if having that kind of strength was as natural to him as breathing. His mind was clearly still elsewhere.

"What is his full name?"

He stood up slowly to look down at her, clear intention written all over him. She was unsure of how to understand his fury, yet she held complete patience for her to answer. The mix did not seem natural. His whole being was of complete authority to take a life and not think twice about it. A part of her respected it. A part of her couldn't help but fear it. It was clear that he was unafraid, to say the least, of taking on such a task.

"He is already dead, Tronan," she said softly.

The look on his face was the same as hers—regret for not getting the chance, for either one of them, to give this ex what he deserved. She could see that Tronan was at a loss for words at not having any opportunity to avenge her in any way. She figured now was the time so that she could possibly help her ex never be brought up again in a conversation, to tell more and get it over with.

"He was the father."

At the last word, she had to look away, full regret on her face for knowing that such a cheap bastard was who she let be the actual father of her child. He could clearly read that she was disgusted with herself for not being smarter. It started to sink in for him the lack of fear she had around him. He thought it was from their natural connection that was of their kind that she simply didn't even know the half of yet. Yet now he saw, from her perspective, that she was simply used to fear from men. She had become, in a way, numb to it. It was written all over her face that she was nearing the end of trying to protect herself. Due to her ex, she hadn't been able to. Then due to her daughter dying, as he could see the memories in her mind now without her knowing that he had, she wasn't able to protect her precious baby either. Instantly, Tronan knew that he had no room to make mistakes with her. Claura made his heart beat again, literally, with just the sound of her voice. She had so much to learn, so much to be proven about her real worth. He didn't know where to begin without scaring her off, without her thinking that he was just sounding crazy. Right now, he simply needed to be there for her.

He still stood before her, clearly lost in his thoughts. She simply waited, rubbing her temples, clearly not in a hurry at all, clearly trying to erase the dream on some level still. Tronan decided to take a small step. He decided now was as good a time as any to open the door for her to realize what world he came from. He clears his throat and slowly sits down beside her again.

"Claura, let me ease your headache. Please."

"How?"

She could see the intensity around him fade, replaced by a soft concern for just her. She could see that he was a man of his word. He just wanted to help her. She figured she'd let him do whatever he was about to do before she asked the very obvious question lingering between them. She kept eye contact, watching him raise his hands, feeling just the tip of his fingers on her temples. She watched him say a few soft words in another language very gently, unhurriedly, it being clear this wasn't his first time doing whatever he was doing. Her eyes semi-widened at the sudden sensation of all the pressure behind her skull just vanishing. She raised her hand over her mouth, looking at him in awe and full of wonder mixed in with a bit of fear.

He cupped the side of her face with one hand, staring at her lips with intense admiration as he let his thumb slide over them, back and forth. The moment made her forget her question—almost. Just the way he looked at her made her wonder if she was in a coma and having the best fantasy ever. He did a slight smile, though not completely reaching his eyes. She could tell he was searching for the right words. She could tell he had a lot to explain about himself—about what was going on between them.

"Tronan, if you are to play a single game with me, I am going to need you to leave now. I've just been through too much."

The words made her throat tighten. She already couldn't imagine not being able to look into his flawless face again. She heard his mesmerizing voice again. His eyes suddenly jumped from her lips to eyes and sent that chill down her spine again. Her breath caught, and she suddenly wished she hadn't said it. His expression was of full ownership, looking back at her, ownership full of love.

But still, ownership.

As much as she felt for him already, her little human mind needed to be realistic. And he respected her for it. She could tell he wasn't truly angry with her, just the situation, as if it simply was not fair everything they were already dealing with between them, as if they were robbed of the happiness they both deserved in meeting one another from the very start. She pressed on, needing him to say something—anything.

"Tronan. Please."

It was her turn to press her small hand on his face, uncaring about his reaction. She needed to touch him, as he made it clear he was quite unafraid to touch her, even if it had been only requisite most of the time. A part of her wished he touched her more, but a part of her simply didn't want to be a fool again.

"I am of a different species, Claura. One that humankind doesn't really know about."

"Species?" she asked, watching him sigh before her.

He clearly wished he didn't have to say any of this, not wanting to have to put her through this, wishing she just already knew. He was ashamed of himself for truly not knowing how to handle this with her. After all his years of existence, he felt he now knew nothing to help him in this moment.

"Yes."

"I am going to need more than a yes here."

"You've heard of vampires?"

"Yes."

She swallowed hard. The crazy part of her brain was already sensing something along those lines about him. He was clearly something other than a regular man. His aura and presence literally screamed of it.

"You've heard of werewolves?"

"Yes." The smashed wolf figurine came to mind suddenly.

"You've heard of shape-shifters?"

"Yes."

"You've heard of…"

"Damn it, Tronan, just say it! What are you!"

"Specii de noapte," he whispered, as if in slight regret of what he was simply out of not wishing to scare her. She inclined her head as if to say, "So what does that mean…?" "It means species of the night," he continued softly.

She was starting to notice that no matter her mood or tone, his voice remained loving and neutral. The small notion was reaching yet another corner of her heart she hadn't known existed. This man was crawling inside her on deeper levels than she knew she even had over the smallest things about him, and if she was honest with herself, it was starting to scare her. It all seeming too good to be true. Her fancy little airport book came to mind, still thinking over what he said. And she saw him nod as if to assert her realization. She looked startled at him in response.

"You know my thoughts?" she asked quickly. She was not being able to help looking suspicious, as anyone in their right mind would be at this moment. He simply nodded, zero apologetic about it all over his expression. Making it obvious it was nothing new to him. "So my book, is it all true? What I've read?"

"I'd have to read it and let you know. But probably some parts, at least. You can ask me any question you want. I am incapable of lying to you."

"Incapable?"

She started to get out of the bed on the other side. She just naturally needed some distance whether she realized she was doing it or not. He stood up again to be able to turn to still face her, watching her pace.

"There are some books that call it lifemate, some true love, others soulmate. I believe your human race refers to it as partners or spouse."

"What do you call it?"

He paused, simply taking her all in. His face held all the proof she needed, his voice holding the most alluring and romantic tone as he said it, "Chibrit."

"English, please."

"Match."

"Match?"

"Though after meeting you, Claura, no term will be near good enough to describe what is between us. 'Match' sounds so superficial now. I never cared before, as I simply gave up all hope decades ago that I'd have that connection with another before I lay to my eternal rest. I am literally unable to provide you with the words of my feelings for you. I can only show you." He paused and waited, giving her a chance to speak again. She only kept staring at him, clearly trying to put all of it together. His tone lowered and became more intense yet caring as he continued. "With my soul, Claura, as well as my mind, my heart, and my...body." The last word was spoken like an intense promise. His eyes shifted to her figure just then and back to her face so quickly she wondered if she had imagined it. Yet a small part of her brain knew damn well she hadn't imagined it and even admired how he did look without needing to ogle. Damn him, even the smallest gray area moments were making her fall so hard for him.

"How long have you known about us, Tronan?" He could tell that she kind of already knew but just really needed to hear him say it from his perspective.

"Since our first dream together," he stated gently, a simple matter of fact he had zero regrets about. "In my bloodline, we all have a talent. I can walk in other people's dreams. I need a connection somehow to their situation or just the person in particular. As you can imagine with you, it was both."

"Where actually were you while we were in the dream together?"

"In my home."

"Where is your home?"

"Not far."

"This is too fast, Tronan."

She began to feel her palms sweat, her body began to feel heavy, and even her stomach started to not feel so well. She put her hands through her hair and crossed her arms tightly over her chest as she sat down in one of the chairs by the window. "You know what I have only recently been through, what I still have yet to recover from. If I can even recover from it!" It was more so yelling at herself than him. She could tell from the energy between them that he just already knew and was not hurt in the slightest and only worried for her. "I wish I had met you a year ago before all this happened. I really think I would have been what you deserved. But not now. Not like this. You simply don't recover from losing a child. I will never be 'me' again."

He did a quick light laugh, barely loud enough for her to hear. She knew she had not imagined it by the look on his face.

"What is so funny?"

"That you think you aren't good enough for me."

"I'm not. I'm boring, Tronan. Traumatized and boring."

"You, sweetheart, are anything but boring."

She looked at him like she was hurt, clearly taking it the wrong way. And he fully understood why she would. He walked over to her slowly knelt in front of her on one knee.

"Claura, look at me."

It took her a few seconds to turn her gaze away from the shadows outside the tall windows, as the image of them together in the reflection alone made her heart skip a beat—of him, specifically. She didn't know men even existed who looked like that. Seeing him kneel before her just made her think how out of her league he was all over again. His next words made her heart jump into a whole new rhythm.

"I love you."

The way he so gently said it was literally making all her pain go away and be forgotten in that moment. The look in his eyes, she had no idea a man could even look at a woman like that. She wanted to say it back, but some part of her wanted to hang onto feeling sane at the same time. Some part deep down made her pause. This truly was not what she had expected to happen during what was supposed to be a quick getaway for a while.

"Sweetheart, your eyes tell me everything. Absolutely everything that I need to know." He read her thoughts, though her face was already giving them away. "Even if I couldn't read your mind."

"That's cheating, and you know it."

She half laughed while saying it. He smiled in return, clearly just thankful some of the pain was fading, even if just for a moment—a moment he decided to take advantage of.

"Let me hold you by the fire. We don't have to talk. I just want to feel you next to me. Let me comfort you, Claura."

He brushed away the one and only tear, watching her as she looked mainly at the rug. He didn't know much of what to do, but he did know that giving her as much time as necessary to adapt his reality and what he was.

"You know what's funny, Tronan?" She looked up and into his eyes suddenly.

"Hmm?"

"That book gave me hope, honestly."

"About what?"

"That maybe it's true. We stupid humans aren't the only ones ruling the planet. I am worried about how much it does not actually feel or seem so farfetched to me. I am beyond sick of the human race after all I've been through recently. To be honest, I wish I could change. Leave. I have always felt like my home is in a place I won't be able to find on my own."

He stayed very still, contemplating every word. She loved that about him—how he so obviously took her so seriously. No one had ever made her feel so special before. Well, one other man came to mind. Roman made her feel important in a way she had never known before. But Tronan was on a whole different level—a level she was having a hard time wrapping her head around while her heart already felt fully content with every inch of him. It was hard for her to trust it, really. She could sense a part of him didn't care, that she needed to just get used to it, as if he had much more important things to worry about because they were truly connected in a way that was natural and just simply out of their control. In that, she felt offended not at all. In a way, the perspective helped her. Helped her more than she liked to admit it did.

"You can," he said, clearly meaning it, clearly wanting it, as if some deep part of him craved it every moment he was with her. Her eyes darted to his again and held all the reaction he needed to know—startled, intrigued, disbelief. He smiled and started to stand up, reaching out for her with one hand. "Come on, sweetheart. Let me hold you."

She looked at him with a hundred more questions in her eyes as she took his hand to help her stand but chose to just walk downstairs in silence with him instead. Enough information was given for one evening. Her mind was about to explode, a possible anxiety attack right around the corner. The last thing she needed was to feel embarrassed again. After all she had been through, a part of her wished she'd still toughen up a bit more. She was starting to feel like it was the least that could happen.

She watched him grab a blanket from a nearby cabinet and gesture for her to lie down first. He noticed her nervousness, deciding not to move until she did, watching her face and waiting patiently. She turned away from his gaze to pick a spot and forgot how to breathe as his hands made contact to move her body to curve against the front of his much larger frame on the cushions. They curled up on the spacious sectional together, facing the fireplace, his heart beat so perfectly strong beneath her back as she lay along his front. The rhythm of it soothed her very insides, calming her very being, watching his every movement as he spread the blanket over them. The gesture felt so sweet. The quiet between them as he held her felt so peaceful, causing her to feel sleepy only a few minutes in. She never felt more comfortable in her life between a pair of arms before. Her mind of its own choosing to take a break from figuring out why he felt so good so close to her.

So soon.

She decided talking would truly be one of the best ways to ruin the moment. She drifted off, unable to recall feeling more relaxed in her life as she fell asleep.

Claura woke a while later, feeling his warm body still against her. His strong heartbeat somehow made hers feel completely whole, as if it had been waiting to be this relaxed her entire life, and she just hadn't known it yet. She could feel him take a deep breath and sense him already being awake still. The obvious question came to mind, and she waited.

"Yes," he finally said.

"Really? No sleep ever?"

"It is needed. Just hardly ever. I've gone six months without before."

"Were you born this way, Tronan?"

Her face snuggled in the blanket more. He paused, unsure of how the truth would help or harm.

"Yes."

He could feel her energy of uncertainty and feel her emotionally pull away just slightly.

"That makes me a little more scared of you. Proves how different we are, how opposite our worlds have been for each of us."

Yet her body felt different, as it decided to snuggle in closer to him even as she spoke the words. She could feel him go very still. She suddenly felt as if she had been too honest—him taking her words the wrong way, for she wasn't scared of him more so than slightly terrified of what he was clearly capable of. His whole being held such an intensity, the way he carried himself, the way he spoke, the way he paid attention to things. She had so much to learn. A part of her felt self-conscious that someone like him would be interested in a woman like her, a woman who knew next to absolutely nothing about his species. About who he really was. Meanwhile, the human race was pretty easy to know everything about. Their entire history was pretty much broadcasted. The remaining silence broke her thoughts, actually missing his voice all of a sudden.

"I did not mean to offend," she whispered.

She could feel his hand move to caress her hair, moving it behind her ear. She felt him lean in closer, despite him already melting into her entire backside, warming her from head to toe, making the blanket seem like too much, yet not wanting to uncover herself much around him due to simply still feeling self-conscious about her post-baby body—well, postpregnancy body, as "baby" wasn't included in the postpackage for her. A lump in her throat swelled up at where her thoughts led to again and again, making her unable to hide a whimper in the silence between them.

"God, I am so sick of crying!"

She felt the warm breath from his mouth ever so close to her ear now, the sound of him inhaling her scent as if savoring her in his arms. She hated herself for ruining the moment with more uncontrollable emotions. She took a deep breath and let it out, wishing he would say something yet not wanting to force the man to talk. She already knew deep down she'd never be able to force him to do anything, no matter how badly she may want or need it. Her raw feelings for him for making so many similar things obvious. She cared for him so much already. She was just trying not to regret anything so soon. She was scared to show her true feelings for fear she'd come off as crazy. I mean, what kind of man fell in love this fast with any woman?

"I am not man, Claura," said softly in her ear, yet sternly.

"Then what are you? I need you to tell me more about you because…"

She suddenly felt courageous and felt like being more of the type of woman a man like him deserved, even if he already thought she was. She turned enough in his arms to be able to look into his eyes. He responded immediately as if not wanting to miss one second of seeing what her expression spoke for itself. It made her pause.

He nodded as if inquiring her on, knowing she was working up the nerve to say something for him. He gripped her chin between his fingers, suddenly looking quite possessive and full-on enthralled with her. Everything about him was so goddamn manly, primal, and so erotically close right now.

"Say it." He had pure masculine seduction in such two little words yet said so tenderly only inches from her face. She couldn't move if she wanted to, as if her own damn soul would betray her and stay in place even if she wanted to move. "Claura, dragostea mea, say it."

"Because my heart already literally can't stand it when you so much as leave the room." *The familiarity of you is making me terrified.*

"Have I left yet?"

"No."

"Exactly."

She watched as his lips slowly pressed to hers—so loving, so genuine, a kiss she had never experienced before, the type of kiss that was truly meant for fairy tales and birthday wishes. His eyes were full of intention, as if not worried at all that he knew exactly how to please her, just simply unable to wait any longer to do so. She moaned as if worried it was not real and just wanted to savor it all with him, coma or not. For if she was in one, may it last the rest of her damn life. She didn't want to wake up. In fact, if anyone did, she'd probably murder them at this point. She could feel him smile against her lips, trying not to break the kiss but unable to help it.

"You're reading my crazy thoughts again, aren't you?" She smiled accusingly, her hands holding his face close, afraid of him distancing himself, for it was the last thing she wanted.

"My chibrit, you warm my heart." He smiled, leaning in to kiss her forehead, lowering back down to look into her eyes. The feeling of worry was so foreign to him that it was slightly a shock to his insides. "What? Have I done something?" She was looking at him as if truly taken back, unsure of what to do or say.

"I've never had anyone do that before. I had no idea how sweet it could be. How loving."

He looked at her intently, like he had so much more to show her, but simply knew she was not ready, and instead leaned in for a quick yet soft kiss, as if just needing the contact subconsciously with her. "Claura, never fear me." He meant for the words to come out softer but failed. His emotions were a little out of control at how her words of fearing him affected him deep down. It truly made his heart hurt and anger build toward himself that she would feel such a way. She leaned away from him slightly, tilting her head to be able to look at him more fully. He let her go, yet she could feel his hands fighting the need to force her to simply stay where she already was—so perfect against him.

"You misunderstand. I fear what you are capable of, not what you may do to me necessarily. It's crazy, but it's like I already know it just wouldn't be possible for you to harm me. How is that so?"

"It's the connection. We do not have the same kind of love that I consider superficial, honestly, as your human race. I would still feel you from afar even if you were just human, as it is literally our souls that call to one another. It would just have been much easier for us to find one another if you were more like my kind. I would have been able to sense you sooner."

"Sense?"

"Yes. Through my gift, which is part psychic ability, with dreams. I would have been able to find you in your dreams much easier."

"Why now?"

"You were simply connected to a relative of my species somehow. I'm assuming Roman. In dreams, I can read some thoughts as well. I saw the images in your mind of Roman being with you on several medical occasions." His eyes skimmed to her lower abdomen as if now appreciating having a full understanding. His palm placed lovingly over her scar again, as if just wanting to comfort the memory in any way that he could. "And then you coming here, to his home, made it so it was literally impossible for me to be anywhere else."

"Ever since my dream...with you, you've been here waiting?" She placed her hand over his, the moment suddenly turning quite intimate. Just the thought of a child between them made her breath catch. She dismissed the thought quickly, simply not wanting to go there. She was unsure if she ever wanted a kid now. Her heart had truly been set on her recent pregnancy and everything that was supposed to come with it.

He nodded in answer. His hand slowly moved to palm her cheek, thumb caressing her face, her lips, as if subconsciously determined to memorize her every detail. She suddenly felt like just lying there, looking up at him, letting their gazes collide for however long he damn well pleased. For she knew for her, it'd be an eternity. She noticed his lips curving again.

"Reading my mind again, aren't you?" she asked softly as if already used to it and accepting of it.

Her mind suddenly focused on why she felt so comfortable with it. Sudden realization in her eyes made his hands still, clearly reading her changed expression.

"What is it?" he asked.

"Psychic ability?"

"Hmmm?"

"I had that when I was a child. I suppose it's time I admit things about myself too. Though you probably already knew."

"I do not get to read everything in your head, Claura. The clarity of your thoughts simply comes in waves for me. The stronger your emotions, the clearer I can read what's in your mind. If your mood is neutral, your thoughts are further away and harder to reach. That's the only way I can explain it. You can be taught to put a block up. It simply takes practice."

"That does make me feel better."

"Good." He tapped her nose quickly. His gaze was full of admiration.

"As a child, I knew right away it was not a welcomed ability. Among my 'species,' I realized even as a child, I needed to hide my talent. Over time, it just faded."

"Do you miss it?"

"I never felt a need for it. So I suppose not. All it ever did was bring something negative, and it was hard to find people like me. I suppose I just willed myself into giving it up, blocking it out, simply to just get through the day like a normal person." She lightly laughed to herself. The thought of feeling "normal" now, if anything, was comical. She took in a deep breath as if unsure of herself, unsure of what to say to him anymore. Sleep started to call her name again. She glanced at the clock, noticing the sun was to be up soon. She quickly glanced at him with worry, only to be taken back by his expression. He was clearly lost in thought for a moment as well, his hand once again placed on her lower belly, looking like he was trying to figure something out.

"Tronan?" He looked into her eyes slowly, as if not wanting to be disturbed from his thoughts but still had full love in his eyes. The way he gazed at her, she already knew she'd be heartbroken if it were just a phase. As if on cue…again…

"We will never be a phase, love." He was as serious as he could be, yet his demeanor still remained relaxed. "You will see. And no, I do not need to leave just because the sun is coming." He laughed as if pleased with himself.

"Don't vampires—"

"My species doesn't. I simply have to remain in the shadows around noon, and that's only when the sun is truly glaring."

In this realm anyway, but he figured that information could come later.

"What happens if you can't get in the shadows, Tronan?"

She was full of worry and fury at an invisible thing now. He took his time answering, enjoying the feel of her body under his hands, lightly massaging her abdomen in such a loving way that showed he had no intention of pushing it further with her. The sensation was wonderful. She didn't want him to stop, already knowing that she'd let him do whatever the hell he wanted with those hands as long as they didn't break contact. The look in his eyes became way more fervid than usual. He was truly fighting with himself now, almost able to hide it. Somehow, she could still tell. Anyone other than her wouldn't have a clue what was going on. Anyone other than her better never have a clue what was going on, for if another woman.

"Claura. Stop. Please."

"Human brain. I can't help it."

"You are my whole heart. Do not worry over something so pointless. It is simply the way we are, and it will never change. Yes, it's sudden, but with us…all we have to do is meet, and it starts. It is nothing to be truly frightened of."

"How do you know that for sure?" She already knew she was sounding silly. But she just needed to hear it. Something inside her strained for reassurance. She was simply still feeling broken, confused, out of her element after everything.

"I need to tell you something. I fear it will push you away." His voice was low, romantic, and unhurried. Something about it reminded her of a feeling of home. At his choice of words, she sat up, brushing through her hair with her fingertips, loving the way the soft light was making his ridiculously perfect features come to life even more. She truly loved just looking at him, as if just seeing him brought her the comfort a woman truly craved and needed.

"Just say it. If anything, I just want to understand more about what is happening here, about anything really."

He pulled himself up a little more, leaning on one elbow now, still on his side. Taking a moment to pull his thoughts together, he lifted his head to face her. She felt the need for sleep start to take its toll on her again, and she lay down on her side toward him, left arm crooked under her head, gazing back up at him. She took a moment to touch his jaw and his handsome features, enjoying touching him the same way he had done with her.

"Despite it may be pushing you away, it is proof of how much we will always belong to one another. I can already see in your mind that, in time, you will become like me. You said no games, so no games." He nodded as if questioning her, wanting her to be sure. She gestured back for him to continue. She lowered her hand, placed it under her head along with her other one, and remained patient. "Sweetheart, once you have just three drops of my blood in your system, as that is literally all it takes, you will be fully like me. Our blood, my line specifically, is that potent."

"Will it hurt?"

"Maybe."

"If so, how much?"

"I will be right there." He had clear determination, but not enough to hide the worry behind his eyes.

"How long does it last?"

"It varies. Everyone's blood reacts differently."

"Could I die?"

"No. You may need longer to heal, but you will not die. That I promise."

"That's all that matters." She could see he had more to say and was pausing. "What else is there? Let's just get this out now, please."

He nodded as if regretting that he had agreed with her. "There is something else that happens that could kill you, though. It has actually happened before." He could hear her heart rate increase. "When we become the same species, you as a female will go through…cycles."

"Cycles?"

"You will go into heat."

"Horniness doesn't sound like a drag." She lightly laughed, touching his lips quickly, playfully.

"I wish that was all it was, sweetheart. The thing that happens, though, is the intensity of it increases each time, so much so that your body reacts dangerously if you are without your Match."

"No one can help this. It has to be specifically their Match?"

The question put such anger in his eyes that he had to look away. She didn't question it nor try to stop it. If anything, she loved it. He truly was hers.

"No." His reaction was getting the best of him. Her hand needed to gesture that his fingers needed to loosen on her hip. He immediately reacted with a whispered chant of just a few words, and the barely a sting that he caused was suddenly gone. He looked at her gently, apology in his eyes.

"You're fine." *More than fine.* She could tell that he wished he could smile at that but continued instead with the sensitive topic—a topic she never imagined she'd be discussing with anyone only just a few days ago. *A damn heat cycle? Seriously?*

"The need for release can get so intense that your system will literally start to convulse, and your heart rate will just keep increasing. It is how your hormones simply react to the cycle, to where even forcing you to sleep will not stop it."

"But it doesn't happen unless you meet your Match first, right? So how could that happen?"

"There have been a few circumstances where the man was unable to accommodate her needs due to death."

"And she died?"

"Yes."

"And you fear you won't be able to be there for me?" *This sounds incredibly...unfair.* His eyes went serious.

"My species is hunted the most. As we have the rarest abilities and gifts, we are the most sought after."

"How do they even steal your gifts once you are captured?"

"Witches."

"Damn. Those exist too?"

"Sorry. Forgive me for this all seeming so natural to me. I am sorry if this is all too much for you, Claura. Please just tell me to stop if you want me to."

"I don't want you to stop. But I do feel like the information here is endless, and I am having a hard time keeping my eyes open again. Must be strange for you to be around someone who needs sleep." She smiled, eyes half closed, snuggling closer again. She felt the warmth of the rising sun seep into the house yet knew it meant nothing compared to the warmth she felt when so close to him. He kissed her temple and laid back down alongside her, pulling her closer against him. She relaxed fully, raising her head so that she could face him and look into his eyes—full of wonder, fascination, and disbelief mixed all into one. She closed her eyes, hearing his voice and enjoying the effect it had on her yet again.

"You are safe, my chibrit."

She smiled, eyes closed. "You wrote that note, didn't you?"

He answered with another kiss on her forehead. His strong, warm fingers brushed her hair gently. He gazed at her beauty as he watched her fall asleep in his arms before him. She smiled on the inside at how she was so oblivious as to how brave she was, simply being in the same room as someone like him. She was right to fear his capabilities. She didn't know the half of it. She had no idea what kind of creature had her literally wrapped in his arms right now.

# Chapter 6

## Believe the Unbelievable

Claura could feel the loss of body heat from behind her before she even opened her eyes. She sighed, sat up to lean on one arm to turn around, and looked behind her on the couch. A very small part of her worried he wasn't real and that she had been dreaming of him again. But she knew better now. Tronan was very real. He was a man of flawless intimidation and quiet strength, and he walked with such an authoritative sense of pure will that she feared for his enemies before she even met them. She knew she'd never be interested in another from just being in the same room as him for five minutes, whether dream or reality. The thought brought on a slight ache in her chest, causing her concern before dissipating only a moment later.

She took a deep breath, silently choosing to believe it was just her hormones. Her heart had, after all, been under some recent strain, along with her body. She looked around the spacious room and welcomed the solitude, actually, and took the time alone to really think it over, her thoughts uncontrollably lingering back to him and all his ridiculously attractive features. It was impossible for her not to notice everything about him. The man was the perfect height, standing at least six feet three. His build was of such a perfect shape and design that it made her knees feel like rubber just stealing a quick glance over any part of his anatomy really whenever she tore her gaze from his eyes. And she had yet to even see him with his shirt off.

"Those eyes. My god," she whispered to herself, caressing her own lips with her fingers while lost in her mental daze.

Her voice held just as much fear as desire. She was feeling taken aback at how easily she fell into them, followed by how hard it was to look away once she did. It was unnerving. She remembered seeing his lower arms with his sleeves rolled up, looking sexy as all hell in just a simple black dress shirt. The strong veins on his arms reached down his wrists and into his masculine hands. His long fingers held more strength than she had yet to realize, the crushed edge of the bedframe coming to mind, and yet the gentleness they owned when any part of her was in their grasp—the memory of her head cradled by him as he possibly saved her life. Any injury to that part of the temple was unpredictable. She slightly shivered at the thought that she'd almost ended up dead or retarded before even getting to meet him in person. Her insides grew cold at the question of if he'd still even have wanted her if that happened. She had so many questions to try to understand him more, but she truly didn't know where to start. And if she was really honest with herself, it was like none of it even mattered. She just wanted him for who he was, here and now. The rest would come in time. Her intuition told her that as long as she stayed near him, things would turn out how they should, one way or another. He reminded her of a feeling of home, and for some reason, that felt good enough for her for now.

She got up to grab just some water as she still had some groceries to get delivered. Turning the corner into the kitchen, she looked up and came to a quick halt. The counters already had some bags on them that weren't there before, and lying next to them was a note.

She unhurriedly reached for it and noticed the handwriting right away.

> I saw the notification pop up on your phone about still needing to complete a purchase and went ahead. See you soon, my love.
>
> Tronan

She had to smile at the little coffee drawing under his name, for he did not seem the type. The thought all too quickly reminded her of how little she knew about him still. She felt so confused with herself. It was so obvious her heart and soul belonged to someone who she barely knew existed just a few days ago. She felt foolish yet knew she'd be happy to die a fool if it meant keeping him in her life. She had been dealt enough bullshit cards for one person, for one lifetime. She deserved this, to be happy, to feel what she was feeling. She suddenly couldn't care less about the consequences of being with him, of being a part of his "species." She could tell there would always be a part of her that would be careless with herself after the pain of losing her infant daughter, but that's where Tronan came in. The way he looked at her was anything but careless.

The image of him so close to her last night came to mind again—his strong, handsome features, perfect jawline, perfect amount of muscle on every inch of him. She loved the feel of his face under her hand. His dark-colored skin was incredibly smooth and completely unexpected. She was almost jealous of it. He was her preference for a white man, but his skin looked extremely dark as if tanned from the sun all summer long outside. His dark blue eyes—almost navy—were like no color she'd ever seen before on a single person. She figured that there must be something different among his kind as well. She had to laugh at herself, at how "his kind" didn't seem so scary or foreign to her. She just wished she knew why. Her head ached when she thought about it too long like she wasn't supposed to remember something and to just leave it be. It was frustrating.

She decided there must be some coffee in the bags somewhere to go along with his little sentimental drawing. She made a grab for it as soon as she recognized the can, it being pretty obvious that a coffee could look the same no matter where you were in the world. Seeing that they were now stocked with French vanilla flavor, as they hadn't been last time, she'd been on the grocery store app. She mouthed a soft thank-you and turned to the coffee maker. She let it brew while she searched for the creamer and sugar. She was being very careful this time as she turned to head back to the living room, eyeing the island corner like she just wanted it removed from the home altogether.

She reached for the blanket, pulling it close, enjoying the scent of him on it still, inhaling deeply, admiring the mixture of what just made him smell like him. She really couldn't put a name on it. She suddenly wondered if she smelled as good to him, and she was now worried she hadn't. She glanced at the clock on the wall, taking in a long, delicious sip, wondering if she had enough time to just enjoy her coffee and shower before he returned. She wondered what it'd be like to share the experience with him.

Her body suddenly inhaled deeply all on Its own, as if subconsciously holding its breath for several long seconds.

"Stop it!"

She needed to talk herself out of being too easy. The last man she wanted to appear as easy in front of was someone like Tronan. She wondered how she would be with him during a "cycle," if even with her hormones and body taking over on its own, and if she'd be good enough for him. The man seemed so intensely sure of himself physically that she literally felt like she was completely inexperienced again, just lying next to him. She had to remember that no matter what species he was, when it came to the physical stuff, he was still just a man on some level, and she was a woman with more than enough experience not to feel intimidated. She laughed.

"Ya right!"

She knew damn well Tronan was way out of her league. In every way, she knew how to be. His mouth alone made her clothes feel extremely irritating. Just being kissed by him made her want nothing but skin and sweat between them. He looked at her like he was more than ready yet so willing to wait for her. The thing is, she felt like a slut in a small way for not wanting to wait already. The man deserved a woman with some damn dignity, at least, and that was what she had to keep telling herself whenever he touched her. No matter how small the contact was. She recalled how his torso against her backside felt as hard as a rock, as if Tarzan himself couldn't hold a candle to being "ripped" next to him. The feel of his toned muscular arms fitting perfectly around her. The notion of every body part below his hips making zero movement, as if not anticipating anything truly sexual at all from her…yet.

The thought made her still. She had been lost in la-la land over his physique, yet it hadn't sunk in what he was going to do with that physique exactly eventually. Her breath caught, and her hands literally started shaking. She placed her coffee cup down on the table before her. She took a deep breath. She tried to stop the very intimate thoughts of being taken by him. His hands were all over her, his body inside hers, every part of him dominating their love making. Her entire body felt hot and so nervous that she was starting to literally feel a slight stomach ache come on.

The picture on the table caught the corner of her eye. She glanced at it for only a quick second, not liking the full 180 her mind was doing. The only picture she had of her daughter was beyond a different topic to focus on, and she suddenly felt like simply taking a day to break from the memories. Knowing deep down she had the rest of her life for them to haunt her, the feeling of missing her daughter every day until she died, even if just for a few moments here and there from sunrise to sunset. It was just a normal part of her life, her day-to-day routine now. It would just never go away. She figured if Tronan had seen the notification on her phone, he must have seen the picture as well, lying only a few inches from it. She wondered what truly crossed his mind when he looked at it. She admired him for being careful when it came to the topic of her baby, simply willing to just listen and not press for details. Made her love him even more. Her love for him was growing so fast, even when he wasn't even around. She needed to hear his voice. The urge took her over, crossing out all other thoughts unexpectedly. She decided to try it, unsure if he would even hear her. Unsure if he was hearing her thoughts this entire time already. Her cheeks blushed ridiculously so at the possible realization.

*Tronan?*

*So you are awake.*

She felt an instant relief at hearing from him—instant relief that he hadn't been reading her thoughts of him this entire time. *Enjoying some coffee, thanks to you.*

*Feel free to still order more if I missed anything. My card is already saved on the account.*

Remembering she hadn't even looked through the other bags on the counter yet. She simply smiled, completely caving into the feminine side of her that he was bringing out at just the sound of his voice in her mind alone was capable of. He made it clear he could tell what was happening.

*Blush becomes you.*

She felt herself stiffen, cheeks heating a slight extra degree at his words. *How…can you see me?*

*I can sense it.* It was a complete affirmation. It was as if not a single doubt he was right. He could sense her nervousness now as well, making him smile too. *Claura, if you'd let me, may I offer an outing this evening?*

*What do you have in mind?* Her uncertainty made her kind of sound distant now. She really wasn't ready to be out in public. She still didn't even want to deal with a drive-through.

*Just one place. And you choose.* He read her so well even when not in the room.

*Okay.* She was unsure whether to ask for more clarification or just wait. She decided to just grab another cup full, practice the kind of patience with him as he so clearly had for her, and waited.

*My home or dinner.*

*Can we just combine them?*

*Afraid not. I don't have a working kitchen at the moment.*

*What happened?*

*I never needed it.*

# THE WINGED WITCH OF MATCHES

A serious realization took over. She almost felt stupid now for not seeing that one coming. Him saying that he had been born this way came back to her now. Clearly, his species did not need human food.

*You will eat with me if I choose dinner?* She wanted him to clarify. She needed to understand but without pressing. She just wanted to relax around him, just let it be. Lying in his arms last night was literally the most peaceful night she'd ever had in her entire life. He felt so ridiculously right to be around. She sensed something about him that she just couldn't put her finger on, something beyond "normal," but something about being in his home still made her nervous.

*Yes, sweetheart. I eat food.* There was a slight humor coming from his side of their mental link.

*Forgive me, Tronan. The last thing you come with is a handbook.*

*You can ask me anything you want, Claura. Absolutely anything.*

*I feel like I already have all I need to know just looking into your eyes.*

She inwardly praised herself for having the courage to admit such a vulnerable thing, slightly using his own words back on him. She felt him smile from afar.

*You truly have my heart, dragostea mea.*

*You never did tell me what that means.*

*Simply means "my love," rightfully so,* he said with complete conviction, as if nothing and no one on the planet would in their right mind stake a claim to her and think to still breathe.

His tone had her feeling something she couldn't quite put a name to. She wanted to question it, yet she didn't know exactly what or how to ask. She figured over dinner, if she wanted to, she'd press him for an answer then. He could hear her sigh on the other end, clearly feeling a bit overwhelmed still.

*I will be there in a couple of hours. I wish for you to just stay at the house.* He tried to sound as honest yet polite as possible. He just wanted her to stay where he didn't have to worry about her. There were a few who may dare cross onto the property, but seeing as it had been decades, he dismissed the thought. He knew he would be able to sense it if someone came to the house and was able to be there in seconds anyway. He could feel her dislike for being told what to do like a child. The sensation of it in his mind was strong. He tried again. *Please.*

The way he asked warmed her heart. She felt slightly crazy for already purely knowing that he was not a man to say that word with that tone to any other being on the entire planet. A part of him, deep down inside, was meant for only her. How he felt she was worthy of his choosing, she did not know, to the point of even questioning it with him seemed unworthy of her. This man was crazy sexy—crazy alluring, crazy intense. Why her? She suddenly realized she may have paused for too long and could no longer read his vibe through their mental link at all. It worried her.

*Tronan, if I asked the same—*

*Please.* There was a clear indication that he would explain if necessary later. She almost felt a little hurt, then thought it silly, for he was only trying to make her stay where she was safe. As if being in this gorgeous house was a flaw. She realized she was being slightly childish, especially as she had no intention of going anywhere anyway.

*I will remain here.* He looked at the picture again, unintentionally. She suddenly thought of how wonderful it would be to say that "we" would remain here. She decided to try bringing it up with him, to test such deep waters. *You saw the picture?*

There was silence, as if he was contemplating his words carefully. *She is beautiful.*

*Was.*

*Is.*

Claura noted that they could discuss their afterlife beliefs later, for she still just felt like taking a day for herself, a day to distance herself from the grief. Getting into such a possible debate was just simply not on the damn menu today. His question suddenly broke the downward mood that she just wanted to stay at least a neutral level, if not upbeat. Upbeat would be nice for a change.

*What did you name her?* He could feel her shaking, literally her heart and mind shaking through their link at just the one simple question.

*I never actually decided. She lived only a day. I debated between two names.*

*Use both.*

She humorlessly laughed. *I should have thought of that.*

*Tell me.* There was genuine authority in just wanting to know about something that was so close to her heart.

*Dayla Rosette.*

*Very few names, in all my existence, have sounded as beautiful.*

Damn. He was good. And then the fear of knowing how old this man may be sunk in. Despite all he had done to show so far that they were meant for one another, he needed to understand that it was just natural for her to fear some questions and answers. She could sense him taking a deep breath, in absolutely no hurry to answer what he obviously saw lingering in her mind. She could tell he was slightly struggling with what her reaction might be.

*You don't have to tell me right now, Tronan. It's fine. I am going to go shower and take a look around, as I haven't even seen this entire house yet. I have been too occupied with needing sleep, and then…you.* She blushed back, a shy smile tagging along. She loved how he never interrupted her. Never in her life had she spoken with someone who didn't interrupt her at least once. That alone spoke volumes of him being from a different time, a different place, and clearly a better place. Humans were so damn annoying, even if just subtly.

He smiled—really smiled. The feeling felt foreign on his lips and strange to his facial muscles. He couldn't recall the last time he genuinely smiled like this. No one had truly given him a reason to in so long. Ever since he saw her in the hallway in their first dream together, he sensed something about her. And then her voice, her voice literally said it all. There was something about it that brought him to life.

*Tronan? How do I know you have "hung up"? For I am heading to the shower first, and I am not ready to have you with me…even if just in my mind.*

She felt like a coward, knowing full well he could see deep in the back of her mind that that just wasn't true. She could sense the conflict in him, his admiration for her finding humor in small doses, yet his desire for her being held on by a thread. She wasn't sure whether she was simply being smart or not, for the intensity of just his damn gaze when he looked at her had to be nothing compared to what it would be when he was inside of her.

*Claura, the next time you speak to me of you in the shower and have such lingering thoughts at times behind those words, I may not have much control despite my best efforts.*

She could hear the apology in his voice, as if he truly was ashamed of himself and feared how she would react to him not being able to stop himself with her, especially after seeing her wake from such a dream earlier. He knew their connection would simply make her melt for him the same way he'd melt for her, but she didn't know that. Even so, even if that weren't to happen so naturally between them both, she deserved better from him. Heat coiled in her lower body from his words, chills were felt down her arms, and her head suddenly felt slightly dizzy. The still-very-human part of her decided she simply needed something more than coffee in her system already. She slightly wanted to blame how she was feeling on simply just needing some protein, for if this was how it was to possibly be for them before she was even turned and then facing a cycle.

*I will be there soon.* She could feel him fighting it and barely winning. She could also feel him "hang up." There was definitely a mental *click* snapped into place, leaving her relieved yet feeling barren.

# Chapter 7

## Frumusetea mea

Claura sat there for a few minutes in silence, unable to know what to do with being disconnected from him so abruptly. She had been hung up on before, but it never hurt. Not until now with Tronan. She took a deep breath and sat up straighter, decided to focus on looking presentable for a dinner outing with him, unsure if it was still even possible for her. She still had only her one outfit from traveling, thinking she'd stop at a couple of stores after she arrived and settled. That had been a mistake. She clearly underestimated the luxury of having her favorite clothing store literally right under her apartment building back home.

She decided to find his washer and dryer, wondering if he even had a set now after learning about Tronan, as her thoughts couldn't help but wonder if Roman was different like him too. It would explain what her intuition was trying to say, at least. She knew something was off about Roman, and she wasn't sure if she should ask

Tronan about him. It was hard to miss how he hadn't bothered to talk much about Roman to her, never wanting more details of why she was here in his home. He said very little despite talking with her so easily about several other things. Suddenly, the sting of being hung up on didn't overwhelm her so much, as she started to recall all her memories so far with him—the way he held her while she slept; the way he spoke to her; the way he listened, caressed, soothed, lingered, touched; and the way his eyes and actions took her so seriously. Deep down, she feared he wasn't going to stick, no matter what he said.

He was just too…perfect.

And she was just too…broken.

She lazily walked back to the kitchen to set her cup in the sink before heading back upstairs, noticing the sun setting into its late afternoon light already out the window, facing the beautiful yet eerie dark woods, feeling zero guilt for sleeping all day. Something about the sleep she just got after lying on the sofa with him made her feel more rested. She looked around her and no longer crept out at how silent the entire house was, about how not a single wooden board ever made even the smallest creak or squeak, no matter where her feet landed. She was starting to welcome it and starting to wonder how she ever got used to all the constant city noise. Even with earplugs and a fan running, she could still always hear something.

Claura enjoyed her shower this time. No tears. No hate for her own postpregnancy body. There was no uncertainty about the cesarean scar on her lower tummy. If anything, she closed her eyes under the warm water, feeling the soothing pressure from the spray hit her skull while her fingers massaged over the same areas his hands had been on the couch together. A part of her was shocked that a man was touching her again. A part of her was sad that it was only the beginning for them, as if she had missed out on so much time with him. She realized it was nothing compared to how he must feel, as it was evident his lifespan had been much longer than hers. She didn't know how old he really was, but he was not from her time. Men from her generation didn't look at women the way he looked at her. All predatory and territorial, yet full of mercy and passion. In her world, it was truly only something for the books.

# THE WINGED WITCH OF MATCHES

She could suddenly feel him invade her mind to see what she was doing as if just wanting to check in on her, then just as quickly evade. The knowing of it was a surprise, as it was so quick. Knowing she would have clearly dismissed it as something else if she hadn't already gotten to know him through a mental link. She started to mouth something…then stopped herself. Remembering his last words. She decided not to push him. If he wanted space to be able to control himself, then so be it. She slowly started to feel his presence again. Only this time, it was a little different. It was as if he just needed to truly collect himself and try again.

His voice first, whispering to her to relax.

Then his hands next.

She felt his arms around her as if from behind all of a sudden, the heat from his palms over her lower belly. She moaned and closed her eyes, savoring the feel of him holding her with the hot water spraying down. She felt his face close, inhaling the smell of her. She couldn't help but wonder just how much he could actually see of her body right now. A part of her feared it while another felt comforted by it. It was no surprise to her that he knew her thoughts by his next words in her mind.

*Claura, your body is still so beautiful. You are still healing. You worry needlessly.*

*You keep telling me that. Yet I can't stop comparing myself to how I was before.*

*Then stop. Once my bloodline is in your system, all is reversed. All is healed. Any trauma that was done is simply undone.*

*That sounds too good to be true.*

*I will be arriving soon. I will give you time to dress.*

*Please don't break from me so abruptly when you leave. Please.*

She was feeling more vulnerable around him than she thought possible for her. If a man were to come into her life again after her ordeal, she expected to be nothing but closed off. Her reaction to Tronan was still feeling…too raw. She could feel his hands linger upward until they were cupping her rib cage on each side, one breaking contact to grasp her face to move her mouth toward his. The kiss was incredibly sensual. It was intensely dominating yet caring. He moved his mouth in a way she didn't know a man could, bringing her right along with him into the perfect kiss no matter how she reacted in response. The man was ridiculously experienced and made her legs feel like rubber in under thirty seconds flat. The control he was having was starting to make her wonder how the hell he was doing it because she was about to give in any second and tell her dignity to go to hell. She honestly didn't know how much time had passed, but it had been some length due to his next words.

*Please hurry and dress, for both our sakes. I will wait. I am already downstairs.*

He let the pressure of him fade slowly, feeling her hold onto his arms a little tighter as he did. His grip on her skin gently became a recent memory now. The shower felt so damn alone all too suddenly. She had to turn quickly and put her hand up on the wall to stop herself from falling backward into where he just was as she felt him completely fade. She rubbed her temple with her other hand in slight disbelief that all this was actually able to even happen. She could still taste him in her mouth, and she literally felt her body beg on its own for more. The ache in her lady parts made it obvious that women could experience blue balls too. And she fucking hated it. She swore to herself for knowing she'd regret it if she didn't hang onto her dignity and get dressed instead of walking downstairs naked and right into his arms right now. Some part of her knew that this shower stall alone would never be the same for her. And he hadn't even been actually present.

She suddenly remembered not actually finding a washer and dryer for her clothes and looked at them scattered on the bathroom countertop with distaste. She really was not happy with herself for not packing at least one extra pair of clothes. Despite them being dirty, she did feel she looked her best in them anyway, so that'll have to do with the wardrobe confidence boost she really needed right now. And they were black jeans with a black cashmere sweater. So that'd have to hide any dirt good enough for now. Having no choice but to leave her hair wet, apply zero makeup, and be grateful she could at least brush her teeth with her finger, she walked downstairs with what grace and confidence she could find. His kiss was all too hard to block out of her mind as she scooted down the stairs and around the corner to see him sitting outside on the patio. He lounged in one of the roomy recliners that seemed too nice of a furniture piece to even be outside. He was facing away from her, staring out into the woods, seeming at peace with himself while being lost in thought.

She slowly opened the screen door, letting it slide across into place, noticing how the noise did not startle him at all. She walked toward his left side, keeping a few feet between them, and noticed how nice he looked the more she stepped in front of him to see his face. Sharp dressed man, a millennial understatement. He had a fresh haircut, fresh shave, and fancy black dress shirt with the top few buttons undone, showing off a chest that would make even the mouth of an experienced slut go dry. She swallowed hard. She felt quite out of her league again. She swore to herself, tucking her hair behind her ear, facing downward to the gorgeous outdoor hardwood. She could hear him take in a deep breath as if taking in the sight of her as well, along with her clear uneasiness.

"Claura... Look. At. Me."

She started to gently caress her lips as if remembering and truly not able to help herself. She suddenly started to cry, feeling herself becoming a fool, suddenly feeling slightly hysterical that there was even a possibility that this man was going to play her and drop her. He was just too good, too handsome, and too great a kisser. He was way too out of her league. This was all just so crazy.

"I can't," she whispered, placing her hands on her hips, shuffling back and forth on her feet slowly, still unable to look back up.

Clearly, she was trying to control her building emotions, trying to figure out if this was another postpartum episode that was possibly being triggered. It all suddenly felt like too much.

She turned to walk back into the house, car keys on her mind, feeling like she just needed some space to deal with her emotions. The man had seen her go through enough already. It was just embarrassing to have it happen again. She was supposed to be enjoying a nice dinner with him, yet here she was, running away, crying, unable to control herself.

Right before her hand reached the knob for the screen door again, she heard a quick incomparable sound and looked up to see him standing inches in front of her. She was close enough to feel his body heat again. It reminded her of the shower again. She blushed for him to see again. His fingertips under her chin, making her look up into his eyes again. For she really did love it when he did that. His touch was so perfect as if made just for her.

"I'm sorry, Tronan." He just gently shook his head no, as if to remind her that she never needed to say such a thing to him.

"You are still grieving. You are dealing with postpartum. You are healing from…trauma." The anger in his eyes was still relevant to needing to avenge her for what Jayson did. "My dear, I am forever. Whether you grieve like this for a year or a century, I am still going to be here." He stepped even closer, leaning his head toward hers more, serious intent all over his face that he meant it. "Understand that even if you weren't like this right now, it would still be very hard for me to control myself. All I want to do is comfort you in any way I can. Be it mental, emotional, spiritual, or"—he put one hand on her hip and pulled her closer against him—"physical."

It was a clear promise of zero regrets. He could read it on her face after a few moments, and she just didn't know what to say or do. Her shyness made it obvious he needed to take it back a few beats.

"Shall we go? I can sense your hunger," she asked.

It clearly meant that could go two ways and that he was there to sate her appetite whichever way she wanted. The look in her eyes made it clear which one came to mind first. He did a small smile, caressing her lips with his thumb again, yet still looking concerned for her more.

"You are not ready for that side of me, for I fear it myself."

"You said I don't have to fear you."

"I meant it."

"Then what…?"

"I don't fear hurting you, Claura. I fear I won't be able to stop."

And he meant it. Boy, did he mean it. A warm shiver went down her spine. His eyes grew even more serious, worrisome, and emotional. She could tell he was fighting with himself, never wanting to make her feel forced into anything with him like she had already experienced before with another. The butterflies in her tummy suddenly turned into something with larger wings, bringing her back into her body and slightly away from the lure he had over her whenever they made eye contact. There was a long pause between them, him still looking at her like he just didn't want to miss a damn thing in her beautiful eyes, giving her every opportunity to speak first and to let the evening lead where she chose for it to go.

"We shall then. Where are we going?"

She wiped her tears dry, clearly wanting the evening to just turn out as originally planned all of a sudden. Deep down, she decided that dignity won still, barely, by the thinnest thread in history.

With a small smile upward into his eyes, her hands reached up to frame his face, her expression of clear confusion as to whether to kiss him or not out of just not wanting it to lead to where they couldn't stop. She could easily sense her hunger, too, her belly doing a little flip. Bringing her back to more questions that she figured dinner would give her a chance to ask anyway. It was like how often he ate, what he ate, and what he preferred. Did he even have to eat human food? The airport book came back to the mind of how she could just point and ask, "Is this true?" and "Is this true?" His most fond memories were where he's traveled, where he's been. It was clearly overwhelming the amount of conversations they could have in just getting to know one another.

"You liked the meal you ordered in, correct?"

"Yes," she answered.

"Well, then we shall just go there."

"Okay."

"Wait here. I will pull the car around." He pulled away slowly and turned to go inside to get the keys.

She looked around her to notice the driveway and how it did wrap around the entire house, and she just had not paid attention before. She hadn't really paid attention too much here really. All she wanted was to sleep and have time alone upon arrival, and then the surprise of Tronan came into her life. The man surprised her on many different levels. He gave her feelings she didn't know a little human heart was even capable of feeling. She hated knowing that it was the death of her daughter that led her here in the first place. Or so she thought. If her baby girl hadn't died, would Tronan have still ever found her? She was sick of having reasons to feel down when all she wanted was to be genuinely happy in this man's presence.

She heard the tires on the gravel come around the house and ended up having a moment of distracted happiness, as if her wish was immediately answered, seeing him come to a soft stop, clearly eyeing her through the windshield. She took a moment to enjoy the sight of the most gorgeous man she'd ever seen driving her absolute favorite piece of machinery. It was funny how things could truly change so fast sometimes if you just paid attention. She walked over to get in the car with a calm confidence that he didn't miss. She sees the door open for him to get out, clearly intending to open her door for her. She put her hand up, admiring the charming gesture but just not needing to be babied. She watched him instead lean over to open her door for her from the inside, making it seem like he had to reach only a few inches to do so, even in a larger framed car. She smiled to herself. Things about him turned her on that she had never even thought at all to notice about other men before. She slid into the passenger seat, clearly content with being close to him again as he reached over her to help close the door, just wanting to still be polite in some way for her obviously. The fact that he couldn't resist himself, even over the small things, had her smiling again. He noticed. He leaned in for a gentle kiss on her forehead, then read her eyes for a moment up close, wanting to make sure she was okay. Make sure she was really fine with leaving the house with him. Deep down, he knew he just wanted to take her to his own home and never come back here. A part of him thanked Roman, giving her such a nice place to stay, at least in the meantime, for she deserved no less. He liked knowing she was safe, even if not on his own property.

He gently squeezed her knee in a loving gesture and started steering the car with the other ridiculously handsome hand. She had no idea how even the smallest parts of his anatomy made her face flush. It felt silly, but she'd be a fool to say she didn't like it either. She enjoyed just looking at him, admiring him, as he looked both ways and drove them onto the highway. His lack of inexperience at using the gas pedal flawlessly was another turn-on. Laughing to herself that, of course, he knew how to drive as well. She saw his lips curve slightly.

"Yes, sweetheart. I do know how to drive."

"I love this car. I wonder how long I am able to keep it actually. I believe it is still in Roman's name, from the airport." She looked out the window now, thinking over all that's changed ever since just the airport not too long ago.

"Do you want to go back home?"

There was ice in his question as if he was unsure if he should bother hiding his feelings about it or not, which means clearly her own home back in the States. He felt her turn to him then and looked into her face as well, just as intently. Both clearly read the other.

"Never." She knew she was a lost cause. And she truly didn't fucking care. Then it popped into her head on another note. "Do you and Roman know one another? You must be wondering how I ended up here. You must want more details than what you possibly saw in my mind."

"I am sorry if I see things from your thoughts that you may not want me to know. I am not able to control it all the time with you, especially when you are the one. I aim to respect the most. It can be a little frustrating for me. I want to know everything, yet I don't want you to feel taken advantage of." He paused. He caressed her knee, lost in thought a little while paying attention to the road. "Hearing things from you directly does bring things into perspective more, with my talent or not, please understand that. Sometimes, a person's thoughts can be blended, and it's hard to make sense of them."

She squeezed his hand that was still on her knee. It took a moment to just savor the sight of him, taking in his words before continuing. "So when it comes to Roman, what have you figured out?" she asked softly, as if simply willing to accept what little or a lot of information he would give her in answer. She could see his face go a little hard. His expression grew a bit dark. Yet somehow, she could still sense some respect toward the man from him all the same. "Your face is very hard to read right now, Tronan," she inquired as if to remind him that reading his thoughts was not an option from her end.

She simply was going to need him to come to terms with clarifying for her much more what he could simply see in her head. Her telepathic gift was simply not as flawless as his. It strained her to use it. Simply speaking, it was still just her preferred choice. Plus, just something about being in each other's head was extremely intimate between them. It could remain casual for only so long.

"You will in time, frumusetea mea. Once you have my blood… in time."

It was as if he simply couldn't wait for her to see into his mind as easily as he could hers, the last two words rolling off his tongue as a whispered longing, more so to himself. As if that would be a relief, and he just wanted to experience it with her starting now. The obvious confession warmed her and how he made it so obvious that anything intimate with her was welcomed by his entire being.

"When it comes to you, I fear the reaction I will get from Roman. He clearly cares for you and yet knows nothing of our connection. Of us." She waited, sensing more—a lot more. "Roman and I have a past, a twisted one. It is still hard to put into words to this day."

"Try."

"Was simply due to a witch, a quite evil one. Her bloodline is one that is rarely seen. She was taken with Roman. Only her affections were not reciprocated. Instead, they were placed upon her sister, whom Roman loved very much. The jealousy, as you can imagine, got heated."

"How so?" She could sense him stiffen, her question forcing him to distance himself. She did not like it. She squeezed his hand as if saying please. "Tronan?" His inhale was deep, nervous, making her blood chill for a split moment.

"He lost his child. The jealous sister…took things too far."

Claura stopped breathing for a very long moment. The soft hymn of the smooth engine was the only noise between them for a long minute. It made so much sense now. The connection she had with Roman became so much more clear. They had both lost a child.

They both connected on that primal grieving level. If only she had known. She had to ask anyway, knowing Tronan could sense it.

"Do you think that is where Roman and I mainly connect? Or do you think there is something else between us?"

Her willingness to be so raw and honest with him humbled him. She expected a bit of anger and jealousy at the assumption, but he gave her the complete opposite reaction, all the more solidifying their connection, their love, and their feelings for each other. She instantly knew that she would never experience the same moment with another man. There truly would be no one else for her. At the thought, her chest did that small sharp pain again, so brief she was able to ignore it. She decided it was simply her body reacting to the stressful thoughts that came from any discussion connected to her late baby girl.

"I think for him, there may be more, but that will change," he said almost remorsefully.

It was as if even, despite their differences, Tronan did not want to hurt Roman. The lack of jealousy made him so much more attractive than she ever thought it could. Calling this man next to her a real man was such a huge understatement. She wondered how she'd ever live up to being the kind of real woman that he so obviously not just deserved...but needed. Someone like him needed a real woman. She wasn't sure of herself yet for fitting that bill. As if in answer and not wanting to get into it further right now, he simply squeezed her hand, enfolding her small one in his much larger one. She noticed him out of the corner of her eye tilt his head toward the building coming up in front of them.

She turned away from the sight of their entwined hands to follow his lead. The restaurant was simple yet beautiful. The second story was for outdoor dining, which was full of outdoor lights, making it look kind of magical. She gestured toward that and smiled. He nodded, giving her a quick wink. She knew she was unaware that he was already a couple of steps ahead of her.

He parked the car and gently shifted it back into gear, uncaring to shut the engine off, instead turning his upper body toward her. She instantly looked up into his eyes, knowing it'd be silly to dry to avoid his intense gaze in such close proximity. Her eyes held the obvious question. She waited and waited. *Damn him and those eyes.* She suddenly just felt like staying in the car with him like this. It was actually a really perfect moment. He already felt like home to her. He just did, and her very soul didn't care to question it.

"Do you have feelings for Roman, Claura?" he asked with a neutral and tender tone.

He sounded like he just needed to hear her say it no matter what the answer was, as he wasn't going to leave her either way. She somehow just knew. She truly felt like no matter what she replied with, he would not feel ashamed of her.

"I did. Now I see why, I think anyway. It's so obvious there is so much I do not know, and I fear I won't ever catch up. Not to someone like you. But I hear you in his voice, and vice versa. I sensed something in Roman's voice right from the start. I sensed you." She looked straight back at him, not wanting to miss his reaction. "How is that possible? Are you both related?"

"In our way, yes. Not like your human way, with a family tree. It's our bloodline. We share the same one among our species."

"But you said you were born this way?"

He nodded gently.

"I was. Yes. Roman was not. He was turned by a witch."

Her eyes grew slightly wide. She continued, "That witch?" His eyes held the obvious clarification. "So I am assuming the evil, jealous sister?"

"I sense you will get the chance to ask him yourself. I see the way he has looked at you in your memories. It would very much surprise me if he did not make a visit."

"He has not come off at all that way. I truly don't see him coming here."

"He will." He nodded toward her purse. "You have a few missed calls from him. I believe he called twice just while we were in the shower." He could see her visage go from such innocent concern to obvious blush. It warmed his insides, her innocence—how she was so clearly a perfect mix of sweet and strong, whether she knew it about herself or not. "May I kiss you again, Claura?" he literally whispered. The gentle yet serious seduction in his tone was unmistakable.

She swallowed…and swallowed again. He looked at her hands, how she was twisting them together, her face showing she was clearly blind to the small nervous gesture. Still, he waited. Her voice came out husky, making it even harder to resist just taking her mouth already and claiming her again.

"I don't know what is happening, not completely. If you kiss me right now again, like you did in that shower, you better just take me home right now, Tronan."

There was literal pleading in her eyes for him to just make the damn decision for them both. The move was completely all his either way. She was already getting tired of fighting it. She was running out of steam to do so. Perhaps it was just a thing of his species where he had a more natural strength to fight it.

"I am not going to take advantage of you, sweetheart."

She actually laughed. "This connection is crazy. I don't trust it, and I can't resist it. It's not meant for humans. It feels almost…too strong, yet just so…right." Her whole demeanor was one of just trying not to be a fool while at the same time trying not to deny herself anything she damn deserved.

Her words actually had him pause, thinking something over that he felt foolish for not considering before. "Maybe you aren't completely human."

The slight shock on her face was hard to miss, yet she seemed full of wonder than fear about the possibility. "It would explain a lot." She just kept staring straight ahead, clearly lost in her own mind and not thinking about a single thing that was easy to see out the windshield. The determination on her face made him admire her even more. He actually loved that look, like she was on just the very edge of figuring something important out.

"Love, let's go inside. Let me answer more of your questions for you, for I know you still have hundreds lined up in that beautiful head of yours. Let me prove to you that you can trust it."

She heard him take in a deep, manly breath as if he knew his thread of control was already gone, and it was only a matter of time before he caved. He swiftly exited the vehicle, walking around to her side to casually open her door, holding his hand out. She put her hand in his, letting him lift her gently, feeling it move to her lower back as they walked to the entrance door together. People on the anterior balcony suddenly hushed a little here and there as they walked up the steps together. She could feel strangers watching her. She could literally sense their nervousness yet inquisitiveness in the air around them. She looked around. Some eyes darted away quickly, and others looked at her with concern. She noticed Tronan avoiding her gaze during the slight stare down as if simply not wishing to pursue it and just get on with their evening together. It was as if not a single person's opinion mattered about them being there. He was worried for her, though, seeing clearly on her face the pieces coming together too quickly when he finally did meet her gaze. She already knew everyone here knew who he was, and everyone here wanted to know who the hell she was. There was zero fear in her eyes, just the startled realization. For the time being, he could live with that.

He held the door open for her, taking full advantage of looking at the stares from others for a split second before following Claura inside. Many of the women looked away easily, clearly being smart enough to see that they should just mind their own business. A few of the men were not as easily swayed. He memorized their faces, taking into note quickly with little effort who needed to be recollected. He let the door make its loud thud behind him, the sound fitting. He turned to Claura to once again guide her on the small of her back, noticing the slight awe on her face. She was clearly admiring the interior. She gave him a quick, genuine smile that instantly made the previous few seconds fade into history, secretly wishing she did that more often. Suddenly, all the pressure of feeling like he was pushing her to leave the house too soon went away, and he realized he wasn't really relaxing until now, finally. He led her down the hallway to the right, up the emerald-carpeted staircase, letting her pause here and there at a painting. She made no effort to talk, her aura making it obvious she got lost in art quite easily.

He stood behind her, hands in his pockets, simply enjoying the easy moment with her. He casually rested his chin atop her head when she lingered longer at certain ones. She moved to look closely at the next painting up the stairway, reaching behind her to lovingly squeeze his forearm, seeming unknowing of the small gesture by the look on her face. He followed suit, completely unrushed. A small, petite female waitress came around the corner, politely asking that they follow her to their table. Her smile was soft, her demeanor tender, and she was clearly a waitress who enjoyed her job here. Compared to the city restaurants, she was a breath of fresh air in her own right. It was only about one in ten waiters where she was from seemed to not hate their job.

"Her father is the owner. She can pretty much do whatever she wants to the place," Tronan clarified.

"Explains a lot." She gave a small laugh. "Her taste is just wonderful. This place feels homey just as much as it does a restaurant."

"Yes. I knew you needed this kind of environment or to just forget it. So I am glad you were okay with such a choice."

He touched her low back from behind with both hands as if to reassure her even more as they rounded the top of the last step together. She turned to smile with an obvious thank-you on her face and set foot with him into the upstairs dining area. There were only three other couples enjoying themselves on the terrace, making it the first time for her to eat out in a non-noisy place. It was way more welcoming of an experience than she imagined it could be, all thanks to this gorgeous "species" behind her. It was scary how he seemed to know her better than she knew herself already. The thought reminded her of her many questions as she watched him sit down across her after helping her slide her chair in. The waitress said her typical waiter greeting, said she'd be right back with their drinks, and left with an extra cheery smile on her face. Claura laughed as if to say, "What was that?" while staring at him in question.

"She knows of us. She likes our species. That is all."

"That is all? So people do know about your kind?" She seemed worried for him instead of surprised, humbling him once again.

"She has proven herself to be…drama-free. Unlike so many do."

"When they aren't so drama-free, what do you usually have to do?"

She acted intrigued as if wanting to know for future reference to defend him, if anything. She suddenly came off as excessively strong-willed to him, leaning her elbows on the table, arms crossed. She slightly threw him off. At his elongated pause, she simply curled an eyebrow, seeming to just want her answer. He silently laughed, admiring really how she was surprising him. She was not as tender as he clearly mistook her for.

"Depends on what they have done."

She shrugged as if to say obviously. She clearly knew she wasn't going to get the details she wanted. He probably just wanted a different and more pleasant topic for them during their outing. She leaned back in her chair, eyeing him. "What were you doing before you knew of me?"

He could tell of her changed demeanor from the way others acted when they walked inside together and how that moment may have brought up this particular question. He could sense her annoyance, but more so her frustration at not being able to pinpoint the reason behind it. He needed to simply direct the conversation elsewhere and get them back to the here and now. She had plenty of time to learn the truth about him, about all his capabilities. It simply did not need to happen tonight. There was only one other thing he was thinking about doing tonight. He cursed himself inwardly for knowing that if she begged even in the smallest of ways, his control would simply be nonexistent. The sweet waitress brought back their drinks, took their orders, and left them be again. It was clear she sensed there was something in the air between them that did not need a third wheel.

"When I called this place to order, the man answering the phone acted quite…off…over the mentioning of just Roman's name."

"Why did you need his name?"

There was a small twinge of jealousy in his tone as if he was simply done with any topic about Roman for one night. It was as if his limit about the man was simply met. It was not in a mean way. He was just clear about it being a matter of fact for him. She could tell there was more to their past than he was letting her know. The slight sting of jealousy in his tone now made her pause, especially after him having none over what they discussed in the car already.

"I simply couldn't remember the address. They said the name may make it come up on file." She looked at him, clearly wanting him to continue with an answer still.

"The owner is a cousin of the witch that Roman had to deal with. And witches are known to not be able to let things go, even after centuries. It is truly their own downfall, and I do not understand how they don't see that." He shrugged as if he truly didn't care to have a connection with them, which, for some reason, stung her a little bit. She decided to brush it off. "After some years, it simply becomes...amusing."

"Every species has its downfall, I assume." She took a sip of her water.

She took a moment to look away, making her miss his reaction. She had yet to ask him about his species in particular. They sat for a few moments, just enjoying being with one another. The lack of awkwardness at no spoken words was so relaxing yet foreign for her. Everything about him was just so opposite compared to what she experienced with everybody else she had come across in her lifetime. She set her glass down, leaned back a little again, and twisted her fingers while deciding where to begin.

"Thinking over everything you said in the car. How are you connected to Roman and his...situation?"

There was sadness in her tone, as if intentionally trying to avoid the word "baby." She could tell he didn't want to address the topic, but she didn't care. It was just too important to her. Roman was, after all, why she was here in the first place. His face suddenly took on a sorrowful, worried look, as if he hated how he had to be honest about it. She hated how she may react. For the first time in her life, she succeeded at a poker face, knowing that she deserved to know no matter how hard the truth was about anything. In just a matter of a couple of days, the man already had her heart and soul thanks to this "connection," which she had the most questions about still. He rubbed his hand over his face. She could tell he was slightly annoyed at not being able to read her that well at the moment. He was clearly used to it being easy so far to do so.

"Forgive me, my love, before I say this."

He looked into her eyes. She simply nodded, trying to appear understanding. She tried to make it obvious that she would be sticking around, too, no matter what. She already knew she didn't have a choice. Neither of them did. He looked around before continuing, making her follow suit. It was eerie how all of a sudden they were the only couple left on the roof, for she had not even noticed a single other couple leaving. She took the notion as good luck really.

"I stepped in during Roman's situation with the evil sister. She was quite powerful and could not be taken on alone. We simply needed one more of our kind to end her, but they were unable to show in time. I simply took it upon myself to still try. I didn't really have a choice, for Roman's child was in the balance. The evil sister, in her jealous rage, condemned Roman's child to only survive if he remained out of her life, never to see her or look upon her even once. She went for the mother too, her own sister. I simply did not know of this curse in time and allowed the mother to intervene. I simply figured she had every right to. She was trying to protect her own child. By the time I realized what was decided—"

"She was able to kill her own niece? Over jealousy?"

His eyes went cold. For the first time, she saw the killer in him. As much as she wanted to admire it, he simply came off as demonic in the moment. Tronan was no longer her Tronan before her. His eyes suddenly met hers, his voice a tone she truly did not recognize and wouldn't have if he hadn't been sitting right here before her.

"Yes. So much happened so fast. I am ashamed, but I am still confused to this day. A witch can make you see what she wants you to see. Despite being there and seeing things happen for myself, I cannot shake the feeling there is something I missed." She watched him take a deep breath, clear regret on his face about more details he was leaving out. "It was made obvious I helped by leaving, is all. So I did." He looked lost as he looked away and down for a few moments, his face looking like he was missing something…or someone terribly and just couldn't put a finger on it. She figured that was enough details of it for the evening by how he was reacting. She wanted to just know one more thing, something inside her coming to the surface of its own, making her ask.

"What was her name, the evil sister?"

"She is dead."

"What…was…her…name." There was zero pause. Something in Claura was coming alive, as if it had claws of its own and was trying to dig itself out of its own slumber. She could see him pausing, trying to figure out why it was so important. Her mirrored gaze made it absolute that she would know this, even if he didn't answer any other question the rest of the evening.

"Moira."

"And the good sister?" she asked with sudden authority, eyes kept down toward her hands now as she played with her nails as if she didn't need to make eye contact to prove how set in stone it was that she got her answer.

"Maya." He was intent on his answers, leading to making it clear why she needed to know. She had absolutely nothing to do with the situation, from his perspective, anyway. Perhaps there was something he was missing.

"Thank you," she said slowly, as if intentionally dragging the two little words out.

She was intensely lost in thought over the information, making him actually feel like the third wheel in a sense now. He decided to try to bring her back to the here and now and started to speak when the phone in her purse suddenly went off. She took her time reaching for it, sighing in regret as if it was the last thing she needed to be distracted by right now. She looked at the caller ID, and her face suddenly looked slightly more awake. She held the screen for him to see. "Speak of the devil." She gestured for him to okay her or not to answer or just wait until later to simply be polite. He simply nodded as if saying it was fine. Deep down, he was thinking over how touched he was with her having zero condemnation for him after his little story and how she was completely focused on the other witches instead. He wasn't sure how to take that. She made no effort to get up as she answered the phone, which he was pleased about. It showed that he was still more important to her than whatever could be going on with Roman.

"Roman, hi. How are you?"

"Just wanted to check in with you. I haven't heard from you in a bit. How was your dinner?"

"It was wonderful, so much so that I am dining at the same place again."

"I am happy to hear you are out already. That is good news, Claura."

"Yes, it's a beautiful place. Probably won't be our last time." *Shit!* She was suddenly scared to look at Tronan. His stiff pause through the phone made it obvious she shouldn't have mentioned that. Was Roman really jealous she was maybe out with someone? Did he actually feel that way? She suddenly looked at Tronan with a worried question on her face. He actually smirked back. She flipped him off.

"Our? Make a friend already?"

"You could say that." She actually had to lower the phone and push it against her belly, feeling slightly awful at not wanting him to hear her fight a laugh. The poor bastard. After everything he had done for her. After everything she had been told about him literally just a few moments ago. Now, with Tronan making that face, he was making it hard to keep hers straight, clearly being proud of himself as she was starting to see that he was right. Lifting the phone back up to her ear. "Umm…you probably already know him." She looked up to Tronan again, this time keeping eye contact. He had the biggest expression of "here we go" mixed with "I will handle this" on his face. His lack of nervousness made her shiver, making her almost worry for Roman. Yet it helped her nerves steady. The moment brought to life the very real fact that she had never experienced being stuck in the middle before.

"I may know their name. Try me." Roman was trying to sound casual and glad for her. He also knew she wasn't dumb enough to fall for the act. He was worried, jealous, wary, and, in a way, had too much anticipation of her answer. He was already sitting down in front of his computer, aiming to have it ready for available flights depending on what she was about to say. He was planning to visit soon, but something in his gut was telling him to see her in person sooner now. Tronan suddenly came to his mind. He inwardly swore to himself, uncontrollably catching himself doing a quick glance at his gun cabinet in the corner. He could hear her take a breath as if about to speak.

"Tronan."

She left it at that. Feeling like a fool would only blabber on more in this scenario. She was full on wanting—needing, really—for Roman to have the next word. She figured he might see her as cowardly for doing so when, in reality, she just wanted to give him the respect to decide where the conversation was to go from here.

Roman literally felt his head get hot. His hands got sweaty. The phone in his grasp started to shake slightly. He heard the slight crack the case around it was starting to make and reached for some control to not crush the thing, for it was his only connection to her at the moment. As if his fingers had a mind of their own, he fired up Expedia as fast as the internet would allow.

"Claura, sweetheart, can you put him on the phone?" His tone made her stomach sink.

"Just one thing, Roman, please. He did possibly save my life. I don't think he actually meant to make himself known unnecessarily. Need you to know that." *I guess.*

She was trying her best to leave more details out, not ready herself to admit exactly what was going on. She was really hoping she wasn't giving something away already. She waited, but no response. It was as if he was having a hard time deciding whether to believe her or not. A small part of him was relieved as much as he inwardly hated to admit it. She clearly was not afraid of the man as so many were. It proved he hadn't done anything to her. Species and humans alike had feared Tronan and his kind for centuries—rightfully so. He wondered how much she knew, how much Tronan had needed, or simply felt the selfish need, to tell her things that she was never supposed to know about—at all.

She pulled the phone away from her ear as fast as she could so that he had zero chance of sensing her slight smirk through the connection. She felt truly horrible for her reaction to the situation. It was simply one of those circumstances like trying not to laugh at a funeral due to it being pretty obvious one shouldn't laugh at a damn funeral. She held it against her neck and bit her lip, slowly raising her eyes to Tronan's intense, watchful gaze at her every move while speaking on the phone this entire time. He seemed unaffected by her mood, as if just trying to deal with his own emotions first. Of all the times for Roman to call her again, it was just pretty awkward to have it be now.

The look on her face made it obvious what she was inquiring. He simply set his glass down and gestured gently for her to hand her cell phone over. She handed it to him reluctantly, unsure of how Tronan was going to handle this, not wanting Roman to be disrespected really. This entire evening so far was full of information she never expected to hear about Roman. That part of her that knew deep down that he was somehow going to be a big part of her life suddenly just got stronger. She felt Tronan's fingers brush hers so quickly, yet somehow, it still felt so erotic in a way, even under the circumstances, as she let him take the phone into his grasp. She started to push back her chair and mouthed that she was going to make a visit to the ladies' room. He nodded and waited for her to depart out of hearing distance before lifting the phone to his temple. He simply cleared his throat for Roman to hear, meaning for him to just go ahead already.

"Bullet or knife. Choose."

"I've already survived both. Try again."

The remark brought back memories of how that was actually true. Roman inwardly cursed himself that it wouldn't be so easy. "What are you doing with her, seriously, Tronan? She is only twenty-four goddamn it! This better be the best goddamn explanation of your entire existence."

"Easy. She is my entire existence."

The remark said it all. Men from their bloodline didn't say such things about a woman unless it was meant for just one thing. He could hear Roman give a huge sigh of regret and how it was so instantly made clear that it would be impossible to obviate her from the situation…from Tronan…now or ever.

"I never should have sent her," he said more so to himself.

He looked around at all the things he wanted to smash suddenly. Yet he knew none of it would help.

"I would have found her eventually, and you know it."

"Sure about that?"

"You know my gift."

"I also know your faults."

His mind was working double time, knowing in the back of his mind that this all started because of uncontrollable circumstances really. He understood how Tronan would be able to sense her through his own connection with her, through just knowing her as her doctor. It was just how strong the bloodline was. No one questioned how it worked. It just was. There was just something about Claura that made him want to protect her. And of all the men to be her Match, fate could not have been more cruel for both of them.

"We all have them, Roman." His tone indicated he really did not want to go there—not tonight.

"Believe me or not, I was planning on visiting her anyway. To just see for myself that she is fine."

He sounded determined to still make the trip despite now knowing it would never go as originally planned for him. Roman had no idea what to really expect when he got there and how he would react to seeing her make herself at home in his own residence that held so many memories for him. Deep down, a part of him knew he wished for Claura to help him make new memories—with him, not anybody else, and least of all, Tronan. He knew he was reaching for the stars, but somehow, Claura always felt worth the effort. He simply just wanted to figure out why, for his own sake, if not hers. He could deal with the feelings never being reciprocated, however strange they were, and how they never made any sense to him. He just needed to know either way, and now the chance was gone. Tronan continued, bringing his thoughts to a temporary halt.

"It's your home." He was making it obvious it was not her only option.

"Just let me see her before it's too late."

"She isn't going to be unreachable just because she is with me. Do you really think me that much of a monster? I would never make her do anything she did not want to do. You have my word."

"You know your word means nothing to me. Not anymore."

"When it comes to her, it damn well does," Tronan said.

There was a long pause. They could clearly keep at this all night. Tronan could sense her coming back up the stairs and around the corner before she even appeared. The worry and confusion were all over her face. He could tell she simply needed to go home already. Her dinner was no longer that important, no matter how hungry she was. He was starting to feel the same way.

"You know you are a damn fool to worry about her when she belongs to me. With me!" The threat literally surrounded every syllable, uncaring if he sounded cruel now. To worry about another's Match in their bloodline was one of the highest ways to be disrespectful. There was literally no one with more power, more knowledge, more strength above them. Moira had simply been the one extremely rare exception. The witch had literally called upon the devil himself to aid her.

"A warning!" Roman snapped.

There was no other way to word it. The coldness in his voice made him sound foreign to even himself. Match or not, he truly hated that Claura was in his hands. The anger was building at the thought of it being literal.

"We will speak to you soon." *Click.*

Tronan could feel the intense vibrations through the phone, and he was simply done. Being questioned, especially about his Match, was just not going to exist.

This time, Roman did let the phone crack in his hand to pieces.

# Chapter 8

## Rising Scents Level 1

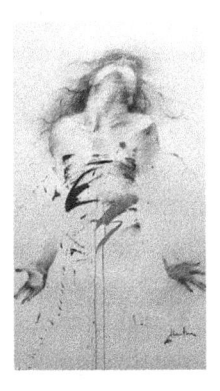

Neither spoke on the way to the car. The stares and, yet again, unnecessary glances from others on their way out were completely in the background for them. It felt silly not to ignore them all. These people didn't even know her damn name. Human or species, she felt the same toward them for sure now. It felt that their judgment was a little high-schoolish. It was funny how, at her young age, she was already able to tell that some people simply did not mature much, no matter how long their lifetime was. A part of her now judged her own race a little less. No more was it all the humans' fault that things could go so wrong sometimes. She felt stupid for not being able to come to such a realization before, even if she had at the time only thought them a myth.

She still didn't know exactly what Tronan was—what his species was. She only knew it wasn't important to her compared to what was sparking between them. It was all she could focus on, and she wasn't sure whether to feel like a fool for it or not. Sometimes, less information was better. In this case, she couldn't decide.

Tronan could sense her slight anger and frustration, her mood taking a serious shift. She just knew that it was inevitable that Roman was going to get hurt on some level through that phone call. The look on Tronan's face when she came back from the bathroom, watching the way he hung up the phone, was all the answer she needed. She hated it. Roman didn't deserve it. Yet one glance at Tronan's face in the car as he backed out of the parking spot and headed out said that he couldn't care less what Roman felt. Despite already knowing the emotions between them, she still wanted to talk about it.

"How did it go on the phone?" Details were clearly wanted by her tone.

"He is coming to see you."

"And you." She was unafraid to clarify.

He simply nodded slowly as if thinking over how to handle it without things escalating. She noticed his lack of need for physical contact this time. No warm and gentle hand on her knee, slightly caressing, expressing such love through such a small action.

"I need clothes."

She wanted to hide her small frustration at her reaction to him not touching her like before, feeling silly about it.

"Sure about that?"

She looked at him. There was a small smile on her face, expecting a smirk on his, only to find nothing but passionate intention. He was as serious as all hell, staring straight ahead as if not wanting to frighten her with what was clearly going on behind his eyes. She felt her heartbeat pick up, her lips suddenly dry. She realized that despite having been with a man before, she had never been with a man like him. She felt as nervous as a virgin—all too aware that the chances of not being what he expected of her being about 95 percent correct. She suddenly wished the only way she could be with him was during an intense hormonal cycle, figuring her body would take over for her while being in heat.

*I'm going to turn into a fucking cat.*

*And his ass will be worth it.*

"At my touch, your body will take over, heat cycle or not," he said, sensing her silence instantly. It was clear she did not know what to say—that she did not want to say the wrong thing and that she was immensely trying not to make a fool of herself. He could sense her intimate question about how many he had been with, simply for the sake of knowing how much more experience he had over her. There was not so much the women themselves. He admired her lack of jealousy as if their connection was above that cliche emotion naturally. He realized he did not want to answer her. It would simply lead to her knowing his real age, and he wanted to put that off for as long as possible. It was only natural that for someone of his long existence, there would be several other women in his past by now. He did not want her to think about it. Compared to Claura, they absolutely mattered not. He was connected to her. He could just feel it. He inwardly cursed his intense longing for her, knowing she was not there yet, not ready. He needed to hear her voice again suddenly, inwardly hating himself for her feeling at all uncomfortable.

"Is there a specific type of store you like?" He noticed her staring out the window, taking in the sights and watching the people along the streets.

Her demeanor was calm. He felt relieved to be able to tell by her face that she was not uncomfortable with him. She was just uncomfortable with how she would come across to him. He was unsure how to handle how opposite she was to the intimate part of their relationship. He wanted to visit everyone in her past that ruined that part of her, no matter how small their actions were when taking part. Jayson was specifically the one person he literally wanted to rip apart. When it came to pleasure with someone you loved, she did not deserve to be scarred at all. It was up to him to change that, only him, and he dreaded messing it up.

"Any clothing store. With my changed body, I just choose what is comfy now."

"I don't understand your worry. You are perfect."

"Everything just fits and feels different after everything my insides went through. It's not so much my outsides I am referring to. I never expected a pregnancy to be how it turned out for me."

She wondered if she could get pregnant once she was like him, no longer human. A small part of her was saddened, yet content, with it being fine with her either way.

She felt the car slow and watched his hands turning the wheel out of the corner of her eye to park along the street. He knew her thoughts but chose not to respond. He could tell the only kind of comfort she needed right now was the one she was not ready for. It frustrated him in a way he had never known before. And that shocked him after all the time he had had on this earth, in this realm anyway, knowing she was far from ready for that truth. She smiled a quick thank-you as he shifted the car into park and got out as if in a hurry to just get this done with. It was written all over her that she just wanted to go back to the house. He figured staying in the car while she went inside would be better for her. Drawing more attention to her by just standing beside her in public was not what she needed again so soon. He could see her through the windows and see that she was trying to just calm down and enjoy buying something for herself. He watched her pace to different aisles in the store, being able to choose quickly whatever she was looking at. He could see her walk up to the counter finally and searched her pockets, followed by an "oh shit" look on her face. Clearly, she forgot her wallet.

He pulled his phone from his chest pocket and texted her to wait just a minute. He could see her reading it through the window and look at him questionably. He looked at the name of the place and found the number with the convenient help of Google. He could see the cashier pick up the phone and go from friendly to nervous as he told them his name and some obvious instructions. Claura watched closely, seeing that Tronan just being on the phone with this person was changing their whole demeanor. She frowned at him through the window yet not accusingly—more so questioning why this person needed to react to him that way. The transaction went as smoothly as one could, and she said a quick thank-you and headed out the door. He leaned over to open her door for her once again, knowing that next time, he was stepping out and doing it for her whether she liked it or not. Something about not doing it for her felt wrong to him, beneath him—more importantly, beneath her.

She inhaled deeply as she turned to put her seatbelt on, stopping when she went to gaze at him quickly, nervously. She could see his hand come up to cup her face and lean closer to her, making their lips meet. His lack of pause turned her on instantly. He felt her immediately melt and could sense her inner confusion at how she couldn't control herself. He used both hands now, placing one on the back of her head, fingers lovingly locked in her long dark hair, giving her no decision in moving away from him and his ridiculously talented mouth. She caved, hard. She couldn't help that the more she lost control, the more he was already a step ahead of her with such intensity and passion. It turned her on more than she knew anything even could. And this was with their damn clothes still on. She suddenly agreed with his previous statement and thought to hell with buying clothes. He started to slow the kiss slightly. She loved knowing that he was unpredictable, that he had the power over her to stay like this for the next hour if he deemed it—right here, like this.

At the thought that he was slowly bringing it to an end, a soft yet deep cry came from her mouth, the sexy sensation of it spreading from her mouth to his, sounding like an obvious uncontrollable plea. The depth of it rocked him in a way he didn't know he could feel. The fact that she worried herself about pleasing him in return was absolutely ridiculous when just a kiss alone was making her react to him in this way. He watched as she grabbed onto him now, trying to pull herself on top of him right there in the car while parked along the street. He inwardly swore as if he had any control in stopping her. The feeling of her straddling him, unable to get close enough, taking over the lead with her mouth, she was clearly oblivious to anything but him. He devoured the moment, taking the opportunity to place his hands in places he had only been dreaming about so far every time she so much as looked at him a certain way. He felt her fingers grasp his shirt and pull. The feel of her fingers on his chest was way more sensual than he expected. Despite all his prior relations, he already knew that Claura was 100 percent going to be a different experience. He felt her body lean away slightly to make more room for her hands to now rip open the lower part of his shirt, breaking the kiss for a brief moment. He tilted his head back and swore out loud, clearly trying to find a way to bring back control and at least get her fine little ass back to the house first. The effort for such faded instantly as she forced his mouth back to hers, feeling her hands all over the front of him as he gripped her sides with pure intention.

Suddenly, the low of her back hit the horn, startling her so much that she literally leaped off him and back into the passenger seat. She wiped her hand over her lips, an intensely startled look on her face as if coming out of a trance. She looked at him quickly with nervousness yet an undeniable possession that turned him on incredibly. He never had a woman look at him like that—like she wanted nothing but to please yet control him at the same time so badly.

"Jesus Christ." He handed over his face, inhaling deeply as if he already knew collecting himself was as far-fetched as the fucking moon. He reached for the handle on the side and put his seat back into a more upright position, realizing he never noticed either of them putting it down in the first place. He took a few moments to just sit there, trying to control himself as best he could. He was literally afraid to look at her, for fear of her expression and how, if it was a certain one still that, he was genuinely lost. Suddenly, her voice broke the heated silence, a mere whisper, as if scared of herself. The unexpected tone made him face her instantly, worried.

"Tronan?"

"Sweetheart?" His heartbeat still pounding in his ears and other places.

"I literally just became someone else."

She looked at him with real fear in her eyes. It was as if no matter how good that just was, she had zero control in the matter. He watched her look at her shaking hands, then placed them under her armpits as if to try to stop it.

"I need to go home. Any home."

She made it obvious that she already knew it was only a matter of time, so why wait? She was his. He was hers. This connection owned them. She figured they might as well own it back.

"Your stuff is already at that house. It is late. Let us simply wait until tomorrow. I do not want it to feel rushed, you coming into my home. I want you to feel ready." He watched her breathing finally slow down and could feel his own match with it. "Love?"

She looked at him quickly as if fighting any cowardly feelings with all her might, literally telling any weak part of her being to go fuck itself. She was inwardly mad at being so out of control, even if it was one of the best moments of her life.

"That's fine."

The look of "holy shit that just happened" was still written across her face. Her need for reassurance from him was literally thick in the air.

"I love you." He couldn't think of any other words of reassurance being more important. He said with such a deep and meaningful determination, as if more than ready to prove it for the next thousand years of their life together if need be. "There is nothing I would not do for you. Do you understand me?" He hated seeing her so scared of herself.

"I love you too." She was not looking at him, but her certain tone was there all the same.

# Chapter 9

# Rising Scents Level 2

He could sense her anxiety literally rising in intensity in the air between them, noticing her whole body stiffen to where it was obvious the only thing moving at all was her mind. Her lack of need to take a breath started to literally startle him.

"Breathe." He was trying to hide the worry. His skills at remaining neutral were dwindling down to coals when he was around her.

"You sound like Roman. He said that often." She could hear him take a deep inhale, turn away, and shift the car back into gear. She noticed him gunning it slightly back onto the main road without even looking to see if another car was coming. It kind of pissed her off. "Tronan, you didn't even look to—"

"I can hear it if someone was. I can hear everything within at least ten miles if I focus enough."

# THE WINGED WITCH OF MATCHES

He kept his face on the road, not wanting to feel any judgment from her about what he really was, and hating himself at the same time for thinking he could keep putting it off forever. He just wanted some time with her. Some normal time. Something in his gut felt like it was just waiting, something lurking to jump out and happen at its own convenient time with Claura. The worst enemies enveloped themselves in the shadows. This was feeling like a completely invisible one altogether. The million questions in her mind were ridiculously obvious. He didn't know how to answer her and keep her from running at the same time. As if she had a choice, which made it worse in her human frame of mind that she still had. It would probably always have. He really was in lost territory, never expecting his Match to not be of his own race. He felt foolish now for not even considering that she would be of an entirely different species. He was so unprepared he felt like a fool. And here she was, thinking she was always ten steps behind him. Little did she know he felt to be about one hundred steps behind her.

"Please don't be scared of me, Claura. I can't stand you fearing me."

"Maybe if you asked questions about me instead. For now."

She could see him pause as if contemplating, his face softening a little at least. "I don't know who my mother is. My father made it clear he wanted nothing to do with me when I found him after being in foster care from a baby until eighteen years of age. I have no idea who my relatives or cousins are. I've never had any family. Moving so much my entire life has made it, so I have no idea how to have a long-lasting friendship with anybody. And I hate that the most out of everything. So I am not afraid of you, Tronan. It's getting to that point with you and not knowing how to move forward…that I fear."

He looked at her lovingly and then back to the road. She watched as his hand slid over to squeeze her thigh as if to just reassure her before lacing their fingers together over her lap. He felt so warm, so full of an energy she couldn't describe. Nothing about him at all was stressful, forced, or fake.

"And now you fear what may be happening inside you, correct?"

Her lips felt dry at his words, yet her mouth felt wet at just the sight of him if that was possible. She was wondering if just caving into her desires with him would be for the better. Maybe it would bring answers somehow. She was starting to feel like fighting the urge to just lie with her Match already, which was somehow making things harder. She was getting tired of feeling confused. It was wearing, and if she was honest with herself, she really didn't have much longer. Even if a curse was over her, was she really getting the shitty end of any deal here? Never had she taken the physical part of a relationship so seriously. She had literally hardly cared to sleep with anybody compared to everyone else around her for her entire life, so what did she have to feel guilty about?

Fucking nothing.

"Claura..." His gentle tone broke her thoughts. He looked at her gently and then back to the road as he slowed to turn into the driveway. "I can literally smell your desire, sweetheart. You are not making this easy for me." He could feel her uncertainty. It was clear she had no clue how to respond to that. The silence was starting to make him edgy, and he was already feeling his control slipping over other obvious reasons. Her particular scent was filling his nostrils, making his entire body go up a few notches on its own. It was making some primitive part of him come alive that he didn't even know he had in him despite all his years of being alive. Never had another woman's personal scent had this effect on him. For obvious reasons, he parked the car abruptly and had already exited the vehicle before the engine even completely shut off. She watched intently as he strode around the front of the car to open her door, but in her own sexual frustration, she beat him to it. She stood up and faced him square in the face as she moved to shut the door, clearly uncaring of his reaction to her slamming it. He went to move closer, taking into account every second of her unease. She saw his hands move toward her as if it was all happening in slow motion.

"Don't touch me." She strode past him and headed toward the house. She grabbed the door handle, only to inwardly swear at herself. It was locked. Tronan was still in full possession of the keys. She turned to look at him, already knowing from the feel of his body heat so close that he did his speed trick again. "Please open the door." As soon as her eyes met his, she could tell he sensed something that she had yet to understand. "What?" He looked so startled that it was making her startled.

"It can't be." He looked her up and down as if in awe yet full of concern, saying it softly more so to himself. He inwardly cursed himself that he knew he wasn't going to be able to stop himself. He knew there was only one more way to confirm it. Only one more way that she was not ready for. Her taste.

"Open the fucking door!" she snapped. He clearly tried not to turn to hysterical level 10 and just keep it at level 3 at least. "You won't answer me, so just let me inside!"

She watched with full-on impatience as he reached around her to open the door, his chest muscles slightly brushing her as he did so. The look on his face was yet another one she was not in the mood to decipher. She just needed him to be straight with her right now. Something full of anger inside her was building, and she couldn't stop it. Couldn't figure out what was causing it. The way he paused and thought over things before saying something was just starting to grate on her nerves, and she had no idea why. She turned around to cross the threshold in front of him and got about three steps before she heard the door slam closed and him pulling her back toward him. He turned her at the last second so her back was up against the door. His crystal-clear intent was to pin her there for a moment—his body against hers in the moonlight in the completely dark house, his face so close, his eyes so serious.

"You are in heat," he clarified with a grumble—intense, hungry, low grumble.

"I'm not changed yet."

"I know."

"How the hell? What the fuck am I supposed to do about this, Tronan? I'm already so lost about all this with you so far. I can't deal with this! My body is literally still healing. I can't even have sex again yet!"

"You're not going to do a damn thing. I am."

The look on his face with those two little sentences made her know instantly she was a lost cause. She suddenly couldn't care less if she was good enough for him. Something about what was going on in her body was making her think the exact opposite now actually, making her question if he was about to be good enough for her. And she hated herself for doubting him, for if he did everything else like he kissed.

Her body literally quivered even more at just the thought alone, heated and tightened. His mouth was all over her now, his hands staking claim anywhere he damn well pleased, making the words coming out of it sound slightly far away. It was as if her body was literally throwing every thought that didn't involve physical contact out the window all by itself. But she could still hear him.

"I will heal you. With one drop, I will heal you enough so that the only pain you feel will be truly followed by pleasure. I promise." The way he was kissing her was made her realize how much he was holding back before. The surprise of it had her feeling nervous now, and she knew he knew his eyes as he looked back at her, proving it. "I am never going to harm you, no matter how badly I want you."

He lifted her chin with his fingers in that way she loved and looked her square in the face. She nodded in response, clearly meaning yes to more than one thing, clearly meaning yes to what was about to be many…many more things. When she spoke, she hardly recognized her own voice.

"How much more intense is your species?" she asked hesitantly.

The worry in her eyes forced him to calm down a little, to just take a moment. He caressed her face with one hand, holding her close against him with the other, placing her hair behind her ear, leaned in, and kissed her forehead for a lingering moment. He closed his eyes and said a silent prayer to himself before sweeping her up and off her feet. With her legs wrapped around him, holding under her bottom with one arm, fingers splayed through her hair to hold her mouth against his as he took them upstairs. He pinned her against the wall for a minute in the hallway in the exact spot where they had first met in her dream. Claura loved the irony of it as his hands got to business owning her wherever he damn well pleased. His mouth was perfectly aggressive as he pulled her back against him and away from the spot she knew she'd never forget how this whole thing started, leading them toward the bedroom. She leaned back slightly to rip off her shirt and throw it right before he gently tossed her atop the bed, watching him take a moment to drink her in—pure lust, desire, yet concern all over his face.

His Match.

In heat.

So soon.

What the fuck was going on?

He could tell by the look on her face that she wanted to know how he was going to heal her exactly—that her mind clearly wanted more details. This was no small thing. It was one step closer to making her like him, and once it was in her bloodstream, there would never be a way to get it out. He took off his shirt, loosened his belt to toss it aside next, then kept a close eye on her reaction as he loosened his jeans. He aimed to do it quickly so as to not startle her too much too soon, as he simply needed to make room. The pressure in his groin was building to uncomfortable lengths already. It was hard to miss the satisfaction written on her face as she eyed his size. He simply looked at her like she was a fool to think she'd be disappointed and was even almost offended. He let his jeans keep loose around his hips as he kneeled down in front of her, pulling her back closer to him to take off her jeans. She lay back on the bed as he did so, raising her hips as if he needed the help, keeping a close eye on his every movement. She didn't miss the small moment of a certain expression across his face as he looked away to toss her jeans on the floor. A look of knowing that if she were to regret this, he wasn't sure he'd know how to fix it. He turned back to her with such love in his eyes before looking at her body again. The rush of her scent, with only her panties in the way now, caused a low and uncontrollable growl from this throat. He clearly was aching to already be doing more with her while not wanting to rush it.

She felt his hands grasp her hips to pull her even closer, close enough to feel his breath on her privates. Something on his face turned completely territorial, primal, animalistic, making even the strongest hormones flowing through her right now slightly pause. She expected him to look up, to take a moment to reassure her, as he so lovingly always did. He was so naturally intuitive with her that it was ridiculous. Never in a million years would she have thought she'd have fallen in love with a mind reader. A dream walker. A different species. She was having a hard time pushing aside and feeling nervous with not just what she was about to let happen, but who she was going to let it happen with. As promised, he did it for her.

One lick.

One suck.

One dominating taste.

Nothing on the bed was worthy of being able to hold on to. The sheer pleasure of her body taking over so instantly and just letting go all on its own was just as incredibly wonderful as the already building climax itself. The feeling of just caving in the car coming back in a rush, only this time she was more ready to welcome it. It was made clear quite quickly how his mouth was pure talent for more than one body part. She could feel him use one hand to move her panties to the side for better access, leisurely caressing with his tongue as he made his way back to grasping her hips and thighs as if determined to hold her this close to him. If he wanted to remind her to breathe again, now would be the time.

He didn't.

Tronan literally had zero control over his reaction to her taste. Even if she hadn't yet, he realized in that moment that if she was cursed somehow, then he was just as much so right along with her. If he thought her voice had influenced him, on his blood in proving she was his Match...her taste held a hundred times more power. It was not the usual flavor of a woman. She was slightly different. Whatever it was, it warmed him in places he didn't know could be affected. Her slightly different moans brought him back into his right mind. She was obviously feeling overly sensitive from still healing. With a quick bite of his tongue, just enough to draw a drop, he suddenly slows to do one long and slow caress with his tongue along her soft and smooth folds. He slightly pushed in with his tongue over just her center. He could feel her just slightly stiffen at the realization, know-

# THE WINGED WITCH OF MATCHES

ing she was in his mind at random moments whenever she could focus enough to want to feel what he was feeling. He knew what he was truly thinking during such an intimate act. He kept his mind as open as possible, wanting her to know the intensity of his feelings for her and nothing else.

She felt his hands move to grasp her thighs even more as her panties disappeared with the help of his teeth alone. It was done so quickly as if truly annoyed by their presence. She inwardly laughed at how they were her only pair and knew now that underwear never really needed to exist for her again anyway because damn, did this man know what the fuck he was doing. She felt his strong body pull hers even closer as he slowed down for just a moment. Her eyes opened suddenly. Despite her fear at what she just innately knew he was doing, she loved it. It was so erotic. She could feel sensations within her body instantly take place. Any and all discomfort she felt started fading, and the soreness started to disappear that she was still experiencing. It was all being replaced with a new ache—an incredible, sexy, and erotic ache. She could feel him start to pick up the pace again as if already knowing his blood would work that fast, every few seconds devouring a little more intensely, a little more deeper, moving to her bundle of nerves with scary precision. He was bringing out moans she didn't know she could make. She felt so good not to have to fake a single one, even in the slightest. She was starting to relate to how he was scared he might not be able to stop because she didn't want him to. She could feel the intense frustration building at just the thought of him stopping and trying to block out the unwelcome thought.

As if on cue, he got even more thorough, grabbing tighter and exploring more aggressively. Her climax built to peak perfection within the minute, his movements matching the building waves to a perfect fucking T. The building intensity made her body, on its own, rise to meet his mouth more, pressing toward him as strongly as she could. She felt him react the same, lifting her entire pelvis by grasping her ass from underneath with both hands. The strength of him turning her on almost as much as the sensations he was creating.

All thoughts other than her climax suddenly and completely faded to nothing. Pure feeling taking her over.

She could hear herself say his name as if an echo in the back of her mind. She tried opening her eyes only for them to feel too heavy, too much of an effort, as her body clearly wanted to focus on nothing but what this man was doing for her. The climax lingered in a way she didn't know could even exist, feeling like it was fighting on its own not to come down like it belonged in her body and had no intention of going anywhere. She could feel his strong hands hold her in place under his continuing exploration no matter which way she quivered, no matter in what direction the climax made her shake. She felt him fight to break contact as she eventually did come back down, truly struggling with letting the taste of her separate from his mouth as he gently lowered her body back down onto the bed. His hands slid down the back of her thighs, tenderly suckling and tasting all of her still quivering muscles within his reach as his hands then moved upward to cage her sides. Half of his fingers on both sides covered her breasts, so gentle yet so possessive. His every touch expressed a hundred things. Clearly still savoring the lingering aftershocks, she looks up finally to watch him move over the top of her, the sight more impressive than anything she'd ever seen.

The man was shaped like a damn dream. This man just gave her the best climax of her life. This man just made her body feel like it never went through any pregnancy trauma with one drop of his blood.

This man clearly owned her and her body.

Tronan lifted her with one arm underneath her, moving her back onto the bed farther to make room for them both, slowly lowering himself between her knees, wrapping his arms underneath her. She felt his perfect hands come up to gently hold her head and face between them, his strong forearms under her shoulders, just gazing at her, reading her, intensely memorizing her. She was still slightly breathing heavily while he seemed to have calmed completely—the obvious question of whether to take this further tonight between them as he kissed her, gently nibbling her lips as he stared right back into her eyes. He wanted her to just say it, a simple yes or no. The dominating expression made her pause at the slight shiver it sent down her spine as she lay so vulnerable underneath him, despite how much he kept reminding her that he'd never hurt her. Something about him was more animal than man, and she wasn't fully certain yet where she belonged in the mix.

"You're fearing me again," he said gently and matter-of-factly. It was a zero intent as a question. His soft yet serious tone suggested he was as well feeling blissfully sedated in his own way.

She sighed, raising her arms to let her fingers play through his dark mocha hair and Admiring how silky it felt. "Yes." She was slightly afraid to look at him as she said it. Most of her thoughts still stuck on how good it felt to have a release—a wonderful, explosive, ridiculously perfect release.

"I wish to change that."

"I already explained in the car—"

"You. Fear. Me."

"I fear what you are. Not who." There was an intensity of his pause after she said it, his face holding almost a glare at her now while she lay beneath his strength, sending another small chill down her spine. Suddenly, she realized that it never happened to her except when she was with Tronan. "I need you to tell me more, my love, about what you are," she said softly, full of soft feminine energy, never feeling more relaxed in her life after any sexual experience.

She could tell he was afraid of how she would react. But she needed to know. She was just extremely intimate without even knowing what he truly was yet. She deserved to know. His eyes softened. He was clearly reading her thoughts. She didn't care. It truly didn't bother her at all when he was in her head.

"I am an omnipotent being, a dream walker. I am the holy trio of the supernatural. I hold the power of each part of this trio tenfold. In my history of species, God's were reliant upon us."

He leaned himself up on one elbow, still leaning over her, and slowly looked away for a few seconds as if in deep thought about how to describe himself next. Without looking back into her eyes, he instead enjoyed caressing her hair behind her ear, admiring her features with his lingering fingers, tracing down her cheek, neck, and over her sternum. "I know it sounds crazy to you. I understand that. There are simply so many things the common human does not know about. Do you need me to say more right now?"

"How old are you?" she asked, looking completely unafraid of his answer, whatever it may be.

She enjoyed his exploration as his one hand now lingered down her side, gripping her curves, admiring her. Despite the seriousness of the moment, she already just wanted to kiss him again. She felt him take control again. She let him take his time in answering, noticing how he needed a moment.

"Do you think you will truly believe me?" His tone was gently authoritative. "It is literally in my nature to not be able to lie to my Match." He slightly cocked his head as if questioning whether she was sure she wanted to know. She looked afraid but like she needed to know, whether she wanted to or not. "My love...," he started, clearly trying to figure something out before he said anything.

"Do you want me to guess?"

He laughed. "May take a while."

She laughed back, though none of it really reached her eyes. "Last I knew, we had awhile." She noticed him stalling, looking down at her body as if studying it with all the patience in the world. His fingers were still lingering as they pleased. "You really don't want to tell me, and it's—"

"January 7, 1100."

His gaze was clearly dead set on not looking away from hers now until she responded. He mastered a poker face like no one's business in anticipation. She swallowed hard. Hiding the shock would have been a fool's choice.

"Explains how you are so good with your perfect fucking mouth."

She gave a wide-ass smile of a troublemaker owning every muscle in her face. His expression in response was pure priceless. Thoughts of what he was just doing flooded her mind, making her scent swell in the air between them again. She watched him look toward her lady V, inhale deeply, and look back up into her eyes. She knew, in a million years, she'd never forget what she was seeing on

his face right now. He looked like he had completely surrendered to something.
 To his heart.
 To his reality.
 To her.
 She, as well, owned him.

CHAPTER 10

## Always Here for You

She went back to casually playing with his hair. She just really enjoyed the peace between them at the moment, admiring his features, the way he looked at her. She had never felt so at ease after a sexual experience. Normally, she would still be feeling all self-conscious afterward, wondering if they thought her good or not. With Tronan, none of that happened. It simply did not matter at all to worry about such things.

"Gods may have relied upon you, but you literally look like one." She gave a soft smile, meaning to play, but her tone was obviously serious too. She really meant it. He was just that good looking. "It's crazy that I am your Match. And I like the term Match. It kind of has a strong sentiment about it." She noticed as she studied him how he felt no need to blink, like ever. "How long can you go without needing to blink?"

"As long as I want."

# THE WINGED WITCH OF MATCHES

"Hmmm, okay." *I will wrap my head around that later.* "Recently, when you saved my skull from possibly being splintered in half by me slipping, if that hadn't happened, how long would you have made me wait to see you?"

"I was planning on visiting your dreams again. Just anything to not startle you. I was terrified of you leaving for any reason, as I can have that effect on everyone."

"Everyone?"

He nodded gently. "Not just humans. But all species that are out there."

"What other species are you like the most?"

"Depends on what strengths I need to draw on, really, for whatever reason. The vampire side, speed obviously"—inclining his head in obvious explanation to the first time she saw him—"and the werewolf for scent and intuition…" He was contemplating, pausing.

"Witches?"

"Their knowledge is very useful. I do give them credit there."

"Least fond of them?" she asked as his tone was suggesting.

"For my own reasons, yes. I try not to judge the entirety of them based on my own experiences, but as they band together so forcefully, let's just say it's been more difficult with them."

"What talents do you share with them?"

"To be honest, Claura, your books are not that far off. Humans do know much. Just not that we actually exist. With witches, you can assume the regular powers with the elements. The give and take with the balance for spells to work. Many of us don't mind that you know things about us as long as you don't know us personally."

"To survive. Obviously." He nodded, then started to move as if tired of the position and started to sit up. He pulled her right along with him as if she weighed nothing. He leaned his back against the headboard, placing her between his legs with her back against his chest, leisurely holding her between his arms. "So your species prefer to simply hide the most?"

"To not want to be acknowledged by those who are already experts at not being acknowledged by humans themselves, in a way, has made it easy for us. There have been times where, for movies and books, we've noticed a slim version of the human fantasy of all the species being mixed. It's always so off-point that we simply don't worry needlessly."

"Not one, like you, has been known to the human world before?"

He stopped rubbing his chin gently atop her head and lifted his hand to her chin to turn her to face him, up close and personal. "Never." The seriousness on his face made her still. She wasn't sure how to react, honestly. Obviously, she would never be the one to put him in danger of being known. He clearly caught that thought. "Claura, there is nothing anyone could do on this earth that I wouldn't be able to stop."

"Moira…"

"She was simply in touch with a power we had not known existed until she used it on us. Knowledge is their strength. And they are very good at not letting the other species know everything. Moira was no youngblood to begin with. There was always something different about her."

"How long ago did all of that happen with Roman?"

He answered, "A hundred and fifty years ago." He could see her trying not to act too startled.

"Sorry to bring this up again. I just have this sense when it comes to Roman and his situation, and I don't know why."

He gave a deep sigh as he let her look away, watching her get lost in thought, feeling the silky dark brown lengths of her hair between his fingers. "Whatever it is, we will figure it out together. I can feel your hunger still. I will go grab our food from the car."

He leaned in close and inhaled, arms holding her tighter. She loved how she felt so much better with him just being near. The thought reminded her of how she felt so much better with just one drop.

"Tronan?"

"Yes?" He letting his fingers explore with one hand, entwining their hands together with the other.

# THE WINGED WITCH OF MATCHES

"I want another drop." Determination clearly overlapped any nervousness she had in asking it of him. "The power your blood has. I can feel it. I can feel you inside me from it."

"The craving will increase like I explained. I simply worry your mind won't be ready for what I'd have to do to your body to help you, sweetheart." She could feel his entire body harden behind her backside as if trying to control himself so much already. She felt him lean in closer to her ear and kiss her temple as if to reassure her before his next words. "What I just did with you was an intense understatement compared to what I will do." She could feel him become as still as stone. The only thing moving was his right hand, still enjoying the feeling of her small fingers playing with his larger ones. The small, sweet gesture seemed ironic against the intensity of the topic lingering between them.

"Even if I fear you, I want you more."

"That's not the only thing, beautiful."

"Hmm?"

"You won't become a vampire, a werewolf, a witch." He could feel her frown, her confusion, and her lingering question. Her mind tried to piece it together. "You will become like me," he said it like he feared for her.

"But that won't happen until the third drop, right?"

"Correct," he answered, admiring her small, delicate hand inside his. The courage he could sense in her was such a 180 compared to the sweetness that he saw in her eyes almost every moment he looked at her. "Only one drop away, though, means you will start to feel the effects already. The third drop simply solidifies what the second drop has already done."

"I see."

He could sense her resolve and her clear need to wrap her head around everything still. He could tell she was slightly annoyed at getting ahead of herself yet fighting with any control over it at the same time.

"I will be back with our dinner. Wait here."

He leisurely moved to stand up, making the space behind her seem so cold and empty as she snuggled against the headboard alone.

She watched him straighten his pants back on and lean down with his fists pressed into the bed to kiss her before turning around to head down the hall. She watched him go just the way the man carried himself had her lower parts aching again. She stared into space at the doorframe, thinking of how he looked so ridiculously good without a shirt on and just black dress pants. She thought over how the evening turned out altogether. She recalled the year he gave his birthdate and reached for her phone to use the calculator. She opened to home screen and felt her heart thump in her chest as she pressed the numbers, knowing the need for such an answer was one truly meant for fiction.

*I can't believe this is happening—923 years old.*
*This is not happening.*

She was unable to believe it—literally unable to know where to begin to let that one sink in. Was it even going to be possible for this relationship with him? She felt like she'd have to know this man for 100 years at least before being able to truly come to terms with just his age alone. She was not able to stop her thoughts at how this Match of hers was 899 years old when she was born. And here, the memory of a previous foster family popped into her head about the need to lecture her one time about dating a guy who was six years older than her when she was seventeen. She inwardly laughed, hand over mouth, feeling some of the shock start to take place. Holding the phone while staring into space again, she felt the small vibration and notification sound and looked at her screen to see a text message pop up. The lost feeling inside her suddenly crept to new levels, making her feel instantly colder and subconsciously reached for the blanket before opening the text thread to read it.

It was from Roman. He never texted—ever. It was short, to the point. "Please let me know you are fine." She wasn't sure whether to respond now or later, whether to respond or not at all. She figured with Tronan away for at least a few more minutes, she'd simply take advantage of the space. Roman deserved a response.

"I am."

"I did wish to speak with you more on the phone."

"You can. When you get here."

"I am sorry."
"For what?"
"Sending you there."
"I'm not."
"I am still always here for you."

It was obvious he was worried for her. He just wanted her to know that she could still talk to him, call him, and rely on him despite Tronan being there with her or not. She was so stuck between offended and thankful she truly did not know how to respond, nor if she even wanted to. The situation with Tronan was difficult enough. To be having so much confusion with two men, she wasn't sure she'd be able to take that on. She could see the dots appear and fade more than once on his end. The guilt over not knowing what to say was eating at her, and the feeling increased as she heard Tronan nearing the doorway again. He turned the corner and instantly read the look on her face, watching her look at her screen, then at him, and back again. He set their plates down on the small table by the doorway and unhurriedly walked over to gently take the phone from her. She took a deep breath, sounding frustrated and wanting Tronan to know that she did not send a message first. The complete lack of accusation toward her on his face as he read the thread warmed her insides. She figured in all his years, he must know how, on some level, to focus on more than one thing at a time and decided to bring it up.

"So 923..." She looked up into his face, still leaning on her side on the edge of the bed, lying under the covers.

The screen instantly became the less interesting topic for him by the look on his face as he turned to read her expression with all seriousness. She knew he was afraid of her response to this one particular thing about him. She knew that this one piece of information was what he feared would make her run from him. She knew she needed to get it over with, that despite the shock of it, she wasn't much of a runner. For once, she felt no need to blink either.

*Must be the drop.*

His expression softened. Her thoughts clearly made his nerves calm down a few levels. He looked back to the phone to simply shut it off, placing it face down gently on the nightstand. He reached his hand out for her to take it, nodding toward their food, waiting while it was still warm. She let him pull her chair out for her, the feeling strange as no man had ever done that for her before Tronan. She watched him sit with old world class yet as casual as a beach boy fully comfortable with every perfect muscle for her eyes to see—more like glare at.

"I just wish I knew…dammit! He doesn't deserve to be ignored, Tronan!" She sounded almost near tears, yet like she wasn't going to give in either. "It's strange having a hard time talking to him. He has helped me through so much, and now I don't know what to even say in a silly text."

"It may be best if you don't say anything to him before I do." He took a bite and looked into her eyes, the worry as obvious as the beautiful color green shown in them. He realized he needed to soften his tone. "Please." He licked his utensil while holding her gaze, noticing the immediate effect it had on her. His ability to hide his smirk was clearly self-resourceful. He looked away slowly to take another bite, clearly conflicted with himself for having to deal with the topic versus the energy between them. It was a 180, and he did not want to have to deal with more than once in one evening with her. The interruption at their dinner had been enough. Roman was going to be in major dislike of a reminder of a particular boundary within their bloodline when it came to Matches. He felt her energy shift, and her next words made it clear as to why.

"I will never catch up to you. Everything you've experienced, been through, all the knowledge you have."

"It all means nothing compared to you," he said sternly. He gave a dead-set stare—dead set at her. It was not a response she was expecting, least of all delivered so intensely. "Forgive me. My harshness is not directed at you."

"You're going to hurt him, aren't you?"

"That depends on him." He looked right back at her, regret in his eyes…yet no regret at the same time. It was quite the conflicting stare. "I'm sorry."

"Are you stronger?" She saw him sit back in his chair and watched him suddenly get agitated about the answer that came to his mind, which was that he was not sure how to verbalize correctly for her.

"Than Roman or others like me?" he asked.

"Both."

She watched him reach for his glass and take a sip. She noticed how his hands were so steady compared to how her nerves were all through her entire body right now. He set his glass down and simply paused for a long moment before looking back up at her. She nodded. Her face clearly asked how that could be. Wouldn't everyone in his bloodline be among the same level of strength in a way, like all the other species were?

"My father was like me, an omnipotent mix, my mother a powerful witch in her own right. Their mix simply made me different."

"How different?"

"The genes of my bloodline are tenfold for me. Whatever someone like Roman has, or any other from my paternal bloodline, it is simply a hundred times more potent in my veins. Hence, the way the others at the restaurant acted toward me, as I know you noticed. Since the beginning of time, people simply fear the unknown no matter what species they come from."

"They have a right to, it seems."

"Yes."

"You must have learned the hard way at some point not to abuse such power."

"Yes."

"And this is why you fear being with me all the way. Your strength."

"A part of it. Yes."

"Then give me two drops. Please." She was fully serious. "For me." She was clearly intent on making it easier for her just as much as for him.

"You don't know what you fully ask."

"I know that I don't. Yet I still do not care." She sounded really frustrated suddenly. The obvious fact between their ages was that she would never know as much as he did anyway—not really, not for a very, very long time, at least. She could tell he knew her exact thoughts by the look on his face. "Where do we go from here, Tronan? Do you really think we can curl up together"—inclining her head toward the California king—"and just watch a fucking movie with what I am already feeling run through me even before you gave me a first drop?" She watched him push his chair back and started to come toward her, reaching out for her. "We have yet to figure out why I already started a heat cycle! And I can feel it building again already with zero control over it!" She let him pull her to her feet, tears pooling in her eyes without dropping yet, seeing his concern for her grow yet again. It made her pity herself in a way. She truly hated what was going on inside of her, even if she did have the most gorgeous man to pleasure her through it. No one in their right mind wanted to be a slave to their own body.

"I am not going to turn you. Not right now."

"Why not?"

"Because I want some damn answers first. I want to know what is happening as well, Claura! Because I have enough control to sate you without causing any harm. Because I am your Match, and it is literally my duty to take care of you in any way, be it cursed or not."

"Is this us, or is this a curse? Because I need to know!"

"I. Don't. Fucking. Care." He growled, pulling her closer to him, watching the hopelessness in her face take effect instantly. He could tell she was already caving, letting it take hold of her again. Her scent rose. The energy between them rose. His blood to all the right areas rising, for he could tell by how she was already melting into him, letting him take possession of her mouth, that he was going to have to give her more this time. Her desire was clearly stronger. He feared only his oral talents would not do the trick this time, and that worried him. For he really did want to mean it when he said he had enough control over her. He picked her up, loving that she was perfectly fine this entire time to not bother with clothes at all again yet, as he could feel her entire body temperature rising. Her breathing made it clear that her heart rate was picking up in a way that had him worried. For some, the heat cycle would seem like a fantasy come true, but in reality…

His heart beat just as fast in return, knowing if he wasn't there for her, then she'd be in real trouble. He lowered her onto the bed below him, loving the feeling of her hands everywhere. He reached down with one hand to feel her…

Soaking. Fucking. Wet.

The growl he made against her mouth had her opening her eyes to look at him, feeling him enter her with two burly fingers as she did so, sending her hips into a circular torment of their own. The feeling of his thumb working her clit while the other parts of the same hand worked magic inside her warmth. The feeling was so incredible. Never in her life had she imagined a man would know how to work her body so flawlessly. Every moment of letting him do what he wanted seemed too good to be true. The cycle was making her hazy, the hormones making her obscure about all details of what was going on other than her increasing waves of another climax coming. She could feel herself grip him more and more as she peaked, her body rising off the bed, making her feel more of him against her as she did so, adding to the sensations. She knew at that moment, literally in the middle of her climax, that she needed the sensation of him deep inside her. She needed him.

Not his tongue.

Not his hands.

Him.

Something in her brain made her realize it wasn't all about hormones anymore. Something inside her needed to connect with him on that level. And it wasn't going away until she did.

The climax started to fade. When she even was in the room started to slowly come back. All she had been able to pay attention to was his skin against hers, his mouth devouring her every whimper and moan, his hands claiming in a way only a real man would know how. She decided to return the favor before she lost her nerve. She reached down in sensual exploration, in a way uncaring of his response. His inhale against her mouth as she felt his velvet tip was priceless. She smiled against his lips, taking her sweet time and enjoying the feel of him in her palm. The size of him was worrying, yet she could feel her body react with nothing but yearning. Longing. Aching. Tightening.

"I'm never going to be more ready, my love. I'm just not." The begging in her voice, in a way, left her feeling completely unashamed of herself. The feeling of him being inside her felt so meant to be it was driving her mad with waiting. She felt him move atop her, such possessive intent owning his face, completely owning every inch of her that he could as he worked down her body. She felt her pelvis raise in anticipation, his hands holding her in place while his breath was felt yet again against her warm folds. His tongue held zero intent on going slow, devouring her like it was his favorite taste in the entire world, wanting the flavor of her heat in his mouth as much as possible and all for himself. She could hear herself as if from a distance, asking him to please just do more already. The exact words she was using were not within grasp, as everything was more of a full-on feeling between them. Words literally felt useless at this point. At her thoughts that she knew he didn't miss, she felt him move back up atop her and grasp behind her head to lift her mouth toward his. She knew she'd never experienced a kiss like it in a million years with another man. It was so fucking loving yet territorial it almost made her toes curl alone. He severed the kiss to look into her eyes better, slightly leaning his forehead against hers. And he knew. Her temperature was increasing more than he realized.

"Sweetheart, stay still for me at first."

"I can't…that's just not…"

Her face was fully showing her defeat in the matter. There was no way she was going to be able to lay still for him while he attempted to gently penetrate her barrier. She could feel him try to hold her with his one hand as best he could, gripping her hip tightly, almost to the point of pain. She felt his fingers almost leave a mark. But she didn't care. Somehow, any mark he made was just not going to bother her. If anything, he really needed to stop thinking he needed to be so damn easy with her.

"It's okay, you don't need…to be so…" He literally tried to string the sentence together.

She felt him then, along with his mouth owning her every moan, feeling her body stiffen in sudden disquietude. His tip was clearly an invasion she wasn't accustomed to. He pushed a little more, felt her whimper again, and slightly pulled away from him. He could feel her temperature rising even more, the cycle in her system getting stronger, knowing he only had so much time before she was burning up…literally. He shifted a little for better access.

"Forgive me," she whispered against her lips.

He watched her face take on a deep level of discomfort as he pushed in far enough to be past her barrier. Pauses. She felt her body want to move but, at the same time, acted like it was too scared. He slowly did it for her. Her arms wrapped around his neck, nails digging into his skin, swearing inwardly at himself at how good she felt already while still dealing with her soft cries as she remained adjusting to his invasion. Knowing the only thing he could do for her in that moment was to move slowly, he pulled her arms away from him gently to be able to watch her face, needing to know from moment to moment exactly when she was starting to feel less pain and finally only pleasure.

"Tronan…" She winced as she inhaled deeply, trying to relax into him. She moved to put her face into the crook of his neck, inhaling deeply, feeling him barely move into her so gently she could feel him start shaking slightly. She realized that this was obviously torment in his own way as well. She looked back into his face and placed his gorgeous features between her small palms, tenderly kissed him. She felt him start to relax against her even more as well.

"My blood erases all previous trauma. Everything is healed and tight again. Remember?"

She smiled against his mouth. Her hips started to move with him. His moan was one she already knew she'd look forward to hearing time and time again. She loved how he still remained at her pace, no matter what level of torment it did to him. The deeper she felt him go, little by little, the more intensely he held onto her. The friction started to truly feel like the best damn sex of her life. She loved more and more every second the reality, the feeling of how just one drop of his blood was making this feel like the first time for her all over again. His size feeling made for her was the biggest understatement, literally. The closeness of him, his scent, his perfect fucking body, his gorgeous eyes, his aggressive yet loving hands on her curves in places she didn't even know brought pleasure at just being touched before knowing him...

"I don't want to wake up. Please don't make me wake up." She closed her eyes, letting her head fall back, letting him just take control. This had to be a dream. It was a silly fictional fantasy dream. And damn, if she woke up later from some stupid coma she did not know she was in, she would savor it now. Moving with him, yet more so just hanging on as her body was clearly determined to do its own thing anyway. Tears fell down her cheeks, eyes closed. Her repeating fear was still obvious. He made no effort to make her open her eyes and look at him. He understood completely and refused to judge her. They came from such different worlds and fell for each other so fast. He had never even touched her once before, only three days ago, and now he was inside her. Her body let him completely own every inch of her, inside and out. The feeling of her particular body joining with his was making the entire experience feel new for him. It made no sense. Yet, with Claura, it all made sense.

He could feel her muscles start to squeeze and release around him, the first waves of another orgasm for her to take over. Her hips were giving into a faster pace now, making it impossible for him not to return the need. He kissed her deeply, then pulled away to lean back into an upright position, pulling her lower half with him. Still lying with her backside on the pillows, she felt him drag her closer to him and lift her hips and ass with his strong arms and hands while never leaving her body. From half-closed eyes, still full-on focused on feeling the lingering waves as her bundle of nerves hit cloud nine, she felt him pick up the pace. He showed that he clearly took the hint that he didn't need to be so damn gentle with her. She loved the sounds coming from him, the noises he was making, as well as completely turning her on. She loved knowing that she alone had the ability to make this man, this species of a man, feel what he was feeling right now, right along with her. In a way, it made her feel powerful despite still being mainly a simple little human. She could feel him get more urgent, more dominating. His thrusts became more intense, making a small part of her brain panic even through her next building orgasm. The memory of him never actually answering her about how rough his species could get. She suddenly started to feel like a fool—a fool having another ridiculously out-of-this-world climax.

She could suddenly feel him in her mind in the middle of her decreasing waves, still making her body rock despite him clearly dominating any rocking that would be noticeable. It was obvious he was able to go this intensely for longer than she was used to.

"Claura, tell me to stop."

"Oh my god…" Her head leaned back, eyes unable to open, toes curling, her body just caving in completely at what he was doing to it. She felt herself grasping her hands over where he was on her skin, sensing instantly that she would never be able to loosen them with her own strength. Despite the pleasure between them, he was fighting with himself. "I can't." The look on her face made it obvious she was fighting with something and losing. That something was controlling her despite it being in the best of ridiculously erotic ways.

Tronan swore to himself. Despite living for almost a thousand years, he never knew it could be like this. On a deep level, it worried him because it was so intense he was truly scared of himself. He warned her. But only a fool would expect her to truly understand what he was saying. He knew of only one thing to do for her. It would make her strong enough to win against whatever she was fighting, hopefully, because perhaps she was right. Perhaps there was something at play here. A damn spell between them, one that was about to turn into a curse if he didn't gain some control. And in doing that, he had to make it so she could gain some as well—drop 2.

# Chapter 11

## Improved Senses

Tronan knew the only way for him to come back down into some semblance of control would be to sate himself first. And he fucking hated himself for it, watching his body lose control within hers, feeling her hands trying to pry his strong ones loose of their grip. Seeing the look on her face that he was slightly hurting her right along with giving her such intense pleasure. Forcing a second drop of blood into her system so soon was the last thing he expected to have to do for her. Too much was happening in such a short amount of time. He feared he'd have to put some literal distance between them after this to start to really feel in control at all and figure anything out. He could feel his climax finally building, her tight muscles gripping him more and more intensely as if to match him of their own will. He had never felt a woman's body do that before, not to this extent. It made his peak so much more ridiculously intense than he expected, the waves of it lingering and lingering until he wasn't sure he'd even come back down. Claura was truly made for him on all levels. At his last strong thrust, right before finally slowing, he felt her whole body shudder, and her mouth unsuccessfully held back a wail of pleasure. He could see she was struggling with herself, needing to come to terms with what was happening while her body itself was indulging every movement between them. He refused to miss his moment.

Tronan moved so that her entire body was beneath his again, forcing her mouth to meet his. He wasted no time biting his tongue, letting the unique and strong taste of copper mix in their mouths. He decided it was literally for her benefit to act now, and he would explain later. She stiffened the instant the taste met her tongue, eyes opening wide, trying to pull away to look at his whole face better. He wouldn't let her. He kept their mouths locked, refusing to miss his chance to do this.

*Take it. Now.*

She could feel him in her mind—so strong, so determined. His will was terrifying her on some level. She knew what he was doing yet was clearly still putting the pieces of the puzzle together as to why. *Tronan!*

*I am so sorry.* His hands were starting to get rough again, the fire building. *I have never not been able to be in control. I am terrified for you. You are not ready. Please!*

*How do I even know it will be enough? You were born as you are. I'm nothing but an experiment right now.*

His body moving inside hers was making it hard to focus, really fucking hard. She felt his entire body go primal, fundamental, and territorial. He had her entire body pinned underneath him in a way she didn't know was possible, not from him. His explorations were getting too intense, too dominant. Suddenly, she was praying to herself that the second drop was going to work as fast as the first. She felt him pause between movements, and as quick as it happened, she grabbed onto the half second of time to try to reach him. Using all her strength to force him to look into her face straight on.

"Tronan! Look at me!" The growl was coming from him, yet the complete look of admiration and love in his eyes had her startled yet feeling slight hope all at once. "Tronan, please."

She watched as his eyes followed her with one falling tear. From fear or pleasure, she really didn't know. His reaction to it was all that mattered. He really stopped then. She watched him fighting something inside him, struggling in a way as if he was determined to figure out, not just for now but for forever, how to control it for good and for the rest of their lives, however long that may be. She felt one of his hands move to thumb away the salty drop from her face. She reached one slim hand down to place atop his other one, lacing her fingers through his as best she could. Unsure if she had found a new strength already or if he was letting go of his own accord now, as his grasp finally stopped digging into her. She felt his arms slightly loosen, his hips start to move away as if meaning to separate their bodies, and she reached to pull him back closer.

"Not yet." She moved with him, toward him, not wanting their bodies to part. Just the idea of him separating from her caused an unusual panic. One she was not proud of in a sense but, at the same time, didn't care. She saw him look down at her body, glancing over her curves in masculine concern, taking his time, clearly in no hurry to look back into her eyes, making her wonder if he was truly pausing on purpose for him or for her. She hated how he was most likely feeling. He didn't deserve to. Despite his nature, it was obvious any harm to her would never be done on purpose by him. She didn't need a perfect man, even one from his species. She wanted Tronan. With all his strengths, all his flaws. Sometimes, it truly didn't matter what amount of years were between two people. Some things were just naturally known—naturally meant to exist. She could tell he thought himself an unnatural being, something too different. But that was just his makeup, his anatomy, his genetics. Not his soul. The look on his face was getting more heartbreaking by the second, causing her to break from her thoughts while watching him, needing to comfort him more than anything. Despite her pleas, she felt him slowly exit her warmth, still keeping place leaning over her.

"I love you, Tronan."

He inhaled deeply, fingers caressing and lingering, eyes still not looking up into hers.

"Don't say that. Not right now."

"I will say it whenever—"

"Don't."

He was clearly more disgusted with himself than he was choosing to show. The anger in his voice and at himself made her fear how to react to him at all. She felt foolish now, embarrassed even, that she couldn't read nor perceive her own Match at the moment correctly. She decided to close her eyes and take a few deep breaths, unsure of what else to do. His entire energy held an authority that he was seeing to check her entire body over before moving off her smaller frame. His hands were the complete opposite of what his voice had just been. The realization that she never had a real harsh argument with a man before made the situation with him right now even more uncomfortable for her. She decided to simply enjoy being with him, feeling him roam her figure, reminding herself that what was making their connection so ridiculously intense so soon between them was neither their fault. They simply needed time to figure things out, and the physical energy between them had been uncontrollable. But she chose not to verbalize it, keeping her thoughts to herself as best she could. The man clearly already knew what she was thinking. She could feel him in her mind, unable to help himself.

"I want to shower," she said softly and quietly, in no hurry to move.

She wanted to just comfort him but was scared as to how to go about it. She just lay beneath him, refusing to even put her fingers through his hair again, choosing to let him do any and all the touching. A small part of her felt like distance may help him, as he didn't even want to look into her face right now. After what he just made her body feel, she hated that he refused to look at her. He kept on with his extremely gentle yet thorough exploration, in no hurry to have a response. She tried to see what he was thinking, only to find a block up that she didn't know he was capable of. He never bothered to block her out until now, and it hurt. It reminded her of her previous stings, bringing her thoughts back to her body and how it was feeling sore.

He moved then, his frame leisurely leaning over her so his lips could press to her forehead, followed by him smoothly leaving her on the bed alone and in the room alone. The air was now cold everywhere where he had just been. She heard the water turn on in the bathroom, the squeak of the closet door closing as he must be grabbing her a fresh towel, and lastly, his footsteps as he rounded the door frame to walk back to the edge of the bed.

She looked up into his face as he outstretched his strong hand for her to take with her own. She noticed how he was still avoiding eye contact, looking only toward her hand, waiting. He was lost in his own head still.

"Join me?"

He simply shook his head gently but finally looked at her. She leaned her head back onto the pillow to look up into his face better, took a deep breath, and responded with a soft okay. It was full of understanding. She put her hand in his, let him lift her right into his arms, and carried her to the shower, setting her down right beneath the spray. He was clearly uncaring of getting himself wet in the slightest. She watched him look into her face as he softly caressed her lips with his fingers for a moment, then turned and left.

She never expected that when he would finally really be in the shower with her, it would have to be like this.

Her heart ached. Her body ached. She closed her eyes and let her head fall back to let the hot water envelope her head and face. She let her hands feel her body as the water warmed her from head to toe. She noticed the changes under her palms and how her cesarean scar felt pretty much nonexistent. Her tummy was back to its pre-pregnancy shape and size, and even her skin felt softer. She smiled. She savored the feeling of what so many women would die to experience all due to two little drops—two little drops that were now forever in her system.

The fact that she had blood from an omnipotent being running through her veins should have terrified her. But the fact that she wasn't scared about it at all was what was truly terrifying. If Roman had been disappointed in her before, she really was in question as to how much his mind would explode now. For some reason, she could already sense that he would be here soon. She figured what it would hurt to ask him exactly when he planned to arrive. Being with these two men in the same house together was going to be interesting enough. She simply prepared herself for it the best she could, which was the least she could do for herself, or maybe just leave, as doing a solo outing for a while may just be the better choice here. She didn't want to see Roman offended or hurt or whatever was going to be his reaction to all this. She didn't want to see an all-powerful being that held her heart on his fingertip lose his shit on someone she cared about. She was in no mood to try to figure out what powers she held now within herself so soon. The last thing she wanted to do was make things worse by just trying and failing anyway.

She shut the water off, uncaring that she completely forgot to use any soap and wash up at all, got dried off, and remembered she had left her new clothes in the car. Swearing to herself for not really wanting to walk outside in a towel nor put her dirty clothes back on for just the quick task, she decided to simply use her mental link with Tronan. And as usual, as she rounds the doorway to step back into the bedroom, he proves he will always be a step ahead of her. The bag was already placed on the bed, with a note next to it.

Just reach out if you need me.

There was no explanation as to where he was going nor for how long. She admired that he wasn't a man who needed to explain himself. It should have bugged her, but she was simply planning on getting some space herself anyway. She decided to call it a night and simply went out in the morning for a drive. Taking a few deep breaths while thinking over the day, she curled up under the blankets and reached for the remote. She knew she wouldn't be watching anything for very long anyway.

*****

The next morning, Claura woke up feeling of still being alone. Despite missing him, the peace of having her own time to think over everything was exactly what she needed. Even with all that happened yesterday, she still ended up sleeping like a baby, pill not included.

She sits up and stares at her bag of new clothes, instantly deciding to start the day where she wanted to last night.

She reached into the bag for her new bra and undies first, both feeling a bit big now. The wonderful pros to his blood in her system were obvious, and she didn't expect it to happen while purchasing the items. She felt she at least had a reason now to go somewhere. A drive alone would feel good. She finished putting on her dark indigo jeans and navy cashmere sweater, loving how none of it felt too tight in any place on her body anymore. It was so nice to just feel comfortable in her own skin again. She grabbed her phone and turned it on as she headed downstairs for the car keys, appreciative of their easy find right on the large kitchen island as if he already knew...again. She smirked to herself. A part of her felt like her complete self, knowing she found someone who was far from any man she truly ever saw herself being with—*for forever*. The thought had her nerves doing a jolt as she opened the door and shut it behind her, looking around at the beautiful scenery.

The woods were so peaceful, the smell was just so fresh and welcoming, and the colors of everything on the property were like a picture from a magazine with the glow from the sun starting to rise, touching everything. Every detail was clearer, whether near her or one hundred yards away. Her eyes were truly making her wonder how much better a hawk would see than what she was capable of now or if the animal simply had some competition it didn't know about. She felt so appreciative of the way she felt so new from head to toe, her lungs literally breathing better, her muscles feeling more relaxed yet stronger than she knew was even possible. She started moving toward the car and pressed the key to unlock and start it even while still a distance away. Leisurely, she slid in, still in admiration of the leather seats that she never got to experience before in a single vehicle. She remembered when she came here, how the heat setting on them felt so amazing, and now she realized it was the last thing she needed. Her body felt warmer than usual but yet like it was the new normal and nothing was wrong. She worried that her temperature alone would make Roman realize everything that had happened. These men were smart, scary smart—the type of smartness that one tried to hide about themselves. She felt humbled really just being someone that they even wanted around. How she got so lucky, she figured she'd never really know. She looked at the gorgeous house as she backed the car around to head for the highway. A part of her was sad that she would not be able to be within its walls forever. She took her time finding anything along the lines of a Target on the GPS before really speeding up on the highway. She figured the chosen destination would be enough to get her near any store that would do just fine. She reaches for the radio button and instantly covers her ears with both hands, slamming on the brakes in the middle of the road, inwardly thankful no one was around to ram into her. The car came to a screeching halt, and she jammed the switch to shut it off with a new speed she was surprised with, yet still more focused on her ringing eardrums.

"For fuck's sake!"

She was still covering her ears resolutely, noticing that despite the pain, it was disappearing just as fast as it had come. Within a matter of seconds, it was as if nothing ever happened. Her human brain had obviously at first gone instantly to thinking she'd have to deal with a chronic earache for days at such intense, immediate pain. She cautiously put her slightly shaking hands back on the steering wheel after a few moments and just stared out into the increasing dawn. The fog was starting to seep everywhere, making it all look serene. Sudden fear crept in as to how she was going to have to be so beyond careful at hiding what she was becoming from the common eye. She wanted to reach out to Tronan for any advice but stopped herself, as she felt stronger about just giving him his space for now. Her mind wandered to the things he had told her already as if he had little worry about protecting her no matter how much she did or didn't yet understand. It was almost to the length of him not even wanting her to know how sure of himself he was, as if that would frighten her alone. Then her mind started to wander back to everything he had physically done to her in that bedroom…and when he…and then…

"Stop!"

She hurriedly shifted the car back into drive and floored it back onto the road into the proper lane. She was mad at herself for her lack of control with such matters, wanting to punch this curse or whatever was going on in the fucking face. She screamed at it to just give it a damn rest already. A woman who needed a break from being a slave inside her own skin was a pretty natural thing to desire. She figured maybe the library might be a good place to stop at, then thought better of it. She dragged any attention toward the topic she wanted to learn about, which might not be a brilliant idea for any commoner to see. She knew Roman had a computer at the house, obviously the smarter bet here.

She glanced at her watch to get a general idea of when the man might actually show, suddenly remembering that she had forgotten to send a quick text at least to ask what time his arrival would be. The time suggested about fourteen hours since she spoke on the phone with him at the restaurant. It was more than enough time to get here, even with such a long flight.

Suddenly, a woman's voice in her head told her to stop the car. The strength in it was eerie, the tone suggesting that not getting her way was long over with. Something about it made her simply just still, acknowledgment alone with zero reaction, as if unafraid or moved in the slightest about it—something about still being beyond resentful with losing her baby girl and now feeling the pristine strength and courage running in her entire bloodstream thanks to Tronan, she was not in the frame of mind, on a permanent level, to feel forced heeding from anyone. From curiosity alone, she slowed the car to the side of the road and shifted it into park. She refused to respond to this bitch who thought she had a right to pop into her head in such a manner—more so, lack of manners. She waited. She thought to reach out to Tronan but then decided not to in case this was just something she needed to deal with alone. The urge to protect even someone like him had an intense stronghold over her. Some part of her told her that that was the case. She could feel her getting ready to speak in her head again finally, as if knowing all of Claura was waiting on the side of the road for sure now.

*I was beginning to wonder if either one of them would ever find you.* Her tone literally held a chuckle as if excited to attempt to get under her skin.

Claura thought to herself, in no hurry to respond. She suddenly admired that particular patient quality in Tronan instead of being annoyed by it. Now she understood the feeling as to why it would just be necessary. *Just get on with it. I already don't like you.*

The bitch laughed. And the sound made not just her spine chill but her entire body. Claura fought the urge to literally shake as if suddenly ridiculously cold. She knew no other evil laugh like this particular one existed.

*If you want to know things about them, the truth is that they will never tell you…*

*Pass.*

*Don't you want to know who your Match truly is?*

*Don't you just speak to people to their face?* Clearly inquiring, she already knew the strange woman had cowardly qualities. She could feel through the mental link that the thought irritated her. Yet chose not to sink to such a cliché level and give an eerie laugh in return.

*Before a time I would have.*

*Time?*

*Before I nearly killed your…what does he say now? Hmm, oh yes, your dragostea mea.*

*I see privacy is no concern to you.*

*Only for me.* She clearly shrugged, as if unbothered by the chosen selfishness at all.

*Unanswered questions are the best way to make sure I block you out. Permanently.*

She could sense that the woman had all the time in the world to play games. She wanted to twist the conversation in a dozen different directions and enjoyed invading, giving straightforward answers.

*Definitely a Match for Tronan. I can hear it in my*—clears throat—*your voice for sure.*

*Goodbye.* She did not even want to contemplate the reason for such a quick correction.

*That's fine. I've perceived enough for now.*

Claura felt the connection break in haste, and it was done in such a way that it was obvious the mental link with her may as well be on a whole other planet right now. The woman was clearly talented in skills that Claura hadn't even had one day to think and learn about, let alone try to use. Yet it didn't matter how much more experienced these other species may be. Her fear was gone. The only thing she feared was what was going to happen with the situation of her being stuck in the middle of such two perfect men. Both of whom clearly had strong feelings for her. Both men clearly had a part of history that overlapped with this woman. She really wished she had just gotten a name. She sensed she'd have to have the woman chained up with stakes within reach to get an answer to much of anything. She sighed, followed by a deep inhale as if her lungs alone needed comfort after not breathing properly during such an encounter. She stared downward at her hands, her slim fingers twisting together, remembering how Tronan caressed them between his stronger ones.

"What have I gotten myself into?" she asked herself gently.

There was zero guilt, just full of concern for herself as to where to go from here with this sudden 180 to her life, again.

Claura put the car in drive and swiftly got back on the highway. She found it eerie yet convenient that no other car had needed to share the road during her now two unexpected occurrences. She subconsciously loved the smoothness of the car and how barely a bump was felt at all from all four tires, finding it soothing really compared to her latest inner turmoil.

*So now Tronan, Roman, and this random bitch…*

"Alcohol…now."

If being a part of this species did anything, it made you need a drink. She decides to punch in a new destination on the GPS, looking for a simple yet not trashy place to grab a margarita. She comes across one named "Class Act" and decided it may fit the bill, and conveniently, it was only six minutes away. As she pulled into the parking lot, she noticed that she got lucky as the front doors alone definitely fit the bill, looking like they were made of real gold. The place was ridiculously fancy. She suddenly wondered if she'd fit in here while dressed in jeans.

# THE WINGED WITCH OF MATCHES

*Screw it.*

She noticed valet parking and headed in that direction. There was no line in front of her, which was nice. She pulled up and casually got out. Turning to look at the guy to simply state she'd only be about twenty minutes and needed the car back, she got silently taken back by his returned expression while looking at her. It was more like staring. She looked him up and down with question in her eyes as to what his problem was. He started stuttering as if nervous in front of his own personal crush, and she realized…

*His blood.*

She clearly looked different above the neck, right along with her lower half, which had been the only part of her body she focused on since she changed. She suddenly felt ridiculously stupid for not looking at herself fully in the mirror.

She held out the keys for him to hold, seeing him act nervous about taking them. She then quirked an eyebrow, angled her head, and jingled them now a foot in front of his face as if to say "Snap out of it." He finally did, looking away as he did so, and stuttered again while asking, "So just twenty minutes, ma'am?"

"The plan at the moment."

She saluted with a small smile and turned to continue up the front platform. She noticed the place to be quite the nice hotel, along with a bar already noticeable through the large windows, inwardly realizing it made no difference as long as she was served a strong one. She made it through the doors and looked up to find the direction of the bar, looking to her left and then right while scoping the place out. Her whole body suddenly froze as she turned into the large room, her eyes looking straight back into his face instantly.

*Roman!*

## Chapter 12

# Bear in My Buick

He made no effort to say "excuse me" to his company on the stool next to him. He simply got up slowly to walk nonchalantly toward her. Every noise in the room suddenly left her ears and replaced by her pounding heartbeat. The man had quite the walk about him, one she had never noticed before, but clearly, other women he sauntered by had an instant eye for. He looked good—more than good. He looked quite handsome in his laid-back dress clothes, black from head to toe. Freshly shaven, her newly heightened senses made his cologne known even from afar. His eyes didn't blink during a single stride, reminding her of another obvious clue that he and Tronan were alike. He clearly had no desire to hide any attempt at reading her every expression as he got closer. He looked so calm yet concerned. There was a firmness about him that she dearly missed as if she naturally leaned on it to feel calmer. She sensed the same thing in Tronan, but Roman didn't see any need to conceal it like he did. It was as if Tronan only wanted you to know things about him if he allowed it, even if they were things that a person simply had a right to use their own intuition and free will for alone already. She watched him slow his pace before coming to a soft stop, still about ten yards from her, his expression changing to concern now mixed with building anger as she watched his nose twitch, looking her up and down. When his eyes lifted back to hers, her blood froze.

His expression was of pure hatred, yet she could tell it was not directed at her exactly. He knew. Just from the scent that she had now, whether from the change inside her veins or her possible scent now after being intimate with Tronan, she couldn't read him well enough for that specific answer. She took in a deep, shaking breath, looked straight back into his fierce eyes, and simply gave a light shrug. It was as if to say sorry, yet not in the slightest sorry. It was one of the most emotionally confusing moments of her life. And just in the past few days, she experienced quite a few. Her small nonverbal response had his eyes softening, barely. He looked completely lost in thought. Almost as if staring right through her. Despite all she knew about Tronan, she did fear on some level that he would stand right behind her, and that was what Roman was truly looking at. She knew better. Instinctively, she knew already she'd be able to perceive him even from afar if he were really here. Honestly, she was thankful to see Roman first, despite what Tronan said. There was a fine line between being controlling versus protective, so damn what his age may be and how much better he thought he knew in handling such situations. She was determined for her own sanity to make sure he knew exactly where that line was—Match or not.

The brightness of her favorite color was so much more brilliant to her rods and cones in her now even more vibrant green eyes caught her attention, distracting her from looking at the bartender dressed in such a hue for the quickest second. A part of her brain welcomed the distraction from Roman's intently long glare. They were only moments away from people around them wondering what the hell was going on between them, possibly thinking them telepathic or else, which was exactly the kind of attention they did not need.

He looked at her like he was reading her thoughts exactly, which alarmed her in a way it didn't with Tronan. She did the most subtle nod toward the bar and started moving her feet. He stayed completely still where he was, letting her pass by him without a remark, noticing she welcomed the small gesture of her sleeve brushing his on her way by. He hated how something so small from her still felt so intimate. It had been a long time since he had to control himself so much. Something inside him was completely enveloped by her different and stronger scent as she so casually strolled by him. He had all he could do not to reach out and touch her, pull her near his body, and force her to look into his face so he could really read her up close. He cursed himself for having such an intense fixation on a woman who already was forever in the hands of someone else—someone he couldn't fucking stand. He stood there for a moment before turning to follow her. He took a deep, burdened inhale, staring into space toward his intertwining hands as he aimed to collect himself. He tried not to think of all the things he'd like to do with them.

Kill Tronan.

Claim Claura for his own.

Not specifically in such order.

He finally turned to follow her then, using his heightened hearing to notice her ordering a Long Island. He was kind of smiling to himself, wishing he liked them too. He knew easily that she was feeling taken back at seeing him, at so many things. She earned the right to do whatever it took to just relax a little. That was, after all, the main reason he wanted her here. To let her get away and enjoy herself. He never had any intention of Tronan enjoying himself as well. The man's mark was all over her. Intimately. And he could not stop his blood boiling in response to the fact.

"After this, I will drive you home," he said.

He nodded toward her obvious choice of strong drinks as he sat down on the stool next to hers. She took a moment to look at him, the obvious thought written all over her face of intense uncertainty. He softly nodded in understanding. "It's fine, Claura." He studied her face as she stayed close to her drink, lost in thought, clearly uncertain about what to say yet wanting to say so much. "You can look at me. My eyes don't bite."

*Other parts of me would be happy to.*

"Apparently, they do."

He looked up then. Her new profound will showed in her eyes, setting him back a beat. His face went from worry to admiration. Despite the circumstances, he liked seeing her like this—stronger and more herself. It was always clear to him that she didn't belong to the human race. Something about her had always been different.

"Not toward you."

"How long are you going to hate him for, Roman? It seems like just common sense that one among us can't choose their Match. It just is. I can feel it." She gently looked away and took a sip. She felt her body warm in response already. She decided to sound cliché, screw what his reaction may be. "The heart wants what the heart wants."

He inhaled deeply. She could feel his energy get more intense next to her. "I know."

She paused, swirling her straw with her hand, taking her time just enjoying his company, really, situation aside. "I have missed you, Roman. You have been one of the few people in my life who have actually treated me the way I deserve and not just because you were my doctor." She looked back up at him then. "This place is so nice. Your home is gorgeous. Don't think I haven't enjoyed it." Her thoughts completely unintentionally led to certain moments within its walls, a blush stealing her face ridiculously fast. Faster than she could look away. She hated herself for it. Knowing by his shifting in his seat and a swipe of his hand over his face as if trying to collect himself. "I'm sorry," she said, almost a whisper.

"Jesus Christ, Claura. We need to leave."

She noticed him looking around suddenly, his face full of anxiety. His instant impatience caused her alarm. He nodded for her to grab her things quickly and guided her to the exit. It was hard to miss some of the better-looking men in the room glaring at her with some kind of determined intention. Some of them were with the female company sitting right across them, full-on noticing the men's interest in her, causing the women to glare at her with furious jealousy in response. She felt Roman give her lower back a gentle push toward the valet area as soon as they were on the other side of the front doors. He leaned in close to her ear, his tone holding a sternness that only a fool would miss.

"Get in the car."

"What is going on, Roman?"

"Your scent."

"What about it?"

"I'll explain in the car."

Just the look on his face had the young valet move in a hurry. Claura could tell the kid had no clue what was going on and was clearly just another human without heightened senses. Her scent affected him at least in the none. She noticed he needed not to saunter off far. In a way, they could have just walked to the car themselves, but it was clear the kid was just trying to do his job. She could hear Roman curse at the same realization. She took advantage of the small window they had before he'd open the door for her. She turned to face him, feeling the weight of his hand move away from the low of her back as she did so.

"You move with such speed like him, too, don't you?" she asked, watching him just nod. "You are a mix of all the species as well, aren't you?" Again, he gave a simple nod. "But you were not born this way?" He looked down into her eyes more intently then, making it clear he hadn't expected Tronan and her to discuss him already, at least not to such a deep detail. It was evident he did not prefer it.

"Are you frightened of me now, Claura? Because you should be." He looked away, rubbing his hands up and down her arms, sensing her nerves starting to get rattled. It was clear the Long Island hadn't helped at all. "For I can already tell that you have zero fear of Tronan, and that terrifies me, proving he has left much out." He said it like he hated the fact yet was conflicted at being grateful for such, for she was never supposed to know anything about their existence in the first place.

She heard the car pull up behind her, watching Roman move to open her door. She turned to get in, already wishing to just be the driver again. It was obvious Roman had no clue how life was without a vehicle. It was such a pleasure. She felt inwardly heartbroken at having to give it back soon. She watched him tip the kid and half hurriedly open his door to slide in. "Nice choice," he stated, looking at the features quickly, then looking at her even more quickly. The moment lingered. It was not far from being as intense as when she was just sitting here not long ago, doing the same thing with Tronan. She could still smell him in the car. Now Roman's scent filled the space right next to her. The mix of them was messing with her mind on a level she didn't know possible. He inhaled deeply and looked away to the windshield, seeing right through her confusion that made him want to just comfort her more, and instead shifted the car as if in an unwelcome hurry. He cleared his throat before continuing.

"It was your scent, Claura. The intensity of it."

"Why would it be…intense?"

Her response made it obvious she had only touched the tip of the iceberg with her pinkie tip when it came to the information she needed to know now. It made him feel that much more protective of her. It made him realize in a sense how Tronan must be feeling. As much as he disliked him, he had a semblance of commiseration for the man now when it came to keeping an eye on her. He knew Tronan would be the ultimate expert at hiding the intensity of his true feelings when it came to keeping her safe. She had no idea, no idea about so much.

"Roman! I need to know. Please." She sounded worn out, like needing to know and understand more was clearly nothing new to her, and she was already tired of it. He wanted to help her but was unsure how to do so without crossing into Tronan's territory with this.

"Your Match," he said with clear loathe. "Because of what he is, everything about his Match…you…will be stronger as well." He hated knowing that no matter how angry he was, Tronan was always going to be able to get more intense and respond with more strength and with little effort. "Thus, your scent was tenfold for all the non-human species in that room."

"So it's not only for Tronan to sense."

"No." His tone made the obvious linger in the air between them.

"How are you controlling it, Roman?"

"Sheer. Fucking. Will. Besides, Tronan would kill me."

"I wouldn't let him."

He lightly laughed. "No one could stop him. Not even you, sweetheart."

"Sure about that?" Her tone had him facing her forthwith, slight shock on his handsome visage. She did appreciate how he didn't try to hide his real expressions so much as Tronan did. It was clearly just Tronan's nature, and she knew she'd be a fool to try to change a man who had set in his ways for literally centuries. The thought brought to mind a question she needed to know. "How old are you, Roman?"

He sighed, knowing that was inevitable. It was just not wanting to go there so soon. It was so similar to somebody else with the same hate for the same question. "Sure you would even want to…"

"I'm fucking sure." She had a look of not needing to be babied all over her demeanor, the energy of it filling the car. "I already know how old Tronan is. He told me." She wanted to simply clarify her reason for her lack of patience. "Baby me and see how fast I'd rather walk back." She watched him remain silent, his face full of anger and turmoil now, taking absolutely no initiative to speak further. She started to make her regret what she said. "Roman, just talk to me! Despite what has happened, I need you to talk to me, please!"

"What good would it possibly do?" he said calmly, too calmly.

"I do not care who I am so-called Matched with. You matter to me, always will, and I cannot explain it."

"Clearly, not enough." His face showed defeat, regret, almost remorse, even for the Claura he knew was gone forever now. He could smell his species' bloodline running through her veins. It was just like his, only extremely more potent. As it obviously would be from a more natural omnipotent being. Roman suddenly lost his cool, slamming his hand against the steering wheel in frustration, unable to hold in his intense grumble of anger that reminded her of a damn bear in the small confines of the car. She waited for his mood swing to subside, but it didn't. Instead, he suddenly slammed on the brakes and brought them onto the side of the road. The sudden movement forced her to grab something. She noticed his right arm and hand move closer as if in anticipation of needing to help her hold on but didn't make contact. He put the car in park in a hurry

# THE WINGED WITCH OF MATCHES

and swiftly got out, slamming the door shut. The sound was so loud that she felt bad for the car. She glanced at the driver's door in slight expectation of it falling off any second. Her nerves seem to shut off their own accord for fear of possible overload. She turned from the door to watch him walking away through the windshield. His masculine stride was just as impressive as someone else who she decided in that moment she really needed to hear from. She wanted time to talk with Roman alone, but it clearly was not going to go well.

*Tronan?* There was worry in every syllable.

*I am here.* He waited. He could sense her troubled breathing. *What is wrong?*

*Can I send you a mental vision instead?* She felt his energy through their link become way more focused and concerned.

*We can. I would normally tell you that you need to practice first, but I'm going to push through that, and you need to just let me, okay?* She nodded on her end, still gripping the door handle, her other hand being squeezed between her knees.

*I take it that's a bonus for us?* she nervously asked.

*Yes.*

He sent her warmth, a feeling of his hand caressing her face before turning his focus to a full-on 360 with her surroundings. She was not hard to find. She never would be. She wasn't far, really. The distance didn't matter. It would always be easy for him when it came to her. She could be halfway across the world, and it wouldn't change a thing, not in this weaker realm, at least. He took his time looking around, uncertain yet as to why she was not in the driver's seat. The small detail made him even more vigilant. He kept looking and stopped as soon as he saw a sight through the windshield in front of her through their mind link.

*I don't know how to put out the flames.* Her tone was breaking his heart, yet even more so, setting his temper on fire. She knew he would comprehend that she meant more than one thing. *It's stronger with you, Tronan, but I can't help it. I don't want to have these feelings for him too.*

*Get in the driver's seat.*

*Why? I'm not going to just leave him out here.* She actually felt him laugh in response, as if worrying about Roman was ridiculous. "I'm serious, Tronan!" she said out loud now, wanting to express how she was simply not going to do that to him.

*Fine.* It was absolutely zero concern for her reaction.

Claura suddenly felt the car move on its own, as if a ghost was driving it. She forgot how to breathe as she sat there helpless to stop it, feeling it floor itself onto the highway. She saw Roman as clear as day still despite the distance he'd put between them now and sensed no reason at all in Tronan to slow down.

"Don't you fucking dare, Tronan!"

She felt a slight squeeze on her knee as if to reassure her, just as he so lovingly did when he was actually in the car with her last. She felt the seat belt be pulled over her in what took the blink of an eye, and then the car spun in a full 180 to head in the opposite direction. She felt the engine speed up even more, as if the main intention was to get her as far away from Roman as possible. She turned to look out the back window, seeing Roman turn to look at her drive away as if he already knew what was happening. The moment made her realize that she had been underestimating how well these two knew each other. She watched him turn back around to continue in the opposite direction. She took a moment to let a real amount of air back into her lungs again. She rubbed her temples. She took a few moments to just think and try to calm down.

"Where are you taking me?" She was unsure how to handle how strange it was to feel like you were riding in a car with a ghost. For some reason, speaking out loud on her end helped things feel a bit normal, as he'd hear her either way.

*Home.*

She let the silence linger for a minute before continuing. "Why do I have a strange sense about going to the real home of my Match, Tronan?"

*It is symbolic that once you cross the threshold, it is done.*

"Done?"

*Our homes are incredibly sacred to us. It is a true notion to anyone of any species that within our particular species, when a Match crosses over the threshold, it is simply as definite as the time that they belong to and accepts one another.* He felt her pause and figured he might as well just get it out and let her know all the information. *Anyone who dares cross into our home with unjust intentions toward either one of us instantly condemns themselves.*

"Condemns themselves…to what exactly?" Her tone lingered on the "exactly" part of it.

*Death.*

She put the pieces together faster than he expected. He could feel it in her mind. Roman asked her to go straight to his house before anywhere else upon arriving. Tronan stated he planned to visit her in her dreams more before making himself physically known in person, as she wasn't on his own territory. The fact that Roman had a right to kill Tronan this entire time without her knowing it, just for being present in his home and near her with what he would have seen as obvious unjust intentions in his eyes. And to think of all the shit they'd done in the man's own goddamn bedroom. Her thoughts just started spiraling.

"I need air. Like now." She could see the city lights disappear in the rearview mirror. Her gut told her that both of their homes would be without neighbors of any kind for obvious reasons. She never thought she'd be house-hopping between two such men. Her own little apartment never felt like part of a past life anymore.

*Almost there.* He put the window on her side down for her.

"So this whole time, in his home"—needing to hear him say it—"Roman had a full-on right to kill you, as it's quite obvious he thinks he and I belong together, right?"

*More like the other way around.*

"What? How so?"

*I see now he would have tried. But as you ended up being my Match, despite being in his home first or not, I actually had full authority to end him. And even if I didn't…* He felt her urge to reach out and smack him, followed by a new anger that she literally couldn't.

At his words, before her anger set in, she felt a new chill run down through her. She was honestly tired of the sensation. She needed a break from it. She could feel the car finally slow and turn gently into a stone driveway as if just having the distance between her and Roman now was good enough for him to calm down. He seemed so in control of himself when she first met him, so unrattled by anything. It seemed the longer he was around her, the more he lacked control, making her wonder if she was even a healthy choice for him anyway if things had turned out differently. Tronan and her still had yet to figure out if what was between them was real or some curse somehow. The last thing she wanted was to realize too late that she had fallen for the wrong man. Roman showing up made things way more complicated than she expected. This was ridiculous. She did not want to live in the middle of a cliché love triangle. If anything, the only love she was really starting to need was her dead daughter. She suddenly craved visiting her grave, feeling such a deep level of mom guilt that she was so far away from it right now.

    She looked at the empty driver seat and back to the windshield, the mature part of her still able to take a moment and admire the property despite her mind going off in a dozen other directions. The driveway was long, with elegantly detailed shrubs on both sides all the way up to the gate and serene and open pastures on both sides. Everything looked beyond peaceful in the warm sunlight. She noticed the gates started to open from quite a distance still, and some part of her started to feel ridiculously excited while another part felt like she had lost complete control of her life. Of the more important choices, one should be able to make anyway. It was not that she wanted to play games between two men, not that she didn't want to choose, but she just didn't want to make the decision before knowing more. Her intuition was telling her to wait, and she had no clue why. These men had centuries on her. It was intimidating no matter how well they treated her or how lovingly they looked at her. There was no way to want both without feeling like that choice would simply be beneath all three of them. This was not a human connection with Tronan nor with Roman. This was not some silly human thing that could be a love triangle for only so long before shit hit the fan, and either the men attempted killing one another, or she finally picked one, or neither. The thought of having neither of them in her life felt like two very easy stab wounds to the heart at just the thought. She hated that she wanted to be selfish. She was already getting tired of this feeling of being in the middle. It was exactly what she wanted to end with Roman tonight. The escalation of it all going in the complete opposite direction had her feeling like the young fool she so obviously was. She was suddenly less angry with Tronan and more embarrassed for herself. She really just wanted some time alone. She looked to the driver's seat with a question in her eyes, wondering.

She felt the seat. There was nothing, making it clear she could claim the seat and steering wheel back when she was good and ready. She was not ready to cross such a threshold if it truly held such an intense meaning. Her heart broke for Tronan and what he would feel when he saw her simply leave as soon as he let go of control over the car, but she knew she needed to take her heart, and more importantly, her intuition, seriously. With her heat cycle finally keeping at bay, as long as she didn't let her thoughts linger, she chose to risk it. The car pulled around a corner, and the home came into view. It looked like a historic estate from the eighteenth century, and the design and layout alone told so many stories. The stone of a dark red was not what she expected. It actually looked gorgeous and fitting against the woodland backdrop. The front walkway up to the doors was immoderately wide, all its stones a dark gray to match the edges of the windows. It looked so welcoming yet so gloomy, the mix making it uniquely alluring. She looked at the large charcoal-colored doors, expecting to see him there. He was nowhere in sight. She decided to take it as a sign. The car parked in front of the entrance and shut off. Her door opened by itself, the small gesture solidifying how this car would never not feel haunted by her again. She just stared at it, unmoving. Her sudden urge to run away feeling silly, as if she was never going to see Tronan again anyway. The thought was beyond humorous. She could feel him in her mind then, a gentle push to remind her of their connection, of how much he loved her.

*I know what you are planning to do.*

*I'm more scared of crossing that threshold than anything so far with you.*

*I understand.*

*Do you?* She felt him pause. Unsure how to answer. *How do I know you aren't just doing the same thing Roman did, if that's even true, as I'm hitting my limit with wrapping my head around things.*

*Please come to me. Come into our home. You worry needlessly.*

With his abilities, he was able to see her facial expressions through their mental link effortlessly. He had no need to physically stand where he could see her from a distance. He simply sat in his study, which was close to the entrance, surrounded by his favorite collected pieces over time. Sitting on his leather Victorian sofa, leaning forward, studying his hands, and remembering how her perfect body felt underneath them. Underneath him. Yet they were still focused on their conversation more than anything right now. She had a 923-year-old omnipotent being wrapped around her finger and simply had yet to realize it. In a way, it terrified him that she already held more power between them both than simply having power over him—his soul, his mind, his heart, and his entire being. It frightened him. And Tronan couldn't remember the last time he felt scared of anything. He was ashamed at how a deep part of him wondered if this was how it was truly supposed to be with his Match. And as soon as she crossed his doorway, it was set in stone for him as well.

*Do I?* she continued, sounding firm in warning of an answer. She made it obvious that if he wanted her inside, he was going to have to be beyond honest with her right now. She needed proof and reassurance.

*You worry about coming into my home more, and you know why.*

He could sense her thoughts wandering. He was learning more and more with time how he needed to gently help her figure things out. Not because she was stupid. Stupid was the last thing Claura was. If anything, she was too smart for her own good and simply just let her heart get in the way. She sensed that it was meant to be pulled in more than one direction, and he could not put his finger really on why, hence their conversation, her confusion. He continued gently, just wanting to see her already. He did not expect some distance between them so he could focus more to end up feeling so burdensome. The distance was making his chest literally ache.

# THE WINGED WITCH OF MATCHES

*There is not a curse over us, Claura. If anything, we are simply dealing with something that is making what we are already feeling just stronger. And it being too strong for you is what is scaring you. I can handle it. I'm simply learning how to handle it in a way I didn't expect to have to. You just need to trust me more. Please.*

For some reason, the "please" always got her. The way he said it, she felt it to her toes—if her soul had toes. She leaned to get out of the car. The door still opened for her as if it'd wait until it aged and rusted if need be. She closed it herself, uncaring that he could so obviously do it for her anyway. She kept her steps slow, knowing that this was definitely a decision to be cautious about. She took a moment to look up, letting the home soak into her memory, having a harder time with the fact soaking in that this was her home now. It did not seem real. Her daughter would have grown up here. And for once, in her memory, she did not start to feel anger or grief; instead, she felt a little sting of peace. It was not much, but it was a start. The thought was that Tronan would have found her eventually anyway if her daughter had survived and brought them both here together. Somehow, the connection with him just made that a fact. It would have only been a matter of time. It warmed her on a motherly level that she did not want to let go of yet just because her daughter was not physically here with her. Once a mom, always a mom, no matter how short their life lived. She took a few moments to envision her running around the beautiful landscape, playing in the nearby woods, and helping to pick flowers to bring inside. If these types of moments were all she was to ever have as a mother, envisioning and imagining, then so be it. And nobody was going to take it from her. She stood lost in such thoughts while turning to see the whole yard, taking it all in, when she suddenly heard the large front doors opening slowly. She takes her time in looking toward them, not wanting to let go of her motherly visions that, for a change, were bringing peace to her heart instead of tears to her eyes. She noticed he was still not in sight, not from her angle, a distance away still anyway. She inhales deeply, already loving the scent of the grounds. She could smell a body of water nearby and instinctively stopped to stand still.

She focused on her hearing, feeling a strange vibration took place from her auricle to her cochlea, and just intently listened.

The stream.

The water moved over the rocks.

The nearby birds enjoyed their home.

It was like music.

She was able to turn the volume up or down with just the intention of it alone. She could feel Tronan smile with her. He was not far from the entrance, waiting patiently. It was scary yet felt so natural to just know such things. The combination of heightened senses mixed with seeing through a mental link was just…positively surreal. It felt like home, like she could get back to herself now. The realization was confusing yet felt like a question that didn't need to be answered. She took another look at the house entrance and started moving forward. A deep part of her just really needed to see him, too, again already.

For some reason, the closer she got to the front doors, the more calm she felt, as if the home was welcoming her on its own, whether Tronan was part of the package or not. Her little apartments back home sure as hell never held the same effect. If anything, their greeting was a lazy city vibe with a sassy, full-on fuck you before you even brought your first box of stuff inside. It was crazy in itself, the feeling she was getting from just being here. She started to wonder if reincarnation was true and if this was her home in a past life. Seeing the inside suddenly felt just as exciting to her, wondering if the feeling would increase at all once inside its walls. She walked up to the door and looked inside, noticing him some yards away, leaning against the impressive marble stairway. His hands were in his pockets, seeming as calm as ever, watching her like he'd waited lifetimes to see the image take place before him. The sight made her mouth go dry.

Lifetimes before her.

Lifetimes with her.

Lifetimes after her?

She stared right back at him, unsure of what to say. She felt him in her mind anyway, noticing his head nodding in a gentle no to her inner question. "When I die, you die?" she asked. He nodded again. "Say it." He admired the sound of her own voice for a change.

Ever since the second drop, she's felt nothing if not more bold and determined, especially when the need naturally called. If this man was truly willing to end his life once she was no longer a part of it, that alone said enough. She was young, but sometimes, the heart just already knew things no matter what age you were.

"Yes."

His poker face was back. He was clearly trying to put her reaction first and worry about his own later. It was not so much with not wanting her to see his true feelings. His eyes relaxed at her smile that finally came. He never remembered a simple one-word answer being more important in his life. He watched her move her feet through the door frame, pausing after just one step to once again look around, clearly needing a moment to just accept what she had just done, even if just one foot inside the door.

# Chapter 13

# Put Before My Own

Seeing the last of the setting sun come through the windows, the warm glow it created made the place feel even more magical. She was feeling more relaxed than expected.

*Another curse in disguise maybe?*

She hoped not yet was in no mood to fight it.

"The dawn will make it look indefinitely prepossessing, I promise you." He started walking toward her slowly, clearly wanting to savor the sight of his woman entering his home with such a loving and relaxed visage while doing so. It warmed his heart all over again.

"Dayla would have loved it here," she said, sounding less grief-stricken at just the mention of her name alone.

She knew Tronan took notice of such instantly. She looked up at the beautiful ceilings as she said it. She looked back down into his face as he came up close, inches from her face. His expression was indefinitely engraved in her memory for all eternity—their eternity.

She felt his fingers move up to frame her face with one hand while his thumb caressed her lips in the way he so loved to do. In that way, she loved to let him do it. The moment of him looking back and forth between her eyes and lips had her knees feeling weak.

"Her happiness would have been put before my own. Same as yours." He noticed her eyes darting away and back again as if unsure of him seeing her reaction to his words and how well they hit home for her.

"I couldn't help but picture her out front, running around and playing." She started to cover her mouth with the back of her hand, tears swimming. "I just… I can't…"

She could see on his face that he was understanding completely. Despite the bad timing of a possible postpartum episode, the feeling of such a home was literally hitting home in parts of her heart. He stepped closer to frame her face with both hands and leaned in and kissed her tenderly, forever cementing this memory for them in their minds, forever knowing that his first kiss with her in their home together was one full of compassion and love. She deserved at least that much, and it had nothing to do with how her brain still thought like a human that needed to be comforted in this way. It did not matter that his blood would bring out elements of surprise, good and bad, from her naturally, no matter that they shared while being one of the most powerful species on the planet due to simply how he was born this way alone. When it came to a woman's heart, none of that mattered. He needed her to know that she was meant to be here with him, not the vampire side, the werewolf side, the witch side…but him. He would love her the same, omnipotent mix or else.

She opened her eyes after letting the kiss linger for quite a few perfect moments, studying him, simply admiring how passionately tender he was being. "I want to go lie down. In your arms." She stared back at him intently for a moment, seeing him move one hand to place on her hip while the other on the back of her head as he kissed her temple. He leaned away to entwine their fingers and started to lead her up the staircase. "Tronan? I meant like you did in the first dream." He gently nodded, and she saw him swoop her up like she was his little omnipotent-in-the-making feather, blinked, then the bedroom. She instantly loved the look of every single thing around her, taking in every detail as he set her on her feet.

"You can change anything you want, my love," he said, smiling as he watched her eyes light up as she looked around.

"Nothing." She circled around and shrugged. "Absolutely nothing." She looked at him to show she was serious. "You do know that I come from foster homes where us kids shared one bedroom, normally five to eight of us at a time, never having much say in the repetitive decor. I've mentioned that, right? Followed by only small apartments when I finally moved out on my own…and you think I'd want to change this?"

She tossed her purse on the bed, took off her shoes to toss, and then she onto the floor. She crawled onto the bed, giving a small sound of pleasure at finally being able to curl up on something so comfortable and just get some damn rest, physically and mentally. The outing clearly turned out to be way more stressful than originally planned. She saw him sit on the edge of the bed, angled toward her, enjoying the sight. Noticing how her outfit matched his navy silk bedding. She curled up on her side, her face curled into the pillow, and just took a moment to study his expression before speaking. She enjoyed the moment so much of being in his home together. She suddenly felt foolish for being almost ready to bolt while still in the car as she sensed him correcting her in her mind.

*Our home.*

"Well, now, yes. For centuries, it's been yours, without me. Will it be weird to share it?"

"For the first time, it feels right to even be in it. I think this home has been waiting for you, and I've just been the guest this entire time. I could feel it too as soon as you exited the car."

"That is a long time to be a guest. Never wanted to just move?"

He shook his head no. "Didn't feel right. Now I see why."

She didn't say anything back for a few minutes. She just loved the feeling of *home* for the first time in her life, truly the first time, and to share it with this man before her. But then she started to feel her eyelids get heavy. She did still want to clear the elephant in the room before falling asleep. "I think he saved me tonight, Tronan," she sniffled as she said it, snuggling in closer to the pillow.

"How so?"

"My scent." His reaction stated the obvious of him wanting the whole story, his eyes growing dark and concerned. "I went for a drink. He ended up being there at that particular place. He started to come toward me and stopped, clearly knowing by just the way I smelled now. My blood or my—"

"Both. He would be able to scent both."

"His eyes, Tronan. I'll never forget it. I never thought I'd see Roman look at me like that."

"Did he make you feel like he was going to hurt you?"

"No. Not for a second."

"I see." He looked away for a moment, and it obviously became clear. He knew Roman would react, but he was just not sure how off the wall it would be. It made no sense. No two men felt like they were Matched to one woman before within their species. It just didn't happen. It was not realistic with how his kind worked. The question of something being wrong with Roman was heavy in the air. Perhaps the curse was on him. Perhaps something was controlling all of them.

"I am sorry I underestimated his true feelings, and now I've made it worse."

"Only worse for him, sweetheart. We will always be fine." She saw him pause, lost in thought while staring straight into her face again. She waited. "So that's what you felt like doing, getting a drink? Is my company so bad?" He noticed her stiffen and how his attempt to make her smile was a big fat fail. "Claura?" He watched her glossed-over expression, it making him worry the longer it lingered until she finally spoke.

"A woman entered my head while driving. Told me to pull the car over. She attempted to talk to me about you and Roman. Saying things like she was surprised it took you both so long to find me. And that she knows things about you both that she thinks you'd never tell me on your own." She frowned, trying to recall it all correctly. "To be honest, I couldn't stand her voice right from the very first word. She felt so...wrong."

"Name?"

"She clearly didn't give a shit to answer a single question."

"And no vision?"

"No. But I'm glad. Her voice alone made it obvious a vision of her would never get out of damn head."

"What else did she say?" He leaned closer, brushing her hair behind her ear. There was concern all over his face all over again. She suddenly realized she wanted to see his face again the way it was when he was making love to her, inside her, even when just smiling and conversing with her. It was an enormous turn-on for her, among other enormous things. She started blushing. He smiled but gestured for her to continue on topic, as it was important obviously. Tronan figured, with her being so new to his world, that he would be the only one in her head for a long time. And now this.

"That I'm definitely a Match for you." She looked doubtful about herself, unsure of the reality of truly being his. It was still a question of worth in her human perspective with everything. Her gut told her something was missing while his eyes alone brought such comfort.

"She doesn't sound all bad."

"She felt so evil. And a part of me feels like I am going to see her again. She made it sound like she will return." She looked from her fingers lingering on the silk bedspread to his eyes again. "I'm actually really terrified. Like there is truly something about her that makes her unstoppable."

"Well, I've lived for almost a thousand years and have been able to put a stop to almost anything and anyone. Some harder than others."

"Anyone ever try to stop you?"

"Of course, but it was how I learned my abilities. To not be tested is to not learn your strengths. For a long time, I wanted to be nothing but tested. I did take it too far on some occasions, as I think any soul would in my position really. It doesn't matter how much power you have. Abusing it makes it inefficacious."

"So in a way, being immature with one's own power can show one's weakness, making it too easy for their enemy."

"Only if their enemy is smart enough to know where to keep an eye out for their weakness. You can look in the wrong library all day for the right book."

"Do you have a library here?" She sounded excited, like a kid about to get a toy.

He simply nodded, enjoying the childlike happiness on her face at his answer. It warmed him, knowing she could still show that playful side of herself even with someone his age. He wanted her to feel like she could show every part of herself to him. The delighted look on her face made him excited about the unexpected with her. She was clearly going to be full of surprises. Her droopy eyelids were getting harder to miss despite him just wanting to keep seeing her smile like this. He leaned in close to her ear, whispering in that voice that she'd never get enough of. Something within it was just so alluring, watching as her eyes closed.

"I need to feel your skin against mine, my love. No more. I promise." His tone suggested he truly meant it.

He placed his arm under her just enough to lift her to pull the blankets down. She let herself watch through half-closed eyes, loving the feeling of being in his arms any way she could get, seeing him wave his hand next and lift the covers over them. The man wasted no time. She felt his skin against hers immediately, his body settling on top of her gently, totally at ease with his masculinity as he felt clearly at home settled with his lower half between her legs. He felt so warm. The perfect temperature. She felt so right beneath him, feeling his hands gently explore, fully satisfied with just being able to touch her skin wherever he pleased. He lingered in every spot he reached, making it obvious the last thing he was going to do was hurry. It felt so good, like the most sensual erotic massage ever. She felt his lips touch places he had clearly been itching to have beneath him again. He made no noises, no moans, as if he wasn't willing in the slightest to lose control again. He kept it simple, gentle, loving. His entire energy was so gentle toward her, letting the sensations help her fall asleep. She was literally only seconds away from drifting off. She could just feel it, despite how she just wanted to stay awake and keep enjoying this. She heard him whisper the words while lost in thought while staring at her belly, lingering back and forth over it gently with the back of his fingers as he lay slanted slightly over the top of her. His other arm was still underneath as if cradling her. The small sentence sounded as if from a distance away with her caving into the much-needed sleep her body was longing for.

"I love you," he said so gently, almost as if he was saying it to a newborn.

She felt him linger for a few more seconds and then move up toward her head again. Wrapping his arms underneath her in that way, he did, cradling her head with both palms as he leaned down to kiss her. The gesture, the way he was holding her, was purely sweet. It had "mine" written all over it. She took one last look into his face before fully caving, feeling him play with her mouth and lips gently with his teeth and those ridiculously talented lips. He stared back at her intently. If she felt lovingly owned in bed with him in Roman's house, this was an entirely different regard coming off him here in this home, in his bed, and in his territory.

She gently kissed him back with what strength she had left, feeling him lightly respond. "Sleep, sweetheart."

*****

Claura knew she was still asleep. Her improved senses made it easier not to get so confused about such things. She knew her real body was still lying with Tronan, fast asleep. This was a dream. For a moment, she felt excited that he may be taking her to this place, sharing it with her. She had yet to experience more of what he could do with his dream walker ability. It was simply another topic among the hundreds she needed more time to discuss with him. The more she looked around, though, the more she realized that this was not the type of place Tronan would bring her to. It was dark, cold, and looked like a cave. There was a very large, wide-open cave, full of even darker cracks everywhere, with water dripping down through most of them. She did a full circle, taking in her surroundings. The sounds of small creatures everywhere, scurrying on the ceilings and walls just as much as the ground. She noticed only two obvious directions to go, neither holding much light. Taking a deep breath, wondering what the hell this could be, she closed her eyes and said a silent small prayer in her mind before deciding to move in either direction.

"Prayers won't help you here." The woman's voice echoed off the walls, making Claura unable to tell at all which direction it was coming from. It was made clear on a chilling level that she was all the same not far.

This bitch.

Again.

Claura cursed under her breath. She started to wonder if she could reach Tronan and inwardly tried. At least now she had a useful vision to send his way. All she felt in response was a cold wall in her mind.

"Reaching for him won't work here either." She made herself known, appearing from around a corner dressed in a white silky-looking robe that completely covered everything but her head and hands. The contrast seemed ridiculously unfitting for her, for the chosen environment. Claura looked her up and down, choosing not to speak yet. She noticed the woman's right hand doing a swirl, a small green light flickering between her fingers as if caressing its owner, reminding her of a petite version of the northern lights.

"Most people are shivering in their boots by now." She smirked, still moving closer before finally stilling a few yards away. "I only want to help you, Claura."

Claura laughed, causing her own echo. And it sounded wonderful due to the fact that the longer it lingered, the more she saw the woman get bothered. "Your little environment here suggests otherwise." She eyes her right back, taking in as much detail of her as possible. She looked quite forward to figuring her out, what she wanted, and how to end her. There was not a single positive thing that could come from a being that had such evil vibes radiating off her. "It's only fair I know your name." It clearly had every intention of driving the conversation away from this being, whatever she was, helping her at all.

"Fair is for losers."

"Fair is for having any integrity at all."

"You truly are just like him."

"Thank you."

The woman looked furious yet got it under control fast. Claura could see it get glossed over in her eyes as fast as it appeared. "I could have killed him, you know. But I chose not to."

"I can already sense you aren't as strong as him. No wonder the failure." Claura had no clue why pressing the woman's buttons was bringing her so much genuine joy. She felt slightly childish yet had no real purpose to care to impress this being at all.

"You misunderstand—"

"What the fuck do you expect, lady, with your words games here."

"I did not say I personally could have. One order—"

"Order for whom?"

"His father."

"His father?"

"Yes. Only the father has the power to kill someone like Tronan."

"All the same, no wonder the failure. A father isn't going to want to kill his own son."

"You would be surprised."

"Humor me. How'd you stop him?"

"I needed you. I needed Tronan to bring you here."

"I don't even know your name, lady…" If she was at all a lady.

Claura started to feel uneasy with not knowing exactly what kind of species this woman was. Was she like Roman and Tronan or like the others that were uncombined? Her mind started to wonder just how long she could be held here like this. Trapped in this dream in this cold cave with this psycho. She started to look around her more, feeling the urge to just leave already, no matter how long it took to get out. It was a whole new level of frustration knowing that you couldn't wake up your own body. She inwardly screamed for Tronan then. And in response, this woman before her actually took on a quick second of full-on fear in her eyes, making Claura pause to try to figure out why. Just then, she felt Tronan pushing through, yelling at her to wake up. From a distance, she could feel her own body twisting in agitation as if fighting in its own way. She could see the woman lift her hand into that wavelike gesture that Tronan had done to her before to make her go to sleep, making her realize she still didn't get a damn name from her before she felt mentally shoved back into her body. Tronan's voice became stronger, closer, more clear. She could now feel his arms around her, shaking her gently, telling her to focus on his voice.

*****

"Claura!"

Tronan was furious. He knew there was only one kind of person who could block him from entering anyone's dream world. But it made no sense as that particular kind of being had no reason to. He shook her, trying to be gentle, putting his voice close to her ear, sending a command into her mind, a hasty whisper full of determination. She opened her eyes, but he could see her pupils still rolling back into her head. It was obvious she was having a hard time coming through, even with his help. Before she even had control over her body again, she forced the words out with complete determination.

"I saw her."

She inhaled as if having a hard time finding room in her lungs, trying to get her body to relax and just fully wake up already. The more she was able to come to and feel his arms around her, the more the dream finally faded and went away. The particular choice of shove the woman used was completely unnecessary, despite being able to tell it was from her fear of Tronan and not specifically directed at her. Still, she had to go through it. She finally relaxed in his arms, cradled on his lap on the edge of the bed, feeling his hand against her temple do something to her mind. Nothing about it felt wrong or uncomfortable, so she didn't bother questioning it.

"Long white robe. Green swirly light in hand. Pale skin. Hair as white as snow." Tronan's entire demeanor changed. She suddenly felt quite afraid to be the one being held between his arms. "You know her?" The answer was already obvious. "She still would not give me a name, unfortunately." She watched him hold her head on both sides over her ears, fingertips on her temples, gently, yet his fingers slightly shaking, making her alarmed. He nodded his head toward her, staring into her eyes as if asking for permission to do something. She nodded yes, placing her hands over his. She looked worried but completely okay with trusting him.

"Close your eyes for me," he said gently, yet like he didn't want to waste any time.

It was as if the memories and her vision would be harder to see with every passing second, and he was determined not to let a fraction of a moment of what happened in her dream escape him. He knew he was risking alarming her by showing more of just how powerful he was and showing how much of her privacy he had the ability to take off his own free will at any time. He saw the realization in her eyes.

"You literally need no one on this planet to answer to you, do you?" she said, frowning slightly as she looked up into his face.

He shook his head. "To try to respect other's free will is all I can do. I will make mistakes with you, Claura. You will have to learn to continually forgive me, and I hate having to even ask it." He clearly meant that he was disappointed in himself for not knowing how to handle it better. He was ashamed that despite his powers, there was always something that he still needed to learn from. He did not want to have to learn anything the hard way when it came to her. He should just already know. She deserved him already knowing. Distress took captive of her face suddenly.

"I can feel her memory moving away from me like she doesn't want to be found. I don't know how I know. I just know."

She gave him a look to hurry up. His speed in response left her brain jolted. She could feel him inside her head remarkably fast, searching and probing. It felt like small needles just tapping around on different parts of her cerebrum. She took deep breaths to work through the irritation of it all, knowing he was hurrying for her sake too. She could feel his resolve, his internal commitment that he was going to find no more no matter how much he searched and withdrew with the swiftness of timeless practice. She felt zero jarring effect as he made his mental exit. Her skull hurt no more.

"Tell me?" she asked, looking worried.

"I will be back."

She felt him move her onto the bed, plant a quick kiss on her forehead, and head for the door. She truly felt she was in the presence of a predator. She loved this side of him yet wasn't a fool enough not to aim clear of it. She felt so hurt that he did not give her an answer. The action reminded her of this woman in the dream. She hoped like hell they weren't related. She could hear his footsteps nearing the front door already despite it being only two seconds, and she knew he would still hear her.

"Where are you going? Please, Tronan! Just one answer!" She could hear him stop and pause for just a moment. "Roman's."

There were no more footfalls, just the sound of the front door slamming, followed by silence. The feeling should have made her feel chilled, but it didn't. Somehow, in some strange and beyond crazy way, she could feel the home comforting her. It was as if it knew of her distress and was trying to ease it like it had a spirit of its own. It brought her back to her own reality and gave her a sense of needing to focus on herself and put aside, even if just for a little while, the drama that the two men brought into her life and into her heart. She literally put one slightly shaking hand over her sternum, closed her eyes, and inhaled deeply.

Repeat.

Repeat.

Just once more.

She looked at her bag that held her phone, wondering if she should warn Roman. She wondered if it would matter as it may already be too late. Just how fast Tronan could move, she did not know—not yet, and then the laughter from Tronan in her head while in the car last night, as if it was truly beyond humorous that anyone would need to worry about someone like Roman. And then just something deep down told her not to worry unless she really needed to, as if something inside her had the situation already covered however the outcome.

"Forget it."

It was silly to try to control any situation that was clearly raw and between two men of such a species. She felt like a fish out of water when it came to know how to help at all. Surely, on some level, both knew that she needed both of them in her life. Surely, they would understand, despite their anger with one another, that she would be destroyed on some level if one were to truly kill the other. Her thoughts led her to wonder how a species as strong as them even died. How was it done? She could feel a whole new level of sadness and depression sink in.

As if on cue to help her snap out of it, she hears the warm shower turn on in a nearby bathroom. As freaky as it was, she just as much felt thankful for the gesture. She slid off the bed and placed her feet on the stone-looking floor, loving the texture and design of the stone tiles, noticing how cold they looked yet feeling the complete opposite underneath her soles. Seeing steam already rising around the corner, she slowed as she entered the large bathroom. She noticed the edge of the white tub in the far corner past the steam, inwardly looking forward to enjoying that for the rest of her days. She already sensed that no matter how long that be, she would not be getting sick of this home. Poor Tronan, this place already felt like it belonged to her more, and she was the one who just got here. She wondered what he had been doing in it for all these years without her. She wondered what he took on, what he studied, and who he invited over if anyone. She was nerve-racking to know that she was the Match for him, in his home, never to leave if she truly didn't want to. She hears the shower head do a loud squeak as if disapproving of her wandering thoughts again. Making her lightly laugh, shaking her head in disbelief, she walked to the shower stall door, gently opened it, and stepped unpretentiously inside. The hot water felt amazing, the quiet of the house relaxing, the genuine enlivened feeling of seeing more of what the home was like afterward. She was feeling more like herself than she ever before had the chance to in her entire life.

She was home in a way, despite not being able to fully explain it...

Just "*Home.*"

# Chapter 14

# Care and Contempt

*The evening before...*

Roman kept walking. Ten more miles was nothing. His fury made his fists tremble, a very rare occurrence among his kind. There was just something about their blood that prevented anything from rattling them. Anything from rattling him until now. Claura wanted to know his age. He never expected to have to tell her, not on his first fucking day back after not even being here for 150 years. He could sense when cars were coming and going, choosing to make himself completely invisible to the eye as they passed. He knew full well that he'd have nothing but a snack if any idiot confused him for a silly little hitchhiker right now. He sauntered off into the woods at the last two miles, welcoming the shortcut. He heard growls from hungry predators that simply ran off in the opposite direction once they got close enough to smell his rage, along with sensing something different about him. Seeing his home come into view brought him to a halt, inhaling deeply. He tried with any control to attempt letting only certain memories come flooding back as he was already on a tight edge right now. He stood there for a few moments, contemplating and even bothering as he already knew who had been in his home with her when she should have been enjoying some much-needed solitude, not wanting to really know just how full-on strong her scent may have gotten in his own home if Tronan had.

His blood started boiling at the thought. Only one other time in his existence had Roman been this mad, and it was at that previous time as well due to Tronan being included in such a situation. "Fucking unkillable bastard." He stared intently at the house, trying to think over what was best to do, and figured he could simply put it on the market tomorrow if he wanted, and started heading toward the front door. A part of him was heartbroken at the lost chance to simply visit her while she was still here before the inevitable happened. Roman wanted so badly to step into his home as the main male figure in her life, comfort, court her, make her feel loved, and show her what he had to offer. The situation of boundaries with Tronan never came to mind to even be an issue. Shit had shifted incredibly fast.

He turned the knob and walked through the threshold. The complete notion of knowing what it meant to simply not be here and watch her do it in person for the first time weighed on his heart. What a fool to think he'd have more time. He stepped in further, eyeing the kitchen with bags still atop it, next rounding the near corner to glance into the living room, noticing the messy blanket lying on the couch and how the cushions were clearly disheveled from more surface area than what Claura's body would do alone. The fireplace was still going on low. Some figurines that were on the shelves and corner tables were now missing. A few spots on the walls with indents made him really pause. He stepped closer to the wall's surface, looking intently for body hair or anything similar, knowing he'd literally attempt to kill Tronan if this signified at all that his brain was set on already assuming. He knew fully what his species was capable of during heat cycles. He rubbed his fingertip along the broken cracks and noticed shards of a broken vase. His chest relaxed, his heart rate slowed back down, and he continued toward the stairs. He was still uncertain as to what the hell happened but was able to put it aside for now.

He turned to head upstairs, slightly sprinting as he did so. He checked the spare bedrooms at first, and neither had a single thing out of order. He continued down the hall to his master bedroom, noticing her particular scent getting stronger as he moved, the satisfaction of knowing she chose his room as soon as he turned and rounded through the doorway. He saw a couple of things left behind, and used towels were still lying at the foot of the bed. The sheets were clearly slept in. He subconsciously lowered the volume on his nasal cavity before even stepping onto the second floor of his own damn home, inwardly cursing that despite his best efforts, her new and very distinct scent was still filling his nostrils. It was more than he could handle. Tronan being intensely mixed with it was more than he could handle. Out of raw curiosity that was still able to take place through his anger, he stepped in further and reached for the towel at the foot of the bed. He held it to his face, his entire gesture more loving than anything. He inhaled deeply and slowly. He felt like a fool. He also felt like Claura was simply meant to be with him—someone she could handle, someone who would not be so damn intense for her, someone who was not literally feared by every other being in existence. Roman simply worried for her. He knew it was a long shot. He just never expected not being able to protect her at all, it being completely ripped from his hands now.

First, his Maya, then his precious baby girl, and now Claura. All three had been taken from him. He was at complete odds with figuring out how it was even possible to fall for another Match. He knew it was completely unheard of. That was not supposed to be possible. Maya was a part of his life almost 150 years ago. As much as he loved her, it seemed like more than enough time to pass to be able to accept a new Match if one came along.

And it did.

She did.

He felt his soul belonging to hers even if the feelings were not being reciprocated. He knew damn well that the feelings were there for her, and all he had needed was some damn time. Tronan was simply getting in his way. Being made instead of born from his species, Roman never fully grew to respect everything about them. He spent many years of his life being a human, like Claura was, before being turned. It was another reason he was able to relate to her so well. Tronan was on the complete opposite end of the spectrum. It would take him decades to be able to truly relate to Claura. He figured if there were a curse going on here over any of them, it still made no sense why Tronan would be chosen for the mix. The man was omnipotent, limitless, and unbeatable. His level of power and control, mixed in with already being a dominant male, was not meant for a woman's heart. And he could tell by the way her face changed, the way she reacted at just the man's name, that Tronan had her heart. There was only one thing left for Roman to do. And it was one of the longest shots of his existence. He needed to figure out if what was even between them was real or a curse. Something was off. Roman could just feel it.

He turned around, regret in his eyes as he stared at his room. He knew that to rid of Tronan's scent, he would have to completely rid of hers as well. He tossed the towel into the bathroom on the counter and walked back into his master bedroom, raising his hand into a quick swipe while saying an easy command he learned so long ago from his precious Maya. His room was suddenly returned to its original state. It looked as if no other person had been here at all. He headed downstairs to do the same.

*****

The following morning, Roman decided to pour himself a strong one for breakfast after having to settle for zero sleep. He made himself as comfortable as best he could on the opposite end of the couch, completely avoiding all bedrooms, even with the cleansing. A small part of him still couldn't fully get rid of her scent. A small part of him didn't have that much control when it came to Claura. The center island held an impressive crack down the middle of it now. He felt utter disgust with himself for knowing he didn't even want it in the kitchen in the first place, and it was the main reason Tronan ended up moving as quickly as he did literally into her life before he could visit even once.

Into her presence.

Into her mind.

Then into her body.

Upstairs.

In his own damn bed.

He spent the majority of his time outside, trying to calm down on the large exterior porch, not wanting his anger to be the ruins of bringing the entire house down to crumbles as he was beyond capable of doing. He stared at his hands as if hating himself for being a species that just naturally could make the Hulk look like a toothpick. Just the headache alone of having to hide who he really was while fitting in in the world was enough to drive one mad sometimes.

And then he heard it.

He heard him.

And he just knew.

The tires came around to the back of his home, where he was sitting outside on the backsteps, watching the brakes get slammed as if it was the last time they would be used, so it may as well be good. He saw Tronan exit the vehicle with a fury that had not met in quite a while, not since that day.

Roman stood up to face him. Uncaring yet fully prepared from simply already having experience with the man. "You could take your fury out on something else, as that car is hers now."

Tronan strode up, wrath owning every muscle. Yet his eyes still held this numb determination like he hadn't truly decided on something yet but was determined to use his last breath to figure it out and do so. "Gladly." It was completely guttural. He kept his stride steady, his whole demeanor single-minded. "Why is she still alive?"

"Who!" Roman snapped, already sick of his presence.

Tronan used his speed to have his hand around Roman's throat and smashed his body up against his own house, crossing the distance flat, the large glass window splintering behind him.

"Moira."

His anger was at such a level he could feel his hands literally burning into Roman's skin, but he didn't care. "In all my years, she has been *my only* threat"—clearly meaning the jab with full force—"and you told me she was killed that day. *Done with*. After my mistake, I left you to be trusted with the task per your wish." He smashed his head back into the glass again as if to reiterate.

He laughed despite barely even being able to do so, looking up into the sky before back into Tronan's face. He clearly took a moment to deal with the memories before speaking.

"She killed my daughter. My daughter! To think I'd lie about such a thing makes even you a fool!" Roman swiped his hand off his body, followed by a swing with his same arm back into Tronan's chest, sending him flying backward toward the woods. He landed almost within the trees. His vamp speed was still clearly impressive for his kind, especially when not even born of origin in their race. It set Tronan back a step—just one. "And I must say it looks good on you."

It was as much of his own unique disgust radiating off him in waves. The energy between them, if anyone was watching, literally sizzled for any eye in the wide world to see.

Roman could see it then. Tronan started to move back toward the house, his eyes coming to life in only that way that an omnipotent being possessed. As much as he welcomed death, he all the same didn't care for it to be from this man's particular hands. He swiped his hand up and did the invisible wall that was common for most witches, yet hardly any owned the skill so quickly, causing another small second of confusion on Tronan's face. Roman inhaled, a full-on manly smirk, full-on impatient with dealing with him, and clarified it for him.

"Maya," Roman said, sounding heartbroken and proud as her name left his lips.

It made Tronan pause. It was clear Roman missed her on a deep level—a level you lived with until you finally died. And to live with such a pain for so damn long compared to how the human race had it, it simply made it worse.

# THE WINGED WITCH OF MATCHES

"Roman, why on earth would you think you'd have another Match after already finding yours?" He waited, sensing Roman may never actually answer. He sensed he just simply did not have an answer yet held zero shame about it. "You know it is unheard of. It simply does not exist." He raised his hands, sending ripples through the protection wall, making it so he could literally see the entire groundwork of the house start to shake. "And as you full-on know"—the shaking stops, and Roman's eyes get wide yet full of regret more, knowing full on well it was nothing but the calm before the mulish destructive storm—"she is *mine*."

Roman knew he was screwed. And he had no idea why some inner part of him, a voice that sounded just like him in a way, was in his head in that fraction of a moment before Tronan blew him to the wind, house and all. He could almost feel it more than hear him.

*Call to Claura. Now.*

With it being his only option, he felt no need to pause. He faced Tronan dead on and inwardly called to her in his mind, praying for a miracle. He watched Tronan's hands count down the very few number of turns they had left to do now to complete his task as he recognized the spell. He had seen it before. Maya and Moira had taught them when they were still learning everything. He was still learning how to use their powers, each of them helping the other. That time seemed like such fiction now. He had a hard time wrapping his head around that he actually existed in those moments and how the tables turned so quickly once Moira clearly had hit her last nerve with feeling second place. He hated himself. He hated that he was, in a way, the cause of his own baby girl's death. He hated that he couldn't stop Maya from being killed. So the release that Tronan was about to give him.

"Fuck it." Roman closed his eyes, welcoming whatever his fate was, feeling more "done" than he realized at that moment, even after all this time remaining alive after what happened.

"Umm…I don't think so, my love."

Claura was suddenly on the other side of the house, staring intensely at Tronan and seeing everything through the glass parts of the walls. They both heard her and immediately paused. Roman spun to see if she was real. Tronan lowered his hands slightly, the crackling power in his palms slightly receding, a numb shock in his eyes. Claura paused for only a second to study them both before pushing her hands forward. Somehow, the power coming out of them was able to bypass the house and Roman and immediately slam into Tronan. She watched him get completely lifted off his feet and fly backward into the car. To her shock, and Roman's, he stayed down. Roman looked at her with exasperated fear of her in his eyes. He looked utterly terrified. She looked him up and down, making no incentive to move closer, noticing his feet starting to move away from her. "I heard you call Roman. I don't know how, but I just instantly knew what was going on." She watched him quickly look to Tronan and then even more quickly back as if afraid to take his eyes off her for too long. She did not like this reaction to saving him. "Roman, it's okay. I'm me. I'm not going to hurt you." She put her arms out slightly and did a light shrug. He almost looked like she didn't give a rats ass for explaining herself as she literally did just save his ass.

"How did you…this makes no sense." He stopped moving away from her but stayed standing defensively a certain distance away. "Your Match is literally an omnipotent being, and you just knocked him out!" He watched her peak over his shoulder to check on Tronan, concern evident on her face, yet no regret. "Jesus Christ, Claura!"

"Chill, Roman! He almost just killed you, and I left him breathing. He will wake up. I just know. Maybe he should control his fucking temper." She saw him clearly not interested in seeing any single part of this funny. She sighed and moved her hands as if to simply collect her next thoughts before speaking. She noticed how just the small normal gesture had him jumping back slightly as if expecting more power from her body any second, and she was startled as to what it could do. "Seriously, Roman?"

"Ya." Very few men in her life gave her a more serious tone—literally only one other.

"I have his blood in me now. I'm sure it's changed things."

"How many drops has he shared?" Clearly, he obviously knew of the magical three.

"Two."

It was all new shock all over his face. "You did that to him before even being fully changed?"

"I guess."

He looked from her to Tronan, clearly in a whole new, unfamiliar territory of shock that the man, his main enemy, was still knocked out and slumped against the car. "No, Claura. This isn't a fucking guess." He put his hands over his face as if never more agitated in the past few decades. "We will figure this out, but I will not be here when he wakes up." He saw her eyes dart behind him.

"Hmm….too late. And quick, Roman, I need to hear it from you before he fully comes to. Why was he about to truly destroy you? I mean, it seems like that time has already come and gone in your past together for that."

"Moira."

"What about her?"

"He was asking why I left her to live."

"Well, why did you?" She watched him turn to her shockingly, eyes darting with an anger she would never question but was not in the mood to back down to anymore either.

"What?" Roman shouted. He looked surprised at his own tone, especially toward her.

"She keeps visiting me. In my mind." The look on his face said he had truly had enough for one night. "You don't believe me." She watched him step closer, his fear of her questionable ability gone for the moment.

"Claura, if you are lying to me right now…" She felt his hand come up and wrap slightly around her throat, giving her a sense of fear for herself that she did not expect to ever come from a single pore of him. "I want you to leave and *never* come near me again." Each word was said with a graveness that sent a chill through her. His face was so close, his eyes so intense, studying every part of her face just as intensely as Tronan had already done on several occasions. Her reaction to it had yet to fade even in the slightest. It was clear his desire for her was out the window. But her feelings weren't hurt. She knew his story. She knew how the love of one's child surpassed everything else in life.

"I am so sorry about your daughter, Roman." She thought her sincerity would soften him, even just a little. *Fail.* Right as his fingers got tighter, she heard movement behind him and made no attempt to stop him this time. Tronan shoved him away from her and through the glass wall, literally growling at him in reaction to seeing anyone's hands around her throat, sending him clear across to the other side of the house through a couple more walls. He turned to her with an aggressiveness that she truly tried not to look turned on about. His expression was beyond full of the obvious that they had much to discuss. Just then, the last words she expected him to say came rolling out of his mouth, still unbreaking eye contact with her as if he was clearly beyond a master at holding down two conversations at once, staring her down yet speaking to Roman.

"She is not lying."

It was spoken with such sovereignty. He was making it obvious that if it was questioned of her again, he was fearless of another attempt at his previous plan. He could hear a muttered "Fuck you" from wherever Roman's body had landed out of their sight. His shuffling became louder. Tronan could see him walking back toward them out of the side of his eye.

"Daemon wants to see you."

"Who is Daemon?" she asked.

Roman came closer, wiping blood and excess drywall off his face with the back of his arm. There was zero limp or bruise on his body. She was secretly thankful. Tronan didn't miss the thought of her concern for this other man. "His brother," Roman answered for her, looking between them both, seeing it clear on her face that she had no clue. Enjoying the moment to push it further. "His older, more powerful brother."

Tronan was still facing her, his eyes alone daring her to look away still. "He asked me to thank you. He has been trying to reach me for some time." She wiggled her cell phone out of her pocket and shook it in front of him. His fraction of a smirk faded as fast as it came. "He only communicates through a dream realm now," Tronan said.

"Why?" she continued.

"He will not say," Tronan said.

"It's true," Roman stated. "He has been unreachable to most of us for almost two centuries now and will not tell anyone why."

"He wanted to tell you, Thank you," Tronan stated a second time, something inside him telling him that she needed to really hear it. He watched her tilt her head and frown at him as if to just clarify already. "For knocking me out. Apparently, he has been trying to reach me for some time." He saw her put the pieces together as he looked away slowly to Roman.

"Because you never sleep," she whispered mainly to herself.

She looked to the floor, lost in thought, then at them both at the realization of them staring intently at one another for an uncomfortably long moment. It was clear they were talking telepathically and did not want her to hear. Utter determination yet remorse holding both their ridiculously gorgeous visages. "Can you please just say something? I deserve to know too. This is all a lot to wrap my head around. When it comes to you two, there are constantly pieces missing," she said to them, watching them take a long moment still between themselves as if wrapping it up.

Tronan turned to her finally. "Daemon needs to speak with you specifically about Moira."

Roman followed the lead. "And he has something of mine."

"And what could he possibly have?" she asked, looking between them, needing either of them to answer.

Tronan took her hand gently with his, brushing her hair behind her ear, the calm Tronan she knew fully back in the depths of his flawless eyes. Her heart slowed, unrealizing until that moment that it had been racing this entire time still. His touch truly was pure magic alone and all for her. Her entire rhythm literally matched his, followed the lead. It was scary yet comforting to rely on.

"He wouldn't say," Tronan admitted.

"Well then, you two really are brothers," she said, scoffing slightly.

The moment lingered, clearly having a ridiculous number of things to discuss between them. Despite the harsh and random circumstances, Roman could smell her scent rising again. He held no hesitation.

"Leave my home. Now."

Claura suddenly strode past him, uncaring of his response, to grab a picture off his living room table. She was completely thankful it was still intact. She felt Roman's energy rising as she did so. He clearly meant for them to leave that second, but she wasn't leaving without the only printed picture she had of her daughter. Roman watched her with impatience and almost went to grab her before realizing what she was doing, only for the look on Tronan's face to completely stop him. It was clear his touching days when it came to Claura, even over the smallest physical contact, were over. He looked back at her, appreciating how quickly she was determined to move at least. He studied Tronan's face again, seeing the man still unblinking toward him, before coming to terms with the fact that he might not be able to touch Claura again, but he could reach out and grab what was in her hand as she passed him. His moment was not wasted as her "scent" came closer, driving him mad in its own way as well still.

"Hey!" she shouted. She watched him dead set on seeing what she was so determined to get. He wondered how the hell he had missed it this entire time before their arrival. The more he looked at it, the more he froze. "Where did you get this?"

"It's mine!" Her small hand tried to reach for it.

"Why do you have a picture of her?" Roman asked, almost growling it.

"That's my daughter, Roman! *My* dead daughter!"

Tronan's eyes never shifted back and forth between two people more steadily in his life. It was a moment that was rare among any species. He caught a slight glimpse of the photo and sighed, ashamed of himself for not realizing it earlier, feeling like something was blocking the memory from him on purpose. She looked just like Roman's daughter.

"What is her name?" He kept snatching the photo out of her reach. "Her name?"

"Dayla!"

"Dayla Laudette," Tronan said gently.

His tone made it clear he felt strongly for the child in his own way already, despite never meeting her. He watched Roman look back and forth between them and decided to clarify for her.

"She looks just like her," Roman said, pure remorse and frustration in his voice.

"Who…what are you talking…?" Claura started.

"My baby girl." Roman handed her the photo remorsefully and turned his back on them to walk back into his home.

"Why is this a surprise? You have seen her before already in the hospital that day! Roman!" She was semi-shouting it at his back, watching him finally stop and only turn halfway to look at her one last time.

"I was busy with you." He eyed her with the most unique expression of care and contempt combined. "Now leave. And don't come back unless fucking invited."

# Chapter 15

## Limitless

"Get in the car."

Tronan tried to hide his desire and failed. There was something off in his voice. For some reason, she knew it was a tone that was even foreign to himself. He noticed her walking ahead of him, with no desire to argue, as she casually strolled toward the car. Her entire walk and demeanor had changed since slamming him into the side of it. The casual confidence was more alluring than should be allowed in anyone's gait. He couldn't tell if this was going to be the longest or fastest car ride home he'd ever experienced because he sure as hell had never experienced any other being of the opposite sex do what she did tonight. And damn him to hell, it turned him on like a motherfucker.

And the fact that her body was responding to his fury the way it did. Her scent was somehow stronger yet the same every time it drove him mad again. He suddenly realized that no other woman he had laid a hand on in his entire existence had one-millionth of an effect that Claura was having on him right now. They both slid in and slammed their doors at the exact same time, an eerie yet simple understanding between them to just get off Roman's property, at least before anything else happened—good or bad. They glanced at each other.

Bad.

Very bad.

She smirked, letting her tongue slightly play with her bottom lip, daring him not to even make it to the road. She no longer felt like playing with borrowed fire. It suddenly felt like she owned every flicker for a change and wasn't afraid to see how well she could play with the flames. He noticed. Starting the car with his mind alone while not looking away from her face as well, he simply powered it to drive its damn self home. She looked at the dash then, slightly in awe, slightly worried.

"How do you actually do that?" she asked, her deep frown making her look uniquely irresistible without even knowing it.

"I honestly don't know. I simply tell it what to do with my mind, and it happens," he admitted.

She looked at him accusingly, like he couldn't be serious like there truly had to be more effort than that. "I'm serious. With me, it just is." He watched her grab onto the door panel with satisfaction as he forced the car to literally floor it back around the house and up the driveway. The seconds literally ticked down in their gazes as soon as they reached the highway and were off Roman's property. Claura was enjoying it, no longer fearing how intense things were going to get when around him. Thanks to his blood, she clearly had new strengths and was literally already tingling at being able to do more with him physically now. The car turned onto the highway with a mechanical temper of its own, and he literally reached for her as she leaped onto top of him. She loved knowing already that she would be in more control this time, for there was simply not enough space for him to move around well. But for her, it was plenty. She smiled against his lips, full-on knowing the reason for the troubled moan he was so aggressively pushing back against her mouth. He already knew her thoughts and how he wasn't going to even make the ride home.

"Just take our clothes off, Tronan! I don't want to wait with still having to practice and whatever—"

She could feel her bare ass beneath his hands instantly before even finishing the sentence. Her cheeks felt so small in his grasp. She wasted no time rubbing up and down his length as if there was anywhere else for her hips to start in the confines of the car anyway. His entire body literally did a light jump as her wet entrance enveloped his tip as she caressed him up and down, over and over, teasing him again and again. She wanted to see him just lose it before even inside her, forcing him to keep kissing her, no matter where his lips were. She caressed his ear with her tongue, purring, kissing his ridiculously handsome jawline. Despite his moans that she loved hearing him unable to control, she was still having a hard time herself with waiting. The feel of him was impressive. She loved knowing how he filled her in a way that most women only hoped for. She suddenly felt him trying to hang on but failing, getting aggressive on a level that was alarming. He wanted to wait, to let her have control. He really did. But he was losing his ever-loving mind with her ridiculously sensual teasing. He reached to pull her hips upward to make room for him, quickly letting go with one hand to guide his shaft into her. The barrier was there, but he felt zero need from her to fight it. If anything, she welcomed the moment of pain before pleasure, and for some reason, the look on her face as she did so turned him on even more. She cradled him as close to her as she could and just enjoyed moving slowly, enjoying the weight of him moving in and out of her. It was stronger than last time, and the friction was more enjoyable and more intense. She rode him at a steady, sensual pace for as long as she could stand. She could feel him coming hard and loved watching his face as he did so, knowing she was not far behind. Completely enjoying how her climax peaked right as he was riding his last waves as if on cue to make him cum twice, with how she just kept squeezing and squeezing, making his climax just last and last. It happened in a way he never knew before, never experienced before. This little spitfire was starting to make him feel like he was the one being schooled in more ways than one this evening. So this is how it felt to not be in control. Mouths locked, bodies enjoying the lingering sensations together, him still inside her, they felt the next driveway underneath the tires. She noticed the expression in his eyes as they near the house more and more.

"Show me what you can do. I always want to know."

The car was parked. He pulled her closer as if needing to hang onto her while he did something. "Close your eyes."

"Why do I always have to close my eyes?"

He laughed, running his fingers through her hair, loving the small circles her hips were still doing with him inside her warmth. It was as if she was just enjoying playing and was determined to do it for as long as she damn well pleased.

"To avoid getting dizzy. That's all." He watched her kiss him, then lay against him, her head resting on his shoulder. "Closed?"

"Sure." She smiled. She knew he could see in their mind the link that she was just playing. She felt him kiss the top of her head. Then there was a swift breeze of air all across their bodies. Then the sheets were all around them. Then he so perfectly took control on top of her and behind her. It was obvious that after her skills were somewhat being shown this evening, no third drop was needed for Tronan to do as he damn well pleased with her curves his time. Her sensual cries and shouts of his name several times over forever etched in his mind for him and him alone.

*****

Daemon knew the particular ignoble mark in his mind well. He craved wrapping his fingers around her throat, causing real fear in her eyes for a change. Despite his anger at the particular witch, a new sense of urgency to not mess up his plan felt like it was literally running a marathon through his veins, adding a unique sense of dominating insistence inside him, mainly inside his mind. He made her wait, as usual, before responding telepathically as his kind was gifted to do with anyone he damned well pleased, this planet or others. He was looking very forward to speaking with Claura finally, for no other than himself was able to give his brother a good knockout in all their long days of existence.

*Moira.* There was full-on contempt to kill in his tone, never caring to hide it from her even in the slightest and for good reasons of his own.

*Daemon. Don't you tire of hating one particular being as much as you do me?*

He glanced protectively behind him, as per his daily routine, seeing the small body still tucked nice and warm in her small bed. His body of its own accord, looking away before speaking again to someone so evil. *Unworthy of hate. Completely worthy of permanent death. Your time is coming.*

*That sounds more promising than usual. I think I know why.* She paused, smirking on her end, giving him all the time in the world to clarify first what they both had figured out. *I have already spoken to her. I know where she is. It is only a matter of time before she is here in person with me so I can have my use of her and end her.*

*Ending her will complete this spell of yours, are you so sure? I mean, it's been around 150 years of you trying to complete it. Are you sure you simply haven't lost your touch, witch?* He could feel her seething from her end.

*Sorry for your soon-to-be…loss…Daemon.* She chuckled. She was full-on and more than ready to get the show on the road, clearly just needing one thing first. *As we both know, due to my favorable circumstances compared to yours, I will be able to reach Claura long before you reach either of them. They will come to me first. And it will be done.*

*So sorry you need more power to get anything done, Moira. On that, I cannot relate.*

He knew with pleasure that she was wrong. Claura would be in his company first. There was no need to chuckle back. Daemon was long done with this woman. Tronan and Claura could not get there fast enough, and he knew exactly what they were up to. He knew his brother had waited too long for a Match to come along, but he needed Claura for his own reasons as well.

And now.

Daemon didn't bother with a single intent at any goodbye with Moira. He just simply shut down the mental connection completely. He made it clear once again, despite her not listening and still always finding a way back through, that he wished she'd just disappear off the face of the earth or, in their case, realm.

He heard a small whimper and immediately walked over to the little person who had been his main companion for so long now, lightly caressing her cheek with his forefinger, enjoying just watching her breathing. He knew that no feeling had ever been stronger inside him than the one he was feeling whenever he looked into her little face, knowing he needed to free her from this curse. He turned to seat himself not far away behind his desk, as a crib was built for her in each main room of his home a long time ago. No way in hell was he letting her out of his sight. Not with Moira constantly trying to use her powers to figure out where Daemon was hiding this little innocent, defenseless person. He could hide with her here forever, but he needed to break the curse and could not do it alone, and enough damn time had passed.

Daemon decided to attempt a connection with his brother, hoping the man would be asleep finally or knocked out again with any luck. He inwardly laughed at how his brother must have reacted to having a Match now, after all this time, and one that would be able to do such a thing.

Fail.

He wiped his face with his hand, clearly agitated with being unable to reach Tronan even with all the powers they held. It was just ridiculous to have to deal with. It all started the day the dilemma happened between Roman and Tronan, so Daemon could only hope that it was just another part of this curse that would go away somehow one day, which meant fully meaning with every cell of his being for that day to be soon.

He tried Claura. Now he was able to reach her due to finally seeing the type of connection that was between them, the particular thread that two Matches carried between them at all times. Despite his abilities, he had to see her through an already-existing connection, Tronan. He inwardly swore at how so much was changing this time around with this situation. Daemon sensed her sleeping and, without hesitation, dived right into her dream world. From a distance, he observed her first, standing tall yet out of her line of sight. He watched as she lay on a beautiful daybed in some random apartment somewhere, her arms holding a small baby, her head against the child's soft, delicate temple while she hummed. He held no surprise that this would be her dream. He could see her memories through Tronan and knew more about her already than she would probably be happy with. He sent a simple whisper so as not to frighten her. He hoped she wouldn't be so terrified that she'd appear to Tronan as having a nightmare again and risk him waking her to end it. He needed literally just a minute.

*****

*Claura?* He watched her quickly turn as if more sensing a threat to the child than herself. He saw her face go sad at the realization that this was just a dream, and it broke his heart. *Claura, it's beyond vital that you find me ASAP.* The way she looked up at him made him pause. It was clear she did not trust him. *Please.* He tried to stand as least intimidating as possible, not moving toward her. It was quite clear that this dream walk thing was still so new to her, even with Tronan. He watched her put the baby back in a bassinet and turn slowly back to stand before him and face him. It was clear she recognized him right away, right from the first glance, as he had many similar features to Tronan.

*Forgive me, Daemon. This is scary for me. All this.* Looking down at the bassinet and then back up, wiping at her slightly wet cheek. *On top of it all, I am still grieving.*

*I know.*

*What is the urgency? How far even are you?* The worry on his face in response startled her. She could tell she was not going to like the answer.

*In a different realm.* He waited, giving her a moment to let that one sink in. He was completely aware of her unknowing about it, among other things—again.

# THE WINGED WITCH OF MATCHES

*Realm?* It was obvious Tronan had more explaining to do here.

*How does one travel to a different realm, Daemon?* She felt the obvious fear a human would feel still in this situation, despite her body being, in a way, already in a different realm with its new blood.

*You will travel just fine now that you have our bloodline in your body. I can see its changes, and it fits you. More well than you realize.* He saw her rubbing her temple and then looked up at him just in time to watch his quick hand swipe, as if to rid of her headache, more so for himself as he really needed her to focus right now. She mouthed a gentle thank-you as she sat back down on the sofa and just waited for him to continue. *So, my new sister, how is it you knocked my younger brother out so swiftly?*

It was an unexpected shared moment of humor between them. She watched him slowly sit across her in a nearby chair. She looked right straight into his smile, admiring the resemblance and how it was actually easier for him to show a genuine one among another perfectly shaped mouth she knew intimately. She could tell by the way he looked back at her and her small blush that she needed not to point out the obvious. That they looked alike, as old as news could be.

*I honestly don't know. I felt Roman, in my mind, needing my help. I already knew where he was, so that maybe helped, I can only assume. Next thing I know, I am there and seeing what was happening, and I started feeling this enormous energy build. It was like its own being inside me, coming to whatever level of strength I needed it to be to do whatever I needed to do...like it was truly...umm—*

*Limitless.*

*Yes.* There was fear in her own eyes first, self-admiration clearly second.

*And with only two drops in you?*

*Yup.*

*How did he react?*

*I don't think he knew how. But for some reason, it heightened our...connection.* As much as she blushed, she also looked even more worried. She stared at her hands now, slightly too embarrassed to look back into his face again. *I don't know. We will figure it out.* She clearly meant to keep it between her and Tronan. He let her stay lost in her thoughts for a few moments before speaking again, as it was an obvious touchy subject. She was clearly conflicted when it came to Tronan. For his own reasons, it humbled him. She heard him clear his throat and sensed him moving next to her, shifting subtly. He watched her face glance to where the baby was. There was zero stirring in the bassinet, as if her reality was still going to be mixed in her dream world, whether she liked it or not. It was completely opposite of what was happening in the one within his own home. He saw her look to the silence of it with pure anger and despair and back to her twisting hands, her face becoming even more lost.

*Claura, I have information I cannot give here. I need to do it in person.*

*Why? Seems like a pretty private place to me, inside my dream, in my head.*

*Moira is able to hide in all places except my home.*

*As your homes are utmost sacred, right?*

*Yes.* There was firmness in the way he said it, as if he'd bring hell to its knees first before what was in his home was found by anyone whom he didn't want to find it. *I can feel you waking. Tell Tronan to get moving. Now.*

*****

There was pure disconnect.

The feeling of having a brother was strange, and not just because it was a brother like him. The feeling of their first meeting being in her dream was beyond strange in that it just felt so normal. It was like she had done it before several times over in a past life. She couldn't shake the feeling she got from the dream, from the look on Daemon's face every time he glanced at the bassinet so quickly you swore you'd imagined it. She figured seeing him in person would make a lot more things clear. She inwardly hoped anyway as she lazily stretched her body in the sheets. She loved the feeling of the silkiness on her skin, slightly reminding her of how his body inside her silky parts intensified everything in and around her on so many levels.

# THE WINGED WITCH OF MATCHES

She turned her head more to see him lying there next to her, eyes open as if in deep thought and simply staring through her. She carefully slides in closer to him, places her hand on his face, rubbing her thumb across his handsome cheekbone. She studied his features the way he had so lovingly done to her more than once already, avoiding his eyes for all intense reasons. And then he made it clear why, eyeing her the way a predator would. The low whisper of it close to her face did not make the threat of it any less intense.

"I do not like my brother being in your dreams while you lay naked in my own bed," he said sternly yet almost in a whisper.

"I think he tried to reach you first." She kissed his nose sweetly, ignoring his intense vibe as best she could. "If only you would sleep."

"I enjoy watching you sleep. Seeing you here beside me now after all this time."

"So now you fear I am the dream that will fade when you awake?"

"I fear many things."

"Like what?"

There was no answer. He simply moved toward her, ridiculously easily sliding her underneath him with his strong arms and shoulders, parting her toned legs for him again, easing into her while holding her perfectly yet lovingly captive under his grasp…again.

"Goddamn it, Tronan. He made it sound like we really need to get a move on." Her head was already rolling back, exposing her throat to his oral invasion as she felt him move deeper and deeper inside her. She loved all the things he did with his mouth, no matter where he placed it on her body. Feeling his one hand moved downward to sensually caress her clit, just the way he did it, being half the turn-on. "The fact that there may be jealousy between you and your brother over me is ridiculous." The words were hard to get out for obvious reasons.

"I will get a move on whenever I damn well please, dragostea mea, however I please."

She could feel him in her mind then, taking control of her body with it, making her eyes widen in wonder. She was suddenly unable to move her hips against him, unable to help her own release come sooner, unable to help her own urges at all, making it feel like even more torment on a whole other level. She lifted her eyes to him accusingly with what focus she could attain in the middle of all the sensations. All she got in return is a smirk hidden behind a very clear intention of forcing her to subdue him in those ridiculously perfect eyes. He slowed his pace and kept it there no matter how much she could feel herself grip him with each rising wave. It was fucking torture. She could feel her body try to quiver in response to the building climax, but in his mind control, he was determined not to cave…and let it build…and build ever so slowly.

Her yelling and pleading of his name sounded dazed, and far away, she literally felt her hand come up and aim at him, her body of its own accord trying to stop its tormenter. She could hear him lightly laugh at her efforts, feel his strong hand gently hold her wrist away from his face as his lower half kept moving in that aberrant rhythm. She leaned on the only way she knew she had left to communicate with him and tried to focus.

*Tronan, please!*

*Just let it come, sweetheart.* He slightly hated himself for how much he was enjoying her fighting him, but he knew he was giving her one of the best orgasms of her life. And he was no quitter—not now, not ever when it came to her. He loved how her scent changed the more pleasure she felt. It alone heightened everything he was feeling in response.

*You motherfucker…* She felt the parts of her upper body that she could still move literally try to levitate and press into him in response. *I can't breathe, Tronan.*

*Almost there.* He felt her muscles clench and quiver around him, her release building. He was way past trying to hide how immensely he was enjoying himself, enjoying the expressions racing across her beautiful face. The feeling of her rocking and gripping around him on the inside in some insane way kept feeling more and more hot and tight around his erection. He never felt more blood rushed to the particular anatomy in his entire lifetime with anyone, no matter how good the sex was. Despite his best efforts, he started to tremble as he felt his own climax starting as hers was clearly now peaking. He was determined to remain at the sensual teasing pace. Determined to make it linger as long as possible, as strong as possible, he could see her literally unable to inhale the entire time she came back down.

"Oh my god." She felt shocked to hear her own voice already. It seemed like such an ache to accomplish getting any single word out. A tear literally fell from each eye, making its way across each temple as she lay beneath him, head slightly still tilted back into the bed, feeling him have one of his best climaxes ever as well—inside her, with her. If he ever topped that, a feeling of just as much worry as excitement filled her mind at just the thought.

He leaned down closer to her, with one strong hand forcing her mouth to his. Palming the back of her head in that sexy, dominant way she truly couldn't get enough of. It was one of his signature moves—one she'd never tire of. She slowly made eye contact with him with only half-opened lids, savoring the kiss first with eyes closed for as long as he did, damn well please. His fucking mouth…

"Sweetheart, in a way, you actually are fucking a god." He felt her smile against his mouth, too weak to really look at him still. He just enjoyed the feeling between them as her warmth still slightly quivered around his shaft. Tiny little aftershocks took forever to fade.

"My dear Tronan, perhaps you are too." He literally laughed against her mouth. Despite it kind of making her feel confused, she loved the sound of it all the same. It was the first time she actually heard that genuine from him. "What!" She was not hurt at all in the slightest if he was laughing at her. She just wanted him to clarify. She chose to still lay completely unabandoned beneath him, feeling the laughter radiating from his perfect chest and arms around her, loving the feeling of him being happy.

"I am just thinking of you sending me backward and knocking me on my ass. I still can't believe you did that."

"So it's settled," she whispered happily.

"What?"

"To do such a thing, I'd have to be some sort of god too."

"Goddess."

"Sounds stunning." She smiled with her eyes closed, leisurely exploring his amorous body with her fingers. "Let me move my hips again."

"You sure? Want me to go again?" He watched her contemplate while staring at the ceiling for a moment and started to move again inside of her as if to push her to just answer him, tell him what he wanted to hear, and lightly laugh at her almost immediate resolve.

"Will this get even more intense still when I am fully changed?"

He leaned away to flip her over onto her belly, gripped her hips, pulled her ass slightly up to enter her from behind, and leaned over her to whisper in her ear, nice and close.

"Yes."

# Chapter 16

# A Curse to Reverse

Tronan watched her catch her breath as they drove up to the front of the cathedral and parked, Roman clearly being in her line of sight already. He himself was feeling a sense of dread about this trip as if he truly could not shake that a major shift in circumstances was about to happen. He was annoyed with not being able to put a finger on it at all, sensing that his Claura had more to do with all this and that he had yet to even understand himself. He hated that he couldn't just protect her from it all better. He glanced out the windshield at Roman as well. It was more than evident the man was tired of waiting. Claura truly wondered if he knew what had taken them so long, feeling slightly ashamed of herself. She opened her door and stood up, hands gently palming over the car door frame, studying him from a distance for a second before completely stepping out of the car. She saw him take one long distant whiff in her direction, turn his face away from her, and stride inside the large building out of her sight. She felt Tronan come close, easing her to the sidewalk so he could close her door for her, and turn and put his palm on the low of her back. She felt his breath on her ear.

"Never feel ashamed." And he meant it. It was as if he had every intention of reminding her only once. She felt him give that subtle guided push despite her feet suddenly feeling heavy. His hand moved down to intertwine with hers, caressing her smaller fingers with his much larger ones, trying to reassure her nerves. She stopped in her tracks suddenly, wanting to ask him before Roman could hear.

"Is there truly no way to bring Maya back for him?" She looked way more sad about it than she intended. She watched him simply study her for a moment and just gently shake his head no.

"Not that I know of." He gestured for her to come on. She suddenly felt a slight nervousness about seeing his older brother again after so long. It was always hard to tell with Daemon just how dire the situation was. There was usually something unexpected that was about to happen whether Daemon reacted accordingly or calmly in response. In all his years, he still found the man hard to fully figure out, related or not. "This realm that I know he mentioned to you briefly."

"Understatement. I need you to clarify much more than he did."

"I had every intention to, my love." He smiled to himself, clearly proud of getting beyond sidelined between the sheets. He felt her playfully nudge his arm to just continue already as they paused, seeing his brother for long enough, so much so she was starting to wonder if Daemon was going to have a word with them about it. "The realm where Daemon's home resides is very unlike earth. The air smelled different. The skies were a constant sunrise of silver and blue hues only, without the sunlight ever really fully rising, the waters being the same hues and making most of the landscape look chronically mirrored around the clock."

"That doesn't sound so nonlovely."

"As gorgeous as it is at first, after some time, it can feel slightly gloomy. Yet it suits him." He took a deep breath, trying to think of what would be useful to her. "You won't see many other living beings here, not in his area anyway. He has around one hundred thousand areas of self-protected land surrounding his home, increasing its circumference every few decades."

"What do they look like?"

"You won't meet them. I don't plan for us to be there that long." He felt her turn toward him while tugging his hand slightly, stopping them on the steps up to the large cathedral doors.

"But *if* I do meet them, just tell me what to expect."

"Tall. Navy skin. Beyond muscular. Some have horns that can be on all different parts of their heads. Some with more than one set of eyes. They all have a unique armor that resembles their individual skill level. They have their own language, so you won't be able to understand them."

"Somehow, that still does not sum it up, does it?"

"No. I am sorry, Claura. I honestly don't know where to begin. Every realm is beyond different from earth. It takes our own species years, even decades, to have the time to study what lies beyond our own place of residence."

"How many realms are there?"

"For our species, 983." He really looked at her then, feeling her hand come up to rub her forehead, seeing her getting overwhelmed. "Let us focus on this one task today. And I will take you to a library later and show you a hidden section."

"Hidden?"

"From the human eye. Only creatures of other bloodlines are able to see it." He pulled her to start moving her feet again, opening the front door with one hand despite being able to do it with his mind. He simply did not want anyone from the outside human world to see. She looked to him in question once inside the doors as to where to go next, for some reason enjoying the heavy yet smooth sound they made as they closed behind them. He inclined his head to the far left corner of the place, taking her hand again as they walked down the center, passing the aisles together, knowing full well what a part of her little lady brain was envisioning. He turns to smile at her, full on love in his eyes, as he raises her small hand to his mouth. She shyly watches as if they hadn't already been intimate together. The sound of Roman clearing his throat echoed over the balcony, making her body slightly jump out of the very intimate moment being shared in Tronan's eyes, lifting her gaze to meet Roman's. Tronan didn't miss the expression one bit. She looked at him like she was truly determined to figure out how to help him get his one love back, but she simply just needed more time to figure out how. Not whether it couldn't be done or not. She looked like someone else had jumped into her body again at the moment, just like she admitted to what had happened to her in the car so recently. He let her hand drop and stepped closer, framing her face with his large palms, intentionally blocking Roman out from her line of sight. "There's that look again." He sounded worried just as much as curious.

"Something inside me, I can feel it." She looked back and forth between his handsome eyes, completely non-intimidated by him—a quality he was still getting used to from her as he mainly knew only how to react to clearly being intimidating to others his whole life. But not Claura. Her lack of fear was more than him simply being her Match and knowing he would never harm her. It went deeper than that. There was another reason. He wanted to study it. He needed to know where it was coming from. There was something different lurking under her surface. As her other half, it was simply his duty to figure out what it was.

"Let's go!" Roman literally rumbled from above.

He turned away from their yet again intimate moment, fed up with it and who it constantly reminded him of, who he was constantly still mourning until his last breath. Tronan turned to see his back already facing them, rounding the corner on the balcony above toward the room they all needed to go to. He turned back around, whispering close to her face.

"We will discuss this later. Follow me."

He led her up to the room and let her walk inside first, closing the door on all three of them. She looked between them for answers, clearly having no interest in her surroundings despite it being one of the most beautiful rooms she'd ever been in. Her mind was already focused on what they needed to do to travel in the way they did. Roman broke in first, stepping closer to her, surprising her as he was normally distancing himself from her more and more lately like she could blame him. "You will feel dizzy and disoriented and may have a small migraine for a few minutes once we arrive." He looked like he wanted to rub his hands up and down her arms to reassure her as he always had done but made no effort to do so. He was standing so close to her, reading her expression, yet feeling so distant in every other aspect possible.

"Did Daemon tell you anything else we need to know in your dream, my dear?" Tronan broke in yet still remained a few feet away. He could see Roman turn to him with slight surprise before looking back to her. The question on his face was clear. He wanted to know what Daemon had that belonged to him. He was at a complete loss as to what it could be and why the man wouldn't just communicate with him directly already as well. She took a moment to think over the conversation, inwardly wishing it could have lasted a bit longer as they didn't really discuss much. She decided to keep it at that. Keep it uncomplicated, as a part of her already knew deep down this was all about to get very complicated for some reason.

She raised her chin, looking between them both, their ridiculously handsome and intense stares. "He did not want Moira to overhear, even risk the smallest chance of it, so he did not say much to me in the dream. Unfortunately. Just that we need to see him ASAP." She watched them contemplate in silence, unmoving in all but their minds. Roman's scent being so close to her still, for some reason, had an effect on her despite it being obvious who she was mated with several times over now.

"Can we go? Please." She watched Roman turn to stand in a circle in the middle of the design on the rug, centering himself in the room. She looks to Tronan, seeing him point to the spot and guide her to it with him.

"Close your eyes, sweetheart."

She looked at Roman one last time before obeying Tronan's gentle command, seeing his all-confusing expression as he stared right back at her—one full of hate yet still full of love. And to think she was about to be in the presence of three of them like this. She inwardly prayed Daemon was full of answers more than confusing feelings. And then she felt it, the shift. Gravity literally disappeared beneath her feet, and her entire body felt like it was spinning uncontrollably, her eyes unable to open, causing her to slightly panic. A soft reassurance was felt in her mind from Tronan. She could hear him counting backward for her from five…four…three…two…one.

Her feet landed while the rest of her body wobbled, her arms and hands reaching out to try to grasp anything before she toppled over like a drunk. She suddenly felt a strong arm grab her right one, while a cold rock was felt under her left palm as she half caught herself. The ringing in her ears disappeared as fast as it had come on. She heard a deep, masculine voice from a great distance as her eyes adjusted to her surroundings. Looking around, trying to bring the place into focus as soon as possible.

"*Finally*," the still far-off masculine voice said.

She could tell instantly the manly growl was neither Roman nor Tronan. And something inside its tone made her pause. Something deep inside her recognized it and was trying to reach for it. She simply shook her head, trying to get back to the reality at hand. She looked up to catch a blurry glimpse of a man slightly taller than Tronan coming toward them. His gait was not gentle. He appeared to be many yards away and then suddenly upon them in seconds. She felt Tronan's grip on her arm to help her up suddenly disappear, his entire frame removed from the corner of her eye, followed by the sound of a body being slammed against a wall behind them, apparently. She stayed leaning on one knee as she turned her upper body to follow the noise, the urgency of what was happening to her Tronan causing her eyesight to become crystal clear now, seeing Roman slightly behind her, watching the scene as well, clearly having zero interest in including himself in the dilemma at all. She turned back to the man holding Tronan up by the neck, anger radiating off him in waves for them to all literally see. As much as she wanted to help her man, she knew she was also a part of the cause of them taking longer to get here than they probably should have.

"Your pace is questionable, my brother."

"It has been a day."

"Oh no." His laugh was menacing, chilling all their spines. "I have been waiting for longer than one damn day."

The air kept thickening around them all, the heaviness of it becoming a creepy invisible entity of its own. She watched as Tronan slammed his arm against his brother's grip, breaking his hold from around his neck but only for a split second before Daemon responded with a limitless fury. The speed of his arms and hands literally blurred as he effortlessly cut off Tronan's air supply with one swift hit from the side of his hand and gripped his neck all over again with his other now. Pulling him away from the wall to simply be able to slam his head back against the rock again. She could hear Roman make a noise of enjoyment behind her. She turned to see him crossing his arms over his chest, pleasure owning his expression, choosing to completely ignore her glare.

"Daemon. Please."

She broke in, standing slowly. She felt slightly wobbly still. While still looking at Tronan with full-on fury yet clearly speaking to her, Daemon made his wishes known and that they would happen *now*.

"I need to speak with you first, Claura." He made sure Tronan understood his next word nicely and clearly before continuing. "Alone."

"Fine." She cut in before Tronan could say anything in response. "Let's go. I need a damn drink." She started in the direction she saw Daemon first coming from, finally looking up to study her surroundings more and seeing a ridiculously tall building come through an opening in the distance ahead, the top of it disappearing into the clouds.

*Damn.*

She headed for it, something inside its walls telling her to do so. She enjoyed the look of the blue and silver hues from the sky reflecting off its stone walls, how the place seemed like such a safe haven despite its gloomy, lionhearted appearance.

"Where to begin?" she asked more so to herself, looking at the huge castle-like structure in wonderment.

She suddenly felt a strong presence came up behind her, a hand brush in front of her face, forcing her eyes closed, followed by her entire body being lifted. Only two seconds passed before she felt landing underneath her feet again, and Daemon's deep voice broke through the silence.

"In my study."

She opened her eyes to see a beautiful old-fashioned office before her. She turned in a half circle to see more of the room. Her eyes suddenly noticed a very large stone balcony a few feet away. It suddenly became clear they landed from that direction, her feet moving before her mind comprehended and needed to see him. She walked out onto the stone balcony and glanced down, seeing instantly their two faces of worry looking back up at her. It became evident who the strongest of the three was, who she was in closest proximity to, in a whole different realm, in his own home. The feeling of being captured suddenly took over, and strongly. She took her time turning to face him. She saw him waiting with complete patience for her to walk back into the room and take a seat. Something about him felt extremely familiar, but she was determined to keep her spine straight and her thoughts on the task at hand. She took a deep breath as she felt her feet move, inwardly reminding herself of her own powers she had as well. She wondered how they would be used. He suddenly spoke, making it alarmingly obvious he knew her thoughts and would continue to know them during her visit.

"Quite useful. More than you can even understand right now," he said, smiling at the alarm on her face, seeing it sink in that he was full of intent on knowing everything that was going to go through her mind while in his home.

She could tell it was for a good reason. She just wasn't sure what reason for yet exactly. She felt the warmth of the room envelop her as she took her last step inside from the balcony, her eyes instantly going to the bassinet she had not noticed before. There was a soft whimper from it, making her blood stop right along with her feet. She looked up at him with full-on awe and question in her eyes. He simply took a sip out of what looked like a bourbon glass, eyeing her intently while remaining standing behind his desk. Waiting. She decides to walk closer, unable to stop herself. And as soon as she peeks into the bassinet up close, she feels her heart leap in a way it's never leaped before.

"OMG! Dayla?"

"No." Her head turned to meet his gaze at an alarming speed. "She is not your daughter." He tried to use a calm tone as much as possible. Seeing her still lingered grief as clear as day across her face.

"She looks almost identical to my dead daughter!"

"I am sorry, Claura. But that is not your child."

"Then who is she?"

"My chibrit." He became as still as stone, even more so than he already was. Eyeing her like her response was more important than she realized. "She has been like this, with me, here in my home… for 150 years." He could see her piecing it together much faster than expected. Her thoughts on the picture that she and Roman so recently argued over. How long ago Tronan had said he had his feud with Roman, but the details were still not all given from him nor Roman. Learning about the two men was like trying to learn chess before even speaking your first words. Her hand went over her mouth. Her eyes widened. She started backing away from them both.

"Roman's daughter?" She watched him nod. "But how? I was told she is dead, like my…my…" The tears started swimming. "Explain, Daemon! Now!"

He set his glass down gently, placing his hands on the very large and dark mahogany desk, leaning forward. Evident on his face, he was thinking of his words carefully first. "Maya was a weaver of Matches, of the thread between mates. She knew she had only a blink of an eye to decide how to save her baby before Moira attempted to murder her. And she chose me." He looked up to her then. He wanted her to know that he meant every word and was not making any of it up. "She created the illusion of her baby dying to satisfy Moira's sick desires, knowing in time she would figure it out any way that that's all it was. But knowing as well it would give her enough time to be able to hide her baby girl away. Never for Moira to find." He swiped his hand, resembling his home. "Here. With me."

"She had to make you this baby girl's Match…why?"

"So I could hide her. It was simply an extra insurance for Moira to not be able to scent any trail. I can keep her safe. As long as she is my Match, I have that right. I can block her from anybody while she is here with me."

"This was so long ago. Why has she not aged? She has truly stayed as a baby all this time?!"

"It was a part of the curse Moira created that Maya did not have enough time to uncreate. It was utmost in her mind to make sure her baby girl simply wasn't killed first, and everything else could come second."

"How does this connect to me? I have no idea how you think I can help."

"For some reason, Moira wants you, to use you. Maya could unbreak the curse, but not while dead. For some reason, you are a threat to Moira as much as you are useful. I can only assume you have the power she needs to complete her curse and kill Roman's child once and for all. If you have that kind of power, Claura, it can mean you also have the ability to reverse such curse instead of choosing to push it forward."

"I would never push such a thing forward. Just the thought alone sickens me." She looked at him with pure sorrow in her eyes. "You have truly waited so long. I am so sorry, Daemon." The pieces of it all still came together in her mind, making it so the conversation could go in so many different directions. She stepped closer to the baby again, admiring her little features, trying not to let it get to her in a way where she would just start crying and not be able to stop. She spoke low to the child, "You poor thing. Frozen in time like this. This is so cruel." The child looked at her with a knowing, like she had been waiting for Claura to show up. The expression made something deep inside of Claura turn even more determined. She truly wanted to help this little person. She was connected to her somehow. She could feel it.

"Yes. But still less cruel than her being dead." He paused, studying her, watching her lean over the baby. "Maya told me all that time ago that the Match of my brother would have the power. I have waited decades for Tronan to find you. Here in my home, with this little one." He shifted to move to come around his desk, placing himself in the center of it, leaning back into it slightly with his arms crossed over his powerful chest. Claura could see that his chest cavity held no need to rise and fall. His eyes were one hundred times more potent in determination than Tronan's. The observation led to the obvious question she knew he already knew was happening in her mind. She simply looked from the small child to him as she moved to sit down in the nearest chair to the small crib. "There are 655 years between my brother and I." He watched her look back to the crib, contemplating how she felt sorry for this baby, for how she could relate to the emotions that came from being in love with someone so much older than yourself. "Claura, the age gap between Matches means nothing. Knowledge of any level can be earned over time. There are simply more important things to focus on between mates."

"Are you so sure about that because I am unable to wrap my head around it?"

"Time."

"Clearly, time can be a curse," she said, sighing.

He could feel her mentally reach for Tronan, needing to feel the connection. Seeing her small smile caused some color to seep into her cheeks.

"I see my brother's main skills still never fail despite the circumstances."

"It is weird that you know." She frowned at him, letting the words leave her lips quickly, accusingly.

"I simply know things, Claura. That is not the difficult part. How you use and handle the information is the real challenge with anything or anyone."

He stepped closer to the crib. She saw him study the small face for several seconds, his expression full of concern, of love. She watched as his strong hands and arms lifted the little body into his embrace. The gentle way he did it was so beyond sweet she knew the moment would be etched into her memory for all time.

"How have you done it, Daemon?"

"Simple. I will be what she needs me to be. And routine, of course." He sat himself in a separate nearby chair, holding the innocent child on his lap to face him, staring down into her face. "With my abilities, I am able to address all her needs, no matter her age. I will not lie to you, though. I look forward to finally seeing her grow, maturing, and able to hold down an actual conversation with me. Never in a million lifetimes would I have expected the beginning of my relationship with a Match to be like this."

"I will end this." The firm tone in her voice had him eyeing her instantly. "I don't understand, though. I can sense you are stronger than Tronan even. How have you not been able to figure this out already?" She used her tone carefully, just wanting some real answers.

To her surprise, he slightly smirked before answering, leaning back into the chair more while pulling the baby against his chest now. He held her small weight in the crook of his strong arm.

"I can see that my all-omnipotent brother has not been completely honest with you. Sorry to say there are actual limits to our abilities."

"How so?"

"Different realms have different levels of power. I was simply born of a stronger realm. Tronan, a less intense one. Where we are born mirrors our levels of power, or strength, despite who we come born from."

"But you have the same parents?"

"Yes. Father was able to jump realms more than most, hence meeting our mother. Most of us only stick to a few realms, cling to the ones that match our own power level."

"She was from a lesser or stronger one?"

"He never did say."

"Seems important to know."

"And now we never will. He is dead. As is she."

"I'm sorry."

"Don't be. Not like we didn't get enough lifetimes with them." His tone suggested it was more than what he personally preferred to have dealt with.

"Moira mentioned only the father could kill Tronan. That's why he isn't already dead. So only those from the same bloodline can kill someone?" She watched him nod. "And you, being the stronger brother, could you kill him if you really wanted to, Daemon?"

Her tone suggested she was terrified of even having to ask. She watched him take a deep inhale and look at her like he was sorry but that she could trust him, and nodded subtly, never leaving her gaze.

"I have no reason to truly harm my brother to that extent. Do not worry needlessly."

"Since we are on the topic of the other two men here waiting for me, for us…why have you not told Roman about his daughter this whole time?" She looked at him sadly. "He deserves to know."

"I needed you to come along first. A real chance at breaking this curse. I saw no reason for him to have suffered alongside me for literally what has been fifteen decades. I know it sounds heartless, but it seemed to let him hold onto his already accustomed grief was easier for him. At least until I could free her from this." *And me.* He was completely able to hide his last lingering thought from her.

"You know I won't be able to keep that secret from him." She eyed the small body against his chest, the little frame looking so tiny against him. It was sweet and scary at the same time. "I'm not that strong, Daemon. I'm sorry."

"Your strengths lay elsewhere."

"How do I keep Moira away?" She got right to the other point.

"The green light you've seen in her hands, don't let her use that on you."

"How do you know about that? How the hell do I stop her?"

"I know more than you are yet ready to learn." He eyed her with regret in his face as if he felt remorseful for some reason. He could see her trying to figure out why and decided to simply distract her by continuing. "As for the green light she uses…figure it out. Same way you let it build inside you enough to knock my omnipotent brother on his ass and out cold for a few minutes finally, which, thank you, by the way."

"I give you permission if I don't succeed with this." She knew he would hate her on a level she feared to see from him if she was not able to save this little one. Able to make it so they could finally really be together.

"I would not do that."

"You know you would want to."

"Something tells me I don't have to worry about it, Claura. So please stop."

The way he said please, she could tell it was very foreign to his own vocal cords.

"May I hold her?" She could hear her own voice crack. "Please?" Her expression turned to terrified, her memories taking over. Claura was unable to block out the emotions rising, the flashbacks of the last little body she held not even being a warm temperature. She saw him instead stand up and walk toward the crib, making her suddenly feel beyond confused and embarrassed for asking. He set the baby down gently and turned toward her, coming close and kneeling before her on the carpet. He lifted his hands to hold her face between them, holding her gaze steady, inches from his own.

"I'm sorry I asked. I can't imagine what she means to you, and you just met me," he whispered to him.

He nodded as if in disagreement, reading her emotions, seeing her memories while just looking into her eyes alone. He sensed she had zero desire to stop him from seeing into her mind, zero fear in letting him do it. "I can feel your relation to her. I just don't know how it is so. So I am unable to trust it until we figure that out," Daemon clarified, seeing the hurt increase behind her eyes—the confusion.

"Unable to trust me, you mean. You are being so confusing right now. You want my help to save her, yet don't want me to hold her."

"I only sense the strength of your postpartum still inside you. It worries me what seeing a little girl that looks just like your dead daughter means for you and for her as well." He wiped one small tear away. "I simply fear whatever piece is missing here. For her sake and yours. Please understand."

"So kill someone as powerful as Moira…then hold the baby." She gave a small laugh, zero humor reaching her eyes.

His expression remained serious, worrisome, intent on figuring something out. She could feel his fingertips do that thing that Tronan did, the tension in her mind fading. The ache disappeared. His hands let go of her skull, moving to stop the slight trembling in her hands next. He was so gentle as if he had been waiting for the moment and refused not to savor it. She was about to question it when he let her go, so she stood up and moved back toward his desk.

"About her, while we still have time, as I sense Tronan's impatience building. Tronan thinks Moira got her powers from the devil himself to be able to accomplish what she did, but I know different." He walked around to the other side of his desk again and sat down in his chair. "Maya was able to inform me of a few things before she… disappeared."

"Different?"

"She got power from her first true love, who was from a very potent realm all on his own. Unfortunately, he was not the first who did not put her first, which is why when Roman chose Maya over her, it was simply too much for her to handle twice. He gave her what power she desired as a way of paying her back for what he did to her, for breaking her heart."

"Did he know what was in the balance? A goddamn child?"

"No. He thought he was giving Moira power to end Roman, nobody else. He had no idea she intended to use it on Roman, Maya, and their baby. Or this is what Maya has informed me of anyway," he said, looking worried over the fact that he was still missing something in all this.

"So he knows now. He must somehow and chose not to help?" Her thought slightly lingered on how he worded it so, saying "their baby" instead of "my match" as it seemed more fitting with how strong the connection was between Matches.

"He has no abilities within the boundaries of certain curses, whether to start or stop them. He can give power, but not use it for the same reasons as others may use it for. It is a flaw that goes back a long time in his particular realm." He watched her put her face in her hands, clearly needing a moment.

"This bitch needs to die. Like now. And I am unable to wrap my head around how this is somehow up to me still to do it."

"Breathe."

She laughed, staring into space at other parts of his office, half-heartedly taking in the surroundings. "Now I have three gorgeous men telling me that."

"I am gorgeous?"

"Fuck off, Daemon. The baggage from the first two has been beyond plenty, now this." She stood up to head toward the balcony, clearly just needing some air, completely missing his expression of "Tell me about it."

She half sat on its ledge, looking down, noticing no one was in sight anymore. She wondered just how much time had passed. She felt him stepping onto the balcony behind her, keeping his distance. She felt the energy from him grow protective but figured it was simply due to sitting this close to the ledge while so high up and choosing not to read into it, knowing he needed her for his own selfish reasons. The sight of being up this high, seeing this much from just one balcony, was obviously old news to him as she felt him continue to stare at her and nothing else. She felt the need to break the silence with what was growing inside her, too scared to want to look closer at why tension was just naturally building. "She is to stay here with you until this is all over?"

"I am unable to part from her." He kept his tone neutral and factual.

"I can understand that."

"I wish to have a little more time before Roman knows. My intentions were to let him know of her as soon as the curse was rid of." He watched her sigh deeply as if he was truly asking too much from her now. "Please."

"I can't."

"Yes. You can."

"I am not promising that! You have no idea how hurt he already is because of me. Adding this on top is too much!"

"He can handle it." He watched her turn to him then, the look on her face making him inwardly shocked at how his body reacted with needing to take a breath for himself suddenly. He felt turned on but, with all his being, chose to hide it under his mask.

# THE WINGED WITCH OF MATCHES

"He shouldn't have to! First, his Maya! Then his newborn daughter! Then having feelings for me and seeing it all meant nothing once Tronan came into the picture! I will *not* lie to him! I won't fucking do it!"

"He already had his Match, why would he—" She could see the realization hit his eyes.

"What is it?"

"Moira, as clever as she is evil. She really did have fun with poor Roman since she couldn't kill him, didn't she?"

"Explain, please."

"It's just another part of her curse. Her spell was made so the baby would die first, but she did not succeed and therefore could not finish it with the parents. So, she must have still cursed them in other ways, thus making him think he is in love with you so he may feel rejection as she did."

"She makes it clear without even knowing her personally why Maya would be the obvious choice. Also, that is good to hear."

"Why would that be good?"

"I was worried I may be choosing the wrong man. This proves I didn't."

He eyed her for what was one of the most unique lingering moments of her life. "My dear, to think you had a choice in the matter proves just how much you still don't know."

"Been a little busy, Daemon." She chose to shrug off how she could sense he maybe wasn't meaning that in the same way that she took it. There was something off about Daemon, and she feared she was too scared to attempt putting her finger on it. The man held such ease about the power he so obviously held. It was alarming. He was clearly as smart as they came, and it intimidated her.

"I'm sure Tronan could agree." He smiled with a smile that didn't quite reach his eyes as he turned to head back inside. "Who will be walking through my door in just a moment."

"Both of them?"

"Yup." She saw him reach his desk and grab another glass, inquiring if she might need one too now. She took one last look out over the balcony, admiring the unique view of another realm. She shook her head, laughing in disbelief at her situation. She thought about how it did not matter how hard she may pinch herself. She was not going to wake up.

"Before they come in, Daemon, please answer me again as to why you could not get rid of Moira already. Forgive me for still being a little bit confused."

"You have every right to be confused." His softened tone put her at ease more than she expected as she walked back into the large office toward him. She watched his hands pour them both a glass, admiring how she could tell they held such power yet were the same hands holding a delicate baby only a few minutes ago. "Moira has connected herself to my Match somehow. If I hurt one, I hurt the other. Another reason I need you to do it instead of me."

"How did you find this out?" She clearly hoped he did not mean the hard way.

"Maya simply warned me. This is why she caused Roman to see an illusion as well. Roman truly believed he saw all three of them die. It was simply another precaution that was, as you can imagine, hard for her to do to the father of her own child. All to make the spell work." She could hear it in his voice, his admiration yet distaste for spells at the same time.

"To the man she loved." She watched him gently nod in agreement. "There is truly no chance that she made her death an illusion as well?"

"I think if she were alive, it would simply have made it too hard to keep Moira at bay, as being sisters they could sense one another always on some level so long as they were both alive. She sacrificed herself for her child. Tale as old as time." He could see the question on her face still, the slight confusion in all the pieces to the puzzle. "What I mean is that in order for Maya to do what she did, it simply took all her strength. Or she threw all her strength into it to make sure it worked. Either way…her own life force was the sacrifice. As I have not seen her since, despite this feeling that she is not gone, I cannot shake at the same time."

"So you do think there is a chance that she is alive?"

"I am unsure." He clearly had a dislike for having to admit he was not able to figure it out. He did not like the many different angles involved in all this. He handed her glass out for her to take. He watched her small, slim hand take it from his much larger one, their fingers making contact for a short-lived moment, watching her remain lost in thought while looking at his desk. He enjoyed the way she so gently took a sip, for the first time risking looking closely at her lips. "Do not be so hard on yourself…sister."

The way he said sister had her blood bouncing and her nerves slightly shaking, her eyes glancing to see his face for a quick moment. He was looking down and away as he poured himself more and placed the bottle back in its spot. The look on his face made her pause. His tone with the one word fully suggested he wished he could call her something else, something more to his own liking. She sensed something, but at the same time, her brain went straight to assuming she was simply important to him as she was the one he saw chosen to save his Match. She had no moment to ask, even if she had the courage to, as two heavy sets of footfalls came closer to the door. She simply decided on a different course, taking advantage of the last three seconds they had alone. "That baby is in my hands just as much as yours. I will be as hard on myself as I feel like. Understand me?"

He sensed how ridiculous it was that they were sounding like parents with such slight bickering. She was terrified of digging deeper as to why it did not feel weird. The weight of his gaze made it impossible to look away. The look this man could give her with only two seconds to spare set her entire body on edge. He simply forced himself to break contact right before Tronan would have seen as he stepped through the doorway.

# Chapter 17

# A Meticulous Price

Roman watched Tronan enter the study in an obvious hurry, full of intent to check on his woman. He stayed behind a few yards, not wanting to be here. He expected them to be on their way back already, the three of them. The one-on-one that Daemon needed with Claura dragged on longer than he was comfortable with. He looked up to see the door remaining open, the light seeping into the hallway, hearing absolutely no voices despite there being three other adults in the room. The quiet had him picking up the pace, only for a soft baby whimper to make him stop dead in his tracks, taking a moment to make sure he hadn't imagined it. His mind raced as to why it affected him so. Some instinct in him burned to the surface, and he started moving again in a race with himself to round the doorframe. The first face he saw was Claura, and the look she gave him set him on edge. It was clear she had information he had yet to own as well, information regarding him. His eyes raced around the room, all the while still keeping his body only a foot inside the door. The noise happened again. He turned to see the other two men standing over a small white crib, Tronan with his back to him, looking down at its contents. Daemon stood protectively over top of it, eyeing Roman with a knowing that sent a chill down his spine. The whimper happening again had his eyes dodging to the spot it was coming from. He slowly moved his feet to see what everyone else was clearly already in acknowledgment of. He saw Tronan move out of the way of his own accord, swearing under his breath at whatever realization he was having. Roman stepped closer to the crib, feeling Daemon's energy rising in response. He looked up at him as if to say, "Give me a break," before finally taking a good peek. His heart stopped, literally. He had all he could do to look away from the tiny face staring back at him to look back at Daemon with furious questions in his eyes. Daemon just stood there, unmoving, unblinking. His face was a mask of pure protective instinct, a hunter studying potential prey with full focus.

"Answer. *Now.*" It was all Roman could get out.

Everyone in the room could tell he was less than a tenth of a second from losing his shit.

"So you know," Daemon stated calmly. Yet his gaze never ceased intensity.

"I am her father. Of course, I know. I can literally feel my blood running through her veins. What is she doing here, alive, with you?" His energy was seething despite being in shock.

Claura started to speak, but Roman cut her off, strictly shouting at her. "Not now!"

It literally made her jump, her eyes instantly meeting Daemon's. Tronan noticed the gesture of her needing to look to his brother for comfort and not him. Daemon remained as calm as ever, simply nodding a very subtle "don't" in her direction, followed by a nod to the door. She shook her head no in response. No way in hell was she leaving.

"Look. At. Me." Roman watched Daemon's eyes jump back to his. He clearly intended that the other two in the room did not matter at all until he got some answers. Not with his baby girl lying here before him, 150 years after he thought she was dead. Tronan and Claura watched with full focus as Daemon raised his hands in a calm surrender before speaking.

"This is all because of Maya. She made the choice." He waited for Roman to speak, giving him the chance before continuing. He took a deep inhale while casually glancing down at the baby between them, making sure she was okay with all the tension in the room. She was as quiet and wide-eyed as expected, looking back and forth between the men above her. There was too much understanding in so little a face. In all his time with her, he could tell her brain acknowledged things, and she increased intellectually over time despite being trapped in her little body still, and it broke his heart. The bond between them was a unique one. He knew no matter what happened, he would always care for this little person. He raised his eyes back to Roman, who was studying him with the intensity of a father ready to slice someone's throat any second. "This was her way to save her."

"Why have you not let me know until now? Why? I should kill you for that alone!"

He lowered his hands to his sides, letting one grip the edge of the bassinet, leaning one hip closer to the crib. "Good luck. As Maya made me her Match."

Roman looked around the room, unable to truly concentrate on anything, with the news clearly rattling him to his very core. He clasped his hands behind his head, his visage facing the floor, his feet forcing his body in stressed circles. "I don't believe this. I don't fucking believe this," he said more to himself while everyone remained silent, just waiting.

Tronan had backed himself and Claura to the other side of the room, still remaining close, yet closer to the outdoor balcony.

Daemon continued, "You know it's true. You know Maya well enough to put her reasoning together yourself. You don't really need me to explain much here, Roman. She did it for your child, to keep her alive, and that's the bottom line."

"Actually, I do. Unfortunately, I fucking do, Daemon! And you know it! You have had my daughter in your hands for 150 goddamn years, yet you chose to speak to Claura first about all this! And why is she still a baby?"

"Moira's curse made her frozen in time like this. Maya simply did not have enough time to fix everything." He nodded toward the two in the balcony doorway. "Claura is the key to breaking what is left of the curse. Maya told me herself that the Match of my own brother would be the key."

Claura felt Tronan look at her in a hurry, confusion and worry in his eyes. "How is this so?"

"I have no idea. Apparently, I am a threat to Moira. For some reason, I have a power she needs to take and use before killing me… and…" She nodded toward the crib gently.

She felt all three of the men staring at her, the weight of it becoming more than she could manage. She suddenly lost her courage to look any one of them in the face before stepping out onto the balcony. It was clear she felt like this was her fault in some way, and just as clear, she feared not being able to fix it. Tronan started to follow her before hearing his brother's voice break the silence in the room.

"Leave her be," Daemon growled, uncaring of the glare he was getting from his younger brother. "She deserved to know more about us, Tronan. More about who she is. Much more by now." He started striding toward him, only to pause and look from the crib to Roman with intense astuteness.

"She is my baby."

His tone told the man, Match of his daughter or not, to go to hell in thinking he'd ever bring any harm to her. He looked away first and back into the eyes of his little girl. Daemon let the look of pure love and disbelief all over the man's face to be enough for the moment. It was clear Roman was in shock and could use a moment with her anyway. He continued across the room toward his brother.

"Claura is none of your concern." Tronan was not showing any signs of feeling threatened in the least, despite feeling Claura's scared energy from a few yards away being as clear as day. It was obvious her mixed emotions were on the very edge and getting the best of her.

"You, brother, have no idea how much of my concern she is, as I need her to lift this curse from that baby girl in there," he said, watching his brother lift his chin with defiance. *Before I make it very clear why.* He simply not wanted to push things too far too soon with more facts. Each word was spoken with menace, as if he dared his brother to take Claura away from him. Away from this task. "And this is because of you, Tronan, in the first fucking place." They could all hear Roman spit out a sound that clearly resembled a you-think-so vibe. The notion made Claura look at her man questionably, the worry increasing on her face as she noticed him hesitant to face her in return. She looked at Daemon with question and back to Tronan, needing an answer from either of them.

"Tronan? Explain!" She watched him pause, still not facing them both. "Please, my love."

After another long moment of waiting, she lifted her arms in the air and looked at Daemon again. He simply motioned for her to wait a moment longer, making it clear he knew Tronan a little better than she did still in certain ways.

"I paused. I was unknowing that I was giving Moira more time to add bullshit to the curse. If I hadn't paused, she would not have been able to freeze her in time as a baby."

"Why did you pause, Tronan? I don't understand."

Just then, Roman came through the doorway, his face making it obvious he wanted Tronan to admit it. The moment was perfect, for he felt his little girl there listening as well. Roman deserved this. And he could feel it from Claura and Daemon that they agreed.

"Say it, Tronan. Turn the fuck around, face me, and say it."

Tronan inhaled deeply, letting his hands let go of their grip on the stone as he turned away from the view of the land over the balcony to face them all. "I let Moira get in my head. She told me that if I kill her, my Match would not be born and able to remain alive. So for my own selfish reasons, I paused at the one moment I had a chance to slit her throat, knowing full well Maya's newborn was hanging in the balance."

"I fucking hate this bitch. And I need to go. I need to go right now," Claura scolded at no one in particular and, without looking at any of them, left the room with such haste that it was clear no one was going to calm her.

If any woman in the world needed space to think right now, it was her. She felt like her head was about to explode with how much information her brain needed to wrap itself around. She was starting to wonder if it was even possible. The mental exhaustion was sinking in. The feeling of another postpartum episode was sinking in even deeper. She walked with rage through the hallways, uncaring of where she was going. Just needing to get the fuck away from the energy of the three of them in that room. She felt a little bad for the baby needing to be left behind, unable to leave the room of her own will if she wanted to, but she also knew that she was in the safekeeping of three of the best protectors she could wish for. The father clearly had lost time to make up for that area just in general. She just kept moving, searching for what felt like a good hour, needing to burn off some steam. She paced everywhere in the enormous place until her feet started hurting, warning her to just take a damn break. She found a hallway full of empty enormous bedrooms and, in haste, simply picked one and slammed the door shut behind her.

Back in the office, the baby started to cry. Roman and Daemon exchanged a glance. Daemon nodded gently and started walking toward her, "I will feed her."

"What is her name?" Roman asked him as he passed by. His low and calm voice surprised to his own ears. Having inner calm after finally getting his karma from seeing Claura be told a certain truth about Tronan was a new feeling for him. He had so much anger toward the man for so long now for numerous reasons. His thoughts returned to Daemon stopping in his tracks.

"She has no name. Maya did not say. I have simply called her 'little one' all these decades." He backed up to be able to look into Roman's face more closely. "I chose to have faith that the day would come for her curse to be broken and let her father name her. I had every intent on telling you, Roman. Don't think I was planning on hiding her here forever. It truly was to keep her safe. Moira is still capable of being everywhere."

"Except here. In your home," Roman said.

Clearly, he already knew every meaning behind it that he already had to clarify to Claura out loud earlier.

"Precisely. Maya's reasoning was meticulous despite what it cost you both."

"And you needed to find Claura. This whole time waiting for Tronan to do so first to be able to even connect with her at all."

"Yes."

"And you did not sense her through me first?" He had no desire to hide his obvious disappointment.

"No." He looked at his brother, seeing him at ease in his silence. A complete one with his own thoughts while still listening to the conversation. "As we all have flaws, Roman, omnipotent or not." He clearly meant for Roman to forgive Tronan someday. "For some reason, I could only sense her finally being with Tronan once she had just one drop. You sending Claura to Romania was the first step to breaking this curse placed upon your daughter. You know Maya is proud."

"Is?"

"She will make herself known to you soon enough. She has simply been waiting for Claura to arrive to show herself, apparently." He felt her presence in his mind the moment Roman walked into the office, warning him to handle it with mercy. The look on Roman's face was one Daemon knew he'd never forget.

Daemon's tone made it clear that the fury he had for it all had been chronic and well-known for beyond too long. All this was new for Tronan and Roman. Daemon had been playing it all out in his head for over a century. Despite his strong will to do what was necessary, if you looked closely enough, you could really tell that the man was fried in dealing with the situation. Roman suddenly felt remorse for him and intense admiration for his level of patience in having to live with his Match who remained a baby for fifteen decades before him, day in and day out. Suddenly, the time zone difference of this particular realm came to mind, making Roman turn and look into the study at Daemon holding a bottle. Feeding the baby in a manner that made it obvious was a most important task to even the ancient ones of his species. He walked back over near his daughter, sitting across them, watching Daemon's huge hands handle her with such care.

"You have many homes, Daemon. Why did you choose this one to remain here with her for all this time?"

"Because if Claura fails, the creatures here may not be strong enough to kill Moira, but they are strong enough to contain her for as long as necessary."

"Does Claura know this?"

"No. I want no room for failure in her mind. She has a power that hides itself. I can sense it. Moira is intimidated by her for a reason, and that is good enough for me." Daemon was truly trying not to give too much away when it came to Claura specifically. He needed to handle it right the first time. And right now, she was clearly on overload already.

Tronan strolled in, clearly heading for the door, stopping halfway to stand a few feet from them both. He stared at the infant for a split second before studying his hands while speaking. "If Claura does not fail, you should let her name her." There was silence between all of them again. "She deserves that. Saving the life of your Match, Daemon. The life and future of your daughter, Roman. She should be the one to name her." He sensed Roman looking from his daughter to where he was standing and faced him in return. "I hope one day you can forgive me, Roman. I simply did not know what to do and then lost my chance to do anything. But now Claura has the biggest chance to fix everything, and I will give my life to make sure she gets it done."

There was silence from them both. He was simply happy with no opposition from them either. Tronan strode out of the room with clear intent not to return anytime soon. He left to take some time for himself as well. He could feel the door shutting itself behind him, uncaring about which gentleman, in general, was doing it. As cliché as it felt, his fury was still aimed at one particular witch—at how one twisted being could fuck up other people's lives so much and for so damn long. And now his Claura was hanging in the balance, her life at stake, her mind still as easily fragmented as a human's would be.

His insides ached at how overwhelmed she must be feeling and how confused. He needed to find her.

Her mind was becoming stronger. He could sense the mental block she was using right now, which was already becoming much stronger than he thought possible. It did not start to happen until they entered this realm. He clearly underestimated a few changes that may happen to her in such a different place. A part of him worried that someone else, once again, was causing the block, making him struggle to reach her. It terrified him that it could be happening to her, even here, where she was supposed to be extra safe from any mental invasion Moira would attempt. He decided it best not to panic and simply use her scent, which in a palace this big was going to take a while. As he looked left then right, unsure of where to start at the end of the next hallway, it became clear that she was upset enough to have zero fears of wandering ridiculously far. Her scent was just gone.

He inwardly swore at his own weakness to find his own mate. Every second that passed made him ache more to just see that she was safe. There were clearly many downfalls as well to her using her powers more and more, for he did not like not being able to reach her at all—not a damn bit. Everything that happened, that changed, that grew, every situation they were faced with, they were supposed to be in it together. He stood in the long dark hallway, staring into space, fear taking hold of it being the complete opposite right now between them.

"Always hated this fucking realm," he swore under his breath.

*****

In the room was a silence Claura didn't know even existed. It was as if the only beings in this realm were literally the five of them in this enormous home. The beings that Tronan kind of described came to mind, slightly making her pause as to exactly how far they would be. Then it became obvious Daemon and the power he wielded in keeping others out. A part of her wondered how much more dominant his powers were compared to Tronan. An even deeper part of her, one that she did truly hate, wondered how much more dominant the man was in general. It was so unfair how confusing the connections were with the men among their species to a woman's heart. First, she thought a certain way about Roman, only to realize she was sensing Tronan through him the entire time. Now she was fighting this ridiculously small, though still existent, hankering toward Daemon. These damn men. And they all looked at her the way a human husband looked at his wife, only on a much more intense level. Was this another Moira curse? If so, it added to her resolve to finish her, if nothing else. On a side note, it also worried her heart, for what if she was cursed, and then when the curse was broken by killing Moira, she realized she was not really in love with any of them?

What Daemon said came to mind suddenly, along with the ridiculously intense look on his ridiculously good-looking face right before he said it, about how she truly didn't have a choice in the matter and was silly to think so.

Or did she?

After all, if Moira saw her as a threat, then that meant she probably had powers enough to choose for herself. Despite the thought instantly feeling wrong on an obvious moral level, it also made her feel some relief. A part of Claura was beyond craving for things to just be easy, to make some sense again. Her mind was tunneling in directions she never expected it to go. And it was becoming harder and harder to shut her brain off. The feeling of her hands in Daemons as he eased her trembling earlier, the way he had wiped her tears away over not being able to hold the baby, the way he walked even if it was only to take a few steps, the way he handed her, her glass and made the smallest of contact in the process, every little thing in that office was coming back to her. But most of all, the way he looked at her.

*He is hiding something.*

Exasperated with herself, she slumped her ass down onto the daybed along the window, letting her face fall in her palms, too wiped out to even shed any more tears. She just felt completely exhausted all of a sudden. Her mouth was of its own accord, flipping through their names as she looked toward the floor, her fingertips subconsciously playing with her nails.

*Roman.*
*Tronan.*
*Daemon.*

The air hitting her lungs a little thicker with the last one. She felt her fingers entwine in agitation through her hair, clasping together on the back of her head, staring into space toward the floor. She looked like she was seconds from laying her head down and just falling asleep. She could tell she was feeling the effects of the realm traveling start to kick in, mixing with the slight buzz from her drink. The knowing of a little girl that looked just like hers, here in this home, really set her emotions on high. The feeling of being jealous of her for having Daemon as a Match made her hate herself. She could not get the man's eyes out of her goddamn thoughts. His voice alone, even when just saying only one damn word, had her body temperature rising in response. Inwardly swearing about it all to herself under her breath, she felt her eyes start to drift down. The thought of where the nearest pillow was came to mind next when she heard the door to the room open and suddenly slam shut. She jumped slightly, eyes as wide open as she could force them to be. Her vision blurred a bit from exhaustion alone, yet she was still able to see a tall male figure striding toward her. Unable to decipher yet his particular demeanor and reason for finding her. She thought it was made pretty obvious that they should all leave her alone for a while—*all of them*. And then he spoke, Daemon.

"Stop! Fucking stop right now!" he shouted. He came toward her abruptly, pointing his finger with momentous intention. She felt her shoulders shrug, her mouth start to form a question, her eyebrows creasing.

"What are you—"

"Stop with those thoughts. I mean it. I will not let you do this right now. Not until this is over. This is already fucking complicated enough!"

"Stop yelling at me, Daemon!" She suddenly realized he did not need to be anywhere near her, much less in the same room, to know her thoughts. She felt foolish for underestimating him so easily. Yet it was not her fault she didn't exactly know how much more powerful he was. She did her best to stand and face him, feeling her body slightly wobble as she did so. "I am just so fucking confused right now! You have no right to make it worse! Get out!" She was full-on giving zero fucks that it was his house with the mood she was in.

"There is no curse in this between us, Claura. Do you hear me?"

He was obviously in the belief of every syllable coming out of his ridiculously tempting mouth. The comment could be taken more than one way by his tone, and the last thing she felt like doing was figuring out why. He was a mere few feet from her now. Clearly, he was able to reach out and shake her if he wanted, as his whole energy was making it look like he was willing to do any second.

"How the fuck would you know? You've been hiding out here for over a century, for good reason, yet still focused on just one curse. How the hell are you really supposed to understand what I am dealing with, curse or not? Huh?"

"I could sense you coming because of your connection to my brother through the bloodline. Do not read into it more than that. I cannot handle more added to everything else right now."

"Well, now that you've really brought it up, Daemon." He leaned her upper body toward him, laughing in his face…at his anger, feeling way past needing to vent. She clearly did not see him as a threat to her at all as he so obviously needed her alive. "Look at you! You crave the touch of a grown woman so fucking bad. Don't you?" She eyed him up and down, uncaring to hide her desire. The man was as fine as they came.

Just like Tronan.

Just like Roman.

No, wait…damn her confused soul to hell.

He was finer. He reminded her of—

"I already don't want to be a part of this world anymore! I will do my best to save your sweet little Match. I really will. But after that, I am so goddamn done with trying to decipher how all of you make me feel. It is not fair to me, Daemon! I want my life back!" There were tears, lots of tears. That affected him not at all despite still clearly taken into account by the look in his eyes as if used to them.

"I know so much more than you realize, my dear. I tried to contain myself, to not have it affect me until this curse was behind us, but you are making it impossible with what I see happening already behind those beautiful fucking eyes of yours."

The level of pure vex in his voice had her holding her breath suddenly, his eyes matching his tone absurdly well. She could feel his body heat from where he was standing, feel it increasing. She watched with way too much fascination as he lifted his one arm to free the top button of his black dress shirt, his strong hand working its way down the rest. She takes a deep breath and puts her hands out in front of her, and with as much meaning as she could use.

"Don't you dare, Daemon!"

She felt her body backing away. Another tear fell down her cheek at her own inward realization that she would cave with this man just as fast as she had done while encased in Tronan's arms and without even fully understanding why. She suddenly knew how it felt to be completely disgusted with oneself yet unable to stop it at the same time. For every step she took back, he simply moved forward. She watched his hands reach to frame her face and pull her toward him, just a little less gentle than how Tronan did it as if he was already more experienced with the gesture and knew her limits, no matter how small or not. He forced her to look deep into his eyes.

"Don't!" She slightly spit it out, her eyes full of fire. "You have no proof for me that this isn't just another fucked up part of Moira's plan!" She was pleading with him not to let this lead anywhere. "She is luring me toward her and using all of you to do so! Stop!"

"I thought that by not letting you cross my actual threshold that, that would somehow help. God help me, Claura. For it didn't do a fucking thing."

She tried to pry his hands away. "I felt it with Tronan already when I entered his home. So I don't know what you are getting at, Daemon."

"I thought I could fight it, at least for a while, at least until we could free the little one. I will be the first to admit I am a damn fool."

"Get to the damn point, Daemon! I can feel Tronan getting closer. I can't let him see this. I can't hurt him like that!" *God, I hate myself. What the fuck is going on? Why is his fine ass so fucking familiar to me!*

"You are my Match from a previous life, reincarnated again. I am in this life now with two of you. So, my dear, if you think you are the only one who is fucking confused and on a very thin edge"—he forced her face close enough to feel his breath on her lips—"think again."

"In that case, we *are* both cursed." She looked lost beyond all repair. "Please don't help me hurt Tronan. I beg of you."

"You have no idea how much you underestimate me. Again." She saw him swipe his hand toward the door, causing the feeling of Tronan being close and almost finding her in this room to completely fade away. She looked at him, startled, followed by anger at what she knew was about to happen, yet knowing she was already just simply not going to truly care enough to stop a damn thing that he was about to do with those hands, with her. Saying there was just something about Daemon was becoming her worst understatement in this entire ituateion so far.

"I am so sorry, my love. But I know you feel it, and I am incapable of avoiding it any longer." She felt his hands through her hair, pulling her head close to make her face him, in complete defiance of her efforts to put distance between them, his mind clearly trying to find a way to still stop himself by the look in his eyes. "I have waited…so fucking long. Going mad with needing to know where you were." Only a few seconds passed between them, and she could already see him giving up as well anyway and could literally feel it in the air between them. "I tried, Claura."

He was begging for her forgiveness already, knowing she was so confused. There was so much information she had yet to learn that would help all this with him make sense, but that would have to come later. He could feel her burning for him more by the second, reacting to their connection on her own primal level as well. Her scent was driving him mad, her temperature rising already as her cycle started surfacing under his touch, to his scent, purely reacting to him the way she had done since the day they met. He had no idea how much he actually had missed it until this moment. He needed to block it out to stay sane for so long.

"I hate you. I really do." She started crying, guilt clearly washing over her.

"I know," he growled with remorse yet love.

He hated how she was looking at him like she would not only never be able to forgive him for this but not forgive herself as well. He picked her up, forcing her legs around his waist, making it obvious he was willing to do any and all work necessary to have her writhing beneath him. His mouth was, in his own way, just as ridiculously talented. She felt their bodies being skin to skin before he even had her tossed back against the sheets, his hands dominating her in places she thought were covered territory already by another. She was clearly mistaken. His whole different level of intensity made her mind wander back to memories of needing a drop from Tronan. Without hesitation from him at all, she felt him move his mouth from hers just enough to bite his own tongue and force her to kiss him back once again. She leaned her head back into the pillows as if to say no, clearly startled, only for his flavor to completely of its own accord make her body do a 180. And it was her wanting it, not something forcing her to want it. She was grateful yet frightened of herself for knowing the difference this time. She started crying slightly harder while clearly fighting with herself, still being completely aware of the connection to Tronan while experiencing an even stronger and more real one with this man atop her. She could feel herself screaming at him in her mind to just stop for two seconds so she could think. But the more she tried pulling away, the more aggressive he got, and the more it made her hate herself for loving every second of it. She felt his hands everywhere, gripping her in a completely different way than Tronan did, his assertiveness leaving imprints all over her curves. His hand cupped the back of her head way more confidently as if he truly had already done it a hundred times over…and more. One strong hand moved downward without the slightest pause as two fingers moved inside. The feeling made her jump, only to realize he was dead set on not letting her move far from underneath him at all. She felt literally locked beneath him in some ancient presiding way. He forced her mouth to fuse to his, taking in her every cry and increase in pleasure. She felt her hips move against his hand, her head tilt back, and his fingers ease out of her right as her climax would have started to really peak. She looked back at his face with pure sexual frustration.

"What are you doing? Keep going!" She glared at him, her face alone telling him that if she was going to go through with this insanity, then he could at least make it good.

"I take it he took an easy on you."

The knowledge the man held in his eyes made her heart leap. He knew too much. She literally, in her human mind, had just met him today. Her heart and body clearly had other proposals that were set firmly in place whether she liked it or not. This was all moving too fast again. Yet it all felt even more natural this time with him.

"Goddamn it, Daemon..." Her body was writhing underneath his, against his, anything to find release.

"Shhh...." He shifted himself atop her while still keeping their mouths locked together in a full-on frenzy. She felt his hands adamantly pushing her thighs apart more, his smooth yet disconcerting tip against her entrance next, his movements unshy in the least as if he'd been inside her body on more occasions than he could count.

"Daemon..." Her face was a mix of passion and worry. He pushed past her barrier as if knowing the exact speed and pressure to make the sting come and go as quickly as possible for her. She naturally felt her hips try to move away to help herself adjust, but his hands were stronger.

"I am not able to stop for you. I need you to relax for me." His voice was one of pure love and determination.

*You are my Match from a previous life, reincarnated again.* His recent words echoed in her mind as she felt him take complete control, knowing that even if he was lying to her...the way this was feeling.

*I am cursed.*

*And fuck me...I fucking love it.*

He pulled his mouth to hers in a hurry, feeling him devour her senselessly. She felt his weight settle on top of her more as he moved deeper inside. His strength saw no real fight in it for him while holding her entire body in place beneath his, not just her hips, as he felt her struggle to move away while her body adjusted to the first two inches before just caving for the rest of him. He looked into her face, gently kissing and biting her lips, giving her one good moment of hardly any movement from him to let her body accommodate to his full size now. He could see all her emotions mixed together as clear as day in her eyes. Her entire body quivered underneath him, mixing with the movements of her chest, rising and falling with her slight crying, completely in tune with her guilt, combined with the inability to control any of it.

"Claura, honey, look at me." He watched her fighting with herself, and it broke his heart. He reached for her wrists, gently pinning her. This situation was a first for both of them.

"What?" Her tone was slightly calmer now. It was obvious she wasn't able to completely fight off the love she was feeling for him, too, despite the circumstances. "Why did you even come to this room? You should have just stayed away." She could feel his hands forcing her head to stop moving and just look at him steadily already.

"I had you first." At the authority in his deep masculine voice, she automatically waited for the shiver down her spine, as it had happened in these kinds of moments so many times before with another. But it didn't happen, and instead of missing the feeling, she felt relieved of it. He made it obvious that despite his guilt, he was never going to regret a second of this either. He was telling the truth. It was simply a truth no one but her knew yet.

"I can no longer do this on my own. I don't know who to lean on now... He is going to completely hate me."

"Let him. I will deal with it." He forced her to really look into his eyes again, choosing to move his body inside hers even more now, knowing already from his past with her that it would calm her down. Some things never change. "My love, you were mine first. You have been mine for several lifetimes over."

She looked at him with love yet untrusted still. "Were you mine, though?" She knew the answer would make or break her, for if it was more of a one-way, she wasn't sure how she was going to react. She held her breath in anticipation of his answer. He simply nodded while folding her hair behind her ear, placing his hand to cup her face, and leaning down toward her to take her mouth with his again. Only this time more gently, as if to match it to his pace between her legs. The friction with him felt so good, making the sensations she had with Tronan feel like foreplay compared to how this man atop her was handling her body. She placed her arms around his neck, forcing him to stay close to hear her whisper.

"I may hate you for a long time, understand me." Her voice held complete conviction. She really needed him to understand.

"I see we are to have another lifetime of you underestimating me." He smiled down at her, yet his eyes held a serious note that he did not want her to miss. "I am sorry I did not find you sooner and save us this trouble. It is a first for us." And of all the people for it to happen with, his own goddamn brother. He knew it was not her fault. With their connection so strong, all she did was sense him through Tronan this entire time. But he could sense that something else was at play here along with her, simply just not knowing. She simply did not know. "You have done nothing wrong, beautiful. I will prove it to you."

And he meant it. Just like what he did with her body for the next few hours. He fucking meant it.

# CHAPTER 18

## Still Always Here for You

*Claura? Can you hear me? Sweet Claura, please hear me.* The female voice was new—gentle, almost like a sweet breeze in the middle of the storm playing out in her mind, her heart, and her very soul. She almost ached to hear it again. It was another dream with another new being. She knew she was still lying beside Daemon yet was unable to open her eyes to look to make sure. Yet she felt no need this time. There was no threat in this woman's voice at all.

*Who are you?* Claura asks her.

The feeling of utmost relief came through from the other woman's end of the dream. *Maya.* At the answer, she could feel Claura really struggle to see her now, see anything. *Please don't fear me. Not seeing me is for both our safety. I need you to just listen. Daemon is going to offer to send you to a safe place for a while, and I need you to trust him to do so.*

*Where could I possibly feel safe? Everywhere I go, something even worse starts to happen. And I really don't think I am the one to be called to being a hero here.* She clearly felt heartbroken that she truly didn't believe she had what it took to save this woman's little baby girl from all this.

*That is where you are wrong. I have been waiting for you to need to go to this place. There is a book, among the emerald section, labeled 210A. Find it as soon as you arrive. Please.*

*Emerald section?*

*I have many confidants there you can trust. You will see. You will feel it. They will help you.*

*I am running out of strength for all this, Maya.*

*Go to this place, and you will be given all the strength you need. Learning about yourself and where you truly come from will light that fire.*

*How do you know that?*

*We are related, sweet Claura. I am sorry for your dilemma, but know that any one of them would still protect you always. I need your help. I need you to free her. Please just focus and follow your intuition. I can sense it speaking to you all the time, even from a great distance.*

*How are you communicating with me if you are dead?*

*I am not dead. I am simply hiding. I needed to appear dead until you came along to keep my spell in place. There are only two places I am able to connect with you finally where Moira cannot find out. When you are in the home of Daemon, as that is where my daughter resides, and when you go to this next place.*

Claura felt herself slightly waking as his arms enfolded her closer and started to bring her senses alive again, a deep part of her fighting to be awake and back in its own body. *How are you not angry with me, Maya? I can tell you now what I have done.*

*I understand more than you realize. You can trust Daemon. You will see. You always do, no matter how long it takes him to prove it to you.*

*Everyone clearly knows so much more about me than I do. It's quite disheartening on top of everything else that's clearly so damn disheartening.*

*Moira did one hell of a curse on us all, but the worst parts, she actually did to you. She has been so beyond cruel to her own...*

*What! Her own what?* She could feel her own hands reaching out in the darkness, her body in itself begging for Maya to just finish that sentence.

*We will talk again soon.*

*****

Claura felt the dream break, followed by an intense inhale of air and her body trying to sit up to grasp as much into her lungs as possible. She felt as if she was suffocating this entire time as if that was what it took to keep the mental link in the dream going. Still, there were so many unanswered questions. The feeling of being overwhelmed just kept increasing. Daemon had no hesitation in sitting up against the headboard and casually pulling her to sit atop him, facing him. He held her face in his hands the way he did, telling her to explain with his eyes alone. She took a deep breath, cleared her throat, counted to three with her eyes closed before looking back at him. "Maya just visited me."

"I figured she would be real soon."

"She's not dead." Her stare dared him to question it, as she could just feel the truth in her bones. "I don't understand."

"She connected with me as soon as Roman entered into my study and saw their daughter. It was a slight shock after all this time."

"I can relate." She forced his hands away from her face, needing to look away, to have a moment. She started to move off him.

"No. Claura. Don't do that."

"Do what?"

"Not lean on me."

"I've leaned on you plenty…" She laughed, blushing and sounding annoyed with her own actions and how she couldn't believe still what had taken place. "Maya believes I am the hero as well and has been waiting for me to come here to be able to reach me," she said out loud, sounding like she needed the vocal confirmation more so than herself to start believing it. She watched his mind spin behind his striking eyes, his hands leisurely rubbing up and down her thighs gently. She saw the realization hit a little.

"This place. It was her safe barrier from Moira as well. Not just for me and her daughter. This entire time, she has not reached out to me, though."

"I have no answer to that. I'm sorry. You would think she would have."

"Tell me what else she said."

"That I can trust you. That you will offer to send me to a certain place to get away from all this for a while. A place she needs me to go to."

"Well then, that proves it." He had every intention already.

"Can't just believe me, huh? Like I have reason to lie about Maya." Her anger was rising. Her frustration was getting the better of her again at what she had done to Tronan.

"Like you don't need proof as well?" He grabbed her hands as she tried to get off him in a hurry, pulling her back to keep her in place. "Proof that I am not lying about you? About us!"

"Can you blame me, Daemon!" She physically fought him to let go of her wrists. Her efforts were clearly untroubling to him in the slightest. "Please! Let go!"

"No."

"Why?" Her efforts started to cause pain. Tears started to swim.

"Because I am about to send you to a place where I have no power in making you come back home to me, not unless you ask it of me first. It will be completely up to you when you decide to return. And I have just waited around 150 years for you to come back to me this time as it is." He saw her stiffen then, reading him in a way that she did not realize that he had already experienced before a few times. "So forgive me, Claura, if letting you out of my grasp right now is a bit hard for me." He watched her face, full of expressions, full-on studying him. "You have no idea how hard it was for me to put our connection aside after seeing you arrive in my realm, to focus on other things first so as not to frighten you."

"How many times have I been reincarnated?" Her face was full of worry and of sorrow. There was an apology in her eyes that he did not miss. She felt embarrassed for not remembering an obvious important detail about oneself.

"You have nothing to be sorry for, so do not look at me like that. You are a witch. Reincarnation became the conspicuous way for us to remain together. Despite its difficulties."

"But the blood in my system, aren't I immortal as well? Like you…Tronan…Roman? I thought that's how it worked."

"For my brother and I, yes. We were born this way. You were born as a Witch. You can live for up to three hundred years at a time once I give you my blood, but you are not completely immortal like me. It is a balance we needed to create on top of the spell already holding difficulties."

"Balance? Difficulties?"

"Something about the spell…it just…sometimes you remember who you are, other times not. And for you to keep your witch abilities, which you made very clear from the start you would not part from, you would not be able to be fully omnipotent as I am alongside me in an eternal manner even with my blood in you. It is simply the give and take of any spell that exists in order for it to work."

"There is no way to fix that?"

"We haven't been able to find a fix. Hence, the library. It has been the easiest way for you to relearn. You made it your main home." She looked at him, startled, not knowing what to think of her having her own home in a different realm this entire time.

"Again, Daemon…how many times…" She watched him pause, look away, worry on his face. "Please."

"There is a particular book in this place where I will be sending you. You have a confidant that has helped you keep tabs on everything you've had to endure through all your reincarnation occurrences."

"Why can't you just answer me?"

"Because I am ashamed to say I do not know. There have been instances where I was never able to find you, and we missed out on finding one another and wasting a lifetime being apart." He inhaled deeply and pulled her closer. "Each time you have to do it, it gets harder for us to find one another."

"So my lives are shorter, at least, like actual humans, when you don't find me?"

"Yes."

"Giving you only so much time to be able to find me."

"Yes."

"There has to be something."

"I have done nothing with my time here, alongside the little one, but try to find a solution. Maya is right. You need to go to this other realm for answers."

"And you could not go, even once, this entire time due to Moira possibly finding you or the baby if you left."

"Yes." The frustration in his voice said so much in just that one little word. "So you see how important you are. Moira needs your powers, but Maya needs them even more. Are you understanding?" There was a genuine concern for her and her need to just know more.

"Yes. Getting there." Looking from his gaze to her fingers holding onto his strong forearms, she relaxed atop him. She loved the shape of this man despite everything else she needed to focus on as well right now.

He let her remain lost in thought, staring into space. The abundance of racing emotions happening behind her eyes was enough to keep him busy for some time. He decided not to intercede at all, choosing to let her come back to him. He saw her mind calm down after several long minutes as if once again reaching her limit in putting the pieces of the puzzle together. Once again, she needed a break from it. She raised her hands to her temples and started massaging, letting her long hair fall down and frame her face as if deliberately hiding from his gaze. She was obviously becoming more and more aware now of just the moment with him, here and now, their bodies still skin to skin. She sensed him smile in response.

"How did you do it? Keep this from me. Really."

"I felt you through my link with my brother as soon as he gave you drop one. I saw that you were happy, and I did not need to rush certain aspects of this situation. You have no idea how just seeing you and seeing that you were safe affected me after all this time."

"I was happy."

"I know. And it killed me. Your memory clearly was gone again in this lifetime. You simply had no way of knowing yet."

"I hate knowing I was hurting you."

"Don't. I chose to stay out of your head as much as possible. Knowing it was only a matter of time before getting you here anyway. And then you came…and I saw what was going on in your mind already so soon, seeing that you could feel it too already…your thoughts…your reaction…just—"

"So this is my fault?" She half-heartedly laughed, sniffling, wiping a small tear away with the back of her hand. Clearly, she still hated herself for knowing how she so quickly threw a man like Tronan to the curb. "I'm terrified to see him. I really am. To be honest, all I want to do right now is be a coward and run." She felt him lean up and pull her closer to him, kissing her lips softly for a second while thinking it all over.

"The place Maya is referring to is the oldest library in any realm's existence. I can send you there, and you will stay for as long as you want. Hear me?" He leaned his face toward her in a way that made her have to look at him. "Time does not exist there. You could go for one hundred years and come back, and it will be like you just stepped out for a coffee for Tronan, who will remain here for me to deal with."

"Because he will wait, for as long as it takes, to see me." There was dread on every part of her face, real heartbreak for the man. "Why did it happen with him, Daemon? Why did it have to happen at all!"

"Whether either of you want to believe me or not, I fear it is just another silly part of Moira's curse. She has her hooks in deep in this with all of us." He made her face him again. "But we have been each other's Match for lifetimes. Literally." His hands got a little tighter. "Understand me?

"She was trying to keep me away from you. Away from the baby. It makes sense, yet there are still pieces missing, as we obviously don't know just how much Moira knows." He could see it on her face, her thought of speaking to Moira herself, actually going to see her and risk walking into a lion's den.

"Not happening, sweetheart."

"I need to go, Daemon. I need some time. Some space. The answers feel like they could never stop coming. My brain feels fried before I truly have even really begun here."

She clearly meant she needed to get a move on to this other realm at least, and already was dreading being apart from him, without him next to her while she discovered a whole new world. What was new to her anyway, despite its history within her past lives. Her hands started shaking where she had them placed over his arms, as if needing him to help ground and calm her, and it just wasn't working anymore.

"I know." He sounded so gentle, so at ease with her before him. It was obvious he was still holding back his feelings about her even being here with him again, not wanting to frighten her with its intensity—of what he really felt. Choosing to let it out and show itself only while doing with her body what he pleased, knowing hers would just naturally return the favor, like a safe zone to really express himself. No matter how much he could remember about her, he was yet again new to her despite their connection.

He started kissing her more thoroughly, making his intention clear of needing to feel her one more time—just once more. "I want to show you something you always loved." He held her head captive, exploring her mouth with his, making it hard for her to even come up for air. Choosing to force her to learn to simply use the breath that he was giving her, somehow making the action sensually erotic and unfrightening. He held her against the front of him, guiding her legs to wrap around his waist as he moved them up and out of the bed. He saw her completely enthralled with just staying connected to him, uncaring to wonder in the slightest where he was taking them. She could hear water running suddenly as if it was from a great distance through a tunnel, her mind clearly devoted to other things. He carried her into the adjoining room to lower their bodies into a large tub of warm bubbling water, it being obvious it was not the first time with him doing such a thing with her in his strong and perfect arms. The soothing noises from the jets spraying everywhere had her for a moment, looking from him to her surroundings. She looked around at the room and the water swirling around them for a second before smiling up at him playfully. He looked back at her like he adored the expression and missed seeing it. He really did just want her to be happy, didn't he? Whether it was with him or not. The notion warmed and broke her heart at the same time.

She watched as he knelt in the water before her, pulling her lower half atop his thighs more, feeling him play with her body gently. He had a look of being in absolutely no hurry all over his features. She felt his hands explore, loving the sensation of not really knowing where they were going to touch next under the water. She watched him fight with himself for control, heard a low grumble from his throat, his eyes so soft yet possessive as he looked everywhere on her body he damn well pleased. Without lifting his gaze back to hers, as if in his own world and dead set on staying there to enjoy it, she felt his large tip start to press into her. The feeling of his grasp on her hips underneath the water alone made her moan. There was something about Daemon that made her nervous, no matter how good he was with his hands or how well he treated her. Her wandering thoughts stopped at the feeling of him going deeper, savoring and playing with her for every inch he gave. It was completely different from last time. She let her body slide down more, feeling the water envelope around her head and neck, her hair floating with the bubbles. The movement caused him to go a little deeper.

His body leaned forward to place his mouth all over her, biting, sucking, caressing her rib cage with his hands. There was a slight nervousness of putting so much trust in him with her body being surrounded by water with this strong man completely in control of her, above her. The feeling of his strong forearms holding her up while he played and seduced him in a way that made her realize no man was going to top this. It was officially Daemon or nobody. She was done with the confusing bullshit, spell not. She was done with overthinking about anything anymore…as her beckoning climax forced her to start doing anyway.

*****

## THE WINGED WITCH OF MATCHES

"Call to me, understand?" He held her close, enjoying the feel of her silk shirt under his hands as he rubbed up and down her arms, trying to soothe her. He felt her nerves start to take hold. He needed her to know that she could reach him in a heartbeat by just simply trying. "I will instantly feel you reach out." *Now that I have finally fucking found you again.*

"I don't know why I am so nervous. Maya made it sound like I would feel at home there. That it will all be okay, truly," she said.

"It will be. You have always loved it there."

"What is the name of a person I can trust over there, do you know?" She watched him smile. "Silly question. Of course, you know. You get to remember everything. Must be nice."

"Please don't think about that. You simply need some time to remember. This place will be good for you. It always was."

"Name?"

"An Allie. You've mentioned her the most before."

"Before…hmmm…" She looked away to the floor, a look of embarrassment. "You must tire of me forgetting."

His smile surprised her.

"No, my dear, it keeps things interesting." She truly underestimated how easy it would be for him to have a troublemaker kind of grin. Under the circumstances, he did not come off as that kind of man to her at all until now. She embraced the moment, trying to make sure she didn't forget it. She wondered if they ever truly had just one lifetime together where they were able to just play, have fun, and enjoy one another fully. It saddened her to realize that if so, she didn't recall any of it. She realized she wasn't giving him enough credit for what he went through, his part in all this. It was all just so much at once. She missed the calm that came with her previous boring life and was hoping this place, being a library and all, would bring back a small semblance of that feeling.

"Can you tell me more about this place? Where will I sleep? Eat?" He put his hands on her hips, fingering the edges of her belt with his ridiculously perfect fingers, looking down at her small waist and shapely hips in admiration.

"I think this time I will simply let you figure it out."

"That's not nice."

His wolflike smile had her startled for a split second. "I don't mean it like that. I mean, I don't want to ruin it for you. I will simply let you judge one of your favorite places for yourself this time, right from the start."

"Or you are truly tired of the repeat. Just be honest." She felt the humor subside, the wolflike smile now completely reaching his eyes in a different way, looking completely displeased with her response. He lifted his hand to her blouse and started unbuttoning it from the top, letting his fingers brush along her sternum and lace bra as he worked his way down, his eyes lifting to meet hers.

"Does this look like I tire of you, hmm?" His intensity made it hard for her to breathe. The complete silence all around them made his voice all the heavier and threatening in a way.

"I need you to find control. As I won't stop you." At her words, she saw him not care to find control at all and started to force her mouth to his yet again. She spoke up right before he made contact. "That beautiful baby girl is waiting. Still." The last word stretching between them, Claura meant to say it with an authority that would make him pause. She saw him get frustrated and then bring himself under control at an impressive rate, step back, and take one long moment to look into her eyes.

"I love you."

He gave her time to respond. She didn't. Clearly, she was just still feeling torn, feeling a need to grieve someone despite him not actually even being dead. She never had a love like Tronan and sure as hell never expected to come across an even stronger and more intense connection with his older brother. She looked to the floor, clearly hating herself, sensing him already knowing why once again. Taking a few moments for herself before looking back up into his eyes, her expression making it clear she was beyond ready to end this curse. She watched him take a deep breath as if readying himself, raised his hand, and snapped his fingers.

Daemon stood there for a long moment, staring at the empty space. Remembering that no matter how many times she had to leave his side in the past, he would never stop hating it. The increasing distance between finding her each time she needed to die and be reborn was starting to alarm him. They figured from the start that it would only get easier with time and what they had to do. Only for the complete opposite to start happening. He turned slightly to look around the room, debating the need to cover up their combined scents in his own damn home. He decided he would simply leave the room and force the door to open for him and him, only to even get in here. He had to smile at her chosen room, wondering if some part of her knew.

It had been where they made love the very first time—so long ago. He had his reasons for staying in this realm, choosing this particular home, as gloomy as it may be to others—reasons and memories no one would dare take away from him.

*****

Roman could feel the shift. He set the baby down, enjoying watching her fall asleep with a thank-you look on her face as if she truly enjoyed and craved her little safe space in her bassinet. He took a long moment to enjoy the sight of her, but only as he could feel his time slipping. He could tell already that whoever was doing the spell to jump from this realm to another was more than equipped with smooth experience. He casually walked out of the office and into the hallway, keeping his footfalls soft so as not to startle or wake her. He closed his eyes, reached within, and found the connection to a faraway part of the castle. He spoke the one word that enabled him to move to his chosen destination, kept his body still, lowered his heart rate, and told his mind to move quickly. He could feel whoever was leaving the place start to really slip away, as if an unseen force was protecting them while earnestly getting them to their destination.

He felt the temperature in the air change and knew he had landed. He opened his eyes to look around, seeing nothing but white space full of nothing as usual. He slightly squinted to figure out just who exactly was trying to leave and go to another realm. A part of him worried it was a being from this particular realm, wandering where they weren't welcome. He itched to take out some of his frustration on someone if he was being honest with himself. He saw his daughter in the body of a baby still yet with eyes that held such wisdom. It was obvious she was trapped, and it sickened him. He heard movement of some sort finally and turned toward it. Then he saw her, the back of her head, as she kept her feet moving in the opposite direction.

"Claura?" He watched her head spin quickly, her long silky hair cascading around her thin, beautiful face, her green eyes looking startled, her thin body dressed in a completely new outfit. Looking like she didn't know whether to believe it was truly him or not.

"Roman!" She looked around her, trying to figure it out. "What are you doing…and where is here? Where are we?" She was clearly expecting a different location, making it obvious she did have a choice in the matter to actually leave. The realization gave him slight relief.

"I suppose it's time you see my gift. The space between realms, when one travels, it's my domain." He could see the question in her eyes. "Just like how Tronan and Daemon can walk in dreams, I walk here. Apparently."

"I would have never thought. Then again, I am surprised all the time. The unexpected is constantly happening in this life I am in now. Can you keep me here? Us here?"

"Yes."

"Kind of in a hurry, to be honest."

"For what, exactly?" He clearly had no clue about this place that was supposed to help her figure things out.

"Daemon is sending me to a realm with a library that will help me figure out what to do about Moira."

*About me.*

*About us.*

*About Daemon and I.*

She tried her best to keep that thought to herself before him.

"That's funny, as Tronan has been looking for you. Intently." He watched her look away, and the expression she was so clearly trying to hide had him stop in his tracks. He was suddenly finding reason to stop moving toward her. He could see that the small action startled her. She started to act more nervous by the second.

"I need you to trust that I am trying to do what is right here, so please, Roman, let me continue to pass through."

"Why has Tronan not sent you? Hmm? I believe you already had your little chat with Daemon."

"Just stop."

"My daughter's life is in the balance of all this. You will be honest with me."

"I am putting her first, trust me. How can I not! It breaks my heart to see her like she is. No one deserves that."

"Agree." He was starting to get angry. She could tell he could sense more.

"Maya visited me." She decided to just lay it out and attempt a distraction. Why hide it? She was not expecting him to believe her at all anyway.

"Me as well." The shock on her face at his words had him half-smile.

"When? What did she say?" She watched him move to pull out a small notebook from his inside pocket and slowly started walking toward her again. The way he held it and looked at it as he held it out for her to take warmed her heart. It was such a small gesture to show what an enormous amount of love he had—and still has—for this woman.

"She asked me to give you this. It has some pages only witches of a certain bloodline can read. Other parts of it are filled in already. I glanced through it, but I honestly can't understand half of it."

"Thank you. And, Roman, you must be relieved beyond anything I can imagine at her not actually being dead. Both of them. I intend to get them fully back." The look on his face was unreadable, alarming her when he so clearly should have shown relief on some level. But she couldn't blame him for possibly just not wanting to get his hopes up. The man clearly knew heartache on a level he so did not deserve.

"She would not tell me where she is, only that I have to stay here for her to be able to reach me and not in a physical manner… yet." Obviously, she was beyond fed up with the fact.

"Ya, she said that to me too. Something about Daemon's home being a safe place to communicate, telepathic or not, as I assume."

"I will remain here with my daughter until this is over." He clearly did not like the idea, not expecting to have his circumstances take such a turn. If only he knew how much she could relate.

"It's a big place, Roman. Not like you won't have your space."

"I want you to name her for me, Claura. Maya agreed on the idea."

"You both have too much faith in me already. Please don't do that. I don't deserve it yet."

"Exactly. Yet." He came closer, standing before her now. He looked into her face like he was worried yet proud. He could see her eyes pleading for him not to make her do it. "Please. She does need a name, after all. After all this time. All she has heard is 'my love' from Daemon for too long."

She could tell he was still immensely bothered by the man being the Match for his daughter. Clearly, Maya had not told all. She didn't know whether to be thankful or not. She could not wrap her head around her reasoning one way or the other. If only Roman knew that the other brother he so obviously already had distaste for as well, right alongside Tronan, was not actually his daughter's Match…but hers. She was starting to feel her temperature rise, her nerves shaking. She needed to suddenly hear Daemon's voice—something, anything from him. He had a calming effect on her that she didn't understand but was happy to use. Roman broke her thoughts before she could attempt to reach out for him in her mind.

"Claura? Are you okay? I am not trying to make you uncomfortable." He was starting to look too worried for her liking. She needed to give him what he wanted from her and get a move on.

"Yes. I am just…overwhelmed." She half-smiled. He wasn't buying it. "Can I think on it for a while, at least? Now that I have seen her and looked into her eyes, I'd like it to be something that pops out. A name that feels like it matches her." The way he was studying her while listening to her every word was making her have to hide her shaking hands. "I am off to a library, after all. It will give me time to research on it a little."

"When will you be back? Soon?"

"I honestly don't know. I'm inwardly praying for this library to help me find a miracle. Along with another book that Maya told me to find first as soon as I arrive."

"You know, Claura, it's precisely inward where your power lies, books or not."

"A manual never hurt." She shrugged. She clearly did not care to try to fake a smile for him anymore. She started to feel a little sick of being on edge about it being completely in Roman's hands to let her get out of there.

"Not that it's any of my business, but you never said bye to your Match."

"I can't have that conversation with you. Not right now." She inwardly knew that if she could just break this damn curse that it would answer so much on its own, and she wouldn't have to deal with it personally. It was just a feeling, a very obvious one, that her being connected to Tronan in a way that should have never been was all part of this bullshit with Moira, and she just needed to know why. How the hell did it benefit her? It would be so nice not to feel stuck in the middle anymore…literally. "Let me continue, Roman. Please. For your daughter's sake." She waited, choosing to be full of patience, choosing the choice that she had no other choice. It took a long time coming, but he nodded.

"Your scent is different." It was full of judgment, yet his tone held compassion still as if he worried about her and what it may mean. She looked at him like he really should not go there. She watched as his eyes became sorrowful, longing even. "I am still always here for you, Claura," he said softly, seeing the recognition in her eyes of the last time he said that to her through a text, followed by watching him raise his hand and snap his fingers before she could do anything or say anything more. Just like Daemon very recently did.

*These damn men.*

*These perfect, intense, powerful, and ridiculously handsome men.*

She really needed to get a hold of her own powers. She suddenly felt a rush come inside her to get a move on with what her own abilities were. Whatever they were. She doubted being able to slam Moira into the side of a car would be enough at the moment.

She felt her body suddenly land. The feeling became slightly familiar now, inwardly swearing at Roman's last comment, hating the entire concept of even having a damn scent at all since being around these men. It was as if her having any kind of slut scent was anyone's fucking business. The judgment for it was undeserved, especially from certain beings who were making it happen to her body themselves, it happening being completely out of her control. She decided maybe there was a book in this new place that would end that bullshit as well. If she can save a child and break a curse, it should be a small task in comparison. Some magical fucking witch deodorant, at least.

She stood straighter and opened her eyes further, instantly enjoying the warmth from the sun, having to hold her hand over her eyes to look around. Maya was absolutely right. One look at the structure in front of her, and she felt so unbelievably at home, with a crazy familiar sense of peace came and calmed over her entire being. Her body inhaled as if her lungs, of their own accord, were saying "home" and had simply been waiting her entire life to return.

# Chapter 19

# Emerald of Memories

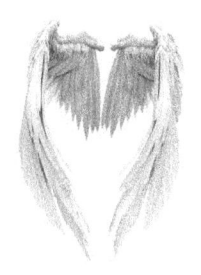

If there was a possibility for your nervous system alone to go to heaven, this was it for her. The scene outside looked similar to a summer day in Venice. The weather was warm and sunny, owning an early-morning glow everywhere she looked. The cobblestone walkway that led up to the bridge where one could overlook the water looked like it was built yesterday, every stone looking new and perfectly leveled. Boats of all gorgeous designs traveled in both directions on the canal, their reflections in the water mirroring their details even more. The water was crystal clear, a beautiful aqua, looking like it was taken from the Maldives itself. The stores and cafés within sight were only slightly occupied by other people, making the hardly crowded atmosphere seem even more welcoming. She took one good, long moment to look up at the perfect structure before her on the other side of the bridge, admiring its size and its beauty. It was one of the most gorgeous cathedrals she'd ever seen, being able to eye shelves upon shelves of books through the enormous windows already. She moved her feet to start walking over the bridge, enjoying the scenery and the smells. She noticed a bakery at the front left of the library entrance, smiling at how the smell seemed so familiar, like grandma's kitchen. She had to laugh at her nervousness about that possibly being true. Was her real grandmother in there cooking up a storm? She let the thought pass as she admired the people looking so put together and just at ease with themselves and their daily routine amongst the streets.

 She decided to take a moment to glance at the book she had just been given by Roman. She wondered with an innate interest in what Maya wanted her to have, feeling a certain kind of connection to the woman that she couldn't put a name on yet. She held it before her, taking a moment to enjoy the beauty of its worn light brown leather. She looked inside to see that the entire book was written by hand, and it looked similar to her own handwriting. She was inwardly questioning it but deciding to just continue on with the other contents. The first page held a rhyming paragraph, reading it more out loud the closer she gets to the last word....

> *For every thunder, there is a rain.*
> *For every love, there is a pain.*
> *For every wonder, there is an answer.*
> *For every forward, there is a reverse.*
> *There will forever be good and bad,*
> *no matter which chosen curse.*

 She frowned while looking down at it, reading it over again in her head. *Hmmm...* She let her fingers continue to the next page. She found it funny to see an index in the anterior of the book yet admired how it kind of helped one get to the point of what page to look for sooner—secretly enjoying the cleverness of the small decision. She noticed many categories of spells mixed with music under M, wondering how that would work. It makes her reach into the small pack that Daemon was kind enough to fetch for her to help her cowardly self avoid Tronan for a bit longer. She felt for her headphones and cell phone, seeing if it would work with her music in such a place. To her absolute awe, it did. She smiled to herself, all the more feeling that this was truly her personal magical space.

"Guess we shall see how this connects later to a spell. I will try to work with a small one first Maya, I promise. So as to help not fuck this up. For all of us."

Suddenly feeling determined, she grasped the book firmly in her hand, as if to dare anyone to attempt stealing it from her, and started striding with confidence toward the main and very large front doors. For as comfortable as she felt here, she did not know anybody. Little did she know that was about to change.

With just one step inside, Claura felt the energy from every single person in the enormous structure and suddenly recognized her presence. Some turned and looked at her for a few long moments, others just a glance before getting back to their reading with a look of satisfaction on their face. Either way, literally every soul in the place recognized her. She waited for a feeling of insecurity, of it somehow being a threat, but it didn't come. It was as if fear in this realm was just not an option. That one simply did come here for peace and for a break. She sure as hell needed it. The feeling of heartbreak for Tronan, mixed with the relief of finding Daemon, was enough to make anyone feel a bit crazy. The two emotions did not belong in the same body, same mind, and same heart. The thought brought her back to her task, giving her the strength to step inside a little more, looking at the cathedral ceilings, recognizing their familiarity yet still loving to look at them anew all the same, studying the theme among the stained-glass windows all over the ceilings and higher edges of the walls. It was truly just beautiful. Her brain didn't care to find a more elaborate word. She decided to bring herself out of the slight trance at just the sight of the place, her heart of its own accord going out to all the rows of books, seeing all the different floors even to yet be explored right from the very entrance. She cleared her throat and, in a shy, nervous gesture, rubbed her fingertips along her temple, looking around and wondering where to even start. She laughed to herself, knowing she had been here before, realizing it was silly to be shy. Everyone probably got sick of her walking through those doors and acting like it was her first time here several of her lifetimes ago.

She looked at the book in her hands, closed her eyes, and reached out to him, needing just a moment of reassurance. The task at hand suddenly sunk in much more than expected with just being here and looking around now.

*Daemon?*

*Yes, my love.*

He could feel her relief, her trying to hold it together, her unknowing what to even say—her need to just hear his voice. He could sense the book shaking in her hands slightly through their mental thread. *Sweetheart, calm your heart. Please.*

She started to nod as if in disbelief of it all, feeling so overwhelmed now. The tears were surely coming, and she did not care who saw. This place felt like home in a way she never thought she'd be lucky enough to experience. She had no genuine faith in herself yet for this huge of a task, and she missed Daemon—more than she should already. It was as if her own soul was telling her she left him too soon after just finding him again. She looked around stubbornly, feeling a sense of ownership of the entire place yet not fully understanding how that could be. So screw whoever saw her walls breaking down at the moment. She felt his arms start to wrap around her from a distance and stepped back.

*Don't! That won't help me hold it together.* She wiped at her tears, clearing off both sides of her face, wishing she could feel his hands do that thing they did right before kissing her. *I just need a moment with you.*

*You are making it hard to remain away.*

The sadness in his tone made her feel guilty. She should be acting stronger right now. She was not here for herself. She needed to get to work for someone else. She had every intention of studying what she could find for the sake of the baby first, herself second. But somehow, she knew she would have to be selfish. A part of her told her that they were entwined already anyway.

*I know. I'm sorry. Tell me…how is the little one?* It truly sounded curious and not like she was just using the topic of her as a distraction.

*She has taken to Tronan, apparently. She smiles the most when he holds her.* She could sense the admirable emotions coming through their thread, his love for his brother despite the conversation that clearly still needed to happen between them. She could sense the protective streak Daemon held for the small child, from their connection due to Maya's plan or just him simply being with her so much for so long, she couldn't tell. *You are my heart. Not her.* He clearly saw her thoughts in her wandering and overemotional mind, even from a distance.

*I know. It's all just a spell to protect her. But what if I can't sever it? What if you always stay connected to her? What will that mean for us, Daemon?*

*We are not going to find out. You will succeed.* She could feel him really fighting not to visit her. *And, my love, do you know why?*

*Hmmm?* She caught her breath again, feeling calmer. She loved how, no matter the topic, just his voice calmed her very soul.

*Because she deserves to find her true Match, as well.*

She smiled, sending the mental waves of it toward him with an intentional push. She wanted to just help him feel happy too. She took a moment to make sure she wanted to say the words, leaning on one hip, caressing the book in her hands while still looking at her surroundings, taking her time. She felt him wait as if it was nothing he was not willing to do for her. *I do love you too, Daemon.*

*I know, sweetheart.* His arms really enveloped her now. She could smell him as if he were actually right there, standing before her. He continued, *Now get you and that sexy little ass to work.*

She could sense his desire, along with his hand, starting to move in the direction of smacking her ass. She somehow knew he would make sure the sound effect would come through into her realm, embarrassing her. Without thought, she reacted and yelled out loud, "Fuck off, Daemon!" while moving away as if he was really there. She heard his ridiculously attractive laughter in her mind as he kissed her forehead and broke the connection. He left her standing there alone in the middle of the enormous library, which now she knew held an enormous echo to go along with it. Her feelings looked of all different varieties followed suit in her direction. She covered her face with her hands, inhaled deeply, inwardly praying for her blush to 100 percent fuck off in a matter of three seconds tops.

"Men!"

Suddenly, soft footfalls started to come closer to where she was standing. She lowered her hands and glanced at the woman walking toward her with a smirk on her face, clearly enjoying the moment before her. Her voice was like warm crystals, if that made any sense. It was just soothing and welcoming, making Claura realize right away that this was one of her friends—a woman who already knew her. The woman looked at her with admiration and love, the feeling of a friend in her almost being an understatement.

"I see you have found him again." She raised her eyebrow, as if to say good job and congrats on having excellent choice in men still. Claura gave her that questionable look, the woman reacting as if it was very solid territory. It was a definite repeat. "I am Allie. Should we shake hands again?" She gave a small laugh.

"I don't know."

She saw her wave her hand as if to say "no biggie," still giving off that warm smile in Claura's direction. "You were always too hard on yourself when you came back again. Let's just get that out of the way first. You don't have so much to worry about as you think, Claura. You are a fast learner and even a faster reader."

"From the many lifetimes of experience, I take it."

"No. Just always were. Right from when you were a little girl yourself." Her tone suggested she kind of already knew what was going on and was clearly planning to help, just by her tone when saying the last three words.

"Do you know about the child?" Claura asked, obviously just needed to be sure.

"Yes. I am so sorry. This is a first for us, but me and the others who will help you."

"First?"

"Well, yes. Every time you came back with zero memories, we helped you study who you are. Now we are here to do that and help you break this awful curse on that baby. It is new territory for us as well. So, in a way, we are in the same boat this time for your return." She smiled, clearly trying to just be reassuring and supportive. She saw Claura debating and pausing, unsure what to say. "Come on. Let me show you your office."

"Office? Isn't this a public library?"

"Yes, for the public. First things first, you own this place. Inherited it from your mother."

"My mother? Who was my mother!" She was unable to stop her voice rising. She saw the woman turn with slight regret on her face. "What?"

"Upon your return in this reincarnation this time, we've noticed a few things go missing in your files."

"Files?"

"Yes. You have your own files you want us to keep so you can reread about your past lives and understand who you really are better for when this, unfortunately, happens to you. This time, we've noticed some of your files now have blank pages, along with our memory of what was on them before," Allie clarified, sounding irritated about it.

"How many?" The blank pages in the book that Roman gave her came to mind as well, inwardly wondering if they were connected.

"We are still reviewing, as we only knew you'd be coming for a few hours now. But where it always stated for you who your mother was, that's just gone now. Completely blank."

"Blank? Don't any of you remember on your own, pages or not?"

The young woman sighed. Looking pissed off about the fact. "Completely blank." It was as if losing the knowledge was completely annoying and triggering for her. "Nobody can remember. And that is a first. Considering we are literally coded in this realm as keepers of knowledge." The distaste in her voice was beyond obvious, as if feeling embarrassed was not suited to her particular liking one bit.

"My father?" Claura asked, looking ready for disappointment with the topic of him too.

"That I do recall we never had information on. Sorry, Claura." She could see her get overwhelmed and started to reach out her hand to place atop Claura's shoulder, wanting to help her. Knowing each time this happened, it was extremely overwhelming for her. She hated seeing her go through it. She went to say something but got interrupted instead, the determination on Claura's face setting her back a beat.

"Maya has a book for me. I need to find it."

"Already on your desk. We know that she can reach us here too already."

"Please show me." Her face was as determined as ever. She could tell Allie had never seen her like this before in another lifetime, but it was obvious why. A baby was in the balance this time. A baby that, as much as she hated herself for feeling weirdly angry at, was attached to her Daemon, and she wanted the forced connection to be broken for good and today. This visit was bound to be different right from the start. She followed Allie to the far-right corner of the building and up the wide stairway all the way to the fifth floor. Each floor let the beauty of the windows be shown more. The view as you looked down from the next floor got even more stunning with each level.

"This is mine? This whole place?"

"The only thing we have in records of your mother is that she left it to you."

"No name on that paperwork, nothing?"

"Just an old-fashioned thumbprint, set in blood."

"I see."

"But you know, Claura, a blood print can be quite useful. It simply must be used correctly."

"How so?"

"Well, in many ways, in many small steps. We have thousands upon thousands of years of knowledge when it comes to curses, and for some reason, when the blood is related between those involved in the curse, it gets harder to decipher. So with that blood print already being a relative to you, it will be easier to use it yet harder to understand firstly how to use it…if that makes sense."

"I have never used a spell before. I have no idea what I am doing." Claura could hear Allie's laugh start to echo and looked up to the woman stopping to turn around and face her while slapping her hand quickly over her mouth. Claura was taken aback, so I was not sure how to react. For sure, she knew that she meant that in this particular lifetime, she had no idea what she was doing. "How many spells have I done before? Did I get good?"

"Daemon did always get a kick out of how you not only underestimated him but yourself as well. Come on. You always glowed when you saw your office. It's one of my favorite moments when you return. Memory or not."

She hurried a little more as if excited to almost be there herself. The last step led down a long emerald green–carpeted hallway. It was clear from just the energy alone that this place was held for utmost privacy—her own privacy. And she was beyond ready for it. As much as she loved the ripple effect that Daemon brought into her life in every possible way when he found her in his home, alone in that particular room, she still felt like she had truly missed out on the private time she so desperately needed and had originally aimed for. Now, while here, just looking down this hallway alone, it made it clear. This was her domain. She just felt it. She stood there, unable to move, her eyes clearly connecting to the particular doorway at the end.

"Claura?"

"Yes, sorry."

"Go on. Just come down when you are good and ready." She turned to head back down the stairs, clearly sensing that this time was different, that she would not be walking into her office with her this time to show her around.

Claura rushed to turn around to thank her, only to see Allie raise her hand as if to stop her and send her a simple smile full of understanding over her shoulder before continuing back down the stairs. Claura couldn't help but wonder why she never aspired toward an elevator in the place, despite it clearly not bothering her at all to walk all the way back down. She turned to face back down the hallway and started to move her feet. She admired the artwork on the tables that were evenly lined up along the walls every twenty feet or so—the portraits of other women who looked just like her along the way. Stopping at one that had a blurred face, the paint actually swirling over the visage on the canvas as if under a spell to keep doing so. She reached up to touch it, then thought better of it. Due to the eerie vibe coming from it, she figured it'd be better not to risk fucking up so ridiculously easy on her first day here. "Let's not get sucked into a painting within one hour, shall we?" She was slightly discouraged at herself for possibly almost messing up so easily.

She continued down the hall at a quicker pace than expected, as if she could sense a deep part of her was tired of this feeling new yet again. She was tired of the personal sequel after sequel after sequel. She took a deep breath, adding the breaking of yet another curse to her list of impossible accomplishments, and stepped through the doorway into her office quickly as if daring anything to put fear in her to do so. A deep part of her was ready to not just feel in control but actually be in control. Other than Daemon not being present with her, her entire being realized that no other place would feel as complete. She never felt more powerful in her life. It was as if every object she looked at, every color of something that captured her gaze, every shelf full of books that covered the walls at random places, and every little thing in its own way was restoring her own power back to her.

She looked to the desk along the back wall and saw the obvious book placed out for her to see in plain sight. She walked across the room with newfound confidence until she stood behind the beautiful piece of cherry wood, admiring its corners full of details and unique designs carved into the wood, and sat down in the large swivel chair that was enveloped in a black velvet covering. She took a moment to savor the perfect height and size of it, a part of herself being impressed with…herself. She clearly held on to her own unique taste in things over the years.

*Centuries and lifetimes, apparently.*

She felt herself swallow, her throat become dry, yet hating how nervous she was at simply just learning about herself. So what if it was for the tenth time? It was her right. And just like Allie had already warned her about, she knew she needed to take her advice and not be too hard on herself. She didn't ask to forget everything in the name of just wanting to stay in a reality where her one true love would be also. And the memory of him stating that they actually missed out on lifetimes together sometimes made her head boil, as having to be reborn over and over was clearly enough to have to deal with. She reached out to him, needing to make the contact, if anything just to make up for lost time for those particular solo lifetimes without him—him without her.

"Daemon?" She chose to speak out loud. She enjoyed the sound of his name. The way it rolled off her tongue sent sparks to certain areas of her anatomy all on its own. She smirked to herself, suddenly in no mood to feel ashamed of anything.

*I sense you are happy with your finding.* He clearly already knew exactly where she was.

*I feel you in this wood.*

*Do you now?* He clearly smirked, intentionally sending images of their recent lovemaking her way. He felt her immense blush yet could tell she was purely enjoying it and actually welcoming it.

*My damn desk, handsome.* She sent a few of her favorite images back. She clearly meant to test his control from afar—sending a few new ones as well, really pushing her limits, showing future wishes of what she really wanted his hands and mouth to do to her.

*My dear...* She loved the warning growl in his voice, at the knowing of him having to excuse himself at a ridiculous fast rate from being around others in his office. She could sense it was bad timing and decided to simply be nice.

*I feel you in this, under my palms. You do wonderful work, my love.*

*I feel you catching on quicker than normal to things. To be honest, it frightens me.*

*I would think one would see it as the opposite of a flaw.*

*I do love it about you. It has simply attracted the wrong company before.*

*That's where you come in. We each have our own ways of saving each other, don't we?* It was not really meant as a question. She could feel him inhale on his end as if truly worried, as if trying to suppress a certain memory he did not want to discuss. *Not going to tell me, aye?*

*No.*

*But I am safe here. I can feel it.*

*There, yes. As long as you do not leave the realm.*

*I have no intention of leaving.* She felt his anger building, yet knowing it was not directed at her. *What is wrong? Clearly, something is.*

*There are others in the adjoining realm with a thirst for powers from the highest witch bloodlines. The barriers have been set between realms to keep the separation permanent. They have not attempted to get through in over a thousand years.*

*Why do you sound worried then?*

*Ninety-nine percent certainty is not good enough for me with you. We have never been able to make sure they stay out completely.*

*I see. And you still let me come here.*

*You have refused to make any other place a home for yourself. You have been adamant about it your entire existence. I simply caved a long time ago, sick of the discussion.* He sensed her getting lost in her thoughts again and decided now is as good of a time as any, as he would be able to see her expression still through their mental thread. *Sweetheart, look in the bottom right drawer for me.*

There was zero hesitation, her entire being just completely unafraid and feeling in complete control of whatever she came across within these office walls. She saw a small leather ring box, the only thing taking up the entire large drawer. Her heart started to beat a little faster and felt a little hotter. *Hmm...how I wonder.* She enjoyed the playful moment through their mental link. She felt his smile, his love for her in a way she truly never thought she'd experience from someone before. From her memory in this lifetime anyway, this would be her first ring. She opened it to see a medium-sized emerald placed in a golden band, it being a long pear-shaped diamond, one small sparkling rhinestone placed on each side. Simple yet clearly unique.

*Put it on.*

*I don't know...is this like your threshold thing? I think we need to get to know one another a bit more. I mean, I did just meet you.*

*Please.* His tone suggested he was waiting for something to happen, that despite her being playful and enjoying it, he was waiting for something that would take place as soon as she did put it on her finger.

She took a breath, admiring its beauty, and slowly slipped it on. The instant flashback in her mind made her entire body still as if she was not allowed to miss a single detail of the memory. It was the first time they met. She saw herself outside in the woods somewhere. It was summertime. Her feet were enjoying the feel of the water as she sat on a rock in the middle of a creek. She turned suddenly to notice a tall figure not far from her, the look on his face making her entire body still. There was a look of such shock and devotion that had her fear him instantly for all sorts of reasons. It was just an instant that she knew what he was already, and he her from the first glance. The memory suddenly jumped to the first time they were making love, him being so gentle, so caring. The scene showed him being that way all night long for her, in a complete and constant fight with himself to stay in such control with her body moving beneath him. The feeling of a drop of sweat dripping on her temple, another between her breasts, had her mind jumping back into the present. She wiped her forehead with the back of her hand, suddenly feeling like she had been holding her breath the entire time, and just waited for him to say something first. She suddenly wanted to look into his actual face so badly. She could tell he was willing to wait longer, wanting to hear her reaction first.

*I umm...wow.* She felt him slightly laugh, yet as well really just wanting to see her. He also still wanted to respect her original wishes in going there to have some time for herself. He already knew it was going to be a challenge to stay away, but he would do anything for her. *I recognize that room. That was the same room we were just in.* She felt him gently nod.

*Another reason it was hard to stay away from you in my own home, Claura. Once I realized what room you had chosen, I just could not stop myself. It was just too damn much of a coincidence.*

*How many other rooms in your home were there to choose from?*

*313.* She felt him deeply chuckle at the fact. He rubbed his hand over his face, using up the will he had gotten so used to having to rely on to do what was right. Their circumstances gave him enough practice for more lifetimes than seemed realistic to be able to handle, even with being one among his species and not some silly human or another race of sorts. His hands were literally shaking with the need to feel her skin beneath them—to feel her close right now. As if on a cue of its own, the book rattled before her on the desk, startling her.

*I believe Maya is trying to reach you. I will leave you to it.*

*This ring, Daemon, was that just a onetime thing?*

*Far from it.*

*How incredible*, she said it in almost a whisper, staring at it in awe as she played with it between her fingertips again.

*My love, do not rely on it so much as just calling to me in the now. I am actually here for you, unlike those memories.* His tone clearly suggested he ached for it, not wanting her to already be apart from him again so soon, hating it really.

She sat back into her chair more, relaxing into its perfect shape, and felt his fingers brush her face as if standing right next to her, lingering on her soft skin, a moment of pure adoration. Then the feeling of the connection let go slowly—the feeling of him truly missing her already. She took a few long moments to just stare at the ring. She thought to herself how she knew she was way beyond the human little way of marriage with this ring on her finger. The thought of having to hide it from Tronan suddenly sprang to mind, bringing her heartbreak and disgust with herself come crashing back. She clasped her hands over her head, leaning forward to place her elbows on the desk, lowering her face toward it, and closing her eyes to just breathe, inwardly praying for a miracle to be hers to own in all this. She lifted her head and reached for the book, seeing it open to a certain page as if anticipating her finally taking the time to read it. She smiled, completely ignoring the fact that this should scare her a little.

Because it didn't.

It didn't at all.

# Chapter 20

## Triss Trass

Roman watched Daemon exit the office more abruptly than usual, seeing how it startled his brother slightly. He himself tried not to give anything away by not being startled at all after recent info highlights with Claura. It was a good moment to have Tronan being distracted by the baby, sweetly talking to her, carrying her around the room, and letting her touch whatever she desired. Her little sounds warmed each of their hearts on a level they clearly were still wrapping their minds around. The effect a child had on you was simply inconceivable until it literally happened to you. It did not matter who you were or what realm you came from. The security that a child required from you turned one into a whole new person, and there was no stopping it.

He could sense Daemon returning to the office sometime later, clearly done with his secretive duty, and decided to meet him in the hallway. His intention was pure on keeping Tronan out of the conversation. He left his baby girl with the man who, for some reason, he no longer hated so much. It was clear he was purely enjoying the little one's company in a way that he never would have expected from such a man. He had never known Tronan to be around a single kid in all his existence. It was just not in his nature. He always dwelled elsewhere in other areas of life—battle and troublemaking being the two main forefronts.

He quietly exited the room, shutting the door behind him in a calm manner, sensing Daemon was already watching him do so before looking up at him and coming back down the hallway. He heard Daemon stop in his tracks some distance away still, clearly able to see into Roman's thoughts on some level already.

"I need to speak with you."

Roman's tone suggested he had no intention of being put off. He watched as the man paused and studied him for a matter of two seconds before nodding his head to go back in the other direction. Daemon turned his back to him, knowing this was coming but not expecting it to be with Roman first. He truly could not pinpoint how he figured it out, if he even had, as he had yet to figure out just how much Roman knew as yet. His mind went to how he would best handle the scenario, remembering how Claura reacted to not wanting to hurt Roman even once more in her lifetime, as he was the first of the three of them that she came across. He was, after all, in this lifetime, the first connection among the males of their species for Claura to have a connection with on some level. He was only hoping that his ring and the memories it held would help her focus on the only beginning that truly mattered, the one she shared with him. He kept reminding himself that she just needed some time again, that it wasn't her fault she was getting more forgetful with each rebirth, and that it wasn't like he couldn't have her for himself underneath him again in a matter of minutes. Memories of the way her body moved with his for hours on end recently made his own body temperature increase at just the thoughts alone. He wanted her more than anything already, once again, after waiting so long to even look at her, to find her, to talk to her, and to see that she was safe, alive, and breathing. Her body was under his hands once again after fifteen cursed decades of being apart.

He cleared his throat as he crossed over what looked like a huge and very unused ballroom, trying to control his damn thoughts, and led them into another private office in the far corner. It was mainly an old-fashioned cigar room, a private place for men on many occasions before. The energy reeked of it.

"How is it, Roman, that you have put whatever it is you know together?" He got to the point of wanting to know how in his own damn home, he had no control in realizing that Roman possibly knew already. The man had clearly been underestimated.

"I met up with Claura on her way out."

He felt Daemon turn to him, looking confused. He looked pissed about being confused.

"Met up?"

He still offered him a cigar despite the circumstances. Roman took one but chose to save it for later. He took a brief moment to just look at Daemon square in the eye as he gently played with it between his fingers.

"The space between realms. My domain," he said without any anger.

There was no need to defend himself. Since seeing his daughter and knowing that she and Maya were alive, his entire demeanor had changed. Roman had, in a way, become a whole new person. It was understanding yet slightly eerie to them all. They all simply chose not to discuss it. He was determined to get them all the way home and come hell if it didn't happen.

"I see you have gotten over Claura, at last." Daemon risked clarifying.

"I see you haven't."

Some anger slid into his voice now. Maya, back or not, he still cared about Claura, and for some deep down reason, he knew he always would. She was being thrown into a hell of a situation, and it was clear Daemon had been hiding his affection for her beyond well. Her expression alone at just the mention of this man's name when he spoke with her said so much but still did not completely clarify the reasoning for it.

"How dare you, Daemon. How fucking dare you think you have a chance to call both your own. I understand my daughter now, as hard as that has been. The connection was to save her life. But Claura belongs to Tronan. And as much as that has pained me to realize, it just is. I see it between them."

"How are you to judge me when you yourself thought you had two Matches as well? Hmmm?" He looked away for a second to light his cigar, sitting down in one of the chairs before a large coffee table in the center of the room, clearly feeling completely unthreatened by the topic at hand, making Roman's blood boil even more at the man's sense of ease.

"I thought Maya was dead. That the connection was completely severed. That's the kind of power she threw into this spell to save our daughter! It's not like I went out and looked for Claura. She literally came into my life of her own circumstances."

"I am sorry you did not know. I truly am. Maya simply told me not to say anything that day it all started. To wait until the time would come. That it was the best way to keep her spell intact for your daughter's sake." He shrugged with his shoulders, as well as his hands, meeting Roman's eyes. "I was simply listening to her, trusting her."

"Why do you want both?"

"I don't."

"Make some sense, Daemon! Enough with these games. I need you to be straight!"

"No games. Other than the one from Moira, obviously." He stood up to face away from the man, walking toward a large desk to set his finished cigar down in the amber ashtray. He puts his hands atop the piece, leaning on it with his palms, his head down as if preparing himself. He was completely unsure how Roman would react. "Claura is my Match. Reincarnated."

"You really expect us to believe that?"

"Every time she is reborn, as it's our way to stay together with what we both are, and her memory gets worse. It's gotten to the point where she barely at all remembers who she is and that I even exist at all unless I can find her. And it terrifies me." It was not like Daemon to show fear at all. Roman actually had no real memory of the man ever showing fear even in the slightest of all his existence. It just didn't exist for Daemon. He was the walking definition of fearless himself. "Just ask her yourself."

"She would not answer much."

"She wants to break the binding spell Maya did on me and your daughter and then the curse from Moira before anything else."

"And Tronan? She literally walked away from him."

"For him."

"How so?"

"She doesn't completely understand it herself yet and has no idea how to tell him to face her plans. She needs time to put the pieces together."

"That's a hell of a way for you to handle this all wrong. Both of you!" Roman snapped.

"There is no right way to truly handle this, Roman! I did not ask her to fall for my brother, as she was clearly sensing me through him this entire time. That is how strong our bond is!" he yelled with a fury now, uncaring at how it may escalate everything. "That is how strong our connection has always been! And no one, even my own damn brother, is going to separate us. His feelings are coming from something else, and we intend to figure out how and why. She simply needs time and space to do such, and I am the one willing to give that to her."

"He may try to kill you. He truly does not see it any other way with her."

"Let him try." Daemon scowled, standing straight again. He eyed over Roman with a look that said he better not try to interfere and go see her and to just leave her alone as well.

"You will go that far?"

"If he does not listen to me, or her...."

"It will take her telling him. He won't truly believe you. You already know that."

"She just needs time. So try to keep your mouth shut, per her request." Roman put his hands up, the attempt to hide his smirk failing, knowing there was a hell of a time coming…and soon—a time that was full of karma for himself, as he had always had a dislike for the brothers on one level or another. Even if it did just boil down to the ridiculous extent of power that both these brothers were born with, it was a good enough reason for him. No one had a right to own such abilities, and least of all, never having to even earn them.

"So my daughter is not your true Match, or they both are? I don't understand."

"Maya has not spoken to you about this yet? Has she not appeared to you?" Daemon asked, looking irritated at having to be the one to voice such an obvious explanation instead of Maya in all this.

"Her moments with me are limited. She says she still needs to preserve her energy to keep the spell intact, as it's starting to dwindle. We never have enough time for everything." His eyes glared into the distance now, clearly hating an unseen force. "She simply told me to speak to you about it to help her preserve her energy." The fear in his eyes was obvious at Maya having to admit such a thing, as she was quite the powerful witch in her own bloodline, making it all the more clear they were running out of time.

"It has kept your daughter safe. That's what the connection was originally intended for. So I could keep her safe."

He glanced at Roman more intently, clearly asking him to understand his side in all this. He owed Daemon that much after he had been here alone with the little one for so long, taking care of her, seeing to her every need, being there for her, talking to her, day and night, seeing it in her eyes that she was beyond frustrated with not being able to grow and converse in return. The dread in such a young child's eyes that it may never happen. His heart broke more times than he could count in the time he had been with her here for all these years.

"Claura intends to sever it so that your daughter may find her own true Match. Whoever that may be."

Roman took a long time, thinking it all over. He eventually sat down in one of the leather cigar chairs, relaxing in it. There was a clear intention of not moving for some time until this discussion was thoroughly done. He simply wanted to know more of all the angles so far with this whole thing, anything to do a part in ending Moira for good.

"I see now."

He watched Daemon follow suit in a chair opposite his on the other side of the coffee table once again. He lit another cigar with a flame thrower before tossing it on the large coffee table between them, letting it bounce and slide to match his irritation. He rubbed his temple as if a headache proceeded. He looked at Roman like he was ready for him to clarify as he sat back into the cushions.

"Maya may have had a push in making sure Claura ended up here, no matter which one of us she connected with. As long as it happened, that is all that was important." He eyed Daemon, seeing him contemplating. "You really can't find her each time, can you?"

Daemon's eyes lifted immediately, his mind clearly focused on the one circumstance he had been hating the most for a very long time. Clearly beyond bothered with not being able to help the matter, hence why being alone for some time he was completely okay with. She tried to truly figure things out for good about what was happening between him and Claura in every new lifetime she came back in while dealing with the curse being placed upon the little one. He knew Claura from a baby several times over in the beginning when the spell held no disturbances, but over time, it started happening little by little. So keeping Roman's daughter company was not a new challenge for him, not by a long shot. It was simply strange to never actually see her grow. In a way, it made him thankful for what Claura was able to receive despite it being through a long-standing spell, as at least she never remained a baby each time. He wondered if her spirit was somehow experiencing a type of dementia. Perhaps the spell was simply trying to tell them that time was up soon for both of them. Roman's voice broke through his thoughts, making it obvious Daemon's expressions were taking a hell of a turn. The man was starting to look lethal. Wherever his mind had wandered to, it was actually starting to make Roman nervous.

"I want to help," Roman said.

"You are already. I did not know how much of a mental break I needed from this task with your daughter until you all came along. I am sorry. It is simply true."

"You have done well. Maya chose you for a reason. And now I see why." He clearly put the pieces together already, proving just how sharp Roman could be when he really needed to. He was not being able to really imagine how it must have been for Daemon to see his Match as a baby in every new lifetime, knowing her time was limited over and over. "I will never doubt your feelings for Claura again. You have my word."

"You actually figured this out on your own and took it better than I expected. I am impressed, Roman. Truly."

"She needs to come back and tell him. And I don't see why the connection was so strong between them if she is your true Match. Why—"

"Moira, somehow, for some fucked up reason. And that is up to her. And right now, she simply needs her space."

"He. Deserves. To. Know."

"Watch your tone with me, Roman. Despite the circumstances, you remain in my home. I will deal with my brother how I see fit."

"He is going to snap any minute now at her being gone. And you know it. So for the safety of my daughter being around whatever hell he is going to bring down when he does snap, deal with it and deal with it now." He stood and started toward the door. He clearly knew how to act like a father, impressing Daemon again already. Daemon simply turned to look at him the way a bear would eye a fox that kept stealing its fish. "Save your fury, for it will be nothing compared to mine if either of you ruin this for Maya and my daughter. If your brother gets in the way a second time, he's done." Roman made it clear he would simply figure out how to be useful on his own time in all this—alone.

He gave Daemon one last look of fuck-off before exiting the room. For once, another man's tone sent a chill down his spine. It was unfamiliar territory, and Daemon was not impressed by the sensation. He could completely relate to the lingering thought he caught in Claura's mind for the brief second while in his arms, her being inwardly thankful at not feeling the chilling sensation with him like she obviously had with Tronan. And the difference confused him. Why would it happen with only one of them and not them both? He suddenly needed to reach for her mind, to feel her presence, and without calming himself first, he made the mistake of reaching for her too bluntly. Originally, she intended to just be a feather in her mind, not wanting to distract her, just make sure she was safe. He could see her at the desk still, reading the same book, looking to be about halfway through now. He felt her pause him as if simply wanting to finish a sentence before she started talking. He waited. He was just pleased with knowing she was fine.

Safe.

In her element.

Back in his life. Finally.

He took advantage of the moment to calm himself while reaching for another cigar. He realized he missed this room. He never really had a reason to use it much anymore, and for so long now.

*What is wrong?* She clearly was not in the mood to ignore anything. She sounded like more of the spitfire suddenly that he knew she could be when she really wanted.

*I may need your help, beautiful. After all.*

*With what?*

*Who.*

*It hasn't even been an entire day yet, Daemon! Surely, somehow you both can give me that amount of time!*

*Roman has been enlightened.*

*I figured as much. He is too wise for his own good. He saw right through me.* He inwardly swore at herself for thinking he may not have noticed, for being that stupid.

*Why would you not tell me of his unique ability?*

*I thought maybe you already just knew.*

*I did not.*

*My omnipotent, perfect man, how did you not know?*

*We are able to keep our main talent from anyone if we truly wish it. It's a privacy that naturally comes with our own unique gift. It's like a natural security layer over top of it, sealing it to our own blood and mind.*

*I wish I knew what mine was.*

*Me too, darling. Me too.* He sounded tired—the kind of tiredness that made her worry for his literal soul, his tired body, which she blushed at, wondering if it did even tire after everything they'd shared. It was not even on the same level of comparison. She sat back in her chair, taking a moment to really try to read him.

*Come to me.*

*As much as I need to feel you again, my love. I fear the two of us being gone from this place at once will simply give it away. And right now, I am not in the mood to be brief with my visit.*

*Yes, you are right.*

She bit her lip. She truly wanted to figure out a way to help. She felt her emotions starting to get the better of her, her temperature rising, and not in the way she preferred after just listening to his perfect voice say such a thing.

"I hate this. I fucking hate this!"

She stood up abruptly, slamming her hands on the desk and letting out a good scream. She lowered her face to the floor, seeing the quick tears fall, taking several quick breaths as if she were about to truly lose it. Just like she had done that first night, Tronan appeared to her. She suddenly looked around the room for alcohol. There was nothing. He sensed her reaching for the book, meaning to toss it.

*Don't!*

*So far, it has helped not!*

*Finish. It.*

*I'm trying! But I can't focus now.*

She let her bottom fall back into the chair, crossing one ankle over the other knee, rubbing her head as if a migraine had just found its new home behind her skull.

*You can. Take a break. I am sorry to have distracted you. You were clearly on a roll. I could feel it.*

The sad feeling in his voice was truly starting to eat at her. She could tell he was leaving something out. Another worry that he did not want her to concern herself with right now. "Don't ever apologize for reaching out to me." He paused before continuing, caressing her lips aggressively, lost in thought. He felt so angry at not even knowing where to start with all this, all alone over here, despite it feeling like it was completely made for her. "We missed out on too much time together. You told me so! And I can feel the truth of it in my bones! This is all so goddamn unfair!" He could not agree more that they still had lost time to make up for. He inwardly cursed himself for knowing he was caving, simply trying to piece together how to not have his absence missed. She could feel his frustration, his need for a break from having to see things from so many different angles. He had been doing it for so long. Meanwhile, she had been doing it for only days. She tried not to let her need to comfort him come off too strong, wanting him to remain there if that was truly what he wished.

*I cannot leave this place, Daemon. My soul won't let me. Something is telling me, deep down, to stay here no matter what and keep searching. I will come to you. For now, just focus.*

She felt his last mental caress come and then fade. The feeling of comfort he offered in just speaking to her made his abrupt absence all the harder to have to deal with. She decided to take a break and listened to some music. The urge to hear her favorite song was taking over. She reached for her phone and headphone pieces and casually walked over to the daybed along the enormous and gorgeous window. The sun was setting, causing the warm rays to shine across it perfectly, as if intentionally meaning to be a natural blanket for her to curl up under. The velour blankets atop it made it look so comfy and inviting. It was clear green was her chosen color, among many lifetimes. She secretly wondered if there was a deeper reason for it—a meaning behind it. She lay down, adjusting the pillows under her head, letting the book rest beside her hip as she clicked Play, letting the start of "Help Me Lose My Mind" by Disclosure and London Grammar take over her eardrums. It helped her troubles to feel at bay, even if just slightly. It reminded herself that she was only one person, and it had not even been an entire day yet. And shit was just happening too fast. She took a few moments to just really enjoy the song before lifting the book alongside her hip back into her hands, opening it to glance through the pages all at once. Letting the edges bounce from right to left. Her eyes widened at seeing colors and letters everywhere on various pages now that were not there before.

"The music…" She felt her lips curve into a smile. Truly just happy that she had figured something out that may be useful, and boy, was it ever. She flipped to a page that had a title in bold writing across the top.

"Uncross Ties," it read within parenthesis below it.

*For Claura, aka Adera*

She sat up quickly, holding the book with an even firmer grip, and started reading the spell in a low voice. Alone in her office, the air literally became more still of its own will, as if her surroundings had, on their own, been waiting for this moment. There was a moment when their rightful owner returned to her own deep roots and returned to what her very spirit needed to do to feel alive. The closer she got to the end of the rhyming spell, the more she just innately understood what it was for. It was as if it was a language that was all intuition inside of her, not needing a single literal damn word to be understood. The book before her was literally just a doorway into its own realm of instinct, of sixth and seventh, continually beyond that, senses. On the opposite page was a spell that was clearly meant to have the opposite effect.

"Balance."

She read it with an instant distaste. It hit a nerve she realized was hell-bent on retaliation in a stronger way that she did not notice fully until now. She read it out loud as well, refusing to be intimidated by it.

*Triss Trass Make It Pass*

*Unbind the ancient*
*Make way for new thread*
*Envelope the mind and soul*
*And body possess*
*alive or dead*
*Heart be taken*
*By new passion unfold*
*Let it be another warmth*
*That fade all the cold*

# THE WINGED WITCH OF MATCHES

*Take this into command*
*Push it set into stone*
*Let them not part*
*From a cell in thy bone*
*Hear this desire*
*Help to rewire*
*Bypass what was meant*
*Let a new love be lent*

Her entire being leaped to action, removing the earbuds from her lobes, standing as if in an absolute hurry to get back to Daemon and show him in person. A part of her was in disbelief that she had found the right spell to unbind already, yet fully trusting Maya. She suddenly wondered why. If Maya could do the spell that connected her daughter to Daemon, then why couldn't she undo it? The question had her stopping in her tracks, turning to her desk, and feeling embarrassed for not asking that question before. She mentally called out to her, waiting a long moment.

Nothing.

"Maya!"

She was unable to contain her newfound strength. She needed an answer before she moved forward. Of all the times for something to come up and cause her to pause, of course, it had to happen at yet another ridiculously inconvenient time. She finally felt her spirit drift into the room despite not seeing anything yet. Then suddenly, the woman did appear, standing in front of the desk, facing her. The image of her made Claura pause. The woman was truly gorgeous. She had those hawklike eyes, the same as Roman's, that did not miss much. She secretly admired the two and feared for anyone who dared cross them, as they clearly held a higher intelligence than most people. She could sense now that Roman was downplaying it so often when around her and how this situation with Moira truly must be to the extreme with how clever these parents already were. Claura, in a way, felt relieved and less guilty for feeling only human still in all this, for this spell was clearly done by someone who did not lose their memory time and time again and was a master with her abilities.

"Claura, to help keep my daughter hidden all this time, it has waned my powers. I am simply no longer stronger than my sister, and I knew that time would come. I knew it might take a while for you to show. It is one of the reasons I chose to connect her to an omnipotent being. His strength is limitless in the way I need it to be."

"Why him, Maya?"

She looked frustrated with the woman despite knowing Maya was truly helping her at the same time. There were other omnipotent beings out there to choose from. Her face held confusion and heartbreak, clearly still not understanding how the distance between her and Daemon had affected her. Confusing the hardship for just everything else going on.

"More like *why you*, my dear."

"What do you mean?"

"You are Daemon's true Match. You have powers beyond what you even realize yet. I need that power to break this curse off my daughter."

"You knew I would find him."

"I made sure you would find him despite not knowing how long it would take. I am the one who made you feel a connection to anyone who had a connection to his bloodline and his species. Roman first, then Tronan, and then finally Daemon. Anything to get you here, where you belong."

"I see." She walked back over to the daybed to sit down, needing a moment. Her breathing started to feel rushed. "This is all so complicated."

"Yes. Moira loved games. That is all this is to her, another game. It is simply her best one yet, but with my family in the balance this time, I will not pause just because she is my sister." Her tone held an ancient authority as her intimidating gaze drifted over parts of the office.

"Please help me. Tell me what to do. I don't remember anything! It is so beyond frustrating this constant feeling of having my being within reach yet never being able to really reach out and grab all the pieces."

"This place is all those pieces."

"I don't have enough time to read this entire place!"
"The third book you need is not here, though."
"Where is it?"
"With Moira."
"Where is she?"

"In her realm, hovering over it. Knowing that if you got your hands on it, she'd be done with all her fun games. So do not fret about her coming here. She may visit you in your mind or appear as a vision, but know that is all she can do. A large part of my powers was used up that day to keep her out of this realm and Daemon's residence. But be careful still, as some of her connections may still cross over."

"How do I get there?"

"Daemon will not let you. It is obvious she will try to use you and then kill you if she feels she needs to." Her tone suggested this sister of hers was completely mad in being able to do such a thing, for a reason Claura could not put her finger on. Maya was clearly leaving something out with reason.

"But I have no choice, do I?"
"Roman will. He can send you."
"Sure about that?"

"We've already discussed it. He knows you are willing to do what it takes to help our little girl, who, by the way, needs a name." She inquired her head toward her as if to say she has had plenty of time. It was as if the little one deserved a name a long time ago. "I can't believe Daemon did not name her after all his time alone with her in that realm. He is truly a man of his word."

"At least pick a letter."
"A."
"Aiyana."
"Lovely." She smiled, seeing Claura look up at her questionably.
"Accepting so quickly."

"I trust the intuition you have. It has a certain...aura." She smiled at her, only for it to fade as she saw Claura get lost in thought while staring down at her hands again. "She reminds you of your late daughter, doesn't she?" Watching Claura started to shake a little.

Her eyes got watery, unable to face her still. Maya, in her spirit form, walked over to sit gently beside her, taking a moment to think of the consequences of telling her. She truly wondered if it would be better if Claura still came to a conclusion on her own if that would somehow make things remain in their favor. With spells, it was always better to let things unfold naturally. But she could sense that Claura was coming to the end of her rope already with everything. Perhaps she was losing her own strength in her own way after being reborn over and over. Maya spoke softly, clearly having made up her mind to risk it. "Claura, do you know why that is?"

"No goddamn clue."

"Would you like to know?"

Claura could tell the woman was being cautious and was uncertain if she should accept the answer with it being no matter how badly she wanted to know.

"May as well."

She glanced up at her then, eyes full of a lost dream at losing her own child.

"I did mention that you and I are related, but I think you misunderstood. We are not related just to the type of witch power we have, Claura. It is not like Daemon and Roman being related by having the same omnipotent blood. We are actually family, and Aiyana…she is your actual cousin."

# Chapter 21

# Brotherly Love

Tronan was done. Enough was enough. Claura could still tell him that she was safe and then get back to having her space. He waited, but he had hit his limit. He strode toward Daemon's office, clear intent in each stride after traveling back home to search for her there. Clearly desperate to look anywhere, only to find nothing. The smell of her on their sheets, through the entire home, drove him mad with worry. He hated that he needed to call on his brother for assistance in this, as Daemon had always owned more willpower in everything with the different realm he had simply been born from. It was a question that their parents never answered: Why could they not have just brought him into the world as well in the same realm? He could tell Daemon was in his office. His scent was full of frustration, among other emotions, that literally was making the entire section of the home smell of it. He rounded the corner to see him behind his desk, Roman holding the little one in one of the nearby lounge chairs, letting her small hand take the little toys from his much larger fingers. The love on the man's face was an image to remember even in the middle of such a moment of needing to find Claura. The two men looked up at him as he walked in and stood alongside the edge of the desk, placing himself between them both slightly.

"Help. Me. Find. Her." He growled, staring at Daemon, a part of him literally begging him to defy him in this, as he was upset beyond what he feared he wouldn't be able to control himself and needed somewhere to throw his rage. He glanced toward Roman for a split second, unable to miss the obvious expression of "Here we go." He watched his brother remain calm behind his desk, clearly unagitated by his mood.

"She simply needs space, brother. So I gave it to her."

"And you had that right?"

"More than you know."

He wiped his strong hand over his mouth before leaning his jaw in it. His head tilted as he eyed Tronan with a look of worry yet determination. He leaned back in his chair, clearly preparing himself while remaining relaxed. He knew Tronan would never truly be able to end him.

"Where is she!" he shouted with enough force to make it echo through the entire room, slamming his fist on the desk, leaving a huge dent in it. The crack was more deafening than expected from the large piece.

"Watch your fucking tone!" Daemon shouted, reacting instantly to match his younger brother's fury. He knew it was coming from his own emotions easily at already having to be distant from her again after not seeing her for 150 fucking years, only to sense where she finally was while Tronan was literally fucking her—his own damn brother. He stood suddenly, sending his chair slamming back against the wall, pointing at his younger brother like his fist preferred doing something else already.

"We should have never come here! I could feel it, and I ignored it!" Tronan shouted.

"I've seen you ignore a few things during your time with her already, so no surprise there. Soon enough, I would have brought her here anyway, with or without your acquiescence."

"I would have loved to see you fucking try!" He just stared at Daemon, clearly wanting to ring his neck already, shaking with trying to control himself. "And what the hell are you talking about? I have ignored nothing where it truly matters!"

"I saw it in her memories, that fucker Jayson," he said the name with such intense disgust. "And then you lost control with her yourself as if a true Match would be capable! I fucking saw it! I could kill you ten times over just for that alone!" Daemon was clearly so fucking furious beyond what he was even used to from himself. "I have already dug your grave for that one. Don't think I fucking haven't." His growl alone while he said it literally made the entire office feel like a war zone, the air thick with it.

Roman's eyes suddenly got sharper, clearly on Daemon's team for the moment with this fresh news. He could see into Claura's memories as well. He already knew who Jayson was from her files while his patient but did not have the ability to see as much as these other two men were capable of so casually. If he only knew…

He butted in, "Is this true, Tronan?" Roman asked. The man was clearly retracing his steps, dead set on examining his memories with Claura more closely. There was no response. He looked at Daemon. "What else?"

Daemon just kept glaring at his brother, trying to decipher if he did need to keep him alive for reasons he was starting to see in the eyes of the little one whenever she looked at Tronan specifically. He truly wished already if it was going to happen or not so he could decide either way what to do with his less omnipotent brother. He needed Claura to work her magic now literally more than ever.

"Did you notice, Tronan"—there was ice in his voice—"how with your blood in her system she reacted like it was natural and went through zero pain? As would be expected, she would suffer somewhat like a human would. Hmmm?"

"She has powers we did not know about. It must have had something to do with that. You know I would have taken on as much of her pain as I could if needed. It is exactly what I was planning on doing." He looked up and into his brother's fury more intently. "Obviously."

"Well, spare me, as I could have taken on all of it."

"Oh, fuck you!" There was a clear distaste for his reality of being born into a less powerful realm than Daemon was for such a circumstance being completely out of his control.

"Why else would she act the way she did in the car that night, having zero control over herself on top of you! Because something inside her, *not her*, was forcing it, you goddamn moron! And I saw the look on your face in her memories during your conversation over your little dining-out adventure. I saw you deep down know that you felt connected to 'something' about Claura, not Claura herself. So spare me the idiocy!"

"Enough! Make your goddamn point!" He knew his brother too well not to know when he was leaving something out still. Daemon's entire persona was engulfed with it.

Daemon knew he needed to just say the bottom line. He was just debating whether to have the baby removed from the room or not first. A small noise from her little mouth owned the quick silence between them. Daemon looked at her quickly, seeing the shock on her face, her eyes darting between them two as they shouted back and forth before her. The moment forced Tronan to look at her as well. The fear on her little face and how she looked worried for specifically him had him pause. Her eyes holding his were suddenly making it hard for him to look away as if he truly needed to reassure her before doing anything else. He watched Roman's hands curl more protectively around her little body atop his lap, clearly ready to leave with her any second. Her small hands were holding onto her daddy's forearm as if for security. Her little face was looking back at Tronan still as if begging him not to make it, so she had to be carried away right now. He inhaled deeply, inwardly trying to tell her to do the same, and to his amazement, she did. He saw the fear start to leave her expression somewhat and turned back to Daemon, seeing him studying the moment between them this entire time with no aim to interrupt. It was obvious Roman was watching it even more intently. For a long moment, none of them said anything.

Tronan looked at Daemon like he truly was determined to figure out how to kill him, that he just needed time to do so, and sauntered toward the balcony out of their view. Roman waited for Daemon to meet his gaze before clearly saying it with his eyes alone before speaking. "What just happened?" He clearly meant the bond his little girl was having with a certain other that was starting to make him wonder as well.

"I have the same suspicion. If Claura can just figure out how to sever this bond I already have with her, then I guess that would leave room to find out." Daemon sounded beyond determined for it to just happen already. He saw Roman close his eyes and lift one hand to cover his face with full-on frustration, truly trying not to lose it with his little girl being held with his other hand atop his lap.

"You fucking omnipotent beings need to get the hell out of my life. This is just…," Roman literally started to laugh to himself like a crazy person. "I can't fucking believe this may be happening."

"Until she is unbonded from me, we don't know for sure. So fucking relax. It's not like he clearly isn't fond of her either way already. I have been around your child for fifteen decades and have never made her laugh and smile the way my brother has in just the small amount of time he has been around her." He started to walk toward the balcony, preparing himself to lay the bottom line on Tronan and stopping for a brief moment as he walked by them. "So, Roman, brace yourself. And deal with it." He gave a quick but meaningful glance to the little one, knowing she would be able to perceive his expression of apology after all the time they had spent together. Her not being able to speak back meant nothing. Daemon and she had their own language, which obviously would happen. Despite him being stronger and able to know the difference between his bond with her versus his bond with his true Match, Tronan had the strength and knowledge to do so. He would always have a need to protect her, even after being together all this time. Daemon had Maya to clarify, and Tronan did not. Tronan had no clue that Claura was not truly meant for him this entire time. This was all a sick and twisted curse placed upon him, and he knew damn well Tronan was not going to be able to see it that way. For Claura's sake, he had to try anyway until she could return. With Maya being willing to help, it should not take much longer. He hoped with all his might anyway for that to be true. Who knew what else would fucking happen in the meantime.

Roman watched him leave from the corner of his eye, still mainly keeping his sights on his own daughter. He tried to wrap his head around the situation once again. "Your mama and I, we are going to have one hell of a chat." He gently poked her belly, making her look at him with those cute little dimples starting to rise. Her eyes were full of wonder. She just stared back at him as if to say she just wanted to be able to talk back already, no matter who she was bound to be with. It was clear to Roman at that moment that even this small child knew there were more important things to concern herself with than who her Match was. He suddenly realized that if anyone deserved to kill Moira, it was this little thing right here. As if on cue, she started to whine a bit, as if sensing where his thoughts led.

"Shhhh…we are working on ending her for good. You won't have to wait much longer." The determination in his tone, his sheer will to do whatever it took clearly all over his face, had her staring intently at him for a long time. Her crying ceased, and she started to look like she was lost in her own troubled thoughts as well, just staring back up at her daddy. He moved the tip of his index finger up and down her cheek, holding her protectively with his other hand still to keep her from falling off his lap, admiring the moment and admiring his daughter. He was still in awe that she was even alive.

Daemon strode onto the balcony, seeing Tronan with his hands on the edge, facing out into the landscape. "Just tell me where she is, Daemon. Please. I beg of you."

"She is trying to help you at this very moment. She thinks that ridding this bonding spell first will be the best way to prove anything to you, as it will sever false ties. Among all of us."

"What are you talking about, false ties? We are here to free your Match in there from her curse and nothing else."

"Tronan, look at me. I will not say this unless it is to your face." He watched him pause slightly before turning only his head enough to make eye contact. "She is Adera." The realization made Tronan's face grow pale, yet his eyes went dark. He turned fully then, the heartbreak beyond what Daemon was ready to see on his own brother's face, realizing at that moment that no amount of physical strength was going to ever hurt his brother more than what his words just did, not in a thousand years. "I have waited for over a century to see her again. Every time she is reincarnated, she loses her memory more, and the gap keeps increasing between her lifetimes. Maya made sure she made her way back to me to save her daughter, making it so she could sense me through anyone with my bloodline…with Roman, then with you. It is truly thanks to you both, being where you were, that she is back in my life. Again."

"You realize I am unable to believe you. I would die for her. I would kill for her. That whatever you are telling me means nothing and is going to change nothing."

"Moira, she did this. She owns the kind of power to make it feel so real."

"You can't prove that."

"No, but I think Claura can. And she's trying. We are still trying to unveil the true reasoning behind all this. Why would Moira make it so you and Claura would be Matched so intensely? It is to her benefit somehow." His tone suggested he couldn't wait to be rid of her, truly wanting to do it himself. He hated that despite all the powerful beings out there that would at least put up a hell of a fight for him, make it an actual challenge for a certain amount of time before he got bored, he was looking most forward to this one in particular. He could sense that something about ending Moira would end more than one curse. Daemon had been around too long not to have the intuition to see shit coming. It was just part of his constitution now, his actual fiber of being.

Tronan repeated the two words "she's trying" to himself, laughing in disbelief.

"Where is she? Just fucking tell me!"

His fury made him seem crazy, slamming his fist into the edge of the balcony, causing a section of the stone edge to start to crumble the surreal distance down. Daemon raised his chin and stayed glued to watching his every move even more intently, wanting him nowhere near Claura when like this. And despite himself, he made sure Tronan caught the thought.

"You fucking bastard." He looked at his older brother with pure loss, pure hatred. Tronan suddenly let himself fall backward, his despair taking hold of his entire being and refusing to stop it—his heart, his very reason for breathing…this whole time belonged to another.

Right at that moment, Roman all at once experienced the most high-pitched scream coming from his daughter, along with Claura trying frantically to reach him in his mind, literally yelling at him, "*Bring me back, now! Now*!" He wasted no time, clearly taken aback by it all and just reacting. He closed his eyes for only a second before needing to open them to see Claura striding across the room in a hurry that didn't seem possible for her size.

She turned the corner to see out onto the balcony, knowing from his thoughts what was going on and exactly where they were, as she tried to connect with Daemon first to bring her back. It was clear he was a little busy at that one moment. She needed him to help her return. She watched his solemn face turn toward her, followed by enormous black wings suddenly coming out of his back, spreading with a fury behind him as if they held a temper of their own for being hardly let out. He took one second to read her reaction before plunging over the side of the balcony toward Tronan. She ran to the edge to peer over, finding it hard to remember to breathe, hearing the baby still screaming in the background. The sounds she was making did not seem normal for coming out of such a small body. She watched as the brothers faded farther and farther away, the distance so far down it was hard to tell just how much time Tronan had left before he hit the ground. It was clear Daemon was gaining distance, but they became such a speck in the distance. It was hard to see if it was still going to be enough.

*Stop underestimating me, my dear.* His level of calm was concerning. *My wings have had some unwanted dust for some time.* He actually sounded almost like he was trying to be funny. She put her head down, leaning her forehead on her forearm, inwardly praying. The need for it was strong no matter how calm this man sounded in her head still, choosing to completely brush off his need for slight comic relief as now was not the time for Tronan's sake alone—for Aiyana's sake.

She looked back to the room, seeing Roman looking like he was having a hell of a time trying to calm her down. His eyes met hers, and she knew he knew. Roman always just knew. The man would be dead before he was even one step behind on something. She could tell he was not happy about it, that it made no sense as Tronan was part of the reason she was under this curse in the first place. Maybe that was the loophole Moira needed. She needed Tronan to pause that day…and only Tronan. Maybe it wasn't Claura at all who could break the curse, but this entire time, Tronan actually could. Her mind was already trying to figure out how to do it for him.

"That fucking clever witch bitch," she said low to herself.

She was unable to hide the look of hate on her face as her thoughts were going in a dozen different directions now, all of them including ideas about Moira and how to end her, along with everything she had caused. She noticed Daemon seeing it clear on her face as he came swooping over the balcony, brother in tow. He let Tronan's body fall on the hard stone, uncaring to be gentle. In his own way, he was furious at the stupid decision—furious at his brother for not being stronger, for not giving them enough time to state what everyone was starting to see. Daemon was pissed, for he knew if his brother was the true Match for that baby, truly was, then he almost condemned her to a lifetime of destitution in all forms that the heart and soul would recognize within their species.

She watched as Daemon's wings disappeared behind him, the action not bothering him in the slightest, which, with their size, was alarming to her. They closed up and vanished into the area between his shoulder blades at an impressive speed, completely disappearing as if never had been. She saw his smirk come through his anger as he turned his eyes from Tronan on the ground to her. *You already know of my alarming size, my love.* She held her hand out as if to say his timing was ridiculously off, and she was not in the mood, hearing his manly laughter in her mind at her reaction. She felt herself blushing and hated it. She turned her gaze away to see Roman returning from stepping inside the room, noticing the baby was not in hand anymore, and her cries silenced. She watched him stride with a calm yet determined fury to lift Tronan by the neck and slam him against the nearest stone wall.

"I wish I could kill you because if it weren't for certain circumstances, you'd already be buried," Roman growled in his face.

"Go on," Tronan said, spitting it out.

The action caused Roman to seethe further, grasping Tronan's esophagus with both strong hands now and slamming his head back into the stone wall hard enough for pieces to come falling down all around him. He watched as Tronan glanced at Claura, the intense look of heartbreak making Roman pause. He knew this was Moira's doing and that she should be the one under his grasp right now. He let go with one hand at least and turned to Claura, as if to say get a move on with it. She looked at him as if truly wondering how the hell he already knew but figured Maya might have just made it known to him already. Stupid not to assume so, as this was all revolving around their own damn child. She hurriedly pulled the book from her side coat pocket and flipped to the page.

Blank.

"Dammit!" She looked back up to Roman, seeing the lack of patience begin on his face. She reached into her other pocket for her phone and headphones. She saw them all look at her a little ridiculously. "Like this is my choice!" She did not dare to look at Daemon, already knowing his wry expression. "Takes two seconds, just hold on…"

"Really, Claura? Are you kidding me?"

Roman was at a loss of what to think of her need for music all of a sudden.

"Yes, Roman! The pages stay blank, as you know. Music makes shit appear apparently, as I now know." She stayed glued to his expression, seeing him figure something out. "What?"

"My Maya." He clearly sounded proud of her, turning his attention back to Tronan, tightening his grip with pleasure. "Moira hates music. Vigorously."

Her eyes suddenly turned toward Tronan's, feeling his gaze. "Claura, please don't." She felt Daemon stepped closer to her, causing more fury to rise in Tronan's eyes at the small gesture of reassurance. "You won't get us back, Claura. This could be a trick. And there isn't any undoing it." She knew those words would linger in her head for a long time.

"I love you enough to do this for you. So please…" She started to cry, finding it hard to hold herself together. It was becoming obvious that this was going to get harder with each line, the curse trying to cling to being alive in its own way. "Can you hold him, Roman?" She hated herself for not being able to look into Tronan's face as she asked it, feeling like such a coward. She saw him nod while still facing him, keeping an even closer eye on the man under his grasp, knowing some serious changes were about to start happening and not wanting to miss a thing.

*You are the farthest thing from a coward right now, my love. Just get it over with. For his own sake.* He touched the low of her back now, needing the connection. He felt her reach behind to grasp his hand while her other one stayed steady, holding the book open. *I will knock him out if I have to. Just say the words. Unbind the false ties. Now.*

She looked at Daemon and shook her head, her face getting even more full of worry. He clearly meant he had to stay awake for this to work. She watched Daemon inwardly swear and step to place himself semi in front of her now, clearly up for the challenge physically but not mentally. She sure wasn't up for this at all emotionally. She started to read the words on the page, the unbinding spell. Feeling it started something within her immediately. She saw the same reaction in the brothers while it had zero effect on Roman. She made her feel like she was going in the right direction and to just keep going. She felt the sisters try to invade her mind—support from

Maya and anger from Moira. For some reason, Maya felt closer. She simply reminded herself of the spell for the courage she came across earlier at the beginning of the book before she needed music at all, feeling it giving her strength at just the thought of it. It comforted beyond sudden as if she wrote it herself.

She saw Daemon step in front of her fully now, intentionally blocking her view of his brother, knowing the look on his face would make it beyond hard for her. She was already having a hard time getting the words out through her tears, as if that was the main intended way to get her to stop saying the words on the pages. As if it was the spells last resort to win. Suddenly, her eyes started holding a green glow, her cries no more, and her stance was still as stone. Daemon turned to her with a look of concern yet more for what it could mean than worry. He knew of her power being like this in the past, but it was never this soon. It never happened before until she was at least fifty years of age and into her next lifetime with him, having time first to learn more about who and what she really was and do it all at her own pace. They learned lifetimes ago that bombarding her with information did actually just make things worse whenever she returned.

He looked back at Tronan, knowing something was different. No matter how much he suffered in trying to fight what was happening, he was just not going to win. Not by a long shot. He could hear Claura coming to an end just by her tone, hearing her do spells hundreds of times, all too familiar with her timing. He watched Roman drop him to the ground, his body being slammed against the balcony's rock floor once again. Roman made it known from the first possible moment who would be in charge here with his daughter's future in the balance, omnipotent being or not, Match to his baby girl or not. They all stared down at him, waiting for his reaction. Claura started walking toward him, feeling Daemon's energy clearly disliking the action, yet he did not stop her. She could feel him simply become more alert. She leaned down to place her hand over Tronan's cheek. She could see him struggling to come to the surface, his eyes fighting to open.

"Tronan?" she said it through tears, yet like she was full of hope for him. "Baby, please?"

It was a mere whisper, wiping her tears with her other hand, it being evident she would always remember their connection. Her heart broke at the feeling of it being severed. It was obvious by the way she still looked at him that she would need time to grieve it all. The more she thought about it, the more it just made her hate Moira for causing it in the first place. She knew Maya would want her connected to them all to help her find her way back to Daemon, but she knew she would never take it this far. This was just cruel. This was pure Moira pulling her strings for her own selfish reasons, treating their hearts like little puppet toys. She inwardly swore, knowing she couldn't wait to return the favor somehow. She heard Aiyana cry, and immediately, his eyes popped open. Knowing he was truly lost to her now, that the undoing of the spell had worked, as he was fully focused on the direction of the small noise and not her leaning down right in front of him. So close to his face still, needing to make sure he was okay.

She simply nodded, more so to herself, and stood up to back away from him. The feeling of knowing she would never have a real reason to be that close to him again suddenly took hold. She kept moving back until she felt the other edge of the balcony against her sacrum, resting her palms on it beside her hips and looking down toward the ground, taking a deep breath with a new determination on her face. The part of her coming to the surface more now was just the notion of succeeding. She felt Daemon smile in her mind, still remaining a few yards away, seeing that she needed a moment.

"You do this every time, my love. Underestimate both of us. Do not let it get to you so," Daemon said to her, his voice full of love and conviction.

"I can't believe I just did that. I can feel it already. Like my heart is more free." She looked up at him, seeing him gently nod, looking so proud of her. She clearly felt the same way. "You should check on her. Make sure she is okay in all of this too."

"I can hear her steady heartbeat. She is fine and in good company," he answered her gently, seeing her shock at having real powers and putting them to use for the first time once again.

He started walking toward her, his body in no hurry, his eyes the complete opposite. She saw his hands reach out to hold her face gently between them, his wings suddenly and loudly taking hold behind him, the sound making her slightly jump. Their eyes met for a short moment before he forced her mouth to his. She could feel the difference in their connection now, as if the thread between them was truly now free of some extensive burden that had been weighing it down and eating away at it.

"Now this is how I have been burning to feel you. I know you can feel it too." He forced her mouth back to his, letting his hands move lower to cradle and hold her between his strong arms. She felt her feet start to lift off the stone floor. She opened her eyes wider, looking around, looking scared of heights all of a sudden. "Calm yourself."

"I just saw how far you flew to get Tronan. I don't think I can handle even half that distance. This is crazy, Daemon!"

"I always loved this part." She felt his mouth smile against hers. His arms tightened a bit more. The realization sank in on her face as she looked back at him with such uncertainty.

"Daemon! No!"

He lifted her into the air in an upward direction first, clearly not wanting her to feel like she was falling toward the ground. Not yet, anyway. She clung to him the way a cat did on the way to the bathtub. Then as he aimed them downward, letting the speed naturally pick up with gravity, she now clung like a cat inside the bathtub.

"I would never let go. You are safe." It took longer than normal for her to relax into his body, but it came. She always did.

"The wind, Daemon! I can't see."

She felt his wings started to widen to slow their speed until he had them literally hovering in the air. She looked over his shoulder, seeing the enormous home, noticing they were halfway to the bottom. She glanced down at the area where Tronan almost just made contact, knowing he saw the concern from the memory all over her face. She felt his one arm move to turn her face to his with his fingers, his other arm having no need to grip tighter to make up for the difference. He simply shook his head no that it would never have happened with him around, needing her to know she worried needlessly. She suddenly got a look of complete trust in him on her face, slightly pushed at his chest to look at him better, and smiled. She saw him shake his head no again for a different reason now.

"I will not," he said sternly, tightening his arms around her more. Letting her really feel his strength.

"Let. Me. Go." She dared him to do it, to prove to her she could trust his speed—this particular ability, really trust it. A part of her wanted to feel the fear Tronan felt. She needed it to help wash away some of her guilt. She expected him to fight her on this…only for the opposite to happen at the realization of the reasoning behind her wishes. He truly caught every corner of her every thought. He felt her grasp on him slip away, signifying her readiness. He leaned forward to kiss her nose, took a deeper-than-usual breath as if preparing himself, and let go. He heard her scream as she fell toward the ground, loving the sound of it, yet his heart dropped all the same at the sight below him. He heard her heart rate increase with every second and decided to still give it another moment, seeing her start to panic. She did say she needed to know she could trust him. He intended to prove it, counting down to himself under his breath.

"Four…three…two…one." He could feel his wings welcome the challenge as if they had a craving for it for so long and were determined in their own right to do this. He moved like the lightning he was born with, doing this since he was a young teen. One moment, Claura saw him still staying where he was above her, followed by a one-second blur, and next, him coming out of nowhere from her right, lifting her back up into the sky, way past the top floor of the palace now, uncaring to accommodate his speed to her feelings anymore. He felt her laugh underneath his arms like a silly little schoolgirl, unable to contain herself, knowing she sounded absolutely ridiculous yet not caring, savoring the turn of events for them both.

"Again! Ahh! Again!" she yelled with excitement.

She pounded his chest with her small hands, leaning away from him, clearly ready, bouncing in his arms with exhilaration, looking all around them and below them again. There was a look of awe and disbelief all over her face at how high up they were. She suddenly started feeling embarrassed of her actions and covered her mouth as if trying not to laugh, her eyes holding a sorry behind the smirk as she faced him. She felt him reach up to grasp the back of her neck, followed by his other arm completely letting go, moving it to relax at his side. She noticed how no pain was coming from the distinct grip as he held her away from him, in front of him, letting a decent enough gap remain between their bodies, holding her there in midair by his fingers alone, so high above the ground. He studied her, waiting for her laughter to come through her fear once again—her trust to take note in her eyes. She tried to fight it, but he didn't miss the small curve of her lips. Her trust was clearly not an issue. His eyes full of concern were bountiful mixed with his wicked grin, the rare expression alone making her toes curl. The strong, intense eyes of her beloved held her in midair high enough to feel the clouds between her fingers if she reached out toward them. She could tell that as soon as she couldn't hold in her laugh anymore, he would let go. He gave her a deadly smile, one full of compassion yet possessiveness, daring her not to keep it together.

"Daemon...." She smirked, closing her eyes against his stare, thinking somehow that would hide the excited smirk on the rest of her face.

She felt herself drop, again. This time, she was less afraid to really scream, meaning to just enjoy it, knowing she was much higher up this time as well. She scanned around her as she let herself fall, feeling her hair float around her face, the soothing cool breeze between her fingers, catching a glimpse of some bodies on a certain level before falling fast past them. Daemon started to move, rushing past her to move below her, not missing the glare from Roman on his way by. It was evident he was not happy, as Claura was still beyond needed to break Moira's curse after breaking Maya's bonding spell. Daemon took note but continued on as if he couldn't fucking care less what Roman wanted right now. His focus was clearly elsewhere, on someone he had been missing for 150 years.

Claura felt him envelope her from behind and underneath, her mind fully enjoying the stars above as the sunset took hold. Pure joy took her over at being halfway there and fulfilling what she needed to do. Not expecting it to be so soon. The part with Maya would obviously be easier. She wanted to help.

*This other bitch…*

She felt his arms tighten as he clearly needed to hang on to her differently while guiding his body to catch her from behind and keep them both soaring smoothly backward, following where her eyes looked for a brief moment, enjoying the feeling of free falling, kissing her temple while holding her against him. He felt the ground come closer and flipped them so he was on top, his back to the sky, her enfolded in his arms, facing the same direction. He took them soaring around the home before landing on a different stone balcony. She looked through the window and noticed the sheets still left as they were, slightly smiling. She was inwardly nervous at how it would be different with him now. She was scared of the unknown, despite it being obvious it would be beyond enjoyable—pleasurable. She chewed on her lower lip without knowing of the small gesture, her eyes making it obvious it was unconsciously done as she turned around to look up into his face. She suddenly looked shy, reserved, and timid. It warmed his insides really how she still reacted to him this way. He loved seeing that look on her face because he loved even more how he knew to perfectly make it fade into something else.

"I want to return to my realm, with you. Please come back with me," she said softly, feeling like she was still catching her breath from free falling.

She reached up to place her soft, delicate hands over his chest, her thumbs caressing his sternum. She separated his shirt where it was already unbuttoned slightly on top, the constant slight tease of what was underneath being something she ongoingly loved whenever he was around. She looked at her hands, watching their exploration, feeling her mouth water. She knew she'd never get over how perfectly shaped this man was, how his body owned her thoughts more than she liked to admit. The noise coming from his throat as he watched her made her gaze jump back to his. She watched him lean down, his face nice and close to hers, and whispered to her.

"I will have you. Now," he said sweetly.

He said it with intention. He said it almost like he was apologizing for something. She looked at him with confusion in her eyes, clearly reading him so well. "I was not with genuine discipline last time. As I have been waiting for so long for you to return." He nibbled her lips, his energy alone making her knees feel rubbery. "I am ashamed I did not handle you…differently."

"I'm not."

"Don't lie to me, please."

"I. Am. Not."

"I saw it on your face."

"The fear fed the flames, my love."

"I never want you to fear me."

"Somehow, it is just another reason why I love you. I do fear you, Daemon," she said it bluntly, meaning to push buttons. She lifted her arms to take her shirt off, tossing it to the side as if annoyed intensely with it. "And I enjoy it." Her face was as serious as it could be, yet her entire demeanor was calm.

"You will be the death of me."

"Just like you have been the death of me, over and over and—"

"Shut up!" he snapped, as if it was easy for him to deal with it more than once. His mind was already on other things of complete opposition to such a dark topic. He picked her up and aimed for the bed, using his mind alone to make the wall vanish for the one second they needed to pass through, uncaring to waste time walking the long way around just to use the door. The feeling caused a cold sensation, as if feeling a ghost walk through you, making her shiver and making her grasp him even closer in response. He moved her in his arms to flip her and toss her onto the bed on her belly, taking a moment to remove his belt the old-fashioned way, enjoying the sight of her bare ass on the bed already. He saw her lean slightly on her elbows and glance back at him.

"Not fair." Her eyes were pure scold, pure fire.

# THE WINGED WITCH OF MATCHES

"There are many things about me, my dear, that are not fair." He said it like he would gladly use the advantage however he damn well pleased, especially with her. His tone made her heart rate pick up a little bit. "But tonight, I will not cave to what I know you are trying to do." She watched as his ridiculously perfect body moved atop her, crawling over her, coming closer until his breath was on her face again, so close to her lips. "You will be caving to me tonight." He took a moment to savor her reaction, enjoying her suddenly looking nervous, as he knew he was about to do nothing but make her body feel utmost pleasure. He wanted to make her feel the way he did their first time, as no other time had been so damn perfect. He placed his arm underneath her, forcing her to flip over and face him, gently moving his fingers through her hair with his left hand before perfectly accommodating her head in his grasp, forcing her mouth to stay close to his as his body settled closer.

"I expect results." She watched him look over her body with such devotion, obsession, and desire—ownership. She saw him take his time to glance back into her eyes at her comment, his worry appearing none, almost making her regret saying it. She felt silly about it. He was clearly not a being who was worried about owning skills. He chose not to say anything, not a word, and that frightened her even more than a stern comeback. He simply looked beyond determined and focused now, so sure of himself with her under his hands. It brought to mind just how well he must know her body, how she had no clue how many times they've—

"You have been mine for 1,700 years, give or take," he answered for her.

"How silly of me to worry about results than."

His deep and slightly aggressive manly laugh said it all. The way his hands moved over her said it all. She felt him pull her closer, growling slightly as he did it, clearly oblivious to it as he was already so focused. Something beyond primal and ancient was coming off him in waves. She could tell he felt her stiffen but was choosing not to want to be bothered by it, choosing to stay in whatever frame of mind he was now in atop of her, knowing she'd just relax and melt into him soon enough.

"I feel more scared this time, don't I?"

"You think I don't know? I can feel you trembling. Hear your heart racing. Your emotions are literally thick in the air." She felt his two larger fingers enter her, his thumb caressing her clit, moving like silk in slow motion, clearly meaning to take as much time as he wanted. She could feel him watching her face as her head tilted back with the already building sensations. "You are more sensitive this time." He continued to eye her intently, seeing how she already couldn't get the words out if she wanted to respond. Her climax was already building in seconds. "In your own way, you have always held the most challenge for me, sweetheart."

"How so?" She was secretly appreciative of needing only the two words.

"You make an omnipotent being have to test his own control."

"You make me sound so powerful as I lay here already feeling so weak." She was clearly beyond happy with the first five minutes here. She was not being able to wrap her head around the next few hours until sunrise, as he clearly had that intention in his mind.

"Now would be a good time to call on some of that witch strength, as I am far from done with you," he said, kissing her neck, loving her soft moans between her words so close to his ear.

"Why not just give me more of your blood?"

It came to mind how she actually had more blood from the wrong brother lingering in her veins. She felt him stiffen and not in the way she preferred while lying under his dominating frame. His body was so warm and perfect atop her, yet the energy around it felt cold now.

"You truly believe you have been given only one drop from me?" He paused his original intentions with grueling difficulty, forcing her to look into his eyes. He was trying to hide the hurt in his tone. After all, sometimes, it did hurt at what she did not remember. He truly wished she used that ring more.

"I am sorry." She knew his thoughts just by his tone, his expression. She was being sick of it herself already—their circumstances. Her voice was breaking, as her heart slightly was at how she felt she was disappointing him.

"You never disappoint me. I never want you to believe that."

"I don't know what to believe about so much still, even after finding you. Even after ridding the false ties just now." She started to put her hands through his hair, her fingers getting slightly more aggressive as her tears began. "I know I have probably asked this before more than once. But, Daemon, please help me." The way she begged so softly made his insides melt. She watched as he gently took her hand, placing his lips against her palm. His eyes closed, and he deep inhaled as if savoring her scent to help himself think.

"We will go to your realm tomorrow. I will help you understand so much more. I promise." Her face was full of tears as she looked back up at him with such sorrow and a feeling of overwhelm. "Right now, I want you to feel as you did the first time I had you beneath me. Trust me in this. You will see."

"I will see?"

He just eyed her with complete adoration, authority, and masculinity. Moving slowly over her in a way that let her know what was coming. She could feel the connection between them being different now—more loving, more full, more pure. She could also feel herself slightly slipping into a dream state as if given the perfect drug, made just for her. His hands on her body suddenly felt even more sensorial, his mouth on her the most pleasurable thing she'd ever experienced. It was as if every sensation was gently climaxing in its own way wherever he touched her body. Then she felt him press against her entrance, her body reacting startled despite her mind seeing it coming. Just the feel of his tip alone, his body was such an invasion for her insides. He watched her flat tummy and hips move in the way that they did, the way that he loved, as he so slowly moved deeper. Her noises in response were the only sound in the large bedroom. It was the only damn sound he wanted to hear. It was the only sound he heard for the rest of the night.

# CHAPTER 22

# A Touch Overdue

*Earlier...*

Maya heard her daughter's wail from afar and instantly knew it was time. She had remained in Claura's office alone after watching her leave first, giving her firm instructions as quickly as she could as they both felt the stir inside them of what was happening from afar. She knew from the panic on Claura's face that she had only seconds to explain how the spell would work, then that turned into only one second of useful time as soon as she saw that Roman was being contacted to bring Claura back to Daemon's realm. She was proud of his ability, yet in this instant, it was just somewhat of a trial to have to race against. She gave it a few moments before appearing herself in spirit form amid the quandary. She had full faith that they would all simply figure it out, knowing they all were intertwined to be here by destiny already, and she was no one to play with that. Only her sister thought she was powerful and entitled enough to play with that, apparently.

Her heart reached out for how Roman had to deal with their daughter at the moment, hearing her screams of desperation come closer as she appeared in the office, simply waiting for the others to be out on the balcony first. A part of her was under control at simply knowing this all meant that her baby was finally so close to being able to be connected to her true Match, deep down knowing that no matter how hard Moira tried to confuse the ties between them all, simply to still feel in control, this unbinding spell would work just fine. She simply needed Claura to do it, and she feared telling her the real truth about why. She truly wondered if she would even believe her, for Moira still might play her games and never care to tell her herself. She literally did anything to remain the one with more power. It was only a matter of time, though. Maya was just at a loss as to how it was going to be possible to play out still.

She saw Roman notice her appear in the room, Aiyana in his arms. He looked up at her with such intense irritation and borderline defeat. She simply gave a small smile, clearly full of worry yet hope for her little one, seeing her upset on many occasions before. She knew that despite Roman not being used to it, it just didn't matter as this time it was beyond different anyway. Despite Roman not liking Tronan, she knew that the man was the key to their daughter's happiness. And she could sense her little heart calm down slightly at the sound of Daemon letting Tronan land hard on the stone balcony around the corner not far away. With their connection, even before the unbinding spell that would disconnect her from Daemon, she could still feel what lay underneath—the truth.

She was clearly not going to be a force to be reckoned with as a full-on adult witch. She watched as Roman rubbed his hand over his forehead, clearly taken aback by the moment, inwardly thankful she was calming down despite it not being because of him. She could tell it only made him hate the man more. He wanted to be there for his daughter more than anything after being gone for so long already. She would always hate herself for having to do that to him to keep the spell strong.

Balance.

Give and take.

Every spell of worth had it.

Witch life was not easy.

She gestured for him to put her in the bassinet, as she wasn't able to hold her in her spirit form. She watched as his strong hands gently lay her down, feeling the relief radiate off him in waves, watching how her little face relaxed a little more at the sight of her mommy looking down at her. Roman did a few paces, looking like he wanted to smash something. The fact that they were both still even alive after all this time still left him in shock on some level. Yet here she was, so close, and he still couldn't reach out and touch her. The fact of it made his frustration boil over.

"My Roman, I know you don't see it right now. But this is a good day."

"Your ability to remain focused has always far outmatched mine."

"I am not happy with him either. He will know that." Her tone clearly suggested she would need his help in this matter in the meantime, as she was not able to do much in only spirit form to him right now. She wanted Roman to do it anyway. He deserved to let off some steam with everything he's been through in this whole situation.

"Roman, I can feel your anger clouding your judgment, and I know that is far from like you. Our baby has been under a spell for fifteen decades to keep her alive. The man that she is truly Matched to almost just killed himself, meaning he almost left her to a lifetime of dissolution and loneliness." She watched his eyes lower to the floor as if not wanting her to read his expression for a moment, his insides literally seething. He could hear her voice get full of absolute distaste by the syllable. It was not like Maya to not be in control of her anger. "I have done so much to keep this spell alive to save her! And he almost just killed her by killing himself when we literally and finally have the unbinding spell ready to be spoken! She would not have survived it, not after meeting him and the bond already starting."

"I wish I could kill him." And he meant it. He sounded like he was still contemplating it slightly. "There is truly no way to bond her to someone else?" He looked at her with utmost determination, tired of this feeling.

"It will never be hundred percent. What is happening here is proof of that already. I am beyond lucky this spell to save her has worked as it did."

"I know."

"It is time. Claura needs you out there. I have borrowed enough power so you can hold him." She watched his eyes slightly soften, it being obvious he was proud of her for acting like such a mama bear. He moved to stand closer, staring into her face with his now too-familiar expression of just needing to be able to actually hold her already.

"I never would have imagined that it was Claura who was the answer to getting you back into my arms someday." He admitted to her gently, his eyes showing slight remorse for having feelings for Claura when Maya was still alive this whole time.

"It took me so much longer than you realize"—her expression showing true discipline of what it took from her—"only to see that it would never happen. I never was able to get used to not being able to talk to you. My heart broke every day." She watched his hand raise to caress her cheek, knowing it would only pass through as it would with a ghost. She saw the hate in his eyes over not even being able to touch her, even in the smallest of ways, yet again.

"This is to never happen again, Maya. Do you understand me? We are ending this." He watched her nod, close her eyes, and take a deep breath. The gesture gave him comfort in knowing she still needed to do that, that she still did have an actual body somewhere. And he was beyond insanity with needing to feel it beneath him.

He followed her lead by looking down at the little form next to them. Hearing her talk softly to her as he walked over toward the balcony, his body of its own would need to feel Roman's neck beneath his hands immediately.

*****

"I see why you don't hate my lost memory so much. I can't believe…" She looked up at Daemon in wonderment, really not knowing what words to reach for.

"I did it with you during our first time. I was determined to do anything in my power to make you mine. Make you want me in return."

"Did you truly have to fear that I would not want you?" She looked startled about it.

"I feared your fear. Of me."

"What do you mean?"

"As soon as you learned what I truly was, you became timid toward me. You were still very young, still learning of your own powers. It only made sense that my powers would still frighten you." He looked at her face, feeling her small body curl even closer to his between the sheets. "You have no idea how happy I was to learn that I am still the only one who has given you such experience." He gently pulled her chin toward him to kiss her, which meant the obvious that he and his brother shared the same gift.

"So here we are, around 1,700 years later, it feeling like the first time for me again." She lightly scoffed at how crazy things were turning out to be still. "I am starting to feel like trying to catch up on my past is what is actually holding me back, maybe."

"How so?"

"I don't know. If I'm looking backward every time I arrive again, then that's distracting me from the more future I could have. I mean, that library is endless. I can already tell it would be beyond easy to spend so many lifetimes there just reading. And I can already sense the books are calling my name, thousands of them just from being in the building once. Maybe there is something I am missing." She felt his hand caress her hair, leisurely enjoying himself, and decided to risk it. "I don't want to do this anymore." She felt him stiffen next to her, invading her mind for more details immediately. "This needs to stop." She felt him sit up straighter, bringing her with him, putting some slight space between them to really be able to face her.

"Don't even think it—"

"I mean it." He eyes were getting watery.

# THE WINGED WITCH OF MATCHES

"Stop!"

"Please! Listen to me!" Her eyes were officially pooling.

"I will never let it happen!"

"I am tired! I am feeling so tired, Daemon! I can feel it getting to that point." Her eyes were officially a fucking river.

"I cannot—I will not live without you. Don't you say it!"

"Goddamn it, just let me explain!"

"Don't you fucking say it!"

She jumped from the bed, reaching for her robe, shaking hands and having a ridiculously hard time tying what was the easiest wardrobe tie in all history as she would know. "It is different this time! I have to stop being reborn. My memory is so far gone to where I don't even remember you at all! To where I don't even know who the fuck you are until I hopefully come across you!" She saw him come near her, pointing his finger, starting to shout as well again and interrupted him. "That is no longer good enough for me! 'Hopefully' is not good enough!"

"Claura, stop this! We have tried so much before already. There is no other way."

"There has to fucking be! Don't you want there to be?"

"Baby, please, I just got you back. Don't do this so soon. I'm begging you, sweetheart." He took her small hands in his, not even liking it when she jumped away from him just now on the bed, let alone being done with being reincarnated.

"How did you find me before, in the beginning?"

"I sensed your first thought and instantly knew where you were."

She threw her hands in the air as if to say, "You see!" She clearly meant to prove her point of how this has gone downhill too far for them both. This spell was simply not going to cut it anymore, not for her. "I am not doing us justice if I can't figure this out. What kind of witch am I if I can't even better my own goddamn spell?" She watched him sigh, clearly uncertain as to state or not what he was thinking. Some deep part of him regretted bringing him up and was unable to recall why.

"What?"

"You shared in doing the spell," he finally said.
"With who?"
"My father."
"Why him?"
"His level of power succored yours."
"Who can't help me as he is dead now."
"Long gone."
"Who is like him that would help?"

He gave a big sigh again, not wanting to share. "The one who helped Moira."

"Let's fucking go then…shall we?"

"He won't help us. Conroy was an enemy of my father."

"Exactly, your father. Not us. Let's go."

"Claura, wait."

"Just say it, please!"

"In order to get to him, you have to pass through Moira's realm. They are intertwined in a way. There used to be a messenger you could use to do it for you, like a realm mailman. Unfortunately, they are no more."

"A fucking realm mailman? Are you kidding me?" She was unable to control her small laugh.

"That came out wrong."

"It's fine. I have to get a book while there anyway."

"I'm sorry, what?" His reaction made her fear of him creep back in just a tad. His head slightly tilted as if in utter disbelief while waiting for her to actually repeat what she just voiced. His degree of deterrence was on a level only Daemon knew how to express.

"Oh ya, you weren't supposed to know."

An *oops* owning her entire face. His expression got less unhappy by the second.

"Do fucking tell." He made her back up subconsciously with how he was walking toward her now mixed with the heartbroken glare on his face.

"The first book Maya gave me and the second book from my realm that I already have back in my office is for the bonding spell and the curse on the baby. This third book I need is in Moira's realm in her safekeeping. I need it to destroy her. According to Maya."

"I think Maya should return fully and go get the damn book herself."

"She made it sound like I would be fine if I just learned a few more things first."

"Oh, did she? Well, I can tell you right now, my darling, the answer is no."

"Why? Don't fucking baby me, Daemon!"

"Witches are a hundred times more powerful when in their own realm. That's why!"

"Roman will send me."

"I'd love to see him try."

"Good, let's go!"

He used his little speed trick to close the distance between them and hastily reached out for her, grabbed her arms, and held her tighter than intended, laughing in utter disbelief at the buttons she was so okay with pushing right now. The seriousness of her actually wanting to go through with all this set his fear to a whole new level.

"What started this, truly?" He needed to know, for he could not find it in her mind no matter how hard he searched. Her mind blocks were getting incredibly better, or she was just getting good at keeping him distracted whenever he invaded her thoughts. Not knowing the difference concerned him. Little by little, things were happening like that with her in this lifetime, this particular contrasting one. He hated how much his gut was telling him that things were never going to be the same this time around with her. And he missed her. He just missed her. He just wanted to enjoy their time together. A deep part of Daemon was begging for just a simple life together, enjoying one another. Yet the more he was around her this time, the more the opposite was clearly going to take place. He held her before him, waiting for her answer. He confirmed his own conflicting thoughts that things were just going to be complicated this time, no matter how much he wanted none of it.

"It feels like my spirit is dying," she said finally. She took a moment coming, but they did, tears at having to say it out loud, at acknowledging it, at admitting it to him, the one person she did not want to have to say it to or leave, ever. "If the spell is obviously getting so much worse every time, then I want no part of it anymore. It's not good enough." She pulled back from him and put her hands up, crossing back and forth with them as if to say she was truly done and determined to move on, one way or another. Just something about this spell and all this borrowed time no longer felt right.

"The answer…is *no*."

"We have had so much more time than other people get to have. Has it truly not been enough? Don't you see it's only getting worse for us? It's getting harder for us to find one another for a reason! And you know it!"

She watched him move one step closer, lean into her face nice and close in that perfect way that he did. "My darling, is this a postpartum episode?" he asked with concern, yet his tone still held too much of a cliché curiosity for her liking.

The anger inside her literally took a moment to come on, as if needing to be brought to a boil first in its own way before being useful. She pulled her hands away from his, stepped back, and cuffed him as hard as she could. She was profoundly proud of the cracking sound she caused as his whole face turned farther than she expected from a hit with just her small hand, yet her heart ached for not being able to control herself due to the look she could decipher from at least half of his face. She felt zero pain, causing her to look down at her hand in wonder, seeing a small green light flickering in her palm. A little mini northern lights show, looking very similar to the only other time she had seen such a thing—in this lifetime, anyway, as usual.

*Fucking memory.*

She was truly beyond done with this shit of forgetting who she was and everything about her. It was not fair. Whether he took her little ass seriously or not with this, she was not changing her damn mind. She looked up to see him eyeing her now, his failed poker face of confusion and anger, yet still a concern. Despite no memory for her this time, she knew deep down in her bones it was the first time

# THE WINGED WITCH OF MATCHES

she ever really hit him by the look on his face. In all distraction, she raises her hand to let him see her little finding as well.

"I think I know who my mom is." She says.

"With your witch bloodline, it's possible many of you have this gift," he said like he really preferred she didn't get ahead of herself here. His eyes tried to simmer down a fire within him, looking at her like she was being foolish for trying to change the subject. He clearly wanted to discuss something still.

He watched her slowly shake her head no as if she was just already being answered by her own inner witch intuition once again. "Maya said that Aiyana is my cousin."

"Who is Aiyana?" Daemon asked, clearly unknowing still of her finally being named.

"Your little ex Match, my darling."

His stare, his entire energy really, was fully belligerent. Yet she could see his mind working at a whole new pace. Her face was an expression of wanting to say sorry, yet she still chose not to. And he understood. Right now, she needed him to take her seriously, and he threw her dignity under the bus. He was ashamed of himself yet did not know what to do for her with the news of this third book now. Its location was beyond ill-suited yet obviously expected. "I want to go back to my realm. Right now, Daemon."

"You know this is always just as much your home as well." He remained in place, unsure of so much suddenly. She stepped closer to him again, lifting her hands to palm his face between them.

"I know." She just wanted to say sorry without really saying sorry because she fully wasn't. He hurt her. For all the people to not take her seriously, it was not just a wound from Daemon doing it; it was an instant scar. He put one hand over one of hers, savoring the feeling.

"Forgive me. We have faced obstacles before, but not like this." He looked away as he pulled her hand down from his face to place a kiss on it. "You not wanting to be reincarnated has set me over the edge, and I fear I will never find my way back."

"Because you won't." She watched as he looked into her face again. "We will."

"You have always had such faith in the unknown. This is the first time I have been unable to support you."

"We want the same thing."

"It is not worth you dying for."

"Daemon, I am already tired of dying. Don't you see? If I can't figure this out, I need you to let me go."

"Never."

"I am going to sever the reincarnation spell! Please hear me on this!" She watched him truly try not to lose it as he backs away.

"I just got done waiting around 150 years to hold you again, see you, touch you. And now after not even being with me for even an entire month, you are talking about truly ridding the spell that keeps us together? Correct?" He watched her nod. "Say it!" His anger at her proposal clearly got the best of him.

"I already fucking said yes! Yes! Yes! Yes!" Her screams were foreign to her own ears. Her throat closed up as she screamed it, emotions making it too hard to almost do so, making her sound like she was in literally physical pain. Feeling determined to defend herself in this.

He slowly walked back toward her. "Then kill me now, Claura. Because that is what you are doing." He put his hands up in surrender. "Just kill me now."

"Shut the fuck up! You are going to help me! We are going to go get that book because I am done! Aiyana still needs that curse broken. I need my spell fixed. I am not in the mood for mommy to be in charge anymore! I am done with this bitch! I am done with this feeling of dying a little more every time I am reborn, as messed up as that sounds! I am just fucking done!" she shouted so hard.

Her voice was bouncing off the walls in a very large room. Her throat already sounded raw, and it was clear she did not raise her voice like this often at all. Watching her made his anger fade completely away. He was officially in unknown territory with his emotions, not knowing exactly how to respond to her right now.

"My Claura, stop. Please. You are truly frightening me," he said gently.

He looked at her with such worry, such ache for not being able to just fix it all himself. He watched her snap, heard her screams, and saw her be so different this time. She knew she had been through more in this human life before coming here. This was not just postpartum. This was real anger and real trauma coming through. And it was all being combined with what she was still learning about herself, what she had just been through emotionally in the past few days—weeks—and what was coming through just naturally from her past lives. It was no wonder she was acting this way. He wondered if bringing it up would make it better or worse. He tried to grab her wrists to pull her close and get her to calm down, but she was having none of it. Apparently, he was late to realize that she truly was keeping it together before.

"Hit me all you like, but you are still grieving Dayla. And I know about Jayson. And I know about that high school jock that got his hands on you after the game where no one was looking. I know about that car accident you got in, which is why you stopped driving not long, even after you got your license, and how long you waited trapped in that car until someone finally came along to help. I saw you had no place to go on more than one occasion, trying to find a place to sleep where you would be safe on the streets before coming across that abandoned chapel. I see it all in your memories. I see you never really let it all out. Depression never really affected you until your daughter happened. So go on. Hit me. Kill me. Do whatever you want. Please, Claura." He waited. He watched her randomly yelling just to get it out, clearly so overdue for this. "Sweetheart, go on."

"I can't! Stop!"

"Hit me. Use your powers."

"No!" She was clearly worried for him.

"You won't hurt me."

"How do you know?"

"You can only hurt me by doing one thing, and you already know what that is. So go on. I'm serious."

"Daemon, I don't even know how—"

"Knock me on my ass, like you did to Tronan."

"Don't say his name. Please."

"Oh ya, why's that?"

"You know why!"

"No, actually I do not."

"Like you don't grieve your connection to her."

"Of course I do, but she wasn't ever really mine."

"You don't miss her at all?"

"I see now. You are afraid you didn't sever the bond all the way because it was your first spell. You don't have that kind of faith in yourself yet, do you?"

"Kinda sane of me not to."

"I underestimated how much you are underestimating yourself, me, us…this time around."

"My faith is dying along with me, apparently."

"Don't speak like that."

"You are tired as well. You just won't admit it. Not even for me." She saw him pause, contemplating. "You really want to see me die over and over again, hmmm? For eternity? You do realize that I can tell that a deep-down part of me already saw this day coming so long ago?" She stepped closer to him, shoving his chest. "We really never had this chat before, hmmm? Not once?" She shoved again, proud of herself for pressing him back, seeing the light start in both her palms now. She took notice of his eyes, clearly taking notice. "How unfair it is to me to forget every fucking thing! Did it ever occur to you ever that someday, I will get sick of this bullshit?" On the third shove, his feet only slightly stumbled backward, keeping her eyes captive with his, the lights in her palms getting brighter. "Because that someday is today, my love! And grieving or not, I goddamn mean it!"

Apparently, omnipotent beings crash through the glass just like anybody else. She walked closer to the broken window, eyeing his smooth landing on his back on the stone balcony, clearly not his first time. He made her worry none as he literally acted like it was an art form with how he did it. He scoffed at the notion while looking down and around the edges, seeing that the glass was actually quite thick. She had zero worry and gave a smirk level 10. She looked up to see him walking toward her as if nothing happened. It was kind of pissing her off with his calm demeanor.

"I've seen you do better. Go again."

"No."

"Why not?"

"We will do it in my realm."

"That's my girl. Catching on fast."

"So just how limitless are you here, in your own realm?"

"Wouldn't you like to know?"

"Actually, I would." She leaned on one hip, and with only one hand now, she raised her palm, holding it out to face him. His smirk only increased, making something inside her itch to rub it off for him. She saw the light start to reach outward now, about a foot from her palm, getting slightly larger in size. She turned to look at him, at the sound he was making as he started to clear his throat, acting like he was actually preparing himself now. It made her happy—very happy, mouthing a smart-ass little "I love you" to him, followed instantly by her pushing her palm out and forcing him to go backward—way, way backward through the bedroom's thick stone wall, out into the hallway backward.

She made it so he was out of her sight for the moment. She suddenly felt another presence come down the hallway toward wherever Daemon landed, hearing them scoff in disbelief at the sight. After his recent similar noise in the office, she knew it was Roman just then. She didn't move, choosing to give him time to figure out what was going on. Instead, she took a moment to study her hand, blowing on her knuckles, giving herself an inward praise. She was in disbelief that she most likely was holding this power inside her for her entire life. She suddenly wished she could go back in time and use it on a few people. She saw a head peek in from the hallway, enjoyment on his face.

"I see you two are catching up." Roman smirked yet still looked slightly concerned.

*Let me guess. Again.* She scoffed to herself. "Roman. Don't come in. Please." She was just not really wanted anyone in her private space right now. As happy as she was with herself at the moment, she was still feeling on edge.

"No plans to, just umm...need you both to come see something."

"Now? Does it have to be now? Kinda busy." She saw him look at Daemon before saying, "Yes," unknowing of why it bothered her.

She heard Daemon still moving through the rubble, making her smile again. She saw him appear in the hole in the wall next to Roman, asking the obvious question.

"What is so important?"

"Baby steps." Roman sounded so relaxed, so proud. Her eyes widened, and she started running. Right as she would have run past Daemon, he caught her around the waist, pulling her close to his body. *We will continue this later.* She looked at Roman for reassurance and help in escaping, only to see him look back and forth between their faces and put his hands up in surrender. She clearly felt there was no need to intercede as he started walking back down the hall toward where he came from. They suddenly heard him yell "Ballroom!"

She faced Daemon with an excited look. "Let's go!" She pulled at his arms to free herself.

He simply stopped her from getting away, his strength making the notion obvious that her efforts were wasted, and he used his powers to transport them both to the specific room before she could argue more. They appeared in the far corner, seeing the others almost in the middle, everyone staring down at something. She started a light jog to get up close, the image of it making Daemon's heart ache yet again for her lost chance at being a mother, for if she was this excited over someone else's child…

"Oh my god!" He heard her say as he came closer behind her. "She is walking!"

Daemon glanced around and saw it for himself, shock on his face as well. "How is this so?"

He leaned down in front of her, looking so proud, rubbing his hand over his face as if trying to hide a tear or two already for her. He watched her up closely, fully focused on her in a way he never thought would happen so soon. He was shaken to his core. He truly was. Claura could see it clear as day all over his face.

"Moira is losing her powers. I do not know the rate of this. She may be in each new phase for I have no idea how long. But the bottom line is, the curse is losing strength, which means its owner is as well," Maya clarified.

# THE WINGED WITCH OF MATCHES

"Did someone beat us to it?" Claura questioned. She clearly meant the chance to kill Moira and not just the curse. "As after seeing what she is capable of, I have no problem killing my own mother." She saw the surprise on Roman's face, along with Tronan.

"We do not know for sure," Daemon chided in, turning to see Maya come closer to Claura.

"How did you finally figure it out?" Maya asked her, standing close. She was clearly perplexed and proud of her niece.

"Witch intuition? You said we were related, but something tells me that Aiyana is not a third cousin." She shrugged. "Green lights in my palms that look just like hers. So far, that is it." She started to scold her. "Why not just tell me?"

"It would lessen your power. It is like cheating, in a way. It is how our bloodline is. The more we figure things out on our own, in our own way, on our own time…the more legit and genuine our skills and powers are. It is just nature's way of—"

"Balancing itself out," Claura finished for her.

"Precisely. You were always smarter than her right from the start. It is one of the reasons she grew to hate you, her own daughter."

"She truly hated me?"

"Oh dear, she'd hate her own shadow if it didn't look thin enough. Moira has always been extreme yet, at the same time, very shut down. It did not take much to hurt her, as well as not much to anger her. You were with me quite often, don't worry. Only that made her hate me even more. You could truly do no right with her. Do not think on it too much." She leaned in to stand beside her, just enough to rub her arm up and down her back. It clearly meant to do the comforting gesture subconsciously, not expecting her ghost body to actually work. The gesture made Roman's eyes go wide at seeing her body make contact, clearly not in just spirit form anymore. "Oh my, how is this…"

She looked at her hands and touched Claura's shoulder in slight shock, seeing her fingers able to press into her deltoid. Roman walked over to her hastily and reached for her hands, in clear shock that he could lift them with his own. He looked down at her with a look none of them would ever forget. They heard Aiyana start to cry as if needing their attention, knowing what was happening. She finally wanted her mommy to hold her for the first time. Tronan walked over to help her little legs that were trying their hardest, picked her up, and helped her get into mommy's arms a little faster. The sweet gesture was forever etched in all their memories. Well, everyone but Claura's. The moment made her even more determined in her wishes.

# Chapter 23

# "I" Need You Still

Claura looked at Daemon, seeing it clear on his face that he did not miss her thought. Stuck between this beyond-important moment with Aiyana and Maya and what was still happening between them. He turned to look at Maya holding her child finally, his eyes not being able to help soften at the sight despite what was going on behind them. Maya turned to look into his face, the expression of thank-you beyond what any words would be good enough for. He simply gave her a reassuring wink back, as if it had been his pleasure this entire time, turning to look at Aiyana and smile. Despite all his years, all his knowledge, and her little face looking back at him right now he could not put it into words. He sighed, refusing to look away, refusing to break the own silent language they had created between them for so long now. She hoped it would be soon that she would finally be able to speak as well. His heart yearned for it, for they clearly had time to make up for it. A part of him needed her to say eventually someday that he did good, that he was good enough for her in all of this. He looked forward to the conversation of apologizing for not being able to do more. For Claura instead to be her main answer still all this time. He watched as her little hand reached out to him, wanting him to take her. Maya lifted her toward him, watching his strong hands reach out and pull her close. He held her small head still as he placed a kiss on her temple, looking back into her eyes, seeing the need to say so much more still. She gave up on her baby noises a long time ago, beyond past understanding that they weren't the words she was really trying to get out. He leaned in close to her little ear and turned her around to have a private moment with her, walking a few feet away from everyone.

She sensed Tronan's eyes in his back the entire time, watching every move.

"I will always be here for you. Do you understand me, little one?" She rested her head on his shoulder, clearly choosing a hug in answer. His huge palm covered her back, rubbing gently, his head leaning softly against hers. "Spell fading or not, we are still going after her. You have my word." He heard her making a small sound as if in agreement and as if saying okay. He gently rocked with her, feeling her fall asleep on his chest in his arms, knowing it was one of the last times he'd get to do it now. The reality of this time was coming to an end with her starting to sink in. His slow movements made him turn and see everyone again, all as patient as could be. He simply let them have the moment to themselves.

Claura heard Tronan clear his throat and turned to look at him. His sharp gaze on Aiyana turned to meet hers, a pure look of regret and uncertainty on his features—of mourning, of thankfulness, of needing to repay her, of not respecting, or even noticing, her amount of courage before she clearly needed to put it to good use. It was obvious they needed to have a conversation, just the two of them. Yet neither would know what to say at the same time. Something inside her told her it was going to happen soon enough and to not worry about it right now. She turned to see Daemon walking back toward her, fully studying the moment between her and his brother before handing Aiyana back to Maya. She saw him nod toward their room as if to say they needed to continue their previous discussion now, in private.

"I need to speak with you, Claura. But we can do it some other time soon," Maya said, not missing the ice between the two. They clearly had some issues on their plate already between them that needed to come first.

"Yes. And in my realm," Claura said.

"Wonderful. Just reach out." She saw Claura turn and go to catch her wrist gently first. "And please, my dear, in the meantime… be careful." She eyed Daemon with the last two words.

"I am not worried."

"I know. And that is what is worrying me. Your sudden lack of fear is quite strong. Your strong will is how it started with your mother."

"What are you saying, Aunt Maya?"

"You are stronger than you think. Being reincarnated has made your powers have to stay simmering over and over again, never fully being able to be let out. Don't let it boil over at the wrong trigger." She looked to Daemon for understanding, needing him to see that she needed to save her energy for more important things. He made it obvious she could sense more tension between them than she let on.

"I need to go see her, see this Moira. But first, we need to make a visit to someone else."

"Who?" Maya asked her, hearing the dare-to-defy-me in Claura's tone, which made her even more concerned now.

"Claura, please!" Daemon was clearly not happy with her not discussing this more with him first, causing more alarm to cross Maya's face at his words before turning back to her niece.

"The one who broke her heart. The first time." She glanced at Roman, wondering if he knew. Duh, of course, he knew. The man never made any effort to show just how much he knew unless it was absolutely necessary. His humbleness was eerie. By Maya's expression, she already knew as well, yet her shock was more of a "hell no" simply because of what he was, not who he was. "I need his level of power to help me fix my reincarnation spell." She paused, her face turning more serious, more sad yet determined. "Daemon knows of no other more powerful. I will ask him, this Conroy, to help me in this. Or else."

"Or else what, my dear?!" She felt the temperature rising from all of them, just waiting for her to clarify what they were already getting at. She looks to Daemon again, facing toward the floor now, lost in thought at his twisting hands. Clearly trying to hold a new level of anger in and not lose it.

"I will not let her," Daemon said, absolute and calm. He was dead set on the decision, no matter what it cost him.

"I cannot do this anymore."

She knew Maya would piece it together as she said it sternly and turned to walk away from everyone.

"Claura!" Roman stepped in, walking quickly toward her. He reached for her arms and forced her to turn and look at him, a little too aggressively for Daemon's liking, causing him to come up quickly and start to shove him away from her. Roman roughly impelled his attempts away with a clear "fuck you" and turned back toward Claura. She watched with building emotions as he raised his hand to point condemningly at her, his tone as firm as she ever heard it. "You will not risk your life in any way, shape, or form. Do you fucking hear me? We need you still!"

"Of course, I will help Aiyana! Something is telling me that I need to see this man first before Moira. I cannot explain it! I know that your need for me matters, Roman, not actually me! Trust me, I get it!"

"How dare you." He looked like he was trying to control himself by not using his ability to separate just him and her from the room to speak alone, and now. Lord knew it was long overdue. He had a discussion with her, alone as it was, ever since he exited the car that evening.

"It is so true." She hissed in his face, daring him to deny it, daring him to do what she could see all over his face, wanting to push his buttons to tempt him. She watched him take just one second to glance at Daemon, already knowing that he was returning the quick gaze with a "don't even" expression.

"To realize that you have been a part of this family this entire time, do you not realize how important that makes you, powers or not?" Roman said to her.

"I. Do. Not. Know. Family." Her tone made him pause. "My own goddamn mother is okay with killing me!"

"It's not going to happen," Daemon chided in.

"No, it's not," Roman agreed, still glaring at her in return.

"I know what I need to do. My intuition is literally begging out of me! And you all keep disagreeing with me in some way!" She hated that she was starting to scream slightly again. She really did not have any intention of losing it in front of them the way she lost it with Daemon earlier already. She felt Daemon's hands reach up to gently push her back, stepping in front of her, blocking her view of them all, and forcing her feet to move backward with him, away from everyone. She made one last attempt to take it farther while straining around his frame to try to see them. "Do you want the all-powerful Claura to help or fucking not?" The sound of her voice broke into a million pieces as they all heard it echo into the distance. Daemon clearly made the decision to exit them both from the room instantly.

All four of them remained staring into the place where they just stood, the silence eerie in comparison to Claura's words and the way she shouted them. Her heart was breaking. It was clear they had all been blind to how much was being asked of her. She wasn't even done grieving her daughter yet. The thought made Roman turn to Maya, both glancing at Aiyana at the same time.

"Seeing Aiyana is still too much for her. They truly do look exactly alike. It's uncanny, to say the least," Tronan concluded.

"There is more to this," Roman added, hissing it between his teeth. He walked over to a nearby chair to have a moment to calm down away from everybody.

"Daemon can handle her," Maya said. She watched Roman stride over to sit down on the chair's arm. She turned to Tronan, not missing the lost, regretful expression on his face, seeing that he wished he could help, still feeling the slight sting of the need to. She chose to walk closer to him and gently hand Aiyana over. "And you have more important things on your own plate now."

"I simply worry for her still." He held the small child in his arms like it was the most natural thing to him now. He saw her lean her cheek onto his chest, clearly still tired but not wanting to miss a thing. He could not imagine only one person being her company for so long, and now all this. Shouting was included on more than one occasion now in the only home she ever knew and in such a short amount of time with them all being here.

"It is different this time. She went through more in this life before finding Daemon and now is going through more after finding him," Maya said. She saw Tronan scoff at her words, at how he was added to the mix in the middle, and how that did not help at all despite how much he truly was in love with her at the time. "She is on overload. We all need to simply be there for her. And unfortunately, she is correct."

"About what?" Tronan asked.

"Her intuition."

"How so?" Roman joined in, letting his own thoughts take a break while listening. "Isn't it still like guessing?" His tone showed he thought the power of intuition was silly on some level and could not be fully trusted.

"Not with her, if she is anything like her mother. Moira was always spot-on when it came to following her instincts. Claura simply needs time to make up for not using the skill as much."

"This all happened too fast for her. All of it." Tronan admits.

"I know. But we needed her back this time more than ever. She will recover from this."

"Sure about that? 'Cause I've never seen my brother look so worried."

"Daemon is about to see how powerful she may be after all, and for the first time. Something is different about Claura now. I can feel it. And to be honest, as frightened as Daemon may be, I am kind of excited." She heard Roman scoff and turned to look at him again. "What?"

"You would be," Roman said, looking humored.

# THE WINGED WITCH OF MATCHES

"I am sorry, my love?" she asked with sarcasm yet sincere interest.

He doesn't answer her; instead, he half-looked at Tronan holding his daughter. "I expect her happiness to look no different upon our return, dear son. For my Match and I, we need to have a talk." He looked up to them both then, striding toward Maya in a way he has been beyond ready to do for so long now. He saw her ridiculously wise and gorgeous eyes start to hold some uncertainty, some nervousness. It was just a small amount. It was just enough to make his smirk return at how he was so pleased, obviously, with being able to affect her so, even after all this time still.

"No, we are not calling him that. Not after recent events." She looked at Tronan accusingly, with a level of hatred that, in its simmering level, somehow held more power than if it were to let it boil over.

"Agree," Tronan scolded right back. He refused to feel guilt over uncontrollable circumstances despite what everyone thought of him. He turned with Aiyana in his arms and strode out of the room to go enjoy his time with her, with his Match—his true Match.

"Why does a part of me still hate that sight so intensely?" Roman asked, watching them leave.

"You are her father. You will always hate that sight." She stepped closer, feeling him wrap his hands around her small waist in response, needing to use her fingers to force his face to turn to look at her and away from his daughter in the arms of someone he so clearly could not stand still. "Leave him be, Roman. It is almost over."

"Exactly. I have some time left to keep despising him."

"He will be good to her."

"Sure about that?"

"He has to be." She watched him incline his head in question. "I put a spell on him." She leaned in close, saying it low, her tone full of guilty pleasure. He just looked back at her like he truly didn't know what to think. A boxing match would have been more to Roman's liking, not some silly spell again. The conflicted expression made her smile, softly laughing. "Oh, my dear, my handsome, conflicted man."

She pulled his mouth to hers. She savored the moment the exact same way she had daydreamed about on several occasions over for literally decades. His arms finally truly wrapped around her body again. The flavor of him returned to her senses instantly, her body reacting already, and the temperature rose. She could feel him fighting his aggression, clearly choosing the more romantic route here, wanting to just give her what he thought she wanted after all this time. He was beyond happy with just having her anyway at all.

"Pick a room, Roman, now."

She felt him growl with absolute pleasure to obey as he picked her up and transported them both. The ballroom was officially dead silent after just holding such salient memories for them all.

*****

Daemon felt her rush to get away from him as soon as her feet landed on the carpet in her office. He watched her act in utter determination to leave his grasp and move anywhere away from him, so conflicted that the person she loved the most was who was going to stand in her way the most right now. She felt so beyond unsupported by him in all this now when her main motives were to literally do this for them. She sat swiftly down on the daybed before the enormous arched stained-glass window, clasping her hands behind her head, her face aiming toward the floor for not an inch of him to see, to read her. He took a moment to just watch her, hoping like hell that just being here would assist her nerves.

"Bad time?" A woman toward the desk broke through their intense, silent moment.

They both look toward the sound at exactly the same time, seeing a tall, thin woman looking beyond comfortable with herself as if this was her own office while staring back at them. She stood in the exact middle of the front of Claura's desk, leaning back against it gently, arms crossed over her midline. She had long pure white hair, hungry eyes, intent eyes, and predatory eyes. She saw Daemon walk toward her, aiming to cause damage. She simply waited for the moment of seeing his hand swish through her spirit form before reacting with laughter. She clearly loved seeing his anger increase.

"No wonder she enjoys fearing you. Sexy." She made it obvious her main desire already was to push any and all buttons. She looked away from his face then, raising her voice toward her daughter. "You did always have good taste in men, honey. I'll give you points there."

"Take your points and shove them up your ass!" Claura snapped without looking at her while completely telling Daemon with her eyes alone not to bother with the "men" reference as he so easily noticed and started to question in her mind. It was just Moira and Moira alone being a manipulative bitch.

"Aww, so moody today. And here I was thinking you'd be all happy, breaking that bond and all." She smiled and looked at Daemon with desire. "And other things." She smiled even more now.

"How could you do this to a child? One you are related to!" Claura got right to the point. She chose not to even find her worth looking at again yet, remaining where she was. "Was this all truly over jealousy?"

"Is that not enough?" she said like it was her favorite emotion to play with. "For you had no idea what was in store for you both if you had not been able to free Tronan so quickly. Shame, I was so looking forward to his level of…jealousy." She saw Daemon scoff, clearly unworried. "Oh no, handsome. It would have been enough to put a little black and blue mark on that handsome face of even yours for a change, trust me."

"No. It is not enough." Claura broke through her bullshit. Her mommy chose an exquisite time to visit, honestly. Now she could take some of her anger out on her instead of Daemon—her all undeserving Daemon. "And you would not be able to know, to be that smart. As you choose to hang onto jealousy worse, then let's say…a 150-year-old child would." She gave her the smallest of glances before returning to studying her hands instead. She chose to keep her head straight and not even bother looking this woman in the face.

"Give her to me, and I will end your poorly made reincarnation spell," Moira said, sounding like the manipulative snake she was.

"You will never do anything for me. Do you understand me, Mother?" she said with contempt as she stood, choosing to walk toward her now. "Come on, dear Mommy, show yourself. Actually show yourself." She saw her pause, enjoying getting under her skin so easily. "Tell me, am I an only child here? The only one you get to torture other than your own damn niece?"

"Sure, why not?" She clearly dismissed caring to oblige in her wants of any truths.

"I see." She recalled how in the book Maya gave her, if one was an only child, it left more room for them to personalize their powers. There was more space to make their spells stronger and more clever, as the family tree and all its power did not need to be shared nor spread out as much. She held up her palm, showing her. She saw the small shock on her face. "This is how I figured it out. You made it too easy to put that piece together, didn't you?" She looked at her with disdain.

"That's not supposed to be…that tint…that green…" Moira actually looked worried.

"Oh ya, why's that?" She looked at her palm as if proud, then back to her, enjoying seeing her nervousness.

"Your father…he…" She raised her hand slightly over her mouth.

"Who is my father!" She stepped closer to her, already knowing she could not physically hurt her in here. Maya had clarified although it was obvious this mental shit was taking its toll equally. "Say his name!"

"That motherfucker…." Her spirit forms clearly needed to take a few deep breaths, too, sometimes. Moira looked away from them both, trying to piece something together.

"I doubt he'd enjoy being that unlucky"—she looked her up and down—"as I'm sure once was enough for him." She could see the solid answer in Moira's eyes, loving how her trap worked. She heard Daemon scoff as if proud of her from behind. "Oh, so I am an only child. Lucky me."

"Your time to test me is limited, Claura. I know of your intentions."

# THE WINGED WITCH OF MATCHES

"I am not worried."

"Speak for yourself." She eyed Daemon again. Just his energy alone reeked of anguish in losing her.

"I will find a way."

"Oh, how's that?" Moira asked, eyeing her with immature enthusiasm.

"Conroy." The bitch took in a deep breath, letting her face rise with it, clearly trying to hold onto her poker face for some unknown reason before suddenly laughing in Claura's face hysterically.

"He will never help you! Thanks to him." She pointed toward Daemon.

"I have no beef with Conroy. My father did." He filled in.

"As if you would take her there either way. It's one of the most powerful realms to exist, literally in the top 3. Even your kind is timid there." She looked back to Claura now. "As my daughter, you are welcome any time without his permission to visit me." She smiled at her while literally licking her tongue over her teeth, giving off the vibe of a true wolf in its other form.

"Why couldn't you just let them go and move on? Like a real woman would," Claura asked, seeing her mother truly face her now, for a moment at least, the fog of maliciousness behind her eyes gone. "Forever is a long time to be hating someone who never loved you enough to hate you the same way back."

"You will never see Daemon let into his realm. He wants nothing to do with their entire bloodline anymore. Therefore, you will have to go alone. Passing through my realm along the way." She inclined her head, studying her, admiring how they were exactly the same height. "To leave Daemon with me while you go on into the next realm...that should be interesting." She leaned her head slightly to glance at him with intense motive. "To risk the life of the one you love so you can risk getting the answer to keep being with him... so complicated." She was clearly in her element, enjoying the reality of things being difficult for others. Claura moved to block her view of him, making the obvious known that he was completely not an option for a torture toy, so help her to hell and back. She truly saw it now, looking into the eyes of her mother up close and personal, seeing the animalistic demonic quality they so subtly yet constantly held. This woman did not know how to just answer and how to let go. She really was a lost cause. In a way, it saddened Claura. Grieving for her had already started to begin inside her. Yet it felt relieving as if she needed to see her up close and personal like this. To have that insurance that she tried and did not fail. Moira was just this way, and it had nothing to do with her, daughter to her or not.

"I will succeed. I will save your death for last so you see me succeed."

"Good luck. As you are far from having all that you need." She gave a small snort, tapping her temple while eyeing her. She obviously suggested her lack of memory alone, putting a big dent in any plan she may come up with.

"Wait…so you…you have a reason to erase my memory then, don't you? It has been you, this whole time, doing this to me?"

"I was not present when you did that spell, so no."

"Or were you?"

"Like you can prove anything, Claura. You don't even go by your original name again yet. You hardly know anything."

"Don't attempt to sidetrack me with stupid bullshit! Who gives a fuck what name I go by, huh! I have reversed a bonding spell that was set in stone for fifteen decades. That's a long time, dear Mommy, for you not to figure out a way around it. And it's because you can't. So to try to make me feel weak just because I just got here is pretty fucking stupid of you! Did it ever occur to you that my memory while here just keeps getting sharper and sharper to make up for the times I did have to let go of it? *Balance*, my dear mother, as you should damn well know." She was going in a circle, making it very clear that she was unafraid to show her back to her for a moment while she looked at Daemon. She just needed to see him, look into his eyes, as if he helped her stay focused just by being here.

He stood across the room still, as still as a stone, arms crossed over his chest. He just watched every little detail happen before him. She eyed her desk as she turned all the way back around, making sure everything was still there. He was inwardly thankful that it was as she faced her mother again.

# THE WINGED WITCH OF MATCHES

Moira just stood there, arms crossed, making an evil clicking sound with her tongue along her teeth that matched her eyes. She eyed her own daughter like she wanted to kill her and taste her blood.

"Watch it, dear daughter. That wall next door holding back a particular realm still has leaks." Her eyes bounced to Daemon. "That may not get fixed this time." She saw him start to seethe with the memory coming back.

Claura calmly looked from her to Daemon, seeing his anger reach new heights at whatever Moira was mentioning. The memory was one he did not want her to know. He clearly needed to discuss it with her now, on top of everything else still, if they could only get this psycho out of her office. She heard his deep voice break into the room, despite him not shouting it, still bouncing off the walls with intensity in its own way.

"I will have your head, Moira. Hear me."

"Put on that ring, dear. I added a few memories myself." She smirked between them both, giving the smallest waves with one hand before fading.

Daemon watched as Claura hardly paused before walking around to the other side of her desk to reach into the drawer for the ring. "Claura!" He walked quickly to stop her before she slipped it on her finger.

"You won't tell me!" She grabbed it and slammed the desk drawer shut. She refused to look at him yet, needing this answer first. "I need to know. I just need to know!" She lifted the box to open it, seeing him reach for it, unafraid to use his superior strength to his advantage. He fights her for only a good second before owning it in his grasp. "It's mine, Daemon!"

He held it out in front of her face. "This could be a trap! You are smarter than this!"

"I am so tired of not knowing!" she shouted at him. She clearly meant more than just the ring, just this one memory that Moira was dangling in front of her. "Get out! Fucking leave me alone if all you are going to do is make this harder for me!" She saw his expression of intense impair, that look coming back that he really just needed to hold her in his arms again already. He was sick of this shit, too, right along with her. "Don't look at me like that. Please. I cannot do this on my own. I already feel you slipping away with this decision. I don't think you understand I have to do this…for us."

She started pacing back and forth before him, one palm over her forehead, her exhaustion kicking in. Despite her look of tremendous despair, he was thankful for the whirlwind coming to an end finally, at least for today.

"Moira will never give you the answers you need. In any form, in any realm. She is nothing but a game with too much power to back her bullshit up." She watched as he tossed the ring box into the garbage. The thud of something so damn sentimental a sound she knew neither of them would forget soon. She went to grab it and got blocked by him, looking up at him in disbelief. "Don't ever touch that fucking ring again, understand!"

"I can probably separate what she has done from it! Let me try!"

"Take it as a sign that I do believe you. I do agree with you. That we do need to move on from this spell and the type of past we have had. It is just so goddamn hard for me to risk losing you…for good."

He could see the recognition on her face. She saw his side to all this more thoroughly, at already having to lose her time and again, and simply fried from the experience. The chance of a final "loss" was too much to bear for him.

"Help me," she said, the despair in her voice breaking his heart. She watched his eyes jump between hers, just reading her for a long moment.

"Call to Maya," he finally said, seeing her start to instantly reach out to her from the look on her face alone. "Tomorrow," he grumbled, reaching for her waist and pulled her closer to him.

"Why not now?" She felt him move his hands upward to pull her face close to his. His eyes held a tenderness, a possession, a fear that did now send that chill down her spine once again.

"Quite selfish of you, my love, to not take notice that they obviously need some time right now. Alone."

"Yes, how selfish of me to want to get a move on with ending the curse placed upon their daughter." He wondered why his comment bothered her more than it should, pushing it to the back of her mind with his next words.

"In waiting fifteen decades to touch someone again, I can relate." He forced her mouth to his.

She started to instantly see it now in his mind that he had come to accept that this was possibly going to be their last life together. In his mind, that is what he truly believed. He was trying to support her to make her happy. He would help her however he could. But he was starting to feel hopeless. She could see he was giving up in response to going along with her wishes and choosing to fail at hiding it. For her Daemon to experience such an emotion, it brought out a whole different level of alarm inside her.

She felt him lean down to lift her ass with both hands and roughly place her atop the desk, leaning into her, forcing her to lean back onto it. His one strong hand guided her head to fall back gently and rest on the hardwood, loving the sensation of something rough on both sides of her, his hands squeezing her almost to the point of pain under his grasp everywhere he touched. Knowing she caused it. The way he was feeling was all her fault. She chose not to stop him, no matter how subconsciously dominating he got. She simply told her witch self to "woman up" as she brought this on herself. The man loved her immensely, and she basically threw it in his face that what he had to offer she wanted no more. She could tell that was how he understood it. His anger at her choices, at what she wanted, at the situation…all of it coming to a boil inside of him. How he abruptly penetrated her next was proof of it.

He was so wrong.

This was officially the lifetime where she would prove to him that he could trust her. The other way around was done. Her entire existence was risking being literally dead set on it.

# Chapter 24

# "Is" His Name

Maya strolled into the office casually with a face full of happiness, wonderment, and feeling in complete tune with herself. That look faded into a complete 180 of concern as soon as she felt the energy of a previous occupant still lingering, her eyes seeing the tension still strongly lingering between the two before her. Claura was behind her desk, looking determined as ever in her chair, watching her walk toward them. Daemon sat in a nearby chair in front of the large and impressive piece, facing her while completely aware of who was already coming up from behind him. His eyes glued to Claura, lost in thought.

"I see," Maya gently confirmed.

"You see what?" Claura asked, sounding on edge more than she intended.

"You both should know that the lingering energy I still feel in this room will affect you. Negatively." She looked at Daemon who was avoiding her gaze as she stood before them both now. "And it already has worked its dark magic." She glared at him, knowing he should be in more control of himself. She knew he felt her disappointment. Claura watched the moment between them, choosing to add her "negative" thoughts into the mix.

"Well, now he can stop hating his own brother for past events, along with you, my dear Aunt, as now he can relate to being a little out of control with me as well due to uncontrollable circumstances." She let the last two words linger off her tongue, making it obvious her connection to Tronan was one she still cared about, despite it being severed. She watched them both look at her with such a distaste yet humble understanding.

"I am sorry, Claura. You are right. We need to focus on what to do next."

"I have already told you."

"No. You are not just going to barge right into both of their realms as if you do not care if you come out!" Daemon barked.

"And if I told you no about last night, would you have listened?"

"You are driving me mad with risking losing you! *You* are doing this to me! I literally do not have it in me to take on what you are asking!" He stood to come closer to the front of her desk as he said it. She saw her stand and face him in return.

"Then leave! And I will save us both on my own. After all, it was your father, not you, I needed before. I may not need you in this entire ordeal, after all, Daemon!" Her sore body unconsciously fed the flames.

"Daemon, please give my niece and me some time to speak." She turned to see his lost gaze, his anger, his fury at the situation, and his tremendous ache to just want to do what was right for her while knowing he could not accept what she was asking. "Please." She watched them continue to glare at one another, him leaning closer to say something before turning to exit her office.

"You will not leave this office without me." He dared her to risk this task without him. "Maya, I need to speak to you." He kept Claura's gaze captive as he said it. Maya looked at Claura and put her finger up. She followed him once he finally turned around. It was as if to say just one minute, and she'd be back.

Daemon waited until she was in the center of the hallway with her, knowing he needed a certain amount of space around them to put up the soundproof barrier. She knew. She stood exactly where she needed to, crossing her hands in front of her belly as she faced him, waiting. He swiped his hand as if dismissing something irritating as he simply cast the spell with his mind, only to hear her small laughter from the other side of the office door come through, intentionally lingering in his mind as well, a laugh that was full of zero real humor.

*Nice try, handsome.* He clearly enjoyed herself behind her desk. She was right about her memory being sharper while here. Daemon could already tell that reading a spell only once was all the effort his little Claura needed to make use of it. Quite different from her first reincarnation life.

He looked up to see Maya, knowing what was happening by the look on his face, and went to try again, only for her to do it quicker and faster. She clarified for him, "She doesn't know that one yet." Daemon's eyes said a quick thank you before turning in a circle, trying to calm himself down. She sensed him failing, then sensed Roman appear behind them down the hallway behind her. Both witnessed the moment Daemon punched his fist into the side of the barrier, causing a mini tornado effect to appear in the invisible wall, along with the entire hallway momentarily shaking as if from an earthquake. She felt Roman start to walk toward them without even having to look behind her and put her hand out to stop him, her eyes remaining intent on Daemon. Without looking back at them both, he made it obvious he knew as well of their visitor.

"This is a private conversation," he asked for some grace here with everything going on, not truly intending to sound harsh.

He heard nothing from either one of them, making it clear they kept the conversation between them mentally, their own private link. He suddenly felt Roman's presence leave, and Maya cleared her throat as if to let him start.

"I cannot lose her. You have to promise me, right now, Maya, that she will not go alone. I cannot have a repeat. I barely got her out last time, even with my…abilities."

"I have no intention of sending her alone. But I can't make her a slave either, Daemon. You have to take her more seriously this time if you truly do not want a repeat. She is determined. Mark my words. She is beyond determined." Her tone sounded sorry about it for her own reasons.

"Yes. This I know. I have never seen her look at me before, in all of our lifetimes together, like she is in this one."

"I know what it cost you last time. To save her. I do." She watched him slowly turn toward her now, taking his hands off the wall and standing up straight to turn and face her. His height suddenly seemed intimidating to her for the first time, and his energy also made her realize that perhaps there was something different this time around about Daemon too, and nobody had really realized it yet but her. Perhaps these two were feeding off each other.

"Do you?"

"If you let her know, I feel it Daemon. She will find a way this time!"

"Don't! I will not live through that heartbreak in her eyes yet again!"

"You want her to stop underestimating herself. Yet you keep doing it for her." Her eyes begged him to see it differently—see Claura differently this time. She could see him fighting his emotions and knew that even after everything she had recently been through, she could not relate to his situation. Not anymore. She put her hand out next to her hip as if to say, "Just listen," and looked away for two seconds before turning back to him to speak. "Just go with her. That is all you can do. Don't deny her on what her very soul seems set on this time."

He took a moment to look anywhere but her face before admitting it. "I am terrified, Maya."

"The storm always comes first. You remember her favorite thing as a child, correct?" She clearly meant to give him an idea.

"The ocean right after the rain." His eyes softened, watching her gently nod.

"Take her seriously, Daemon. Follow *her* this time." She swiped her hand slowly to dissipate the invisible wall around them, as if wanting to help him more, but there wasn't any other main advice she could really give. She left him to his thoughts as she passed by him to walk back into the office, gently shutting the door this time.

Instantly, Maya felt the still lingering awful energy within the room and regretted not ridding it quickly before leaving her niece alone, as she clearly needed it out asap. She took a deep breath, closed her eyes, and spoke a few gentle words that made Claura feel the negativity in the room fade instantly. Looking at her aunt with questions, Maya simply pointed to the book on her desk and, without having to even touch it, opened it to the page of the spell she just did before her. Claura looked down and read the whole thing despite the first line, making it obvious what it was used for. She slightly laughed to herself.

"I know you love him, but some time to focus here on your talents is what you need."

"I have been trying, and things just keep happening. And then the more shit that happens, the more questions arise, and I am unable to keep up with it all."

"I spoke with Roman about a couple of important things"—her eyes looking away to attempt to hide her blush—"I spoke with… dammit." She covered her face, smiling behind her fingers.

"That good, huh?" He found it funny.

"You have no idea." Her blush increased, yet her face tried to hide something, knowing Claura would simply see it as something else easily at this moment. "As well as you have no idea how happy it made me, Claura, that he was not one of the chosen ones in that area with you, despite my willingness to risk it to get you here. I knew with us being related, he would sense me through you." She looked away as she said it, noticing that Claura noticed her lack of eye contact, knowing she would confuse it for her, just trying to hide her blush still.

"You can thank his chosen profession for that. It was obvious that a doctor should not sleep with his patients."

"Yes, he has always been drawn toward healing in all its forms."

"I can see he has healed you." She winked at her.

"Thanks to you."

"No, it's not. I was tempted, trust me. The sexual aura these men hold in this bloodline is just…ridiculous." She heard Maya lightly laugh. "But this is all due to your genius spell to save Aiyana. I am sorry it is so hard for me to try to have a connection with her. She just looks too much like my own for my liking. I hate not being able to work around that. I really do."

"And on top of it all, she is with Tronan, who you still clearly care for."

"How can I not? In my mind, in this lifetime, Tronan was still my first great love. And I hate how that makes Daemon feel, as he was truly my first. I just don't remember it! I can't keep redoing this. I just can't. I need to be able to stop forgetting. I can see the situation taking its toll on Daemon as well. He just won't admit it."

"I understand. Truly. Something about that first time, feeling that way. It sticks." She looked away to check out the office decor, walking toward some of her books now, reading the titles, gently touching them as she scanned down the row. "Sticks so much that that is why we are here in the first place. Moira being so hurt from her first love denying her."

"It must have been epic, to be honest. Because I am already burned out with her games, and we haven't barely begun."

"Oh yes, we have. Tronan being with his true Match now says so much more than you know about your level of power. They are at his home now, as she needs to stay where she can be protected by him specifically."

"I feel so foolish for not putting that together before. Of course, with the unbonding spell being done, she is no longer able to be protected by Daemon in his realm anymore." She inwardly hoped that the home had the same welcoming warmth for the little one as it did for her, knowing she deserved it immensely, enjoying the thought of her seeing new places finally, and with no better man. Tronan was a wonderful Match to have, and she loved knowing deep down that they were true Matches this time for him. They both deserved nothing but happiness. And she intended to keep giving that to them by finishing this.

"Feeling so overwhelmed will do that to you. That is why family *is* important, Adera. We look out for one another." She looked at her again, wanting to see her reaction to being called her real name.

"Not feeling it." She had a stone expression. "It's beautiful, but not feeling it."

"That's a bummer. As it was always Daemon's favorite no matter what name you were given in each life before finding him, once you started not having your memory more and more, little by little."

"I think Moira is a part of that downfall."

"I would not doubt it," Maya strongly confided. "But do not jump to that conclusion. Despite how much we hate our enemies, it is always more important to keep your head on straight than to be consumed by such hate."

"Among other things, as well."

"Like what?"

"Like why would she need me attached to Tronan so strongly? Why would she play that game, huh?"

"Well, to keep you away from Daemon, I assume. Your powers are stronger when you are with him. And to make Roman jealous so he would know the hurt she felt. The hurt he caused her in choosing me instead." Daemon's words of her not leaving this realm without him, being dead set on remaining close to her throughout this whole ordeal, clearly crossing over Claura's face. "Daemon is only trying to keep you alive, you know."

"He seems so dead set against ridding this failing reincarnation spell."

"It is all he has at the moment to keep you in his arms. Do not be so hard on him. He won't admit it or want you to know unless you absolutely need to, but you have always actually been more strong-willed than even him, my dear. It is your loss of memory getting worse now that has made you not recognize that."

"Another reason I need to end this. For good."

"I understand your reasoning. I do."

"So you will help me." She watched Maya sigh, but her eyes were already holding the answer. "Daemon said her powers are a thousand times stronger in her own realm. Does that affect me when I am her own daughter? Wouldn't mine be able to multiply as well?"

"Unfortunately, there is only one way to find out. As everyone's abilities are slightly different." She saw Claura pause, trying to think over the risk of what she may be missing. "Let me suggest using Roman's talents. Perhaps he can realm jump you to the small loophole that is placed between Moira's realm and the one where Conroy resides, bypassing her realm completely."

"Can he really do that?"

"Again, unfortunately—"

"Only one way to find out." She was contemplating. "Is there a way to help keep Daemon safe, no matter where we land?" She watched her aunt smile, once again waving her hand in that way, making the book open to a different page now. "You have already done more work for yourself in your past lives than you realize, which is why I know if you just remind yourself of things, stay here, and don't leave for a small amount of time, it is what will help you the most. As your *family*, you can trust me on this. Okay?"

"Aren't you in a hurry to get your daughter hundred percent free?"

"Of course I am. But, Claura, Roman meant what he said. You are more important to all of us than you realize. Your needs do come first too." She watched her flip through to the next page, standing with such unique confidence behind her desk while looking down at the book, taking a moment, a deep inhale, before looking up to face her.

"I am sorry. To both of you."

"It is okay to snap. Sometimes, that is what it takes to let more parts of ourselves be known. Do not hold shame over it."

"My brain cannot move forward until I get some things out of the way."

"Shoot." She sat down in the chair now where Daemon had been, facing Claura as she sat down in her chair behind her majestic looking desk.

"Why was Tronan able to help me through my heat cycle, which happened before I was even turned, if he was not my true Match?"

"Wow. Moira made it that strong? I did not know. I am sorry."

"He kept me alive, Maya. I will always remember that."

"I know, but so has Daemon on more than one occasion. Your connection is still more than what you understand. I think that is why Tronan was able to sate you during your cycle still. That part of him that is like Daemon, being brothers, it was just strong enough. It somehow came through for you still, even while in another's arms. For that, you are beyond fortunate, for Moira was probably hoping to kill you with that plan alone."

"Well, she fucking failed."

"Being here, in this place, is helping you already. I can see it. What else?"

"There is an occasion I am naturally more curious about for some reason. One he will not discuss with me is about a nearby realm that we have to keep at bay here. Can you tell me about that?" She could see her aunt's body go stiff, her eyes go dark and full of sadness. "Please, Maya. I am begging you. It is my own damn memory to have as well, seeing as I was a part of it."

"Okay." Deep inhale, her hands grasping the edge of the chair, rubbing back and forth as if nervous about where to begin. "That nearby realm is basically minions and servants to people like Moira. They live to find loopholes. Moira originally owned this realm. Before all the drama, she did actually do some good for you, believe it or not. She signed this place over to you to have for yourself, letting you create your own realm. Your own sanctuary."

"Jump to the sour part, please."

"Don't want a single reminder of a good, happy mommy memory?"

"Waste of breath."

"Perhaps Daemon should be here for this."

"Why? Just tell me!"

She watched her aunt lean forward in her chair now, clasping her fingers together, contemplating before looking back at her. "She saw how much smarter and wiser you were becoming, and it made her jealous of you. Her own daughter. She saw how people of wisdom from all different realms were coming here, happy to give you more of their knowledge to share in this peaceful realm, which to this day still holds the most wonderful library that anyone knows of. She watched with suspicion and bitterness as so many others grew to like you. Knowledge is power, Claura. And your power grew to not only match hers but started to succeed past. Her jealousy grew into rage. She started to want this place back for herself. And she went to great lengths to try to convince you to give it back to her."

"Do tell."

"She saw your belly growing," she said softly, as if to balance out the reaction she knew was about to happen before her.

"I'm sorry! What!"

"You and Daemon had a son. She used him as leverage to get what she wanted. Give her the boy. You keep your library, you know...how a psycho thinks. Her little minions in the next realm, before the wall was up...as there wasn't a solid reason for it yet before all this happened, helped her try to achieve her goal."

"We had a child together! Is he alive?"

"He is. But he was sent to a different realm. The balance in this case, my dear Claura, was his life would remain intact if you both never saw him again. But he is alive. And she lost."

"Who chose that? Who did that? There must have been another way!" Claura was standing now, pacing, slightly shouting. Maya stood up and came around to her side of the desk, her hands gently reaching out to still her and calm her.

"Daemon did. Just like I had only a small amount of time to choose for Aiyana that day, Daemon had but a moment to choose a spell. He had to choose between keeping you or your son in his life. He chose you."

"Me? But it's our child!"

"He knew he would be fine, truly!"

"How do we know that? If we can't even check on him, how do we truly know, Maya!"

"Because he sent him to one of the most powerful realms, where, unfortunately, no one has been able to cross into for some time. Daemon wanted to give him the chance to be in the most powerful realm to be able to protect himself against anybody, as he would not be able to protect him himself."

"We have to find a way, Maya. Do you really expect me not to try?"

"He is fine. He really is. If he wasn't, Daemon would be able to tell, as he made that part of the spell."

"Truly?" There were tears in her eyes. Maya gently wiped them away with her small hands.

"Yes."

"Why would he not just tell me? I deserved to know this!"

"He has seen you try before. Your heartbreak and not being able to figure it out happened more than once, as you tried so many different things. He simply did not want to deal with that heartbreak again. You must understand, okay?" Maya started to cry a little, too, unable to avoid the pain on her niece's face. Claura's eyes of shock and sorrow darted all over the place. "Claura, take a deep breath and know that you need to focus on your reincarnation spell first. It is not selfish to do so."

"I want my son."

"I will help you. For now, let's make it so you and Daemon can remain together, never having to part, giving you a better chance to take all the time you need to focus on getting him back." She gripped her harder, making her listen even more. "*He is safe.*"

"What was his name, do you know?"

"*Is* his name."

A masculine presence suddenly filled the doorway. Claura was afraid to look at him yet unable to help herself at the same time. He started walking toward her, seeing Maya distance herself. Her expression made it clear she would leave them alone and return when called again. She gave Claura one last small squeeze of reassurance on her arm before vanishing into thin air, returning to Roman. He walked slowly toward her, his expression one of such longing, of love, of worry. Looking as sharp as ever, his demeanor a whole new kind of intensity. The intensity of a father coming through. She felt foolish for not wondering sooner if they'd ever tried to have a family before. Of course, with how much she loved this man, she would want to see him happy with a child of his own—their child. She looked near tears again, wanting to know more already, needing him to answer her with motherly desperation. Her eyes were begging. He rounds her desk to stand before her, his scent calming her slightly. His hands remained at his sides, the small gesture so unlike him. He was clearly trying not to repeat mistakes, clearly hating himself for being rough with her the last time she was in his grasp.

"Valek." His hand raised to let just his index finger caress down her cheek. "Our son's name is Valek."

"I am so sorry." She held his face between her hands. "As much as I am feeling overwhelmed, you are just as much so, for reasons I can't even remember. For reasons only his father can remember." Her face was full of hate for herself, for what kind of mother forgot about her own son, no matter the circumstances between them! She backed away, needing space to think again, unsure where to even start. Knowing he had already seen this happen more than once made it even harder for her to know what words to choose.

"You chose to keep this burden upon yourself, to truly never share it with me again? To never ever let me know of him?" She felt so conflicted herself now in all this. She made them officially more on the same page than they've ever been. "Is he truly fine, Daemon?"

"You know I would have only sent him if it were so." He pulled her close, letting her next array of intense emotions come over her as he held her close in his arms, feeling her tears through his shirt as she rested her face against his chest. "I chose you, Claura. I found a way to keep you both safe and keep the love of my entire existence alive and with me. And I do not regret it one bit."

"How did you do it? How did it all happen?" She lifted her head to face him again, seeing him look up toward the ceiling and take a deep breath as if preparing how to explain it all.

"None of it is what will be useful for us in the future, for when it comes time to be able to reach him again."

"You are tired of telling me." It was written all over him.

"I thought I lost you both for a moment. It is a moment that has stuck with me to this day. I simply do not wish to discuss it, not when it isn't truly necessary." He sees her nod in understanding, inwardly thankful she was willing to not press further once again. This was the first reincarnation that she actually did not. "I saved you both. That is what is important."

"Just tell me why you sent him there, to that specific realm? Was it truly the only option for him being safe?"

"The balance with the spell was that in order to send him there, we would have to sever contact with him. That was the deal."

"I don't understand why."

"It is simply a realm that does not like to share their superior knowledge. They don't answer much. But their power is above everyone else, so I know he will have the strength to defend and protect himself from anyone in any realm. I could not bear to see our son go where I would not be able to protect him." He lifted her hand to place a kiss in it, causing her to just notice then that she was trembling. He looked back into her face, already seeing the determination to get to him someday, causing him to smile—to feel proud of her.

"What?"

"They let you have him be born right in that realm. It made me immensely proud. They were very fond of your thirst for knowledge, the realm you upheld, the sanctuary for all creatures and beings that you created. It was as if they were proud to call your son, our son, into their home for safekeeping."

"Now that makes me feel better. Couldn't have just started with that?"

"He is safe."

"I gave birth in one of the top 3 most powerful realms in all of existence?"

"Yes."

"Did I get to hold him just once?"

"No, your injuries from fighting with Moira's minions left you coming in and out of unconsciousness. Your body still persisted into labor. I found you and spoke the borrowed spell to transport us to the realm he is in now, just minutes before you gave birth. I held him." He looked down between their bodies now, for once afraid to let her really see into his face. "Once."

"He was fine, healthy?"

# THE WINGED WITCH OF MATCHES

"He was perfect."

"Who took him?"

"A woman who helped you through the entire ordeal, me beside you, taking on all of your pain. She healed you while I held our son. I could see she took her time for obvious reasons, watching me hold him as if already protective and admiring of him herself, knowing the moment was of…momentous importance to me, for us."

"Understatement." She looked at him like she was beyond worried for him, her eyes so full of love.

"Immense understatement." His voice was barely enough for even her ears to hear, even with him standing so close. The sight of tears swimming in his eyes as he remained looking toward the floor, away from her gaze, caused a determination inside her that she knew would only grow from this moment forth. He saw the question in her mind and answered it for her. "He has been there a little over three hundred years." The cost of not seeing his own son for that long, in his eyes, was what no man should have to go through. Her mind put it together that he had waited around two hundred years for her to return to him this time, thus meaning her son was born to them in her last reincarnation. He looked up at her then, seeing the yes in his eyes, answering for her. He meant that despite so much time passing, this ordeal was still raw for him.

"Tell me what to do. Please."

"I beg of you. I cannot lose you both."

He looked at her again. His expression caused a chill from her head to her toes. He looked so angry, so full of a fire that he had literally been holding in for centuries, Maya's words coming back to her. She was suddenly very disbelieving that she was the one with stronger will between them. One of the hardest moments of their existence she was not able to be there for him, not present the way he needed. He had to say goodbye to their son for the both of them that day. Shoulder that alone. He saw her slowly nod as if lost in such a deep state of refusal to fail in any of this, just simply trying to figure out where to begin for them—all three of them.

"I need to speak with Roman." She leaned on her toes to slowly kiss him. She felt him actually remain a statue, hardly moving in return, staring at her with such intense energy. "After." She took his hand and led him to the large daybed, gesturing for him to please sit, taking a moment to just look down at him. How he hid this fatherly energy from her was clearly from practice, as she would never be able to unsee it now. She had every intention never to unsee it again, no matter what it took. By the expression on his face, he could see her decision being made not just in her mind but in her heart.

Her visage expressed it quite clearly as she watched him casually sit before her. She was sorry for not just underestimating the powers they both owned but everything that was between them this whole time. This man had been so much more deserving than what she had been giving, yet that was precisely her goal now despite him hating her plans. She just wanted to give him everything he deserved, tenfold. She wanted nothing but to comfort him, be close to him, and show him how much she needed him now more than ever. She would fight until her last breath to make a way of life for them in the way that they deserved. And if she failed, well, then she needed to make the most of the now. Of the moments she had left with him.

She brushed her fingertip over his lips and lifted her hand next to do a quick little snap with her fingers, letting it fall back along her now naked hip. Letting him remain fully clothed, loving how the man looked so fine in his black slacks and dress shirt, cuffs rolled up, top buttons undone, moving to cradle herself before him atop his lap, noticing his strong hands refusing to make contact. His eyes thoroughly watched her every movement, yet somehow still keeping a complete eye on her face. He let her hands do any and all the touching, the playing, the sensual exploring, forcing his mouth to belong to her whether he wanted to react yet or not, enjoying the unknown of just when exactly he was going to cave. Her face started to own a sadness behind her growing hunger for him, and her eyes were already starting to plead for him to just touch her in return the way he so perfectly did again already.

"Please, Daemon…please…"

Her movements got a little more aggressive atop him. She held his face between her hands as she forced their mouths to fuse together. She saw him in no way unrelenting to remain in control of himself.

# THE WINGED WITCH OF MATCHES

The man was as still as a stone despite his handsome jaw returning the favor for her mouth at least. She felt his shoulders move and got excited, only to open her eyes more to see him lean back on his hands into the day bed as if to make himself more comfortable, in no way making an effort to touch her—his poker face one of the masters as she looked into his eyes, flustered for more than one reason. Her temperature rose, her scent increasing. She knew it was affecting him. Eyeing him with a combination of sarcasm and question as she reached to undo his pants, the craving inside her of its own accord was already too excited and full of selfish demands to control itself. She grasped him and stroked, feeling his thick and impressive readiness as she clearly did not need to check her own. Her insides were more than ready, aching, feeling hot as if the friction was already happening. She loved this man's body. Just looking at it was all it took for her to feel completely turned on. The way hers reacted so quickly was ridiculous.

Without looking into his face, focusing fully on the sight of their bodies joining, she completely shook literally with the immediate sensations as she slid herself over him. Slowly enveloping herself around him, eyes closing at how good it felt from just the first inch. Her lower half felt like it was vibrating from waiting, and now she was finally able to stop controlling herself and just let go and finally get what it so desperately needed. She felt him remain still other than his breathing other than sliding down slightly to let her have better access in taking all of him inside her. He watched her face, taking notice of how she completely avoided his gaze the entire time it took her to build up to her first climax, completely fine with being one with what his body had to offer and paying zero attention to him.

He could feel his hands digging into the daybed's mattress, knowing the imprints he was making were permanent. After what he did to her the last time he was inside her, his entire being was dead set on not laying a finger on her for as long as he could hold out. He felt her movements start to slow as she came back down, saw her lift her hand to her mouth to lick her fingers in a sensual way he had never seen her do before as she gazed down to enjoy the sight of him moving in and out of her. Her other hand grasped his thigh for support.

The sight of her enjoying herself like this one he knew he'd never fucking forget, even if he did lose his memory for once. He felt his own climax starting to build, regretting he'd have to cave so soon, for he would love nothing more than to let her go like this all goddamn day before him. He could see it in her mind that she did not actually take notice of his obvious rising climax, and it was for purely selfish reasons that she alone started to lift her body off him.

He watched as she turned around, standing before him, letting her sexy little ass remain in his direct line of sight, taking a moment to fix her long hair, completely oblivious as to what the sight alone was doing to him. He swore inwardly at knowing he had only a moment more of control before grabbing her and having his way when she began to move back down to sit atop him, her back to him, letting her hair fall over her back as she reached to grasp him once again. He felt her small hand hold him in place for her as she, too, slowly for his liking, penetrated her yet again, taking her damn sweet time, hearing him swear behind her out loud now. She felt him pulsing inside her, already climaxing at just the feeling of being fully within her velvet heat again, smiling and enjoying the sound of her husky voice as her craving for him was still building. She waited until his climax was completely over before even picking up the pace at all and without turning to look at him, uncaring really if he heard, for it was his problem if he missed it, as she was clearly in the mood to be selfish for a while.

"You may want to call on some of that omnipotent strength, for I am far from done with you."

"Try me." He grabbed her hips now. His hands moved up to grasp her sides, her breasts, exploring gently yet firmly from behind.

"You misunderstand me. I am trying out a new spell." She felt him lean closer against her back, starting to take control now, just a little.

"Try. Me." He gently bit her ear, wasting no time using his dream skills.

"You're drugging me again."

"You like it."

"Fuck ya, I do."

She felt his arms get tighter, her body being lifted and turned to be tossed face down onto the daybed. His two hands alone made it very clear where so many parts of her anatomy would remain in perfect position before him, underneath him. And damn did he make it feel perfect.

# Chapter 25

# Tip of Death

Maya walked into the living room, admiring the fireplace and the enormous glass walls that she so dearly missed. She loved the feeling of being in Roman's home again, their home...with him. It was so surreal for her. With her daughter not far away at home with Tronan, her daughter that she could finally hold within her own arms for real, as well as the man she loved, she should be happy. After all this time, she knew she should be happy. They had both waited for this day for so long. She watched Roman round the corner from coming downstairs and started walking toward her, seeing her face full of emotions. Looking so forward to this day as well, her guilt washed over her at seeing his reaction to her mood. He deserved to be so happy right now too.

"What is wrong?"

"Claura."

"Daemon with her?"

"Yes."

"Then he can handle—"

"I am afraid he can't…this time."

"Why not?"

"She knows."

"Clarify, my darling, please."

"Their son." She watched his face do nothing for a long moment before becoming full of shock.

"Son?" He swiped his hands out as if to say "hold on." "This entire time, Daemon has been holding that secret as well?" He looked away from her gaze for a moment to think. "And you've known this, haven't you, my dear?" His eyes moved back to hers slowly, as if unsure how to handle this information being kept from him.

"It is not my business to tell."

"As are many things, apparently."

"No. Don't! Don't you dare, Roman! It was to save her!" Her tone made it clear she refused to be swayed for her own personal reasons in this. Her eyes became sad yet full of fire.

"It is only because I have been able to hold her as a father should and touch you now that I have been able to finally calm the fuck down Maya, at all, about you not letting me know for so goddamn long. I could have tried to help. I am her fucking father!"

"You helped by not interfering with the spell that I had but two seconds to decide upon. More than you, even you…know."

"I find that hard to believe."

"I know. And I was willing to pay that price."

"What else do I not know, hmm?" He saw her look away quickly, clearly needing to immediately avoid her eyes from his ridiculously intuitive ones. When it came to Conroy, it was Claura's business to learn. It was expressed all over her face that she was determined to mind-block him on certain thoughts. So he started for her.

"When was he born?"

"He is around three hundred years old."

"Where is he?"

"In a different realm." She saw his face simply do that stern "just continue already" look. "Daemon saved both of their lives, another

Moira situation, by having to let his son go to a place where they would have to break contact with him."

"Permanently?" She gave that look again, that look that said she did not want to answer, did not want to at all be put in the middle. He caught that particular thought, at least. She could feel him constantly probing to get through the argument out loud along with the one through their mental link, making the rising tension that much worse.

"Being her aunt and the only main one around to help her at the moment with everything in her own realm, you already are in the middle. So please."

"It all depends on…" She paused and refused to finish. It was resolute on her face and in her mind.

"On what?" He came closer now, just a step.

"I can't tell you, Roman! I can't risk her knowing before she finds out on her own, which she is so close to doing. I won't risk it! She needs all the power she can get from doing this on her own. So stop, please!"

"What is it with you witches…" He clearly meant her bloodline alone.

"It's just how it works for us…" She eyed him like she dared him to question it further. She was immensely proud of her bloodline no matter what anyone said and would defend it with her life. She could see him put that one on the back burner for another day. "You can help her and Daemon."

"How's that? Seeing as she clearly needs a damn break before more is to come. And we all should be respecting that." He inclined his head as if to say them specifically, as hard as it was to wait to end all of this.

"My gut has never been as spot on as Moira's and Claura's now, but I can sense that if you and Daemon combine your realm jumping skills…yours specifically as you can contain people in the in-between, you can help her." She watched him scoff, turning around to step away again, needing to take a moment.

"Forgive me, Maya. But this time, I simply do not understand. How is this supposed to help defeat Moira? Containing her does not kill her."

"Distraction." She saw him slowly turn now. "I saw it in Claura's mind while she was out on the balcony that Tronan may be the loophole here to actually break the spell on Aiyana. I just need Claura's help in figuring out how. You and Daemon can find Moira between realms when she moves, and with your combined strengths…keep her there and unable to jump back into her realm. Claura and Tronan can retrieve the book we need and get out."

"If the book even helps."

"It will."

"She needs to see Conroy first, so she said."

"Yes."

"Are you so certain she will come out alive from that first to even be able to do this? That being, *if* I can even bypass Moira's realm in the first place to get her there!" He looked away slightly, a small amount of shame on his face for still caring for her, worrying for her so much.

"Absolutely."

"You are leaving something out. Again. And I really don't appreciate it."

"I know." She saw him look at her in disbelief that her short answers were seen as good enough from her perspective.

"You are the only person in my entire existence that I have been able to be confused by. And right now, my darling"—leaning in close to her face now, his breath on her soft skin—"you are pushing one of my last buttons."

"Good. I have time to make up for anyway." She winked.

"Distraction with me will not work."

"Because you are smarter than even my evil sister."

"Goddamn right I am. I was beyond close. I had found a way before Tronan fucked it all up!" He took a deep breath, thinking over his next words.

"And for that, I am immensely proud. It was another reason why it was so hard to leave you out of it the second time around in trying to save her."

"How the hell did he not see yet that our daughter was his Match back then? He had literally already looked upon her."

"Aiyana had not cried or made a sound in front of him yet. She was still so new, so little. Sometimes, that is all it takes, yet exactly what it takes for the connection to be recognized. She was simply not around him enough yet in time. And Moira knows which lies to choose to get her manipulative way, obviously. So let's use distraction, her own trick, back on her. Shall we."

He finally took a moment to put more of the pieces together. So much time had passed in not being able to just simply talk to her and make sense of more for far too damn long. Seeing her wait with all the patience in the world while eyeing him up and down, clearly not willing to give up on her other motives here with him. Her eyes stated the obvious that they had much to make up for in many forms. As much as he wanted to touch her again already, he knew this conversation needed to be done with. "I am not okay with Tronan being put in the middle again after last time." He strongly clarified. "Whatever you and Claura come up with, it needs to be crystal fucking clear that it will work."

"I know."

"Despite Moira being the main workings behind our daughter's curse, he fucked up. Do you really want to risk that again?"

"Yes."

"Why?"

"Because I know she will have more help on her side this time."

"How do you know that?"

"I. Can't. Say."

"Enough! I will not stay blind to another situation that may risk losing both of you *again*!"

"Stop! Please just stop!" She held her hands out, wanting to comfort him, but she was afraid to touch him as she wanted what was happening between them to be completely different right now.

## THE WINGED WITCH OF MATCHES

Maya simply wanted time alone with him, the time she had been craving for so long now. It was clear on his face that he was determined to rid this situation for them both and remain in complete control of himself until it damn well happened. He was thinking of them in the long run, and all it did was make her love him more and want him more. It did not matter that he was not omnipotent on the same level of power as Daemon or Tronan physically because he was truly just as smart. She knew it from the first moment she laid her eyes upon him that day, seeing him walk through their hometown with Moira by his side first.

"Tell me!"

"You will know soon enough. Once you and Daemon have done your part." She watched as he turned to grab something and throw it against the wall. Despite her eyes looking uncertain, as Roman did not act this way with her hardly ever, her body was able to suppress its need to jump in response. "Roman, please. I am begging you to trust me. Do not do the same thing Daemon is possibly doing with Claura right now by not following me in this. I am begging you."

"This is different. And you know it."

"It being different this time is my point! Claura agrees!"

"Claura has only been back for not even a month. She has so much to catch up on. We are throwing her into the lion's den! The least we could do is have a set plan with zero fucking loopholes this time."

"And there may be only one loophole at play here. It will simply be harder to find. Claura is dead set against any more games. She truly does want to end her, Roman. Her own mother."

"How do you know she won't change her mind, hmmm? What if Moira pulls a fast one that is that good on her?"

"Daemon won't let that happen. They have been without their son for twice as long as we have with our Aiyana! On top of that, I never had a stillborn as she did, and that was not even that long ago for her. Claura never even got to look into the eyes of either of her children, not once! I am doing this for her! And just like her right now, I am doing this with or without the help and support of my Match! Despite me desperately needing him." Her voice was begging, pleading, and he knew it was for more than one reason. Her scent made it obvious. She watched him grip the edge of the back of the sofa, hearing it start to break under his grasp, his anguished face toward the floor. Without looking back up to her, his tone once again calm, completely surprising her.

"Aiyana is calling to you." He saw her from the corner of his eye, took in a deep sigh, centered herself, and started to turn for the door. Despite being able to appear instantly over at the other home with her powers, it was obvious she was going to enjoy a walk through the woods right now first—alone. "Call me when they are ready." He refused to look at her before heading back upstairs, needing to think it all over as well. He made it clear his decision was already made despite their intense disagreement in all of it. "Maya?" He sensed her pausing without turning around. "Promise me that you will use a spell that will at least take me with you this time." He said it like his heart was already breaking at the chance that this was all going to go sour so soon again for them. "Even if in death, if it comes to that, we are going together. Do you understand me?"

"Promise," she said sadly, shutting the door behind her.

Roman hated the sound of her leaving so soon after all this time. It became beyond evident that none of them would be able to fully be together the way they deserved until her sister legitimately and permanently expired.

*****

Tronan could feel her coming, walking slowly through the woods, and decided to meet her in the yard. Aiyana's sights were set on the exact direction her mommy was coming from even long before she appeared without Tronan's help at all. He was unsure of the unsettled expression on Maya's face as she walked through the opening in the trees, making him concerned as this should be one of the happiest times in her entire life. He looked at Aiyana, seeing her being set back as well by the energy her mommy was bringing with her.

"It's okay, honey. I highly doubt any of your mommy's anger is directed at you. Welcome to having parents. At least you don't have to deal with grandparents, as my mommy and daddy, in particular, are long gone." Aiyana looked at him with an expression of confusion, as if she was truly wondering why he thought such a thing. Her face was full of "of course, I have grandparents." It took him back a moment, making the need to talk to her already that much more of a longing. He was starting to understand some of the frustration that Daemon had felt for so long, inwardly realizing he needed to talk to him about how he did it. But that could wait. It was not the most important thing on the table right now, as her little body was still growing. And that would have to be all that mattered until he heard from Claura. He was determined to know absolutely everything he could about his own Match on his own, anyway. So far, his time with her had been literally the sweetest moments of his entire existence.

"Tronan. Aiyana," she said with pleasure as if the sight was more reassuring to her than they realized.

"What troubles you, Mom?" She heard Aiyana make a small, quick laugh out loud to match his inward one.

"Well, firstly, that," she scolded him, smiling at her baby girl in his arms. "Hey, baby, I see your significant other is already teaching you to have a little sense of humor, now, isn't he?"

"Anything to make her smile." He handed her over to Maya. "News from Claura?" He was not missing her small scoff, full of tension, as her instant response to the question caused him to worry. "Is she okay?"

"She will be."

"What happened?"

"Did you know they have a son, Daemon and Adera?"

"She is going by her first name now?"

"Answer me."

It was clearly not knowing how serious she was, making it so his answer was already given really. His eyes got serious now, the depth of how serious this man could be before her once again. It was obvious he was enjoying his time with Aiyana, and she was rubbing off on him, softening him, and making him act completely different now with her around and in his life for good.

"Time frame? Age?"

"Three hundred-ish." She watched him think it over.

"I was away at the time, literally across the world. Upon return, I knew something immense took place and my brother simply never chose to discuss it with me."

"So you did not know either." She made it clear now, in partial at least, what she was just having a heated discussion with Roman about in their own home.

"He has never mentioned I am an actual uncle, not once." His expression was one of pure understanding, zero condemnation. Daemon clearly would not have done so if it was not necessary. "So she has lost two," she said softly.

"Yes."

"How long did they have him for before Daemon needed to obviously make a very hard decision for whatever reason?"

"Moira. She is the reason."

"Again? She fucking caused this too!" He faced her more now. There was fury in his entire stance. "I need details, Maya, and forgive my tone, but I need them now."

"Forgive me for cheating, but I am fried after already going over this with Claura and then Roman just in today alone." She swiped her hand while saying a few soft rhyming words before him, seeing it take about ten seconds for it to all take place behind his eyes. She watched him glance at her, then quickly away as if not wanting her to see his expression suddenly. He clearly wanted to kill something at that moment. She was thankful they were outside still, knowing she'd have a repeat of him throwing something against the wall like Roman just did. She saw him look around anyway as if needing to have the same reaction with something, anything within reach. She saw him turn around fully and walk away from her a few steps before stopping, still as stone, and contemplating.

"Tronan..."

"No. Please wait." He put his hand out as if to say, "Just a moment." He heard Aiyana make a noise as if she needed a question answered, making him turn around. He looked into her little face, admiring her beauty at such a young age already, watching her smile at him as if just looking at him whenever she needed was enough for her to feel better. Her body had grown to the size of a two-year-old now in just a short amount of time, making it clear the curse on her was fading fast, at least in all this. Her every glance his way warmed his heart. "You too, my darling."

Maya nodded, turning around to enjoy looking toward the woods, the birds, and anything that made her Aiyana smile. She took a moment to see herself enjoying all the new things in this different realm here called earth.

"You are leaving something out. Just say it." His tone was thick, with everything that was happening behind his eyes still, unable to stop himself from putting the past together more now while still wanting to know what the future was to hold in all this at the same time.

"I have an idea. A plan."

"And Claura is in agreement?"

"Working on it. She and Daemon clearly need some time. Again."

"She's truly dead set on all of this, isn't she? Even if she doesn't come out alive?"

"Put yourself in her shoes."

"Put yourself in Daemon's shoes. Willing to lose Roman?" He saw her start to lose grip of that strong-willed witch wall Maya so boldly and expertly held up, and the tears were swimming. He looked at her with an expression of "sorry," not meaning to touch a nerve on purpose. "Maya…" She watched her hold Aiyana a bit tighter, turning away for a moment.

"He is so angry at me for leaving him out of all of this for so long."

"Can you blame—"

"No!" He looked quickly at Aiyana with an apology for yelling before her, still holding her. "Yes!" She gestured toward what, or who, was in her arms. It was as if to clarify the obvious behind her hardest decision. He sat her down, giving her little butt a pat as she headed toward some outdoor toys nearby on the porch. Tronan gestured for Maya to please sit, choosing a spot where he could keep an eye on his little one.

"You do not need to feel guilty about anything, Maya. Nothing. Despite your powers and your abilities, that being no matter…you are still a mom. And as a mom, you made your decision. End of story."

"You are so forgiving. Aren't you angry at all with me for attaching her to Daemon for so long?"

"It is my failing."

"Really?"

"Yes. You think I don't remember her, but I do." He looked at Aiyana, watching her playing with some colorful cubes, already looking bored with what stimulus they had to offer. "Roman and I never got along, even before the ordeal. I simply chose not to press it until she was older and chose me for herself in front of him. And I chose to make sure I did not hear her cries, as you both know why, and because I knew she was safe with you both anyway until she was simply older."

"Clearly, we failed as parents."

"No. You have done the exact opposite. The determination you must have had this entire time alongside Daemon. I truly never gave him enough credit."

"And you fell for the bonding spell with Claura so easily as your mind told you Aiyana was dead."

"I truly felt like Claura was my only chance at a Match at all. I was simply responding to how she was reacting to me as well."

"Why did you pause that day then, if you already knew Aiyana was most likely your Match?"

"Moira mentioning anything about my Match would have made me…any man…pause. She knew the one second I needed to contemplate her lie was the only second she needed to curse her." He looked into the forest for a moment, wondering what his options were in all this now. "I want to kill her myself, Moira." His tone suggested he was adamant about it. "I can see it in Aiyana's eyes that she is truly the one who deserves to do so, but as she is so young—"

"As if you'd let her try anyway."

"Of course, I'd...question it." He looked at her again on the porch, seeing her watch him with a deep level of curiosity while examining a new toy at the same time. "Her face is so expressive. So beautiful." He felt Maya's eyes watch the moment thoroughly.

"Claura thinks you are the loophole. Actually."

"Do tell."

"If Moira needed you to pause to start the curse, it may be you who as well ends it. This entire time." She saw his intent gaze as if he really did not want to go down this road unless he truly could finish it. "I am sorry for not seeing this before. It is truly...scary...in a way how smart Claura can be."

"She does own the most magnificent library in all the realms. Perhaps it is time we all stop underestimating her for good. After being connected to her the way I was, I do not want to see her have to part from us. I can't imagine what it puts my brother through every time."

"You did not recognize her, Tronan? That she was Adera, truly?"

"No. I was simply gone that much. Being from two very different realms made it so. Despite being brothers, we always had very separate lives with different responsibilities. I only saw her a few times over several centuries. And her reincarnation spell made her look slightly different each time she was born again. I simply had no idea it was her, no idea about Moira's game. Truly."

"I see."

"You can ask me anything, Maya. Please."

"What came to your mind first when you saw her in the office in the bassinet alive?"

"Shock."

"Obviously."

"Remorse. Shame. Confusion."

"I am sure confusion the most." She watched him softly nod in agreement.

"I now see how Daemon felt, how it was for him being connected to two at the same time before the unbinding spell was done."

"You did not know who to choose?" Her tone held no condemnation.

"How could I, Maya? I truly thought she belonged to Daemon and that I maybe had made a mistake. Daemon is stronger. My fight for her would have been inevitable death. And what I felt for Claura, in my confusion, I clung to that. In how my brother felt torn, I could relate."

"You were more torn."

"Yes. I am not as strong as my brother, unfortunately."

"It is okay, Tronan. Despite you almost killing yourself literally minutes before Claura was able to say the unbinding spell, we do understand."

"Roman will never say that."

"Well, fortunately"—looking to Aiyana—"us women can be a bit more forgiving." She smiled down at her daughter, who started walking toward them now, looking between them as if she did not know who to go to first, then suddenly pointing into the distance while trying to shout, "Dada!"

They both turned to see Roman walking toward them, pausing for only a slight second to make sure he actually heard what just came out of her mouth. Maya looked at her beloved, smiling. "Well, my love, that being her first word should make up for a few things."

She watched him pick up his pace again. His face went from concern while watching Maya to full-on love and adoration for his daughter, watching her walk and lift her little butt down the steps backward, one at a time, to start walking toward him, little hands in the air, her smile as wide as she could make it across her small visage. Maya turned from the moment to study Tronan, clearly keeping his sight on his little beloved still. Unknowing of his smile, he was so in tune with just whatever was happening with her.

"Tronan, is she liking this place as much as a certain other had?" Maya asked.

"And you know this how?"

"Forgive me for seeing too much sometimes in her memories. It is only because she is my niece that it makes it easier."

"Go on."

"This used to be Claura's house." She could see just the reminder of what took place with her here affecting him on a deeper level than he let on. He noticed that she noticed, taking a moment to look away before admitting it.

"I am afraid to speak with her."

"She misses you. She really does."

"I regret how I...handled...some things."

"Well, now Daemon has too." Her tone suggested regret yet a dire need for them all to just move on as well.

"Excuse me?" Tronan asked.

Roman walked up onto the porch with Aiyana in his arms, standing in place before them both, in no hurry to sit before more clarification was met here with this discussion, looking at Maya with serious questions in his gaze.

"Moira." The men looked at one another, clearly on the same page with this bitch just needing to die already. "She left some unwanted energy in the room after her little visit to Claura's office, knowing fire would feed the fire with them already arguing."

"That conversation must have been interesting," Tronan inquires.

"Am I the only fucking one who would have been able to treat her right!?" Roman unapologetically chimed in, raising his voice intentionally as if he didn't give a rat's ass about anyone's reaction. Maya took notice as to even her, intentionally hiding her knowing expression of what it meant.

"Well, not all of us have your control, my dear," Maya said darkly, eyeing him with slight contempt after a moment of looking away to collect herself.

"No. Clearly." Roman eyed them both back for separate reasons. Aiyana, in his arms, started laughing a little through the tension, slightly surprising them all. "Well, someone sure knows how to not be bothered by us silly adults, now do they?" He smiled back at her, nibbling her fingers playfully, causing giggles.

Tronan crossed one ankle over his other knee while leaning back into his chair more, leaning his jaw on his hand, clearly calmer than any of them had ever seen him before—like ever. "Despite what everyone thinks, Claura can handle herself." His tone fully expressed he was over the ordeal. Claura was a grown woman with his blood in her at the time, and he was starting to look back on the times he had with her with more love than regret. And no one was going to take that away from him. "Has Maya spoken with you? The plan?"

Roman looked at him like he couldn't believe he even asked. Of course, she did come to him first. He saw Tronan actually laugh at him in return with his eyes alone.

"What, dear son?" he said with obvious dislike still.

"Like it's my downfall, my own Match can't speak yet."

"Actually, it kind of fucking is." He looked at his daughter as if to say, "Duh," seeing her actually join in with the same expression as they both looked back at Tronan at the same time.

"Roman. Don't," Maya softly tried, knowing the warning was a waste of breath as soon as she said it.

"Oh no, hell no"—pointing with his one free hand at him—"Moira or not, he knew what he needed to do and still got distracted. I don't care that it was for only one second."

"I listened to you, Roman, more than you even realize to this damn day, whether you see that or not. Unlike the third guy, I actually showed. It was one goddamn second! And she wasn't mentioning just anything about anybody. She was bringing up something that had to do with her!" He nodded toward Aiyana briefly as he stood up to walk closer to him. "Stop holding me accountable for what was done when I was there with you, in full support to try to stop it, just like I am today! Again!" He waited for Maya to finish taking Aiyana from Roman's arms to shove him backward toward the woods where he came from. "I will be who ends this! And if you mess *that* up for me this time, I will fucking bury *you*!"

He saw Roman literally laugh with such rage and disbelief, Maya bringing Aiyana inside with her out of the corner of his eye. Taking notice of how they were out on the lawn now, Tronan was clearly in the mood to beyond defend his loved one and his home, no matter whether Roman was her father or not. "Well, this is a long time coming, isn't it, son?"

"Don't fucking call me that! I am more than twice your age."

"I'm sorry...well, with even my short years, who figured out how to defeat Moira the first time? And who fucked that up? Please remind me!" Shoving him back now. "We could have all been saved this bullshit a long time ago!"

"Moira would have just caused harm elsewhere, as Claura makes that obvious herself with her situation. At least Moira is dumb enough to choose to do it with someone like you, Roman, in all honesty."

"Meaning?" He clearly took it the wrong way.

"Because you're fucking smarter. You're smarter than all of us! The fact that you come from the human world baffles me."

"I was changed by Moira. You think I like knowing I am how I am due to that psycho?" He heard Maya in his head mention how she was baffled. They weren't slamming each other into trees yet, taking a split second to see her holding Aiyana through a certain window.

"Well, Maya was next in line, so...same result. And you know it." He rolled his cuffs back up, fixing his collar, his tone making it clear he was set on honesty and not really meaning to push buttons. "Why the hell did you choose Moira first, huh? Didn't see it? With how smart you are, really!"

"Well, we are all pretty stupid in choosing our first love, aren't we?"

"I was under a fucking spell by that bitch. You were not." He eyed him, daring him to defy it.

"No. I was."

"Hmmm?"

"I was stupid once, Tronan. Okay! It's called being human. Not all of us can be born this omnipotent being."

"Where did she get the power to turn you, all on her own?"

"That is what she said."

"And you believe her?"

"I don't believe a fucking thing she says anymore. Never will." He headed toward the house now, leaving Tronan facing the woods alone.

"She is mine, Roman," he said without turning around, meaning every word about how Moira was his and his alone to end. Sorry yet not sorry for taking the opportunity away from the father in this scenario.

"You'll get first dibs." He turned back toward the house again, deep down knowing it had to be him anyway. He heard Tronan slightly laugh from afar as he neared the house, followed by an eerie silence.

"I am sorry I failed, but so did you." Tronan figured if there was ever a time to throw that in there, now would be it. He heard Roman stop again, sensed him turning around this time, and turned to face him as well. "Out of respect for you, I distanced myself from Aiyana after she was born. I already knew, Roman."

"I'm sorry, you knew!"

"Your dislike of me was…not easy. I made the decision to leave her alone until she was older until she chose me for herself in her own way. I would have been able to have that control for her, whether you believe me or not."

"I don't."

"I know." He eyed him like he dared challenge his words anyway.

"Wait…so in a way, you think this is my fault just as much as I think it is yours? Are you serious right now?"

"Very. I could have let the connection start from one of her first cries, brought her to my home, and kept her safe."

"I did not know."

"Would it have made a damn difference!" He saw Roman turn in a circle, refusing to look at him while he thought it over. "Answer me! Your turn to turn the fuck around and answer me!" Tronan literally growled it. His recent moments with Aiyana made him truly realize just how much he had been missing out on, the connection being able to be whole now.

"Yes." He faced him again now.

"Oh really?" He scoffed. "Liar," he said it, just one word, with such distaste.

"It's true. Maya would have made me accept it."

"Why do you think she mentioned me that day to help save her? Hmm?"

"Because she already knew, didn't she?" His face showed clear disbelief at how smart his Maya truly was, at how he missed this little fact this entire time. Yet another part of him was getting real tired of her just not being more honest with him about things. She was different compared to before this whole curse on their daughter happened.

"She was getting ready to tell you, not expecting Moira to force her to have to take things so far, to have to make it look like she and Aiyana died to protect her! You took that chance away from me to just keep her safe in the first place. Daemon became the obvious choice due to the rising level of power that Moira somehow got her goddamn hands on! And I had to face losing my Match as well, thinking she died before I even got to feel fully bonded to her for one moment!"

"Why did you never tell me?"

"What would it have mattered after thinking she was dead? I decided to hold out in claiming her for my own out of respect for you, and it was the biggest mistake of my life. I will never put anyone first other than Aiyana so long as I am still breathing. Understand me?"

"Do you know why I have always hated you?"

"No. And I honestly don't fucking care anymore."

"Moira."

"Don't blame this on her. Daemon and Claura have enough reasons alone to end her, let alone the rest of us having to continually add to it."

"It's true."

"Fine. Enlighten me." His tone suggested making it quick as he already was feeling the need to check on Aiyana for himself again.

"Before she changed me when I was still a lousy little human. I thought she was the love of my life. And then one night, she sees you and looks upon you with such lust."

"Jealousy. Just like what started this whole thing with her, apparently."

"Yes."

"Maya knows?"

"Some things she does not need to know. So please."

"I see now."

"What?"

"Why do you still hate Daemon and me so much when it comes to Claura? It brings back those feelings of jealousy, doesn't it?"

"Not proud of it already, Tronan. Don't need to rub it in."

"You have one of the most gorgeous and smartest women as your true Match. Why do you still care so much for Claura? Hmm?"

"Claura is smarter. For some reason, that gets under my skin."

"So sure you are correct about that?"

"I am missing something when it comes to Claura, but I will figure it out."

"Perhaps you should leave it alone."

"I am sorry. I can't."

"Daemon will make sure you 'can.' Mark my words."

"I saw her go through things, Tronan. It has simply already marked me."

His tone was actually sad. He was feeling disappointed in himself suddenly with everything Tronan had just made known on top of other things still. Things he wished were not so obvious, but you could only hide so much, super being or not. His heart ached for how much Maya may actually know, not wanting her to feel less than what she truly was to him. He was holding on to the hope that once all of this was over, somehow, someway, things would just get back to how they should be.

He clearly meant the time he had together with Claura before this life was brought upon her when it was just Claura and Roman, patient and doctor, being there with her as she went through what she did. "I saw her sleeping on a bench in the park with not even a blanket when she was in her second trimester. I saw her go to a coffee shop, not having enough money for a drink and food and simply had to pick one or the other. I saw her window shop with tears in her eyes, constantly wiping her cheeks with dirty tissues while admiring all the baby items she could not afford. I watched her roommate give her back her own key to her own goddamn apartment when she saw fit after having a guy or two over. I kept an eye on her more than any of you know. I saw her live a shitty life. All of you don't understand why she keeps underestimating herself but I know why. I looked forward to her hospital visits because I enjoyed watching her walk into a safe environment. I enjoyed taking extra time for her appointments, extra care and blood work, and extra time to sit and chat with her. And it may be because I sensed Maya through her this entire time, as they are related. I don't know. I simply do not know. But there is one thing missing here, in this world with her, and I will figure it out."

"You should speak to Daemon about all of this. For he has seen her go through things too, so don't be a fool here, Roman."

"That bastard can see it in her memories. He doesn't need me."

"Your jealousy needs to stop, or else Moira can use that to her will in this still. She is one of the smartest witches we have ever known, and Claura is her own blood. Claura is getting stronger, despite what you have noticed or not of her yet in *this* world."

"While Moira is getting weaker..."

"We don't know what that means. Moira could simply be dying from a different enemy as we speak. Lord knows she has nothing but an endless line of them."

"Or there is something else...something I am missing..."

"Roman, when it comes to witches, there is always something missing. I can sense something different about Aiyana already, but I refuse to push it. I know it will be shown in time when she is ready."

"That's because you will not push her to do anything, understand me?" It was clearly okay with the topic jump here. It was clear as day, meaning that despite his daughter having the mind of a much older being than her body matched, Tronan would wait, so help him God.

"I will not lay a finger upon her in such a way until she is at least sixteen years of age. You have my word," he said softly yet full of meaning.

"Twenty." He raised his face as he said it, stepping closer to Tronan, watching him slightly smile. "This isn't funny."

"The fact that you think I even am capable of doing anything to her that she doesn't want me to do, *true* Match this time, is actually funny. Come on, dear Roman, you should know the women hold the real power here, with their heat cycles…as is clear by your dear Maya, which, by the way, you need to take care of." He sniffed, pointing out the obvious. "Take her home. *Now*."

Just then, they both heard the sliding glass door on the porch open and shut. Roman still eyed Tronan for a moment before turning to face her, his intense gaze of dislike for him still coming to the surface out of pure habit, eyeing the determined smirk mixed with seriousness on Tronan's face. Maya's expression made it obvious she was busy with her daughter and truly did stay out of the majority of their conversation. He was completely oblivious to their tension, walking toward them with motherly happiness on her face. He smiled as she came closer. He looked up at them while stating, "She is down for a nap." He looked between them as she came to a stop before them both. "What?" She watched Tronan laugh to himself as he walked by them both and headed inside. She only slightly watched him before turning back to Roman with questions in her eyes. "Please tell me you didn't talk about me?"

"A little." He slowly moved toward her.

"Are you ready to go talk to Claura? Come with me this time." He tried not to look at his body for obvious reasons, the man's stubbornness coming to mind first. Looking like she was tired of putting her needs on the back burner during this situation, but if that was what made him happy, then so be it. Roman was worth the wait—a 150-year wait, to be exact.

"It can wait."

"Really? You wanted to get a move on with all of this, and now that conversation about seeing Conroy can wait?"

"Uh-huh." She came closer. Her eyes were getting more serious. She saw his one hand reach out to grab her around the waist, forcing her close as if her resistance in the matter meant absolutely nothing to his strength.

"Do not tease me, my Roman. I beg of you."

"I can't just touch you, hold you close?"

"You are pushing one of *my* last buttons." Her tone was trying to be funny, but her eyes were completely not. Her expression is one of pure sexual longing and frustration.

"I'm not worried. I'll find more." He winked at her. He leaned in toward her ear now, letting her feel his body heat nice and close, his breath on her skin. "And I will find them now."

"Then why aren't we moving yet, huh?" Her eyes closed at just being able to feel him this close again. It all so surreal still. His actual body touched hers finally after all this time. Despite him already having his way with her, it was just more of a warm-up after all this time they had to make up for. She hastily grabbed his face with her hands and forced his mouth to hers.

"Because you can travel us back home faster. While I do other things faster." His face smiled at her reaction to him having to pull away just to talk to her. Her temperature rose, and the heat cycle got more intense.

"You have always enjoyed teasing me until the literal tip of death, my love, and it no longer feels funny."

"No? But you know what it does feel?"

"Damn good." Her hands were going crazy for him now, feeling his get rougher in return as she felt them appear in their own bedroom.

CHAPTER 26

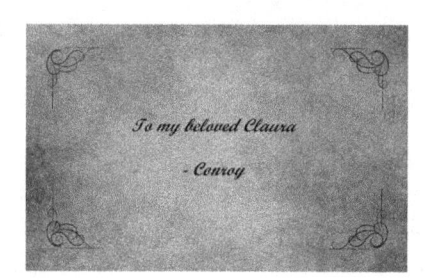

## Magical Letter

*To my beloved Claura*

*- Conroy*

Claura continued to lay in Daemon's arms on the daybed long after morning hours had come and gone. She enjoyed feeling him breathing next to her, her head on his shoulder in the crook of his arm, letting her fingers play over his chest muscles. She watched as he barely needed to breathe at all. There was silence between them all morning, enjoying one another over and over again, loving how his body could just keep going and going for her. The entire morning was nothing but a honeymoon in bed, really. And she hated that she had to get back to work and find a way to finish the task at hand still. She noticed the sun getting higher in the sky, feeling it get much hotter on the velour bedding that was wrapped around them, suddenly looking to the clock and then his face with concern.

"Relax. It is Tronan that said he burns around noon and noon only. Not me." He felt her not relax beside him. "And just mentioning him was wrong of me, I see." There was still silence. He felt her rest her head against him again, making no incentive to say something. It caused his eyes to open in worry, slight wonder at what that could mean. He stared at the detailed ceiling now, letting his fingers caress along her hip, enjoying the curves that were so uniquely hers.

"What if I am wrong about him being the one, the loophole here? What if this plan gets him killed?"

"You have yet to even research how it is possible he even would be."

"My gut—"

"Is sexy as hell."

"My intuition—"

"Is annoying as hell."

"Daemon, stop! I need your help in this."

"Moira is growing weaker. She may not be as hard to kill as you think."

"Something tells me she has a witch generator." She heard him laugh.

"Well, we will just kill that too."

"I can feel someone coming."

"Lock the door." He slightly sat up to lean over her now, grabbing her in all the right places again, making her smile right as she slithered out from under his grasp and walked for the door.

"My darling, at least dress yourself before you open the door. As much as I hate to ask." She heard him snap his finger and looked down at a pink silk robe wrapped around her.

"This is clothes to you? So help me." She looked at him with a fake dislike, watching him wink in return.

Claura could hear her name being yelled from down the hall before she even was close to the door, her shouting making it become clear quite quickly that something important was happening. She turned to Daemon with worry now, seeing him already dressed in some Levi's and a black tee and walking toward the door with a clear intention to open it with her.

"Allie?"

"Yes. Come now! We have a visitor." She looked at Daemon with fear, knowing he was not going to like who it was. They both turned to look at his face now, seeing him sniff, followed by rising anger. Claura looked back to Allie with a question, already being able to tell that Daemon was action before words at the moment, seeing him start to exit the office and walk down the hallway toward the stairs.

"Allie, who is it? Why is he smelling them?"

"The minions on the other side of the wall always smelled potent and strange…very, very strange."

She saw the fear cross Claura's face, making it clear she was already informed of a certain part of her past. She noticed how her fear quite quickly turned to anger and determination about it, though this time, and started running down the hallway to catch up to Daemon. As she cornered the office door and started walking, she looked up to see Daemon grabbing the edge of the balcony and jumping over as if the ten stories below him were nothing to have to deal with. She picked up the pace, already knowing he was fine by their mental link, yet still trying to come to terms with what he was capable of. Just by the small whiff alone, he clearly knew exactly where this visitor was on the very bottom floor. She looked over the balcony to see pretty much every being there looking in one direction, backing away from the scene. She turned to look at Allie with the obvious question of how the hell they got down there faster with a spell of some sort. Allie nodded in her direction, reading her face with zero effort, swiped her fingers in a little detailed circle, and let a book appear between them. She started to toss it to Claura, seeing her barely catch it while trying to keep an eye on the scene below.

"Open it. Page 67. Read it."

"I don't have time…"

"He is fine. Only one came through. You need to practice."

"Okay…"

Claura's fingers couldn't move fast enough. She opened the book to the said page and felt instantly thankful it was but two lines. She felt Allie grab her hand as if to say they were going together. She finished the last two words and lifted them to the bottom floor. Claura felt the fog of the spell dissipate in just one second and looked around immediately, feeling Daemon from a certain direction but not seeing him yet. She followed her intuition, her feet moving already before her mind even told them to. A part of her was frightened, very frightened, but also very angry. These beings were part of why her horrible mother almost got her way...why her very own son is apart from them still. Despite the bastard having the balls to come back here alone, as that could mean so many different things now, she first wanted to know how the hell they even got through. She turned the corner to see a weird-looking figure with green skin and very strong arms being held up against the wall around the neck, Daemon's fury alone making her top a few yards from them.

"Stay back." His warning to her made the being turn and look at her. Daemon responded in not-so-kind way, slamming the being's head into the wall and forcing it to look away from her with his thumb alone. "You have one minute, and you don't get to leave alive, no matter what you say."

"Conroy wants to see...her."

"You are coming with news from Conroy?"

"Yes." He held out a small envelope inside a shaking hand.

"Why?"

"I am a mailman for him. He only let certain people know of my use."

"I can smell Moira's realm all over you. You are literally asking me to kill you right now."

"I don't expect to leave alive. I know." He sounded like he welcomed it.

"Your services are beyond useless."

"She needs to decide that."

"It is fucking decided!" He slammed his head into the wall again.

"What is it for?" Claura butted in, arms crossed over her chest. She looked worried yet determined all the same. "Why is...this... useful?" She nodded toward the envelope that was now on the floor, as clearly, Daemon wanted nothing to do with it.

"He is a liar. You can't believe their kind, Claura."

"I am not in her realm anymore. Not since..." If there was a way for this little minion to trigger Daemon even more, he found it. Daemon let him start to fall to the floor and backhanded him with a closed fist so hard he started flying, literally flying, before sliding down the aisle between books.

"I already know a thousand ways to kill you." Daemon started walking toward him.

With his back to Claura, she decided to risk walking toward the small envelope, studying it.

"Allie?" She quickly came up behind her, still staying close this entire time.

"Yes?"

"Is there a spell to open this without me touching it?"

"About 130 to choose from."

"Good. Please choose one for me. Hurry."

She looked up to see Daemon reaching him now, placing his hands on him again. It was far away from her enough to make her have to use her heightened hearing skills now to know what was being said between them. She decided against it that Daemon could handle him, whatever he truly was, leaving her alone to deal with this little white envelope that held the energy of a damn bomb. "And, Allie, please choose wisely. I am sorry I cannot assist in this due to losing my fucking memory over and over."

"I have never disliked a lifetime here with you. Not once."

"I appreciate that, for this may be my last." He felt her pause at once next to her.

"But you have so much knowledge—"

"That I keep forgetting!" He looked at her aggressively, seeing that she was being too blunt by the hurt on Allie's face now. "I am sorry. But if I cannot find another way, I am done...alongside with this failing reincarnation spell."

"I have truly underestimated how different this time is, but at least now I know how to be of more help."

"How so?"

"To be blunt back here, Claura, you need to keep me more informed."

"Noted. I am sorry. Now how!"

"The row down there that they are in right now, that section alone holds clues as to how to fix spells." She looked at the books surrounding the two like she was worried for their spines first, the actual living spines second.

"I need more than clues, Allie. I need answers. Which is why I am going to see Conroy and then make a visit to Moira."

"Why him?"

"Intuition."

"Is that all that is guiding you?"

"It is all I have. And my aunt Maya. She is beyond supportive in this, despite everyone else not being." She looked up at Daemon, knowing Allie did not miss the expression toward him.

"I have never seen a man go through more heartbreak. I truly hope you know what you are doing."

"I don't. It just feels like it's my only option. Can you please find me information on his realm and Moira's realm? Please."

"Consider it done."

"Thank you. And, Allie…"

"Hmmm?"

"I look forward to knowing you are more than my assistant. Do not think that I cannot tell that in other lifetimes, we had more time to be friends."

"Noted. Now let me help you with that envelope."

Claura watched and listened closely as Allie did a soft-spoken spell as if to let the envelope know it was not going to be harmed and it was okay to open. She gestured for Claura not to get too close, seeing her follow her advice instantly. They both looked at the now-floating envelope, seeing it open and a small piece of paper unfold before them. They both lean in closely and read it out loud at the same time.

Dear my Adera,

Do not hesitate nor be afraid to finally visit me.
I have been looking forward to it for longer than

you know. Please excuse my particular mailman. Not many were still up for the task. Talk soon.

Conroy

"My Adera?" What the hell...

"Apparently, he already knows you are coming. And knows you," Allie said.

"He makes it seem like I don't actually have to fear him. Why is everyone so afraid of him? Do you know anything about him?"

"To be honest, I have never heard the name before. I think it will be quite difficult to find information regarding the top 3 realms. As those are the only three places that have stayed wary of adding their own intelligence to your library."

"And we don't know why, do we?"

"I am sorry, Claura. With your memory or not, this is one of those things where we just don't have the information anyway. Perhaps he is that information himself, and speaking to him is exactly what you need to do."

"Tell me about it."

"You need to tell Roman to try to get you past Moira's realm. And soon."

"Agree. Something tells me I am running out of time."

"Yup. I can sense that too."

They both look at the note still floating in the air, glancing past it toward Daemon and the other being still having a chat. Claura could tell the little guy was tough, for he was still holding his own... barely. She saw Daemon look at her and notice the opened envelope, his face a whole new level of worry and anger. The green being before him turned to follow his gaze. She expected a smirk from him for seeing that he got his way, knowing she wouldn't be able to resist. Instead, he looked grateful and relieved despite his current beating. She watched him close his eyes as if thankful his mission was finally accomplished and remain closed long after Daemon let him fall to the floor with quite the rough thud. Daemon stood tall and faced her, remaining where he was. It was obvious he was worried about what might happen next with that opened envelope. Suddenly, they all felt a presence behind them, two in particular.

*****

## Slightly earlier…

 Tronan closed the sliding glass door behind him. There was silence. Other than her soft breathing and steady heartbeat, he could hear from the distance between them in his home. He decided now was as good of a time as any to shower and then make some dinner for them both before she awoke. He laughed at himself for not even knowing what she would like to eat now that bottles were out of the question already so soon. Even the sippy cup phase was coming and going much faster than expected. His little Aiyana was a fast learner. He smiled at knowing how most parents probably wished certain days would go by as fast, especially Daemon. Bottles and diapers for fifteen decades, all because he couldn't speak up to Roman right from the start. Tronan did not try to hide his fear of Moira, but he also knew there were now more powerful witches in existence. And something kept shaking his insides about one of them being right upstairs now, fast asleep. He peeked in on her for a few moments before he let himself enjoy a hot shower, seeing her sleeping so soundly. He admired her ever-changing features as they changed little by little on a daily basis now. He leaned in close to whisper to her little ear how beautiful she was, kissing her forehead before grabbing what he needed and shutting the door behind him.

 He took his time washing up, enjoying the sense of peace that was coming from the change of events. Thinking over everything that had happened and that was to come, his mind focused mainly on how to keep Aiyana safe in all of it. He hated that he wasn't sure what exactly he'd have to keep her safe from. Moira was as manipulative and tricky as they came. He reminded him of how lucky they were to have Claura, the woman's own daughter with similar abilities and powers, on their side. He realized he did not know as yet just how powerful Maya herself was, as he never had to pay attention to her that much until now. For still needing Daemon to help her with everything, and then Claura now too, he wondered if she was losing her strength, too, like Moira, and was just better at hiding it. And if so, why? He paused, thinking he heard her waking, only to be able to tell she was simply just moving in her sleep. He wondered if using his dreaming ability with her now was too soon. The last thing he felt like doing was scaring her. He decided to simply leave her be, that there would be plenty of time for that to come. Her steady breathing was enough to reassure him that she was fine.

He hastily dressed and headed toward the kitchen, halfway there, deciding that he would just wait now and simply ask her first what she would like to eat. On that note, he walked back to the bedroom and peeked in, only for his heart to stop. He opened the door wider and walked toward the bed, his face turning more serious as he stepped closer. Seeing a larger frame underneath the blankets, feeling in shock at what was before him. A young girl still, someone who still looked just like Aiyana, only to be about ten years old now. Tronan just stood there, unsure what to do and unsure what to think. He watched as she slowly stirred awake, her eyes searching for him immediately, her expression going from relief to confusion by the look on his face.

"Sweetheart, you have grown again."

"I…uhhh…" She leaned up on one elbow quickly and looked at her hands next. The shock on her face started to show. "Tronan!" The sound of her own voice being able to say his name made her sit up now, looking even more startled. She started feeling her face, removing the blankets to see more of herself, staring at her own body in awe, looking like she was afraid to touch her own skin. He could see the fear start to creep in real quick. "Tronan!" She looked up into his face with pleading eyes. She saw him kneel before her now along the side of the bed, reaching for her hands. His face was an expression of shock and love at hearing her say his name.

"Are you in pain?"

"No."

"Nothing hurts?"

"No."

She moved closer to him, clearly needing the reassurance she had already gotten used to getting whenever she was scared while being so little, needing him to hold her. He recognized the expression immediately and gestured for her to "come here," enveloping her in his arms for a hug. "This is scary. This is so scary. I can't believe I can talk." She felt him squeeze a bit tighter, taking in a deep breath, inhaling her unique scent. She knew he felt her slight shaking at not being able to hold back from crying a little. "I feel silly like I don't know what to say now that I can finally say anything!"

"You can tell me anything."

"I've waited so long! I have waited…so…long!" She was hyperventilating through tears now. It became clear she did not know where to even begin. She leaned back out of his grasp for a second, feeling his one hand on the side of her face while looking over herself again. She looked back into his face with complete disbelief. His eyes held such compassion, such love, such admiration. "Tronan, I am so sorry. I don't know where to begin." She watched him smile.

"Already like your cousin, I see, apologizing when you never need to."

"Claura? She was in my dream…along with a minion."

"It was just a dream."

"No, it wasn't." She looked at him with worry.

"How do you know?"

"I just do." She started to get up and felt him gently stop her.

"Slow down. Please." She saw the worry fade from her face as if she was naturally meant to follow his lead in every way, shape, and form already. It warmed his insides and softened his heart even more at how she was just so okay already with taking him seriously. And so naturally.

"Okay," she said softly.

"I have waited so long to hear your voice. And it sounds so beautiful." She watched her give him a shy smile.

"I recognized you, you know."

"When? In the office, with your father and Daemon?"

"No. Long before that." She saw the realization sink in on his face, along with the shock, the guilt.

"You truly knew, even then, as well?"

"Yes." He nodded while letting his much larger hands take hers, looking at him still kneeling before her.

"Sweetheart, I am so sorry. I am so beyond sorry I let this happen."

"Moira made her choices. This isn't really your fault."

"I already don't deserve you."

"It is true, and you know it. Despite what all of you come up with in this messed-up situation that I have had to watch take place on my back…not even sitting, at least most of the time…on my back in a bassinet…this is all Moira. I blame you for nothing." She put his face between her small hands, forcing him to remain looking into her eyes. "All of my rage is going to go toward her. Nobody else. Please know I mean that."

"I cannot imagine what this has done to you."

"It has made me ready."

"For what?"

"Everything." He could tell she was choosing not to be specific on purpose.

"My darling, you need to give me a better answer. Please." He watched her take a deep breath, looking away as if working up the courage for his reaction and not necessarily the task at hand.

"To kill Moira."

"Oh really?"

"Oh really."

"I don't think so."

"I will be—"

"Out of harm's way."

"Despite being cursed for so long, trust me…I have had plenty of time being out of harm's way. Your brother did too good of a job, to be honest."

"Good to know. We can go thank him together."

"Fabulous. I can sense the minion is still in her realm with them. We need to go now."

"Minion?" The pieces came together more now, thanks to the information Maya shoved into his mind earlier.

# THE WINGED WITCH OF MATCHES

"Please trust me." Her tone made his reaction to her grow even more intense. He could tell she had been needing to say it to him for some time. "I can't have them hurting her again. Even just one of them beings is dangerous. They are extremely hard to kill."

"Daemon is with her. He knows this. How do you already know this?"

"Daemon read to me."

"Oh, did he, about evil minions?"

"He understands me." She was not meaning to sound mean. It just came out. She felt her heart hurt more than expected at his quick glance away from her face. "But more importantly, I understand him. You get more information from just listening than you think."

"Aiyana, you do understand that you still need to listen to me, please."

"You're not going to take me, are you?"

"No, we will go. I just…sweetheart….I…" He let go of her hands and stood up, walking away from her a few feet to face in the opposite direction, trying to get a hold of his emotions.

"I won't go near the minion. I promise."

"Thank you." He faced her again, gesturing a regrettable "let's go" with his hands, watching her jump off the bed in a hurry and head for the door.

Taking a quick moment to wonder if he should let her parents know of their first adventure out of politeness, he decided against it, as being polite didn't get him for the first time. He used his speed trick to catch up to her down the hall, grabbing her around the waist to lift her into his arms right before realm jumping them to the front doors of Claura's majestic enormous library. Tronan and Aiyana felt the energy and smell of the minion as soon as they arrived. Both walked simultaneously toward the particular aisle of books.

*****

Daemon, Claura, and Allie both turn to see Tronan and Aiyana saunter toward them. The look of pure shock on Daemon and Claura's faces one Tronan would have forever etched in his memory as soon as their eyes landed on Aiyana walking slightly in front of him toward them. They all stared without the right words as she walked only a few feet from them, eyeing the minion behind the two ladies and seeing Daemon standing over it. They were clearly determined to end its life, and they were just unsure of how to do it yet. His look of shock at seeing her, knowing instantly who she was, gave her the moment of pause that she needed to do with the minion as she pleased all on her own. She could feel Tronan stepping closer now as if warning her not to risk doing anything stupid as she lifted her right palm toward the green creature, saying a few soft words with determination, her brow creasing as she pushed her palm outward just a small degree. The lights she owned looked just like Claura's had, only purple. They all saw the power radiating from her palm toward the creature before anyone knew what she was even truly doing and could stop it, the moment being completely unexpected from her. She inwardly commands Daemon's feet to step back so as not to take any of the blasts as it hits the creature, causing his thick green neck to make a hell of a "snap." His already-closed eyes stayed that way for good.

She turned to Claura, being unaffected by the look on her face. "They will never touch any of my family again." She looked to Tronan next, seeing his disbelief and slight anger that she would be so careless with her safety and her powers so damn soon. "I said I would not get close. I never said I wouldn't kill it." She just kept staring into his face, with zero guilt for her actions. Her sternness in this matter clearly threw him off.

Daemon saw the look of shock on Tronan's face. It was clear he was having a hell of a day too. He felt his brother in his mind as he faced him in return over Aiyana's head, the accusation strong.

*So you read to her, hmm?*

# Chapter 27

# Croissants to Die For

She saw the look on Daemon's face, not knowing where to begin, trying to piece together how helping her education was a bad thing. She simply deserved to have her mind filled with information as her ability to think and reason grew despite her body not growing along with her for the entire time she remained in his home for so long. *Yes. Almost every day.* Daemon's tone held zero apology. *You were not there to see it in her eyes, Tronan. So don't question this. You do not understand.*

*I know I have yet to understand more. She has made that clear*, she said with a humble distaste.

*A person, still in the body of a baby or not, can only take a happy little fairy tale so many times. So yes, I read to her. Every damn book I had. Every topic. Everything. And I am proud of her for paying attention, to be honest.*

*Proud that she knows how to kill already? Seriously!*

*Like you're not impressed. She is clearly not the only one who will be able to so easily knock you on your ass.* He wiped some of the creature's blood off his face, eyeing Tronan with amusement. *Relax. We were both here despite the outcome.*

"Stop, you two. I can feel the argument literally hanging in the air about me. I knew what I was doing." She looked between them now, seeing Daemon's expression of satisfaction alongside Tronan's expression of complete…dissatisfaction.

"So you learned how to kill from being read to? Quite the leap my darling. I am not fond of this risk you are so casual with taking so soon."

"So soon? Seriously!" She laughed at him. "I have been waiting…"

"I know, Aiyana. But please have patience with me. Those creatures hold so much strength, and I have yet to know what powers you own, if he got his hands on you…"

"He didn't. He did not even try."

"If he did!"

"I am not scared of them!"

"To be fearless is to be foolish. Listen to me!"

"Listen to me, Tronan, now that you finally can!" she shouted at him, her small voice breaking slightly, clearly affecting him in a way he was unfamiliar with.

She watched him turn in a circle to look away from her for a moment, trying to control himself here. She glanced at Daemon for a moment, seeing him smirk at his brother, sensing Tronan not missing the expression as well. *Welcome to having a True Match, my brother.* She saw Tronan laugh in disbelief with no actual humor as he faced her again.

"Aiyana…" Claura stepped closer to her, trying to break the tension a bit. "How long have you known you could do something like this?"

"Decades. Obviously."

"Decades? I see."

"No you don't. But I wish you did. You need to go see Conroy."

## THE WINGED WITCH OF MATCHES

"You wish I did? What do you mean?" She watched her sigh as she leaned down in front of her now. "Please, Aiyana, just be honest with me." She glanced at the brothers for a second, then back. "With us."

"They told me—"

"Who?" Tronan quickly intercedes. He watched Aiyana look at him with impatience to just let her finish first.

"They told me not to tell you until after you see Conroy."

"Honey, please. Who?" Tronan tried to sound calmer.

"I can't say." She felt Daemon come closer, leaning down now before her, gently touching her arm, admiring her beauty…her size now, making her face him.

"Little one, we need to know."

"I suppose I can tell you how they told me and communicated with me. I don't see how that would be cheating you from figuring it out on your own…so much." She looked to Claura as she said it. She made it obvious she already knew that the witches of their bloodline needed to figure things out on their own to contain more power. That annoying balance that they all had to deal with.

"Go on." She just wanted her to say some sort of answer already.

"This person came to me in my…dreams." She looked back and forth between the brothers now, not meaning to give away such a big hint. Seeing that it was obvious, though, she needed to tell them something. Daemon stood and turned toward Tronan, hands on hip, the debate clear between them mentally.

"How long has this person been doing this?" Daemon asked, still keeping an eye on his brother. Seeing it clear on his face, he needed help with all of this. He was just so worried for her, so unsure of how to handle this situation.

"Since Moira cursed me."

"What have they been doing, telling you, in your dreams with you?" Claura asked.

"They taught me. Just like what Daemon did for me when I was awake."

"Teach you what?"

"Everything."

"That's her favorite answer." Tronan scoffed gently.

"They helped me get through it, just like Daemon did. Just like my mama did, visiting me sometimes. They made me feel important. Special."

Seeing Daemon and Claura move out of his way, Tronan knelt before her now, holding her face between his hands.

"My love, you are beyond special."

"Just like you are special to Conroy, Claura. I would not wait much longer."

She looked at her cousin while placing her hands gently over his much larger ones, as if savoring the feel of them on her body, completely missing how sweet the small gesture was to Tronan at the moment.

"Why do you say that?" Claura asked, eyeing her back.

"I just know he is going to help you despite what everyone says about him."

"Please tell me he did not visit you in your dreams as well?" Daemon asked sternly.

"No. Just the other one."

"The other one," Tronan said, clearly not liking getting no name. He saw her look back at him like she really was sorry she could not say, that she hated not being able to just tell him, begging him to understand and to trust. "When did this person visit you last, in your dreams?"

"I have not seen them since the false ties were severed. They told me once I have you in my life again, I will be fine and won't need them anymore. It always felt like they were protecting me." She refused to look at anyone but Tronan before her as she said it. "It is because of this person, not Daemon, that I know of my power. They helped me learn about it so I could protect myself and all of you."

"All of us?" She saw Daemon question her with enthusiasm yet still taking her seriously.

"They come from a…different place." She held Daemon's gaze captive, seeing his serious poker face take over, his mind on a roll. She saw him start to open his mouth and interrupted him, feeling like she had already said too much. For if anyone knew how smart the man was, she did. "They taught me how to have the power to kill Moira."

"*No*," they all chimed in at the same time.

They saw her laugh with a grown woman kind of expression in response, not one of a child, taking them all back a beat. She eyed Tronan, looking dead serious.

"She is actually mine, my love," Aiyana said while already turning to walk away. "I need a snack."

She headed toward the front doors where the nearby café still kept the majority of the library smelling like granny's kitchen. They all watched her go with her unique and confident little stride, clearly overdue to even do such a thing as still walking around. It was obvious Aiyana had more going on in her little head this entire time than any of them anticipated. Tronan stood up slowly, keeping his eyes on her until she was far down the aisle in the distance. He turned the corner toward the entrance. He felt Daemon slap his shoulder as if to say they are really in for it with her as he walked by him, following Aiyana.

"Me too," Daemon said.

"Really? A snack?" Claura asked, arms crossed, watching his fine ass in those jeans stroll away from her. She inwardly laughed at the few bloodstains on him now like it mattered not at all to him.

"Yup."

She walked away with a clear intention to speak of someone in earnest. Claura slightly knew as soon as Aiyana mentioned being visited in her dreams but decided the question could be answered later. Daemon wanted to continue the conversation, and she could see it clear in his mind he may want even more than a damn name. She took a deep breath at the turn of events, already sensing the underestimated connection between Aiyana and Daemon, and she watched him turn the corner out of sight as well now. She saw Allie and a couple of the other ladies take care of the green body while the rest of the library got back to normal. It was obvious this scene was not so out of place here. She turned to Tronan, seeing his lost expression, slightly smirking but feeling sorry for him.

"Apparently, I made it real easy for you once upon a time, didn't I?"

"That once upon a time will remain with me forever, Claura. Do not mistake that." She looked into her face, meaning every word with how serious he was right now.

"Me too. But you know what's funny?"

"What could possibly be funny?"

"The surprise that awaits Roman in all this. His daughter clearly will be a challenge for him." She smiled at him.

"Ya, about him…" She looked down and away with slight regret.

"What?"

"He still loves you, Claura."

"Oh, you two had a little chat finally? That must have been interesting."

"Quite."

"So why would he possibly still feel that way? He has Maya back."

"Something about how you are even smarter than her. It gets to him."

"Oh really? Well, I think the smartest one of us all, who is still in a smaller package, enjoying a cookie at the moment, will be easily turning his attention elsewhere soon enough."

"I don't understand it."

"On a day like today, you will need to clarify for me here."

"Why does he feel that way? There was no bond to sever between you two. The false bond was between us."

"Are you suggesting I ask him with everything else going on? Not sure I could handle that kind of chat on the same day I want to go see Conroy. I fear none of us will ever even wrap our heads around Aiyana alone first."

"No question there."

"I feel your guilt in not knowing how to handle this with her… and maybe a few other things. You can still talk to me. Please know that." She watched him stand up straighter, face her more, step just one step closer. She reminded her of things she had thought were left in the past already.

"I knew Aiyana was my Match before I met you."

"I'm sorry, what?"

"I thought she was dead, Claura. I truly thought she was dead…"

"So you already knew I was second choice, this whole time making me feel terrible for making you feel like second choice. Hmmm?"

"Please understand."

"I do. Trust me, I do. All Moira here still…ay."

"Spell or not, I loved you, Claura. I really did."

"Stop! Just stop!"

"I am sorry. That is all, I am just sorry."

"You know I hate myself more every day, knowing I was originally born from someone like her."

"Don't say that."

"I will say it all I want. She makes me hate myself. What if it's only a matter of time before I become like her, huh? After all, according to Maya, she wasn't always this way. Which one of you—no, wait, it'll clearly be Aiyana who can take even me out here…how are you going to react to that?"

"Now you need to stop." His energy got tense. His tone even more so.

"What would you do, Tronan? Who will it be?" She shoved him slightly. Her temper started to rise a bit, trying her best to suppress it for the sake of the nearby public in her own realm, which was supposed to be a safe haven for everyone.

"Stop," she asked with his last ounce of control, saying it softly. She put his hands up to block hers.

"Say it! You know damn well who is more important to you. So fuck off, Tronan. You come at me with this still, seriously? Have I not been through enough confusion with the feelings I have had for all three of you! Don't you dare come here, to my own goddamn realm, and start something over like that. Don't bring up Roman's feelings for me again. He can speak to me about it himself! And I still hurt over us, I do! But you can't come to me saying these things. I am still holding on by a thread here despite knowing Daemon is the one, as

I can just feel that all won't be corrected fully until my own mother is in the ground."

"I understand."

"Sure? Then *say* it."

"Enough." His tone was even more firm now. Knowing he'd remember her face of swimming, tears and anger mixed together for some time.

"Ya. Enough."

*****

Daemon caught up to Aiyana with ease, standing behind her in line. The energy alone between them clarified she already knew who was standing so close behind her. She felt him lean down slightly to talk closer to her ear. "You need to have a little mercy on my brother, sweetheart."

"You know what is stupid? Us. Here. Right now. Waiting in line at a little café like this, with all the power we're holding. Acting like we're at a silly Starbucks back on earth."

"I highly recommend the peanut butter brownies."

"You don't say."

"Also, the oatmeal cookies."

"Go on."

"The croissants are always warm and to die for."

"What else?"

"And the fact that you need to be nice to him. I am serious, Aiyana. I feel your pent-up rage and him being the easy target for you."

"As my Match, he should be able to handle it."

"As his Match, you should not want to hurt him."

"Is it weird not being tied to me anymore?"

"I have no buttons left to press today. So good luck." She knew the topic switch was to immediately get under his skin with her tone.

"No?"

"I am sorry, Aiyana. I really am. That none of us know how to handle you."

"Then don't try." She ordered her food and got handed her brownie. Daemon quickly snatched it out of her hand and started eating it, leaning against the counter and giving her a wink. She simply asked for another one. He took that one as well.

"I'm actually really hungry, *brother-in-law*."

"Don't care, *sis*."

"You think I know where to begin with all this, Daemon? 'Cause I am just winging it. Other than killing Moira, who did this to me, I am winging it. And I do listen to Tronan already. I know I should be scared. But I have had so much time to be scared in my head already that now…you can't even imagine the freedom. Not even you. I will simply not pretend to be afraid when I don't have to be, just to appease everyone's little adult feelings."

"Simply discuss things with him first."

"Why? He has yet to learn how to even communicate with me correctly! I am in this stupid little child body still. And as much as I approve of the change happening finally, that is all he sees."

"You haven't even given him a day to get used to these"—pointing up and down toward her figure—"changes."

"Don't be like them, Daemon. Don't baby me. I beg of you. You are the only one who can wrap their head around my situation. They have not been there, Match or not."

"Oh, I won't be. Hence, this little chat that comes with a warning."

"Oh ya, what's that?"

"Give me a damn name. Or else."

"I can't."

"I think you can."

"I can't!"

"You really want to test me now that I don't have to literally baby you?" He pulled his hip off the counter, walking slowly toward her now.

"Don't test me! Just shut it and eat your fucking brownie! And here"—she grabbed one off the counter herself and tossed it at him—"have another!" She watched him swiftly deflect everything as if he saw it coming before she even decided where to throw it. "You need to trust that I know what I am doing."

"Forgive us for having a hard time with such as we all just started being able to speak with you today alone."

"I don't need anyone's help. The advice given from any of you will not change the outcome."

"Maya and Claura, not just Tronan, want to help guide you. They have been waiting to help you learn how to use whatever powers you have. You need to let them have the chance at least once. This no-name you speak of, they may have helped you in your little dreams, but reality is far different little one."

"Maya, yes. Claura, no. I fear her slightly."

"So you do fear something."

"She has an obvious wall up with me. It's plain to see my looks that remind her of her own dead daughter do not help!"

"She knows that is not your fault. Just give her time. She will come around."

"She has already come around plenty. I can still smell her on Tronan."

"I see."

"Do you?"

"Yes."

"Because you can relate."

"Yes."

"So you understand."

"I understand it is still not either of their fault. You need to see past that."

"I am trying!"

"Try harder!" He saw her start to shatter now at his tone. She did not really know him in this way yet, being able to actually communicate, let alone shout back at him. "Aiyana, look…" She followed her to a nearby bench along the wall, appreciating her choosing a private location with few others around now.

"You don't get it. Not really. I could feel him, even from afar. Them from afar."

"I did too."

"Huh?" Her expression was of doubt and disbelief.

"When Tronan gave her the first drop, they were—"

"They were…?"

"Come on, Aiyana, don't make me say it." His voice was low, and his eyes averted.

"How did you control yourself?"

"Had no choice. I had to stay with you in my realm."

"So Moira is not the only one to blame for things. As well, I also see."

He got up to put some distance between them. He clearly had heard enough for now. He simply sat up straighter, watching her walk away from him, knowing it was of no use to get her to stop and just finish the conversation. Aiyana might not be good at a poker face, but her energy and emotions were. For all his knowledge and his time with her, he was finding it hard to read her right now.

Aiyana came around the corner, expecting Tronan to be in the same spot, only to find nothing. There was not even the green body anymore, nor the bloodstained carpet. The books that were splattered everywhere from Daemon's efforts to kill the being were all picked up and back in order along the shelves. She thinks for a second to just reach out to him mentally, then decides against it. Feeling so in love with him was so hard when he looked at you like you were a child despite already living for fifteen decades. She wanted to chat with Daemon more but inwardly knew she just needed to know where Tronan was and needed to feel his reassuring presence. She was sorry but did not know how to show it. She inwardly swore that she was already more like her cousin Claura than she cared to admit, both were stuck between a rock and a hard place, needing people to support them in their efforts. She needed to find a way to be taken with them when they went to kill Moira, but she knew she had time as the task here at hand first was to visit Conroy. It gave her time. Little time. But still, she would make use of it. She learned how to make use of her time in her lifetime to a degree that she figured very few people knew of.

She looked around the aisles, admiring all the books, and looked up to admire the detailed ceiling. She spotted him. His eyes instantly met hers as if he had been waiting for her to notice him. He was on the top floor leaning over the balcony, looking down over everything...over her, with Claura a few steps behind, still coming up the stairs. She felt his fingers caress her cheek before turning around to follow Claura down whatever hallway they were in. It was clear on his face he needed just a few moments to speak with her, and it would not be long. She decided to take the opportunity to show him that she was okay with taking his advice at least and started walking back toward Daemon, knowing she still needed to thank him for all he had done for her. Between the expected question from him and her brownie tossing, she never did get around to it. She saw him still sitting in the exact spot, leaning forward with his elbows on his thighs, enjoying his sandwich now. Smirking as he turned to wink at her, making it beyond obvious that he knew her more than she realized, even if he was grown and talking now.

He stood from a distance still. "Thank you." He patted the still-warm spot next to him and took another bite of his food, watching her with ease as she walked closer and sat beside him again.

"I'm sorry, what was that?" He held his hand up to his ear.

"Thank. You."

"Wait...one more time."

"Thank you," he whispered, tears swimming. She saw him finish his last bite before pulling her into his arms quickly without even looking at her. She took a deep breath, pulling her even closer to him after a long moment.

"I love you, little one. Don't you forget that. I will always—"

"Be here for you. Ya, ya, I heard you the first time."

He laughed. "Yup, Tronan is definitely in for it."

"Or...am I?"

"What do you mean?"

"Being bonded doesn't mean I know him. I know only you, Daemon. I am scared to get to know him. It is different now...growing now. I am so used to a baby phase, I don't know how to deal with actually being like"—she gestured toward her figure—"this."

"You are already terrified of your first heat cycle." He chose to be blunt for them both. "I can hear it in your voice."

"What if you always know me better, Daemon? What if I feel like you just will always know me better no matter how much I love him? Hmm?"

"I will."

"You're not helping."

"Yes. I am."

"How so?"

"By being honest."

"And confusing."

"No. Not intentionally. Being honest with him in *all* things is all you will need between you both. Trust me."

"Are you honest with everything with Claura?"

"I truly try."

"I am sorry about your son." She knew he had to hold back with Claura in being honest about that recently.

"How do you know about him?" he questioned her half-second pause before answering.

"I can see it in their memories, through my connection with Tronan once he was told by my mom. And through Claura, as she is my cousin." She saw him stare at her for a long moment before nodding and looking away. "I can't imagine keeping that secret from her."

"No, you can't, Aiyana. You don't have a child. Yet." She saw how his comment made the fear creep back into her face. "He is incapable of hurting you. You have nothing to fear with that."

"You hurt Claura."

"Well, goes to show how powerful Moira is. All the more reason for you to speak with us before you do anything. For my brother's sake, at least."

"I can end her."

"As can I."

They stare at each other for a long moment. He saw her raise her one hand with a huge smirk on her face and quickly followed her lead from her thoughts—rock, paper, scissors. Both lose. Both start laughing.

"I am serious, little one. As we may get only one chance. Who knows what the bitch has been up to."

"I can find out—"

"*No.*" There was a long pause, feeling her smile at his thoughts. "Fine. How?"

"No-name says on a full moon, I can draw a certain wolf energy to help me with a certain spell. I can spy on her."

"Does it actually let you see where she is at that precise moment?"

"Within five minutes."

"Not good enough. A lot can happen in five minutes. She could be anywhere in just one minute."

"My father can hold her. I know of the plan."

"Sure about that? I have yet to ask Roman if he has even tried before."

"Let him try with you." She watched him scoff, slight humor at the suggestion. "Seriously, Daemon. Who here is stronger than you at the moment? Other than me?" She winked at him.

"Well, your head grew again, at least."

"I have had help for decades in learning about my own powers."

"Have some patience with us, as no-name has not kept any of us informed, alongside you not being able to so much as say more than goo-goo-ga-ga."

"They did that for all of you. Knowing timing was going to be everything."

"So while in your dreams, they already knew about all of us?"

"Yes."

"Are we related to this no-name, Aiyana?" She looked at her again after a long moment of her not answering. She saw her look at him with swimming tears, seeing one fall, and her small hand swiped it away quickly. Her face wanted to tell him so badly, in that moment proving that she literally couldn't. "You are holding back for Claura's sake despite your dislike of her right now."

"No." She saw him turn to her with a sincere question in his eyes. "I am holding back for the both of you. It will be my gift to you, my real thank you, you will see."

# Chapter 28

# Fearful Changes

Tronan let Claura pass him in the hallway as he slowed down to notice the portraits along the hallway. He saw her turn to him slightly, slowing in her tracks.

"You have never been here before, have you?" she asked.

"No reason to be. Until now." He still faced the wall, taking in everything.

"Truly, Tronan, not even once?"

"I was never important to you before this lifetime, Claura. Our paths crossed for only a few moments, few and far between, over the centuries. I always had responsibilities in other realms, in other parts of other worlds. I was hardly ever near Daemon and you. Why do you think I did not recognize you?"

"Can't believe I did not think about that more."

"You have been busy."

"Well, why didn't you?"

"Your reincarnation, your beauty changed each time."

"My beauty?"

"Beautiful every time." He turned to her now. He let the image of her looking so powerful, so at peace, in her own realm, be framed into his memory to keep.

"Did you know you were an uncle?"

"Not until Maya informed me just very recently. I am sorry."

"Don't be. I am getting him back, for good."

"And how do you plan to do that?"

"I don't know, Tronan." She shrugged, as if so tired of this feeling inside of her yet knowing it was the only thing keeping her moving forward. "I just feel it. And as Aiyana grows more, the feeling gets stronger. I can't explain it more than that."

"You think my Aiyana and your son are connected?"

"Truly do not know, but nothing is out of the cards for me anymore."

There was a long pause between them, each keeping to their own thoughts, staying out of each other's heads. The feeling was cold compared to what they shared once. She gently gestured for him to just follow her, watching him need a moment before moving his feet. The small action made her nervous now, as it was not like him to act like he couldn't trust her. She turned the corner into her office, heading straight for the desk, completely avoiding the daybed for obvious reasons. Suddenly, she wished she had cleaned up a bit, but what use would it do really? With their abilities, he would still smell something. She inwardly swore at how many spells there probably were to fix the small problem that she simply could not remember, regretting not asking Allie for the small favor first. She sat behind her desk and watched him walk toward her, looking around, still close to the doorway.

"This is gorgeous. I can see how it felt like your real home all this time. It has you written all over it."

"Thank you."

"The library I had in mind for you was truly a joke compared to this. I see now it would have been nowhere near good enough."

"Never know. One book can change a lot." She gave a small smile.

"So you need just one book to finish mommy, correct?"

"As Maya tells me. My mother does not part far from it, like the coward she is."

"Coward, yes. Clever, definitely, yes. Don't underestimate her."

"I am so sorry she did this to you both. I hope you know I plan to give my life if that is what it takes to finish her."

She saw him glance down after a second, not wanting her to see his rising emotions. She saw the conflict inside him for caring for her yet knowing he'd always have to put Aiyana first now. She watched him walk forward slowly to take a seat in one of the large chairs before her desk. She leaned forward, hands clasped together.

"What can you sense about her?"

"Her power? Or just in general?"

"Let's cover both," he said regrettably.

"Let her get her pent-up energy out, and it will get better."

"I know. I am just unsure of how to keep her safe in the meantime. I simply do not know what I am up against. Moira has always been a mystery, and now my own Match is just as much of one."

"You doubt your skills, and I hope it's not due to simply being the less omnipotent brother here. You kept me safe, Tronan. You have an entire planet called earth where every normal human being on it would fear what you are…while some creatures already do, among other realms, I am sure. Why are you underestimating yourself with her? She is beyond lucky to have you. Even if she is more powerful." She saw him eye her more now, making it clear she found the sore spot. "I see. You already think she is more powerful than you, and that scares you."

"Daemon doesn't scare you?"

"Our powers are used differently. They have their own uses. Does not matter which of us is more powerful."

"Some other person has been helping her for decades in her dreams, on top of Daemon protecting her for long himself. I simply fear I am too far behind to be what she needs me to be."

"I think you two have a hell of an interesting start, and you can't let fear own all of it. You have yourself a little firecracker, Tronan. Don't waste it."

"You are right."

"Now, as for in general…definitely knows more than we do, but that's only thanks to this no-name person. Daemon has taught her everything else. So we haven't failed with her, Tronan, not in the way that you think."

"I have failed her. Tremendously. She deserves to take it all out on me."

"And to think you aren't up for that task is foolish of you."

"I admire your courage in me, truly."

"I admire how you kept me alive, Tronan. The heat cycle alone that you helped me through was probably just another angle for my own mother to try to kill me. I will always be there for you until the day I die, which may be soon." She sounded like she almost wished it to just be quick if anything, not really like she hated the idea.

"You sound too ready. What is truly wrong here?" He stood up to take a peek at the book on her desk. Her fingers kept intently brushing over it, his face getting dark for a split second as he recognized it from the day on the balcony. He was thankful for her averted eyes for the moment while she spoke.

"I am just always missing something. No matter how much I read or do, I am still always at step 1 it feels like. It's so goddamn frustrating!" She looked up at him again after a long moment, noticing instantly where he was starting to gaze away from. Her guilt instantly sank in. "Tronan…oh god…"

"Perhaps you just need different music this time." He tapped it gently, looking at her with slight sadness before turning around to walk around her office more. He took his time looking at things. "So what were you listening to that day, hmm?"

"I just hit replay of 'Help Me Lose My Mind' by London Grammar…as in the moment, I did feel like I was losing my actual mind having to say that spell. Whether you believe me or not."

"I do."

"I think killing her completely will end…everything."

"Sure about that? What if we all still feel this way about you? Roman and I? Despite having our Matches? Because trust me, Claura, you are not the only one who tires of this confusion."

"It has to be residual due to Moira still being alive. She is keeping her pain in the ass spell somewhat alive still somehow because she is just that strong. And I think it's just a damn distraction. But..." She paused, afraid of his reaction.

"Go on."

"You know who I think is stronger?"

"Don't. Don't even think about it."

"Aiyana," she said her name slowly as if disliking how damn obvious it was.

"She will not be given the chance."

"Well, then"—laughing slightly—"you better keep an eye on her because it is clear she plans to take the chance, no matter what she has to risk."

"As her Match, it is my responsibility to end Moira for her. You have yet to even clarify how I may be the loophole here."

"I don't think we need the loophole anymore." She leaned forward, crossing her forearms, and she looked at him like he really needed to just get on board here already, for all their sakes.

"She will not go near her."

"Have fun telling her that."

"I came here hoping you could help me. Not rub what I already am starting to see in my damn face."

"Let's backburner this, shall we? Until I get back from seeing Conroy."

"If you even get back. You don't know what he really wants from you. It is not a joke to go to a realm like that."

"Oh really? Because he is in one of the top 3 realms, correct? That's why everyone fears him? Know who else is? My own goddamn son! This is a reason for me to be close to him, even if it still is one or two more realms over, so I am fucking going!"

She tossed the small white envelope at him. She saw him catch it with ease, his face proving he did not know that piece of information about his nephew while doing so. He took a moment to read every word, to think it over before walking back to her desk on her side of it now, setting the note down gently. The small gesture reminded her of the moment in Roman's home when he so gently placed her cell phone back down on the nightstand after reading Roman's texts. How so much has happened since.

"I will support you in this. But Aiyana will not be a part of it. So forgive me, Claura. I hope you find a way without her. I just got her back after barely having her at all the first time she was in my life. I will not risk losing her."

"I will not be the cousin who holds her back, as I can relate to everyone doing that for you." She looked up at him slowly, seeing his intense expression of mixed emotions. She felt his hand move toward her face, gently letting the back of his fingers brush down her cheek before lifting her chin to make her look at him more closely. In that way, he did.

"So help us, Claura, for we may never be on the same page again," he said like he truly wished with all his heart it wasn't so. Yet she was no fool to ignore the very real, despite subtle, threat beneath the surface.

"Until this is over." She reminded him with her eyes alone that she was willing to risk her life here, not so much Aiyana's. "She is just my mom still despite how powerful she is."

"Your mom is the only witch who has ever caused this much trouble for those of our kind. If you underestimate her, you may as well just pick out your own damn gravestone now."

"What shall it say, Tronan?"

"This is not funny."

"Never said it was."

"Find the damn loophole. Please."

"What if I can't?" Her eyes were getting watery, doing that complete 180 he was so familiar with still. "You think I want Aiyana to risk not being safe? She deserves a happy life more than any of us. I know that, Tronan. I do."

"How could the loophole work? You must have something."

"She needed you to pause to complete the spell, right?"

"Yes."

"Meaning she needed you...you specifically to start the spell. Therefore, she may need you to end it if she wanted to."

"How do we get her to want to?"

"We have to get her to leave her realm for something so we can get the book while she is gone. We need a distraction."

"Simplify."

"We need something more important than the book. We need Aiyana."

"Goddamn it, Claura! Listen to me!"

"If Aiyana is more important than that book that has the power to destroy Moira, then doesn't that say something? What does it say!" She walked toward him now with a fury, following his steps back toward the door.

"Fucking stop!"

"It means she has the power to destroy her herself! Daemon only thinks that my mother is scared of me for some reason, but I already can sense that my dear mommy is terrified even more so of Aiyana. Why else would she put such a horrible spell on her!"

"If you involve her in this, so help me God, I will make you fucking terrified, Claura! Do you understand!"

A sudden breeze was felt in the room. Claura couldn't turn her head fast enough to keep up with the motion of Tronan moving backward behind her. She turned to see Daemon already holding him up against the wall, watching a few of her favorite things fall to the floor around the commotion. The men became a blur as they shifted back and forth before her, it being obvious they had done this before but with way less meaning...until now. The entire other end of her beloved office was smashed to pieces as they fought. Her heart broke at what she just had to hear come out of Tronan's mouth, literally shouting at her. Her heart broke at knowing he was just trying to protect the one he was truly meant to be in love with. Her heart broke at knowing the fight wasn't even an even one, at knowing this was all more drama none of them deserved due to her sick mother.

*Daemon, my love, please...*

The no answer in the face of a dilemma, this time had her extra frightened. *This all still boils down to more drama from Moira, so stop!* She heard footfalls come running down the hall and through the door, already knowing who it was, looking back at her face with remorse and regret. Claura saw it on her face already that words were not going to help, admiring her for being smarter than herself at this moment. Aiyana was, after all, much older than she was mentally. Her heart broke again for this person before her, who had been dealt so much, thanks to her mom.

She saw her raise her palm, yet again in just one day alone and said a soft command under her breath, secretly hoping she would not take more out on Daemon than Tronan. Then again, she might do just that to make it fair. Unsure of how to feel about that, she watched the purple light spread in her palm, the tiny blast used once again, stretching outward before her to become anything but tiny now, lighting up her entire office with it. Taking into account, anyone looking at her window right now would see this for many, many miles, completely blocking out the site of anything that was warped in it. It shook the entire room for a good ten seconds before it goes sucked back into her opened palm. Claura looked at her, watching her magic fade back inside her, the lights completely gone now. They both look at each other and then at the far wall where the two men just were.

Gone.

Both of them.

"Where did you send them!"

"They are fine."

"Where, Aiyana!" She faced her more now, her face demanding an answer, determined to make use of being taller than her for however longer that may be.

"We need to have a chat." She eyed her with the same enthusiasm, height clearly of zero importance here.

"Fine." Claura knew that if this little person was already informed by no-name how to take on Moira, then what a foolish move to think she'd be intimidated by her right now. "Just answer me, please, so I don't have the question lingering in the back of my head for our entire conversation." She refused to let Aiyana's strong will have an effect on her where it did not belong, for she deserved a damn answer—the mental link with Daemon being of no use for whatever reason just yet making her worry.

"As I know, you still need to have a chat with my father. I'm sure he will be happy to update you later on how their arrival went."

"Oh really? Why there?"

"Because he still hates them. And I find that funny. Now he can deal with them while they are like this."

"You know, Aiyana, men only have so many buttons to push before they actually do start to lose respect for you."

"Is that why they all still have this *respect* for you because you hold out on pushing buttons?"

"Oh, my dear, I push plenty of buttons. So fuck off, dear cousin."

"Touchy subject. I get it."

"Do you?"

"You are not the only one who still has feelings for the one you used to be bonded with."

"It will all go away soon."

"Yes. It will." Aiyana agreed with zero hesitation, eyeing her just as intently.

"Are we seriously fighting over men we are already Matched to, Aiyana? Are you jealous I get the more powerful brother? Hmmm?" She leaned forward now at her desk, forearms crossed over each other, smiling at her smaller cousin. "Buttons...," she said slowly and with pleasure.

"Why would I be when my power towers over both of yours... combined?"

"You really believe that, don't you?"

"Oh yes."

"Good. I won't hold you back, cousin. I am not your overprotective Match."

"Don't want to support Tronan in protecting me anymore?"

She laughed slightly hysterically, smiling like she was thinking about still punching him herself after how he had just spoken to her in her own realm, in her own office. "Fuck. No." She set things aside on her desk now, organizing out of habit. "Such a shame too. I was looking so forward to our little chat after everything we have been through...you know...together." She eyed her. "Buttons..." She smirked.

"Claura, dear cousin, it's going to take more than that."

"Oh, okay...well, let me tell you ahead of time, honey. Stock up on some Gatorade."

"Like I know what the fuck that means."

"Such language for such a young lady." She raised her eyebrows at her, faking a shocked expression. "I got to experience both, my dear. Let me just say I am not getting, by any means, the shorter end of the 'stick' here."

Aiyana literally starts laughing. "If it's a 'stick,' I don't want it."

"Oh, you will. Trust me." She winked now and meant it. She saw the look on Aiyana's face change, and she saw her notice that she was being more serious now. And then the fear crept in all over her little expression. He made Claura pause for real now. "What is wrong? Really?" She watched her in the chair before her desk, turning her blushing gaze away, looking at the back wall as if she wished she didn't send Tronan away suddenly. "We are cousins, Aiyana. We have plenty of time to push each other's buttons later. For now, be serious with me. Please."

"I already talked about it with Daemon."

"I see. And he helped, truly?"

"I don't know."

"You are fearless when it comes to killing my mom, yet with this Tronan situation...you are frightened." This made her wonder if what Daemon said was true earlier, about maybe Moira wasn't so hard to kill anymore after all. "Why?"

"I only know Daemon. He is all I am familiar with."

"I know."

"No. You do not." Her voice cracked, looking around like she could use his presence too now, for different reasons.

"Hmmm...okay. Well, this is great." She looked so tired of the scenario, not meaning to sound funny at all. "Look, you are Matched to him for a reason. And in time, you will see."

"I have had nothing but time. We both have."

"Now it won't have to be time apart. It's a whole new ball game now."

"What if I don't care to play?" Looking serious, knowing Claura knew exactly what she meant.

"To be honest, you will be missing out then. And that makes me sad for you. It really does."

"Of all the spells I was taught from no-name, I never was able to find one to help me fend off my heat cycle that will happen someday."

"Why are you so terrified of such an act?"

"I simply want it to be my choice, not my body taking over."

"It will be both, actually."

"Not good enough."

"A controller, I see. Well, that will be fun for dear Tronan once you do get past this fear."

"You aren't going to take me seriously in this. So forget it."

"There are very few things in life that will be more worth your time. I simply don't want you to miss out on one of the best experiences you could have with a Match due to fear. And if it makes you feel better, I enjoy any fear I get during the act."

"Does not make me feel better."

"Because he is incapable of truly hurting me. Rough sometimes, yes. But not in a way you'd actually have to worry." She saw the resolve in Aiyana's eyes, clearly choosing to put the topic aside for now.

"So the one who visits you in your dreams..."

"I can't tell you his name, so don't ask."

"His. Interesting." She eyed her quickly before looking back to her spell book, glancing at it casually as she kept her part in the unique conversation here. Seeing Aiyana's look of "shit, I fucked up" all over her face.

"How did these dreams go?"

"He took me places. Made it feel real. Like Daemon and Tronan can."

"Every night?"

"Almost, ya."

"What place do you remember in particular? Did you have a favorite?"

"Yes. There was a place on the oceanfront. The sun was always shining, the birds…the smells…it was a nice change from the confined spaces within Daemon's home."

"Sounds perfect." The dream felt awfully familiar for a reason. "So how did he teach you things, spells and such?"

"As you would imagine, really. Sometimes, it was just a wide-open white space of nothing where he would teach me archery and knife throwing, with and without the use of magic. That ended up being one of my favorite things. It was really an endless experience. There was always more to learn. He taught me to read and speak and took me to places where I could experience swimming. Poor Daemon, it was why I was always truly bored with the bathtub he put me into. He just did not know." She slightly laughed to herself, looking away into the distance, subconsciously studying the objects on the office walls. Broken and not broken.

"So for all this time, you have been learning spells and all about your own skills, on top of basic knowledge?"

"Yep." He saw it sink in on Claura's face just how far ahead Aiyana was here with learning what needed to be known…again. "He kept me sane, as did Daemon. But Daemon is no fool. He could sense something was going on by my changing expressions and gestures. I think he simply may have thought it was possibly Maya the entire time if someone else were to reach out to me in some way and chose to just leave it alone."

"So you have gotten to experience a nonbaby body, just not during reality while awake."

"Yes. But it's not the same, as I see now. As fearful as I am of these changes, I am beyond grateful."

"Understatement."

"Sometimes, the simple words are still the best to choose from."

"Agree. Now may I jump to the chase..."

"He taught me everything Moira has ever learned."

"So you aren't stronger, your equals."

"Oh no, I am stronger."

"I need proof before I take you anywhere and risk Tronan killing me for it while Daemon does a replay...and you will be too busy to stop them next time. So details, please."

"I fear that will give too much away."

"Of course it would. Something, Aiyana, give me something here."

"Can't. And it's for your sake."

"Get out."

"Seriously!"

"Very. Dead-end answers mean dead-and-done conversations. Out."

"Where am I to go?"

"For a walk. You want us all to treat you like more of an adult in that ten-year-old body than go for a damn walk by yourself. Or stay and answer me. Your choice."

"Damn cousin..."

"I am tired, Aiyana! Tired of feeling like my own brain is hiding from me, from having everything just gone from my head over and over! I have been beyond drained from feeling like this is all on my shoulders, only for you to now come along and make killing Moira sound like part of a pre-dinner plan during a weekend outing...*and* only for it to be a huge risk to even see if you are right. So yes, not answering me is a trigger. Now go. I need to think."

"Maybe you should be the one getting some air right now." She gestured that she was welcome to come with her as she neared the doorway. The look on her face made Claura's heart sink slightly. It was clear how thirsty for company she was after all this time being stuck as a baby, seeing pretty close to nobody for so long. She just must naturally crave female company now that she had the chance to even get a taste of it. She realized, in a way, that she was honored to spend some time with her now that she was grown like this, as her very own mother still had yet to even lay her eyes upon her today. She figured she'd be showing up any second really.

"Yes. Let's go. Shall we? I have yet to even try a café, in this lifetime anyway, outside this building."

She watched her slightly smile at her as she walked toward her and down the hall together.

# Chapter 29

# Find the Weakness

Roman felt the energy of the two bastards coming before they even fully appeared, looking at Maya's reaction as well over his coffee cup as he took a sip, knowing their very relaxing, satisfying, and quiet solo time in their own home was coming to an end. He watched her laughing to herself while pouring herself a cup of coffee, taking no interest in hiding her smirk.

"Oh my, Roman, perhaps just see it as an opportunity to hit two birds with one stone here."

"I'd rather be doing other things." He stood up to walk around the center island, wrapping one arm around her small waist as he savored his last sip, squeezing in places only he was allowed. He turned toward the porch, seeing them land simultaneously from somewhere in the sky and hard, even for them. She made him unable to control his slight laugh at the sight.

"Well, isn't this interesting? Aiyana must be with Claura, I assume?"

"That strikes me as odd. She has yet to even want to really hold her, let alone babysit," Roman stated, unable to hide his tone of being disappointed with Claura in a new and unique way with all of this.

"Give her time."

"Well, if anyone is patient, it will be Aiyana."

"Unless all that time has had the opposite effect."

"We shall see."

"That we shall."

He put his fingers through her hair and pulled her head toward his, savoring one last kiss before setting his cup down and heading outside, feeling her instant moan through his own mouth, making him have to break the kiss early for obvious reasons. He heard her small giggle as she watched him head outside, enjoying the sight as he went, appreciating neither of them making an effort to come in. She watched as he opened and closed the sliding door and decided to just head upstairs to enjoy a bath. Choosing to leave all the troubles to Roman to deal with as he deserved it after making her wait…again.

Roman stepped onto the porch and closed the door gently, hearing his Match's thoughts clearly in the back of his mind, making no effort to walk closer to either of them, seeing them standing straight now, eyeing each other with deep disdain. Their clothes were beyond scuffed with random blood stains.

"Where is my daughter?"

"With Claura, in her realm," Tronan answered.

"Why are you both here? Looking like you want to kill one another? Which, be my guest."

"Claura," Tronan answered again.

It was clearly okay to put some blame on her name first. She watched Roman look between them, reading them both at the same time. The man was too good at hiding his shock at Tronan's next words and just trying to figure it out already.

"Aiyana, she has grown again."

"Aiyana," Daemon chided in, correcting him as to the real reason why they were actually here.

# THE WINGED WITCH OF MATCHES

They watched Roman hold his hands out as if to say, "Hold it," looking out into the distance for two seconds.

"Claura sent you, or Aiyana?" He walked closer to them both now.

"Aiyana sent us here. My conversation with Claura got heated—"

"Heated?" Roman inquired, really wanting him to clarify and to do it now.

"You stay away. Hear me?" Daemon growled to Tronan, eyeing him intently.

"Someone tell me what the fuck happened!" Roman shouted.

"Claura has a plan. It involves using Aiyana. Tronan is simply making it obvious where he stands in the decision," Daemon said.

"Using my daughter? She is"—looking to Tronan with slight anger for just not knowing already, for the mind block inside Tronan's head at the moment was made of pure brick—"how much has she grown?"

"She is around ten years now," Tronan said.

"Her body," Daemon said stubbornly, eyeing his brother with a clear intention of an obvious problem here in how he was already treating his Aiyana. "I highly recommend you two don't baby her." He gave a quick glance to Roman. "And she is damn powerful. She took out a minion that was from a higher realm."

"What? She has grown from being two to ten and is killing now?"

"Yes," Tronan answered. "She sent us both here with her powers alone. Apparently, someone has been teaching her things." He looked at Daemon again.

"You taught my baby girl to kill?" Roman made his anger obvious.

"Both of you can kiss my ass. I did what was right for her. Despite her staying in that small body, her mind needed stimulus. And boy, is it fucking stimulated. So don't come at me, trying to correct what I have done. You have no idea what you are in for, Roman." He watched Roman start to come closer and say something before Tronan interrupted.

"She has had a dream walker this entire time, helping her from a different realm," Tronan filled in, seeing Roman summed that up behind his eyes.

"Must have been for a reason this no-name came back into her life even before you could, Tronan, because at least he took her seriously." He was uncaring of how much that would enrage his younger brother. Aiyana needed him to catch up to who and what she was, and she needed it now. "Do not fail her in this, brother. She needs you to understand her."

"It angers you, doesn't it, that you can't be there for her the way I can now…after all this time," Tronan said, his calm tone slightly eerie. "I went to speak with Claura with the complete opposite intention in mind, but she would not stop pressing. Put yourself in my shoes. You would react the goddamn same!"

"You are fucking up your chance with your own here, and now you are seriously fucking up with Claura and me! Speak to her like that again, and I won't stop no matter what realm I am spiraled into." He gave Roman one last quick glance before disappearing, his eyes begging him not to be a fool in this alongside his brother. Tronan and Roman remained silent for a good minute, both thinking over the situation.

"Of all the places for my daughter to send you both, she chooses here." He laughed to himself. "You are in for it, aren't you, son?" Roman asked with slight humor as he faced Tronan now from the same spot Daemon just stood.

"As are you. She knows, Roman. She recognized me as well so long ago, and despite her wanting to take her anger out on just Moira…so she said, trust me, you got it coming too."

"Oh, do I? Well, I am not threatened by pent-up energy and anger from my own daughter."

"You should be. She is more powerful than Claura."

"Is that what she said?"

"More than once. She wants to be the one to kill Moira."

"I can trap her."

"You will do no such—"

"Moira! Not Aiyana." He eyed him for a second. "You are lost, truly, aren't you?" He watched Tronan walk away, his back to him, giving him the answer he needed, studying him from a distance now.

"You are agreeing with Claura then in this?" he asked without turning around.

"I am saying let us give her first dibs." He saw him remain silent. "Let me give you some advice, Tronan. To try and control the witches of their bloodline is like trying to grab the wind."

"I am unable to agree to this."

"Think about it."

"I am unable, Roman!"

"You will be with her, right there the entire time."

"I can't stop Moira. I may not be able to save her. Please do not ask this of me."

"Claura will be with her, already willing to end her somehow herself."

"Nothing in this is guaranteed."

"The only thing you are guaranteeing here is not giving my daughter the revenge she deserves."

"It is not worth her life."

"I can already pick out the day's events from your memories."

"You're welcome. Now get out of my damn head."

"I hate this too. I really do."

"Please tell Daemon that I beg of him to find a different way when he goes with Claura to see Conroy."

"I see you two are officially enemies until this is all over."

"And all thanks to Claura."

"This is not her fault."

"She is asking too much!"

"So are you, from Aiyana, by holding her back in this. Please see that, Tronan. Put yourself in her now larger shoes." His tone was suggesting he was eager to see her. "Does she still look just like Dayla?"

"By the way, Claura looks at her still, yes."

"And they are spending time together as we speak?"

"Yes."

"That should be interesting. Let me have some time to speak to them both. I will have Aiyana reach out to you to bring her home." He heard him scoff. "What?"

"Like she needs me. You still don't understand."

"I am talking about the gesture here, not that she is already powerful and smart enough to do it on her own."

"I don't even know how to stop her from traveling to see Moira already on her own!"

"She may not know."

"I doubt it."

"Then why hasn't she done it already? Hmm?" He smirked while still looking serious. "You underestimate her, clearly, but it's not your fault. She is obviously intent on not giving us much time to catch up with her here. But overestimating her may be just as big of a mistake." He watched him think it over. "We all have a weakness. She has had a lot come out of that little mouth today alone, none of it pointing to her main weakness. Find it." Roman takes only a moment to give him time to respond before heading back inside. "What if she does not have one?"

"Every one of us has one. If we didn't, Moira would truly be able to ruin our lives forever. We found a way once. We can do it again," Roman said, giving him one more good look before stepping back inside and shutting the door gently, leaving Tronan alone with his thoughts before disappearing a moment later on his own.

Roman was already reaching for Maya, and in his mind, they needed to go see their daughter soon. He was unsure just how much she stayed out of the conversation again this time as well. For some reason, she was doing that more often, uncaring to linger in his thoughts. It was not like Maya to not be fully concerned with what was going on, especially now with her own daughter in all this. Perhaps she just needed to be told of the update now to care. Or perhaps she already knew more than she was letting on. Either way, the smell of her naked in the bathtub as he walked upstairs was putting his mind more at ease. He figured some more time for Claura and Aiyana together might be good, despite how it went, and decided that now was more time for him and his Maya, knowing full well how it was going to go.

He turned the corner into the bathroom doorway and leaned on the molding, watching her play with the bubbles through her wet fingers. She was thoroughly enjoying herself, still seeing how happy it made her just to be back in her own physical body.

"Do I dare ask?" she said casually without looking up.

"Our daughter has the body of a ten-year-old now," Roman said, seeing the shock instantly on her face.

Watching her need to move on and get out of the tub already, he put his hand up to tell her to wait a minute.

"She is fine. Claura and her should spend time together." He felt her invading his mind now, wanting the memories of his recent conversation with the two as fast as she could get them. He walks toward the tub, leaning down next to her, with zero hesitation in letting his one hand explore the water's surface. He reached her lady zone immediately as if he could see right through the bubbles, making her jump only to instantly relax into him a second later. "I am sorry, Maya."

"For what?" Her eyes closed, and she softly moaned. Her hips started to move already in response to his touches.

"For making you wait after already needing me for so long. When you clearly needed my touch last time, it was cruel of me."

"It is not easy, having this be our main weakness with you men."

"Weakness...," he said more to himself. He swore inwardly now at the possibility of what it could mean for his own daughter. "My Maya, for once, I actually wished I was more confused."

"I see your thoughts. Leave this one to me."

"Gladly."

"As your responsibilities are relied upon elsewhere at the moment."

"Beyond gladly." He watched her rest her head back against the tub more, her body sinking below the water another couple of inches, her face becoming fuller of the sensations taking place. She felt him not care to tease at all, letting her come to her climax as quickly as her body desired, all on its own. "I love how you just let go with me."

"I never had a choice with you."

"Would it have made a difference?" He saw her peak now. He needed a moment before answering.

"No...pe," she answered it breathlessly.

She felt his hand remain exploring, not moving away from her at all, even long past the last little aftershocks. She opened her eyes again, seeing his direct stare, taking in everything the way he always did. His fingers moved to her inner thighs now, massaging gently. He just enjoyed looking into her face for a few moments. Nothing was happening in their minds, just peace and quiet for once between them. He slowly stood up and removed his clothing, moving her to let him lay behind her in the large tub, letting his hands explore once again. One hand came up to gently grip her jaw and force her mouth to meet his. Taking his sweet time, he explored her mouth with the familiarity that no other would be able to provide. He enjoyed being able to feel where he pleased with his other hand, not wasting any time once again. He was not letting her face escape his grasp through her entire building climax and long afterward for her second time around. Her moans and movements rubbed on top of him under the water, almost making him climax himself alone. He let go of her face to grip her with both hands, making her face him now, looking down at him. He saw her beyond relaxed, satisfied, just completely in her element right now before him. Maya always had his heart full from their very first time, succumbing to him so ridiculously easy as if she truly could not help herself. It drove him to his very core, the soft sensuality of it in her face every time. The fact that she would always remain his no matter what he did or said. She would just always forgive him and always want him like this.

He gently held her face close to his, his hands through her hair, forcing her mouth to obey his oral commands. He felt her lift her hips upward to be able to accommodate him as she slowly lowered herself over his length. He watched her still slightly quiver at the pleasure it brought after all this time, no matter how many times. The feeling made his hands get a little rougher, his arms a little tighter, while letting her hips completely take over the pace for them both.

"I will let you have your karma this time, my love." He felt her face instantly smile against his lips.

"You know you deserve it."

"Uh-huh."

"You know I will make it worse for you."

"Can try."

He felt her move his arms to lay on the sides of the tub and gestured for him to slide down a little and relax a bit more. He obeyed. He instantly realized he couldn't move himself out of the position now. Her powers made him immobile. He leaned his head back, his expression going from trying to hide a small amount of worry to full-on determination and trust. "Go on, beautiful. Pleasure yourself, and don't stop until you are done."

"I will never be done with you." She gave a soft warning, her eyes holding a unique worry that was actually for him at the moment. Seeing him avert his eyes for a moment with a half smirk on his face, his expression of trying to find the right words. "You are asking for it." She saw him about to say something and started moving again, very slowly, taking only his tip into her over and over again for several minutes. She literally let him come to a finish without even being half inside of her. "You taught me how to tease well, my Roman. And now you may regret it."

"Loosen up on your powers, just a little. Please."

"No." She watched his head lean back, eyes closed, hearing him swear as she moved him all the way inside her now.

*****

Aiyana and Claura strolled along the boardwalk along the canal. They were not saying much, just enjoying the sites together. Each had plenty of their own reasons for just enjoying the momentary feeling of simply living. It was a sunny day. The feeling the realm lent everyone so freely was enough for them both. It was a break they so desperately needed. Aiyana pointed to a boat below that was parked alongside a dock. Seeing passengers getting off, their tour was over. Claura smiled and gestured for her to go first, seeing the look on her face of wanting to enjoy a boat for the first time in reality. They headed down the steps together and noticed that they were the only two next in line. The driver gave off an easy smile, reminding her of someone, the feeling giving her a slight pause. But she decided what harm could come from a simple boat ride where they were right now.

"Where to ladies?" he asked them both, looking between them as they settled into the back seat.

"Anywhere the sun is still shining." She saw him smirk and look away real fast. She turned to Aiyana, enjoying another brownie and giving her a small smile. "You really like those, don't you?"

"Sometimes, Daemon is right about things."

"That so? Let me try." She watched her reach into her jacket pocket to pull out another one for her, still wrapped and new. She took a bite with her. She instantly sighed with pleasure at its richness. "Damn. I have a good cook in my little café, don't I?"

"Simply my first one, so I will just have to agree."

"So where do you want to travel first when all of this is over?"

"I just want to be next to Tronan. I don't care where we go."

"Settling into the thought, at least I see."

"Of course I am. It's just so new, with him actually being here now."

"Maybe aim to have your next conversation with him be about some other things for a change. I know he would like that. He just wants to get to know you, you know."

"I understand. I just already..."

"Hmm?" Claura watched her blushing again, looking slightly away. "He won't pressure you. He really won't."

"I feel silly saying this, with my young body still, but it is not him I am worried about here."

"Oh really?"

"I just jumped close to a decade in one nap. I could do that again tomorrow. It could literally start tomorrow...the craving."

"For your sake, I hope so." She looked at her and winked.

"It's not what you think."

"Then enlighten me. I never expected to be the one learning from you here, that is for sure. I actually look forward to you helping me catch up on stuff."

"More than happy to."

"Excellent. Now tell me."

"No-name mentioned with my extensive powers, I have to succumb to a balance."

"Yes, the balance thing with us. It can be a pain. Especially figuring things out on your own all the damn time, which slows one down…incredibly." She clearly hated that about her witch self.

"It is not so bad. Wouldn't you rather know you were smart enough to figure something out rather than just being told over and over again? That would feel lazy to me, to be honest."

"True." She paused plenty, giving her all the time she needed to still say her answer. She sensed she was nervous.

"Well, my balance…during my heat cycle, I lose all of my powers. I am frightened it will happen before we can end Moira. You know…your mom." She said the word like she couldn't believe Claura was so okay with this, despite it all, as it was still her own mother they were planning against.

"Does not bother me one bit." She saw her thoughts in her head briefly. "She is the reason I am unable to see my son. The reason I am losing my memory more and more in every new life. The reason for so much. I won't hesitate. Have no fear there. Please."

"Okay."

"So your powers…gone for good, or just during your cycle?"

"I think just during, but that is still enough of a risk. And Tronan, being from a lesser realm than Daemon…I am just so used to someone like Daemon being able to protect me. I hate how this would all make Tronan feel like he isn't good enough to protect me the same way. When deep down, I don't want anyone else doing it, truthfully." She sighed, finishing her brownie now. She put the wrapper back in her pocket with haste. She watched the boat go under a bridge, causing it all to get dark now. She made them both look around and at each other. The air became cold. They saw the driver start to turn to them, smirking at his semi-strange features, turning away as he spoke.

"No worries, ladies. Sometimes, the sun fades in this particular… spot."

She saw Aiyana look at her with sudden worry, shaking her head a big fat no, saying that "hell no" it did not get dark spots in a realm like this. She shoved it into her mind, the quick lesson of how every realm had a hidden loophole door somewhere. The realization sank in on their faces, and they both stood up quickly to jump out of the boat. They step onto the back of it and get ready to leap together when he shouts back toward them, "Too late!" and turned to smile once again. Claura instantly shoved Aiyana out of the boat, telling her in her mind to find Daemon. She knew full well that a one-second pause was all that was needed for shit to go south after what Tronan dealt with so long ago. She watched her come to the surface of the water. It being intent on her face, she just wanted to go with her to help. Claura suddenly felt herself getting sucked into another realm, the image of Aiyana in the water before her suddenly no more. The cold air around them suddenly got even colder. The boat sped up as it went through some invisible wall as if the man was in a hurry to show off his delivery. Claura could see a cave-like structure appear—a very familiar one. She reached out to Daemon, unsure if he would hear her or not. Her body shivered, unsure if it was from fear or the dark and cold environment she felt trapped in now. She brushed away one tear, trying to get a hold of herself. She still wanted to make sure Aiyana was okay again, even if she had even made it to shore.

*My love, help me.*
There was no answer.

# Chapter 30

# Canal Loophole

Daemon appeared in her office, fully expecting her to be there—both of them, really. His moment of panic set in as he stepped into the doorway only to see the room empty. He glanced to the back wall, seeing the debris all over the place due to very recent events, wondering why Claura may not have taken the time to simply use her magic to fix everything yet with one spell alone. She tried to figure out where they could have possibly gone together. She hated having to reach out already so soon to him.

*Aiyana with you?*

*She is supposed to still be with Claura,* Tronan answered instantly. He gave Daemon a hint that perhaps he was coming around after all with needing to let Aiyana include herself in all this.

*They are gone.*

*Can you reach either one?*

*Not Claura.*

He felt his brother through the distance swear inwardly at the notion, knowing Aiyana still needed to learn just yet how hard it was for him to give her space to come to him on her own. He knew reaching out to her right now would only make things possibly worse in their already-icy relationship. He hated feeling this distance between him and…both of them. *Aiyana, sweetheart, where are you?* He sensed her need to spit out some water from her mouth before answering, making his awareness increase even more through their mind link.

*Swimming. In the canal. Very close to a loophole that just took Claura.*

She felt him invade her memories instantly to know exactly where she was, feeling his presence land in the realm only seconds later. Looking up along the edge of the water, she saw him pace toward her. His eyes watched her swim away from a certain direction that headed under a dark bridge, having a small amount of difficulty with the current. Unable to miss how his body looked, he dived into the canal from above, landing only a couple of yards away, pulling her close to him. He saw the worry for Claura all over her face.

"The driver…he tried to take both of us. Claura shoved me into the water and then faded behind a…wall!"

She was upset with herself for not knowing how to describe it better at the moment, hanging onto him, appreciating his body heat in the cold temperature of the canal's water.

"What did he look like?"

Her Tronan officially looked like a killer. She knew this expression, just never while staring directly into her eyes. This was a first for her, and it sent chills over her body that had nothing to do with the cold water anymore—feeling his gentle hands on her body, trying to reassure her, knowing what she was already thinking as she started to answer.

"I fear he was transforming himself, so it does not matter. There was that particular slight shimmer to his frame at the last moment. Just like with the wall as Claura disappeared through it." She felt Daemon closer now, looking up to see him glance down at them both. She watched Aiyana point toward the dark bridge, her face saying that was all she knew. She looked at him like she was so sorry, seeing the same killer expression unfolded into his entire face now as well. She watched him glance toward the area where she had just pointed, his entire demeanor an intense inward debate before he turned around to head back to the office. She looked at her for just one more glance before doing so, checking her over for himself as she floated there in Tronan's arms. His face made it clear he already knew he would not be able to follow Claura and had to find another way to reach her. He saw this anger about it build as he walked away in a hurry. She felt Tronan's gaze still glued to her face the entire time.

"Sweetie, calm yourself," Tronan said gently, feeling her rising tension, her body shaking even more now from being so upset.

"I am so sorry! I did not know what to do! I have all this power, but I did nothing! I have been taught so much…Daemon is right!"

"About what?"

"About how reality is so different from learning and practicing in a safe little dream world! I had so many spells in my head to help stop her from disappearing and no time to choose one!" She looked to the bridge with fear and then back to him. "And you. I am so sorry, Tronan! I have spent so much time listening while a damn baby that I just did not want to do it anymore, even with you." Her eyes begged him for forgiveness. She felt him grip her body closer, his hand on the back of her head, pulling her against his larger warmth, feeling his embrace meant more to her now than it ever did.

"Listen to me now. Okay." He felt her head nod next to his, her crying making her shake. "This is not your fault. I mean it. Hear me?" He gripped her closer with one arm as he grabbed the nearby stairs attached to the dock, lifting them out of the water together as if she weighed nothing. "Come on, let's get you some new clothes." Reaching for her parents in his mind. *Roman! Claura's office, now!* They knew they had more than enough catching up to do with her, with all of them now.

Tronan just stood there, feeling her smaller frame wrapped around his, her arms holding on tight around his neck, her legs wrapped around his abdomen. He held her close, intentionally making his body heat increase, inhaling her scent with his face in the crook of her neck. He savored the moment despite its cause.

"You don't have to say sorry to me, little one. Do you understand?"

Her harder squeeze her answer in choosing.

"I have to tell you something. It is not the right time, but I still want to tell you." She moved slightly away to look at him now, facing him, admiring his gorgeous features. She looked at him the way she knew he was still unsure of how to take as long as she was still not fully grown yet but uncaring. She decided to take Daemon's advice in just being honest with him. His eyes held complete patience for her words, looking over her features, clearly admiring what she had to offer as well. "I am terrified of my heat cycle…"

"I know."

"But you don't know why."

"I would never force you into anything. You know this."

"It's not that. My balance in this with my powers is I lose them during my heat cycle. I am unable to protect myself or anybody during. I am terrified it will happen before we can end her." She watched his face closely, seeing him turn it over in his mind from both of their perspectives.

"I understand."

"You do?"

"Yes." He laid a small and platonically admiring kiss on the side of her small mouth. "I will always understand so long as you are honest with me. Please don't stop doing that for me. For us." He leaned his head in that way that said he wanted her to say out loud that she understood and that he needed to hear it.

"Okay," she finally answered softly, reading his eyes for a long time. She nodded after a moment, touching his face with her small palm and enjoying the moment for one more minute—just one—before they had to deal with everything else. "I just want to go home right now. Isn't that selfish of me?" She laughed at herself while wiping one more tear off her cheek as if she was embarrassed by it. She felt him lower her to her own two feet to stand now.

"It is where I have been waiting." He looked down at her gently, touching her nose quickly with the tip of his finger. Seeing the notion made her smile, but it kind of bothered her, as it was loving yet something you do to a small child. He took a deep breath and raised his hand to try again, this time letting his large fingers cup her chin while his thumb brushed lightly over her lower lip.

"You are so beautiful to me. No matter what form. You know that, right?"

"Yep." She felt some funny stares from some people now while they were out and about in their routine. They did not want things to get weird, for they had a home they could be in together, just the two of them, while they figured this out. She took in a quick inhale as if to intentionally need it just to break herself away from his gaze and looked down over her body, snapping her right fingers. "I may not look older yet, but I can at least dress it." She smiled up at him, seeing his eyes try to hide something. "What?"

"Seems you are more like twelve or thirteen now. Taller. Curvier." He looked from her figure to her face with pause yet determination, the mixed expression making her nervous.

"And what?" she asked, seeing it clear on his face he was still holding something back.

"And any day now, or minute…puberty."

"Damn." He clearly looked terrified of hormones. As usual, he was afraid of quite random things and was never the main threat in this entire scenario. She truly was unafraid of Moira, and Tronan was still trying to figure out how to feel about it.

"No, my love. It is much more than hormones between us."

"Will be. Not is. Not yet."

"Standing corrected."

"Good. Get used to it."

"In time, my darling. In time." He looked over her head now at the bridge for a quick moment, eyeing the spot intently, before coming back to her with a gesture that they get moving. He saw her need to take just one moment and a good deep breath over what was about to come with Roman and Maya seeing her like this.

Tronan and Aiyana saw Roman and Maya come out of the office and headed toward them down the hall in a hurry. Their whole demeanor made it clear Daemon within the office had filled them in on everything already. Roman took instant notice of their hand-holding, along with his daughter's new expression of acceptance toward the man. Somehow, it brought him comfort, yet he still hated it. He noticed Maya pause ahead of him in the hallway for a moment, as if in awe of the sight before her, before moving her feet even quicker now toward them as she took in the full sight of their now young teenage daughter.

"Oh my…my beautiful girl! Look at you!" He pulled her in close for a hug before holding her back to look at her some more. "You are so stunning!" He literally was squealing it. It made Aiyana look up to Tronan with a look of humorous displeasure, rubbing her temple with her right hand, her eyes clearly saying, "*Help me.*" Tronan simply smiled back at her. *Let her have this moment. She has waited so long.* She humbled him by listening instantly, pulling her mom back toward her for another big squeeze, eyeing Roman over her mom's shoulder. He walked slowly toward them, taking his time, reading the entire scene before him. He saw that he was already made aware apparently of her not being happy with him for making Tronan not claim her asap the first time so long ago. His face showed that he was ready for the accusation, ready to just finally speak with his daughter no matter what the conversation was about. He looked at her with such love and admiration yet question. Maya pulled away to give Roman his moment now. Aiyana looked up slightly more and more as he comes closer, feeling his gaze as he just stood there for a minute, eyeing her intently.

"Dad."

"Daughter."

His one had moved to reach out and cup her chin in his grasp, gently making her look more into his face. The moment was quite serene yet serious all at the same time. "Forgive me." His voice was almost a whisper.

"I prefer the argument first before the apology." Her eyes alone held her smirk while the rest of her face remained professionally poker. He saw one side of his mouth smile slightly in response.

"Another day."

"Good." She looked serious now. She wanted him to know she meant it. She heard Tronan clear his throat next to them both, his whole energy full of pride and pleasure in his Match, clearly beyond pleased with her.

"I see you two have found common ground finally," Maya said. She smiled between Tronan and Aiyana, receiving a quick glance of accusation from Roman. She eyed him in return with a look of "whatever," followed by a wink. She held her hand out toward the office. "Shall we?"

They all walked back into the office to see Daemon facing the far wall, obviously busy with something and with no intent to turn and face them.

"Oh my…her more precious belongings were along that back wall. You know this Daemon, correct?" Maya sounded stern, as if angry for her niece. She knew that she needed certain possessions for certain advanced spells, and now they were irreplaceable. She wondered how she missed them before, eyeing over everything more intently now.

"As are mine." His tone made it obvious his mind was half elsewhere, keeping in constant touch with what Claura was dealing with from afar. He hated that he had missed her plea for help earlier while traveling between realms. It was literally a three-second ordeal of horrible timing.

She looked back up to his hands, seeing past them now at the wall shimmering before turning into a hidden arsenal. He lowered his hands to his sides, looking left and right, choosing where to begin. He took only a very quick moment to do so before stepping forward to start placing them all through his attire. He used his powers to hide blades in his literal forearms on both sides of his arms as if it caused zero pain to do so. Daemon felt Aiyana stepping closer to him, looking extremely worried for him and wanting to help. He was unsure where to start. He read her intentions as clear as day, as clear as he would for forever after their decades together. "You will remain here, waiting to help with the next task. Stay with Tronan."

"Nothing? Really! You are giving me nothing here in helping, knowing what I am capable of!"

"I already know where she is. Seeing exactly what she is seeing from moment to moment takes away half the work. I will have her back in time for dinner."

"Your weapon choice suggests otherwise. Knives over bullets, really?"

"I'm faster. And knives are just plain fun, little one."

She winked at her yet was unable to hide the still-smoldering fury he contained by a thread here in need of getting her back. She wasn't in one of the worst realms, but she still had yet to prove to him she could use her powers to protect herself enough in this lifetime again.

"He is right, Aiyana. He can do this alone," Roman chided.

"Well, usually anyone but you is." She turned to face him now while remaining at Daemon's side, glaring at her father. Seeing his sudden interest in remaining quiet pleased her immensely. She saw her mother cover half of her face with her hand now, looking at the floor in deep thought. The part of her face that she could see was torn between a smirk and heartache.

"Aiyana!" Daemon sensed what was to come between the two and just did not want to deal with it at this specific moment. "I know this is new to you, that all you've ever seen of me is when we were in my home together, but you are not the only one with pent-up energy"—shifting his belt to add more weapons before looking back up into her face—"or rage." His face showed that he understood completely, but her father also already understood that "another day" was literally genius in the matter. "Little one, go home." He gave her a look that he just already knew, whether he saw it in Tronan's mind or not about what she recently said outside. Daemon looked at her like he just wanted her to be happy and to let him handle this in the meantime.

"If I say call to me if you need me, would you take me seriously?"

She watched him pause for a moment, looking into her eyes, reading her while feeling Tronan start to walk toward the wall on the other side of him. He eyed the weapons up close.

"If I say have a hot chocolate waiting for me, would you take me seriously?" She smirked, knowing she loved that in her bottle from time to time, not so long ago.

"This is not funny." She saw him step closer, making her have to lift her gaze to keep eye contact.

"You may be more powerful, but that doesn't mean you get to underestimate us. What are you to do whenever something goes wrong with any of us, huh? Step in and take over every time for the rest of all of our lives? What kind of life does that give you, Aiyana?"

"I may enjoy my first *real* knife fight."

"Oh, you will. On another day."

He leaned down to kiss her forehead and briskly walked around her toward the door. He heard Tronan clear his throat loudly as if to say, "Forgot something," seeing Daemon turn to catch the sharp-edged chakram with ease. It was as if the blades all over it meant nothing to work around as he caught it perfectly from Tronan's toss across the large room.

"Thank you, brother." He gave him the quickest of glances that held the possibility of a hundred different meanings before turning back around to exit the doorway for good this time, leaving all their sights.

Aiyana rubbed her temple, seeing her father not miss the sorrow in her eyes over watching Daemon leave to do such a task alone. The emotion made her have no room to express the full 180 she felt toward her own father, instead leaving it as if her mind was clearly elsewhere. Tronan stepped closer to her, gently pushing her hair behind her ear, letting his index finger caress her cheek before lowering his hand back to his side.

"Are you ready?"

His soft tone was full of the obvious suggestion of just going home together now. She had dealt with enough for one day in her new body, new environment, and new life. She gently nodded while aiming for Claura's main chair, going to sit down. She heard her parents say it together next.

"No!"

"OMG...what!" She looked at them like they were truly being the cliché, annoying parents all teens dealt with, making it clear she still chose to sit despite their efforts. "I am just sitting!" She saw the shock on their faces.

"What is wrong?" Tronan asked, eyeing between them. He watched Maya start to speak and then pause, turning to Roman to see if he'd like to clarify. He noticed it evident on his face that he preferred just not saying anything anymore for the time being, watching him turn slowly to walk toward the door.

"Only Claura can sit there," she said to them. She faced them both now after watching Roman leave with regret. She was unsure of how to help him with this situation with their daughter.

"And why is that?" Aiyana asked.

"Umm...unsure. The chair has a mind of its own for a reason. It shocks anyone but her who sits there."

"Did it come that way?" Tronan asked.

"Yes," Maya answered.

"Well, where did it come from?" Tronan continued. He watched Maya put her hands up as if to say she simply did not know.

"Well, no shock here," Aiyana stated, seeing them both look at her with a question. "What! You think I know why? How would I know!"

"We can just ask Claura when she returns," he said.

"Is he being truthful with me, Tronan?" She looked up at him with real worry.

"More than you know." He touched her chin affectionately, gesturing for them to get a move on. He was more than ready to have some time with her in their home—alone.

"Aiyana, honey, can I speak with you before you go?" Maya asked gently.

"Sure, Mama. What's up?"

She felt like herself behind the desk, touching and looking at a few things before she looked up. She enjoyed trying out "mama" for a change in the real world. He saw Maya's expression of "Alone, please" written all over it.

"He is my Match. You can just say whatever it is in front of him."

"Not this." She saw Tronan's look of concern as she glanced his way momentarily. She saw her daughter read her thoughts already without even being in her head, impressing her, showing her level of natural intuition. Clearly, she was already more like her cousin in that way. Maya inwardly hoped Claura's intuition was serving her for the better at the moment.

"I have already spoken to him about it. And how do you already know?"

"You are my daughter." She eyed her intently now, letting her know that, as her mother, she would always know more than she let on.

"Well, as your daughter, I have it taken care of." She watched her mother stand straighter as she eyed Tronan with a new worry, seeing his face daring her not to trust him with this.

"I simply want to teach you spells that will protect you during. Shields."

"Good enough to stop Moira?"

"Possibly."

"Possibly is not good enough."

"We will find something. Besides, this no-name did not teach you a spell strong enough to already know how to help this matter?"

"They said I needed to leave that up to my Match," she said, her tone proving she did not like how her own mother was making her own Match feel like some sort of threat with this.

"Really?" Maya asked, watching her daughter just nod, seeing her nervousness beneath the surface as any inexperienced young woman would own. She knew her place was limited here but just wanted to take advantage of it the best she could all the same. She just wanted to be there for her as her own mother despite the type of woman she was already. "Your father and I look quite forward to meeting this no-name you keep speaking of."

"You will."

"When?"

"If all goes well, soon. You, in particular, won't be the first to meet him, but you will."

"That so?" Eyeing Tronan, seeing his look of overwhelmed and disbelief at how his little Match was just so completely full of faith in the matter. Being able to relate to the feeling with him, glad they were at least on the same page about that.

"No-name told me that beings from lesser powerful realms are known to sometimes have…unexpected skills," Aiyana added, tilting her head slightly sideways, eyeing her mother's response closely.

"Let us hope so."

"I plan to end Moira first still anyway. Simply waiting…more so now on Claura and Conroy to have their little conversation still."

"Claura is okay with you going with her on this mission, truly?"

"She told me herself. Are you not?"

"I do not doubt your powers, my daughter. I simply have some doubts about you knowing how to use them."

"Sounds the same to me, kind of."

"You already know better. And you know you already know better. Do not try to confuse me. It will not work."

"I have quite the parents, don't I?" She glanced at Tronan for a moment, her voice sounding proud yet like she was suddenly feeling too tired after today's events to be up for the challenge. Knowing that Tronan noticed.

"Maya, let's call it a day. Please." Tronan tried to say it as politely as possible. She knew Maya just wanted time with her daughter finally yet unable to ignore Aiyana's eagerness to just go home and rest now.

"Fine." Maya's expression made it clear she was truly catching up to her daughter's unique situation despite how she looked on the outside. "If you hear from them, please let us know. Daemon does not always update as quickly as I'd like."

"Will do," Tronan said.

"You both could do Claura a favor and clean up before you leave. That's if you know a spell for it." She turned to glance at her daughter in the doorway for just one moment before finally really leaving. She saw her lift her right hand and, without any pause, snap her fingers, her blank glare hard to miss. The entire office went back to normal. Even the irreplaceable objects. "Impressive."

"You all keep mentioning how we should not underestimate Moira. Same goes for me, dear Mother." She kept her face as blank as possible, clearly intent on reading her mother's expression too much to have one of her own.

"No-name did good, didn't they?"

"You have no idea."

"No Aiyana, I don't." Looking sad through her gentle smile, turning away from both of their gazes to leave. Maya looked up to see Roman waiting still in the hallway, leaning against the wall, arms crossed over his chest, face downward. He looked at her with the same expression she knew was already on her face.

Exasperation.

Confusion.

Longing.

Unconditional love still despite it all.

Parenting sucked.

# Chapter 31

# Emerald and an "Ex"-Mystery

"May I have just five minutes to look around before we go?" Aiyana asked. She saw him nod, watching his eyes take notice of a particular book on the desk before quickly glancing away. He failed at hiding his expression and knew it. "This is that book, isn't it? The one that broke the false ties?"

"I believe so." He watched her open it. "Need headphones."

"Why is that?"

She held the spine at the angle needed to glance through all the pages casually. Her eyes focused as they moved from right to left.

"Claura needed music to see what was on the pages. Many remained blank otherwise. Was part of some spell your mother did to keep Moira from reading it."

"Really? Because I see not one blank page. Do you?"

"Yes, many, in fact. What I see is only the first half of the book being written in."

"I am seeing the entire book being written in."

"You are truly remarkable, aren't you?" He pressed his hands onto the desk beside her, leaning down to look closer as her beautiful eyes took in the sights on the pages that she alone could see. "Do you recognize any?"

"Several."

"That is good."

"Actually, all of them. I kind of already know this book by heart." She scoffed at herself. "I wonder if the other book she needs…if I already know anything that is written in that. She may not even need to go get it." She looked up at him, hopefully.

"Well, the only way to find out is to unfortunately get it and see what it even entails."

"Yes, unfortunately…that is true." She took in a deep breath, sighing, sounding tired.

"Quite a day for you, hasn't it been?" He saw her tired eyes look back up into his. He saw her shift in the mysterious chair more slightly to look into his face better.

"Well, I did enjoy the swimming."

"Oh ya? What else?" She returned her joking smile.

"Brownies. Tossing them at Daemon."

"Really?" She saw her nod, smiling at the memory.

"Boat ride, before…ya know."

"Go on."

"Being held." Her tone suggested it was nice to finally know the experience with him in a way that held no fear around it. She watched him think it over, staring into her eyes before saying anything back.

"I will hold you, and only hold you, until you literally beg it of me to do more." He saw her forget to breathe now, and it reminded him of another cousin's habit she clearly had in link to Claura. "You have my word, sweetheart." She watched her face, seeing her look uncertain of what to say. "Let me take you home. Come on."

He held his hand out for her, stepping back slightly. He watched her slowly close the book and look around the desk as if she really did want to just bring one thing home with her for some reason. She noticed the trash can as she turned to get up, saw a small ring box in it, and reached for it.

"What is this?"

She bent back up slowly to stand before him. She held it gently as if already sensing it held some sort of power within its case.

"Perhaps it is best to leave it alone," Tronan said, watching her move the small box around in her small hands, looking at his face for a brief second before deciding to open it. "Wow. This is truly… just beautiful."

Tronan followed her eyes, unsure of why the sight before him was causing such unease. It was, after all, just a ring. Perhaps Claura threw it in there despite a heated argument between her and Daemon at some point. He was, after all, aware of their recent heated argument that took place right here in her office thanks to his conversation with Maya so recently.

"In case she wants it still, we should just leave it here."

"It was in the trash, so I doubt it."

She moved to put it on now, feeling his hand stop her.

"No."

"Why?"

"I don't know. It just does not feel right. Let me just clarify with either one of them first, okay? There could be a thousand reasons why it's in the trash, plenty of them being good ones. For your safety. Please."

"Okay. Fine. But I am taking it with us." She moved it away from the tip of her finger to put it back in the box.

"Fair enough. Now come here." He watched her move to stand close to him, fiddling with fitting the ring box inside her leather jacket pocket. It brought his attention to his earlier question that got put to the side. "Leather, my darling?"

"Yes. You don't like it?"

She saw his gaze hold a moment of a grown man with full-on admiration. She felt his hands on her gently as he moved her hips to have her turn in a circle for him. His eyes on her body made her more aware of how alone they were now. She felt him grasp a little tighter around her waist as she faced him again, question in her eyes. Tronan saw as clear as day how she was so unfamiliar with all this, literally looking at him like she was possibly disappointing him in a way with her clothing choice. He was completely oblivious as to how her new and growing curves were affecting him in leather from head to toe. Even underneath her jacket, she chose a leather corset, so help him.

"I didn't say that."

"Say something then."

Impatience crossed her young face. She stared into his eyes while he remained studying her features, looking at her lips as he touched them gently. She finally understood those books that mentioned butterflies with people. She admired how gorgeous he was yet too shy to make it known out loud. She hated her inexperience. It was not fair. She had 150 years of knowledge, none of it able to help her with this feeling she never experienced before now that she was with him—really with him. His body was so close, his fingers touching her gently, his eyes looking at her in such a way she was finding it hard to put into words. He was taking her breath away already.

"Tronan, please say something."

"I love you, Aiyana." He felt his fingers move through her hair now, holding her head between them next, forcing her to keep looking closely into his face. "I love you."

"But not my clothes?"

She tried not to smirk at him, completely failing. She made it obvious she wished she knew how to respond but just didn't.

"It's okay. I know you won't feel comfortable saying it back for a while." He smiled back at her yet not reaching his eyes as much.

Aiyana instantly stopped smiling, seeing the seriousness on his face. She felt the embarrassment of knowing she didn't measure up to what a grown man like him needed at that moment. She looked down and away now, grabbing his hands from her face to let go of her, trying to back away.

"No, don't do that."

"I hate my fear on this. It makes me feel weak."

"You are not weak. Look at me." His hands made her look back up into his eyes again, shaking his head no gently. "Feel no shame. Please."

"I am so inexperienced and have been waiting for too long… it has made it so much worse for me than the average person." Her frustration and humiliation mixed so clearly on her face, all through her voice.

"Your inexperience makes me so goddamn beyond happy."

"What!"

"My darling, to know I am the only one who will get to touch you in that way, that alone brings me so much pleasure. Please do not underestimate that. You have no idea how happy that makes me." He watched her relax a little at his words, even leaning slightly more toward him now. "We do not have to talk about it now. We don't even have to talk about it."

"I can't help it."

"For tonight, please practice not worrying about it. For me. Because I cannot wait to prove to you that you worried for absolutely nothing." Her eyes bordered on a tear or two, looking away and back to him and away again.

"Okay."

She pulled herself together—for him. She felt him pull her even closer now. She knew instantly that it was for the purpose of traveling home as he held her closer like this for their arrival earlier. She felt her feet land on the outdoor porch at his home a moment later, his arm still wrapped around her for a long moment before letting go.

"You hungry?"

"Yes, actually. All I've had today are mainly brownies. I fear they are too much of a favorite already." She walked through the door he was holding open for her, clearly loving the sight of her entering his home. The happiness it gave him was tenfold compared to how it felt with Claura that day not so long ago. "Not even sure what else I like yet."

"I can take you out for dinner tomorrow. For now, at this hour, we will have to improvise. Any hints?"

"Hot chocolate?"

"That is not a meal."

"And for that, I am beyond grateful." Her eyes found the bottles and sippy cups on the counter, feeling her feet move before she could control them. He grabbed every one of them and tossing them in the nearest garbage. "You have no idea how good that felt."

"We can have a bonfire and burn all your onesies."

"I'd love that."

"Bassinette next?"

"Absolutely."

"What else, Aiyana? Tell me." He walked slowly over toward her, looking at her like just helping her in any way he could right now was the only thing he wanted to do—the only important thing to focus on.

"Umm"—leaning her back into the center island now, putting one hand through her hair—"we shall see. I suppose." She looked at him with a longing she did not know how to take care of.

"Go enjoy a hot shower, stay in it for as long as you like, and just come back down when you are ready."

"Okay, what are you going to do?"

"Mac and cheese."

"What?"

"You'll see. It's a cliché favorite." He stepped next to her now, holding half of her head in his one palm, pulling her toward him to kiss her temple. "Go. Enjoy yourself."

She watched him turn to pour himself a drink first, eyeing him without moving, seeing his eyes smile. His hand now reached for another glass.

"What is it?"

"Bourbon."

"Why aren't you filling it?" She heard him softly laugh in response as he slid hers over to her gently atop the counter.

"You'll see." He turned to her now, leaning on his hip on the counter, taking a swig. He looked forward to this. "Just a sip."

She smelled it first and didn't actually react the way he expected. She studied his gaze for a second before choosing to take one big swig as well instead. She instantly regretted it, hearing his laugh in her mind as well as out loud as she turned toward the counter, looking for a sink to spit into. She slapped the marble with intense distaste as she realized she needed to just swallow and get it over with.

"Tronan! That is not funny. It fucking burns!"

"I see I have a champagne girl on my hands."

"And what is so wrong with that?"

"Nothing."

"Then why not just start with fucking champagne!" She saw his pleasure in this moment all across his face. She stood to face him now, wiping the back of her hand across her mouth. "You wait."

"Oh yeah?"

"Yeah."

"I already know your weakness, my darling." His tone made it clear he was unafraid to use it…in their future.

"I am your walking weakness. So how about don't fuck with that?" she said as she started to walk away to head upstairs.

She felt a sudden breeze of air, knowing it was instantly him using his speed ability to stand before her now, blocking her from the stairway.

"Excuse me?" He was not laughing anymore. "You will never risk your life, for anyone or anything, just to get back at me. Do you hear me?"

"I was just playing along. You already know I will be bad at this." Her guilt and embarrassment combined in her eyes pulled on his heartstrings. "Maybe for forever."

"You can't say things like that to me. It brings something to the surface that I cannot control, as your Match. Please understand."

"When it comes to you, Tronan, no-name left everything out. Even Daemon had a hard time reading such books to me. He never finished them. It is very frustrating, and embarrassing, to have so much knowledge about everything…until you." She looked too shy to face him despite his face being within inches of hers at the moment.

"I am glad. Our relationship does not concern them."

"But I need help in this. I clearly do."

"I will help you." He watched her look toward the floor, shaking her head back and forth as it tired of feeling inadequate before him.

"I don't want to shower. I don't want to eat. I just want to go to sleep." She looked up into his eyes, seeing him contemplating her words. She closed her eyes and lifted her hands to rub her temples, feeling him gently remove them to let his fingers do it for her. The ache and tension instantly faded into nothing. "I never want you to feel like I underestimated you, Tronan. I hate that it will happen so easily with my kind of powers and after having someone like Daemon to protect me for so long."

"You let me worry about that."

"That is a topic that includes both of us. Not just you."

"A topic for tomorrow."

He lifted her into his arms, moving slowly toward the same room she was in earlier, enjoying any moment he was able to have her in his grasp like this. Feeling her head on his shoulder, knowing her eyes were already closed. He laid her on the bed, pulling the covers over before just mentally removing her clothing, lying atop the blankets beside her, pulling her small curves into his arms. She turned to face him then, eyes still closed, curling into him, her one arm wrapped around his neck. Her face curled in close to his chest, inhaling his scent as if subconsciously doing it. One deep inhale and sound asleep. Tronan lay there awake for the rest of the night, enjoying every breath she took, admiring her beauty and how, by the hour, it literally kept changing before him.

*****

Daemon always hated this realm. It was always raining. If anyone thought his preferred realm to call a home was gloomy, all they had to do was come here to be proven wrong. He landed himself on the roof of the building she was in, taking a moment to look over all four edges, taking note of how high up he was. He saw how the place had remained the exact same as it was during his last visit centuries ago.

*I will see you in just a minute.* He tried to reassure her. He felt her nerves on dire edge.

*They are moving me. Again.*

*Let them, and don't argue with any of them. The majority of beings here don't even speak English, and not speaking their language tends to piss them off. I will follow. Do not worry. Focus on your body temperature. Your heart is starting to have to fight.*

*Feels like a brick is not just on my heart, but inside it.*

*They dosed you.*

*Dosed me?*

*Sorry, love, not all drugs can be as wonderful as mine.*

*I can't believe you right now.* She felt him kiss her freezing forehead from afar. *Please hurry. I don't think they are planning to kill me, but this is bullshit all the same.*

*Kidnapping is one of their favorite tricks. Don't take it personal.*

*Oh, yes. I'll do that. So you have been here before, have I?*

*No.*

*What would they want, Daemon?* Her fear rose in her voice.

*Have you been able to read enough spells to at least put up a barrier around you?*

*I have not.* She felt beyond frustrated with herself for not focusing and reading more like Maya mentioned she takes the time to do. *Everything I have focused on has been to help end Moira. Now I fear I have even wasted my efforts in that thanks to Aiyana.*

*My love, you underestimate yourself. Still.*

*I am not ready to deal with this. I am just not. Perhaps in past lives, but not this one.*

*Your power is lingering, as if in hiding and ready to come out when called. It has been simmering for far too long, and I can feel it wanting to be let out when I am around you. Simply reach for it. It is there.*

*I cannot focus since you told me of our son. I have been unable to really focus on anything since.*

*I know. But picture him from afar, watching you. Waiting for his mother to use this opportunity to be the badass that she really is.*

*Unbelievable.*

*I will not let you be weak right now.*

# THE WINGED WITCH OF MATCHES

*There are too many around me now in this room. I have no idea where to begin, even if I did want my powers to stop simmering and just be let out already.*

*When they have stopped moving you, I will be there. I cannot risk being sucked into a loophole trap. It is one of their tricks.'*

*Loophole trap?*

*They know I am coming.*

*Who is they*

*Devalia. I can already sense that she has come a long way in this realm. And she used to be besties with your mother.*

*Fucking fabulous.*

*She is nowhere near as powerful. Do not worry so much.*

*Good. I am not ready to take on a Moira counterpart.*

*I meant you.*

*Your faith in me better be realistic.*

*Since day one, my love.*

Claura could sense his hands double-checking his weapons as his body held the urge of a cougar to pounce. She looked before her at the group of people leading her somewhere and saw enormous metal doors up ahead start to open, a person shoving her back to assist her along a little quicker. Inwardly, she was already looking forward to her future moment with whoever was behind her, smiling to herself now. Daemon, in her mind, helped more than she let on, still fearing how this would have gone down for her without him being able to reach her still. She inwardly wondered if there was a way for people to still be reached during realm jumping. Then again, every weakness also had a strength.

"Balance...," she whispered to herself, knowing her brain was working on witch-drive now, in a timely manner all on its own, figuring out how to best handle this situation.

She suddenly felt no fear and more anger at just not being able to be home right now with a delicious snack. She decided to do whatever she could to make this become a part of her past as soon as possible. Just being told this person in charge used to be besties with her mother had her instantly craving all this as a delicious warm-up before the real battle. She suddenly got shoved into a metal chair. It actually felt warm compared to everything else in the environment. It was a quick moment of the Jacuzzi time with Daemon popping into her head, making her smile despite the weird energy coming at her from everyone surrounding her in the large dark room.

"What is so funny, Adera?"

Well, she clearly already knew too damn much, whoever this woman in charge before her was. "Name?" She looked into her face with impatience, seeing if she'd answer her or not of her own will. Her look of a displeased killer just wanted to put a name to its prey before it drew blood.

"Oh yes, you are definitely Moira's daughter." She eyed her back.

"Correction. Moira's enemy."

"Well, I guess you can take that up with her. She wants to speak with you too."

"Let's just go together." She smirked at her, watching her pull up a chair to sit on it backward and face her.

"I see you are back with…your man."

"You can say hello soon yourself."

"I know. You were just bait, my dear. I don't really care about you."

"Bait? Can't just reach out to him yourself?"

"Banned from your little realm, just like Moira. My days of visiting there are long gone. But that loophole, you put that there lifetimes ago yourself. We can't go in, but we can bring you out," she said with pleasure, as if this was all just a fun little game.

"Did I?"

"You forgot to redo the spell that needs to be done each time you return to keep it off-limits to everyone's use but yours. I see your ability to focus is waning."

"Bait me to try to befriend me now with this advice? Really?"

"I see her in you. So trust me, we will never be friends."

"Shame. Usually, a common enemy brings people together."

"Not this time."

"What do you want with Daemon?" She felt his presence now coming up behind her. She felt beyond relieved as the drug was getting slightly stronger instead of wearing off.

"Answer her," he said.

He walked through the doors with determination. He looked straight into the woman's eyes. Claura looked up into her face again, her head feeling too tired to hold up, her neck feeling incredibly sore, intentionally putting up a fight with the drugs in her system, for some unknown reason, uncaring if it made it worse or not.

"Ya, Devalia. Answer me." She smiled at being able to make it obvious that she already knew her real name as well. She saw her eye Daemon with thirst, and it was evident memories were returning behind her eyes. They had a past, and Claura already was beyond not thrilled about it.

"Cuffs? Really, Devalia? So afraid these days." He raised his hand to cast a quick spell to dispose of them instantly as he looked at Claura's wrists. Eyeing the woman as the metal fell to the ground, the sound of them hitting the cement floor echoed through the large room that looked like nothing but a large abandoned warehouse.

"Can we do this quickly? This place fucking smells," Claura stated.

"She is just like her. I can already tell Daemon. You may want to watch it."

"Your fear of her already is quite the stench, dear ex."

"I'm sorry! Ex?" Claura did her best to eye him now despite the pain of turning her neck and looking at him still slightly behind her.

"For a reason," Daemon stated without pause.

"You see, dear Adera, I could not have children. Other than that, we were perfect for one another, weren't we, Daemon?" She stood to walk closer to him now, looking at him like she missed him but also wanted to just torture him. "Do you know what that does to a woman, Adera?" She still read his face, stepping closer now. Her tone was low yet full of emotion, full of a lingering hate.

"Makes her see what should be the clearest fucking sign ever?" She did not even care to look at her as she said it, hating how close she was to Daemon right now. She knew easily what was going on in her thoughts. Her lust for him was beyond obvious.

"Get out of my head." She was unhappy with how easy it was for Claura to get inside it.

"Like I am going to listen to a damn thing you tell me to do." She felt a pretty good hit suddenly across her face before she could even finish saying the last word. Hearing Daemon growl next as he lifted her by the neck now, glaring at her.

"I knew that would get you to touch me." She smiled down at him, her hands around his forearm as he lifted her, squeezing her esophagus.

"You were better than this," Daemon hissed.

"You ruined that." She glared back at him with emotion now. She felt herself drop hard to the floor. Her choking sounds filled the room. Everyone else around them was still as quiet as mice, just watching. Daemon looked at Claura, seeing her expression of question. He saw her wanting to understand if this woman truly deserved any of this or not after what she had just said. His eyes told her there was much more to the story. They both looked back at her at the same time, seeing her stand with easy confidence as if she dealt with being choked on a daily basis.

"For your own sake, Devalia, I suggest you get the hell out of this neighboring realm. And never come near again, loophole access or not."

"When was this?" Claura wanted to know. It was eating at her to know.

"Before us." Daemon's tone made it clear she need not worry an ounce.

"Oh yes, dear Adera…before you. When he was different."

"Different?" Claura asked.

"What did we have, Daemon, a good 150 years together or so?" She watched him look at Claura, seeing her turn her face away from both of them. The hurtful reaction brought Devalia pleasure. "And it was fun."

She dragged the last word out, wanting him to remember, eyeing him like she was ready to receive anything he wanted to dish out, as long as it was coming from him. She saw the back of his hand coming long before it made contact across her face, letting it happen, choosing not to move despite having the ability to do so in time. The crack sounded like a whip as it knocked her to the floor for a second time.

"Oh boy, does that bring back memories." She laughed while wiping the blood off her bottom lip, feeling the slightly split skin along her cheekbone, eyeing him with contempt.

"I can go at this all night," he growled.

"Oh, I know." She winked, watching him walk closer to try and knock some sense into her again.

"What do you want?" Claura asked quickly, not really caring to see more between them already. She sounded sick of this realm for fucking forever after not even being here for that long, just wanting to leave now. "If what you both shared was so long ago, how the hell can it still matter now? Honestly, you should be embarrassed."

"I want you to kill your mother, as well." She still eyed Daemon from the floor, leaning back on her hands now.

"Couldn't just send a letter?"

"No." She stood up now, cracking her neck, straightening her jacket. "I wish. But no."

"Why do you want her dead?"

"She is the reason I cannot have children. She cursed my insides."

"Why?"

"She once upon a time wanted Daemon for herself before you were born." She already felt Claura's intense stare, knowing the memory of how Moira reacted to him while her spirit body was in Claura's office that day. Her evil mother's comment sank in a little deeper now. "You see, dear Adera, she curses us all who want your man here. And she won't stop. It has nothing to do with power. It all boils down to love." She looked him up and down with sad regret before turning her back to him to walk a few yards away.

"Daemon?" Claura needed him to clarify here. Say something. She watched this woman get a laugh in at his need to pause.

"So you really let her think still…yet again, that dear Moira mommy was just evil and hurt over other men? Really, Daemon? Isn't that card to play getting a little old?" She turned to see both of their faces now. "Do you know why he left himself out of the full truth yet again?" She eyed her quickly before glancing back at him. "Hmmm?"

"Stop. This does not truly concern you." His tone made Claura feel colder despite the words being said to one another. Just listening to him right now was making it obvious that once upon a time, he truly was "different" before meeting her.

"It does. In a small way, but still."

"How so?" Claura asked.

"Do not," Daemon said almost over her, knowing where this was going. He looked at Devalia like he was about to slice her nearest artery if she said it.

"My dear handsome Daemon, I do not need to say it." She pushed her palms out, one toward each of them now, using her powers. "I can simply show her." She saw him try to stop her with quite intense aggression now, coming closer. She simply sent a blast of power toward Claura, watching as it made her look like shards of glass were piercing her skull, shoving the memories into her brain as fast as possible. It blasted Daemon away with her powers from her other palm, sending him flying backward and across the room, just enough to give her enough time with Claura here. He looked into her face now, having no reaction to the pain all over it, uncaring to feel sorry for her in the slightest. "You see, little Adera, my own particular ability is I can hold one's memories for my own keeping, and I don't have to give them back until I damn well please. And right now, it pleases me." She smiled as she saw Daemon coming back closer to them now, knowing it was too late for him—far too late. She looked back at Claura, standing more in front of her now. She saw the memories take hold in her mind behind her eyes. She knew it was the best way to prove her point and prove her words. "Daemon was the very first one to break her heart, and he was the first one to break mine." She let it sink in, enjoying the silence between the two before her. "You got yourself quite the little heartbreaker in your grasp still, Adera. There must be truly something unique about you."

"It's simmering."

"Well, time to boil the fuck over."

"With pleasure." She eyed her with a new level of hostility.

"I have a weapon that will help."

"Use it yourself." Claura scoffed.

"Unfortunately, only one with purple power has the ability to do so."

"Then it is useless," Daemon stated.

"Oh no, I won't go near her. I needed you two to bring it to her."

"Who's that?" Daemon asked more seriously now, moving closer to her, a unique fury coming to the surface that only a protective ex-Match would hold.

"We knew of her level of power from afar as soon as she killed that minion," she said like she was actually sorry she knew but even more sorry for knowing just how much Daemon and all of them had on their hands now in protecting her. It was as if she even needed it. "Aiyana."

"Ya, I'm fucking done with this."

Claura stood up in a hurry, feeling the sudden need to protect her cousin and the new memories unfolding in her head that held more facts about her Match as the official "boil over." She walked toward Devalia, unliking the lack of space between the two ex-lovebirds yet again, and blasted her to the other end of her own goddamn realm—out of both of their sights. Somehow, she just inwardly knew that the spell she used she created herself, making it easy to use so spontaneously. She refused to look at Daemon. She looked around the room at everyone and shouted.

"Who can go fetch this weapon? You got two fucking minutes and I leave without it!"

The sound of her own fury bouncing off the walls felt somehow familiar, bringing her witch instincts joy. She turned her back to him and walked away a few yards, saying nothing. She was not sure where to even begin with yet again more information. She felt him wait, his eyes on her unmoving, his need to actually breathe gone in the way he did when his mind took over as if his body was strong enough not to even need air. But Claura knew that was all she needed right now—space from him and some goddamn air.

She heard someone come walking back into the room, being one of the few to scatter and find this so-called weapon. She saw a small rectangular briefcase in their grasp, stepping toward her with caution all across their face. It suddenly felt silly to Claura for even worrying about protecting herself here in this realm, as these people were more like just troublemaking rednecks in a way despite any power they held. She simply gestured for them to just please hand it to her so she could get a move on, and then it sank in that she did not know how to realm jump yet to get home. Her mind reached for Roman with zero hesitation. She felt him respond the same. She turned to stare at Daemon, looking at him with hopelessness. She was grateful that he came to her rescue, yet she needed time alone to wrap her head around things more now. She wondered if he had already seen this expression on her face before. She suddenly felt like her own damn Match she could not trust. Suddenly, she sided with anyone in any realm who truly believed that leaving the truth out is still linked to lying somehow. It hurt. She was damn hurt.

"You. Need. To. Let. Me. Explain," he said, watching her back up three steps for every one he took forward toward her.

"You had that chance. You already had it." There was hate in her eyes as she looked at him like he was now a stranger again. The trust was gone. Daemon was looking back at her like he already had a dozen knives in his heart, with her facial expression alone. "I am a game to you, aren't I? That is how you did not get bored with my reincarnation over and over. You decided to switch up what I should be reminded of each time I returned. Playing with me, playing with my own damn memory!"

"It was so long ago."

"It happened, Daemon! And let me guess, you were sensing me through her!" His expression answered her. "I am done with this! I am so fucking done with this! I don't want a connection with any of you! If this is how it happens, to this extent, I do *not* want it!"

"I will never want anyone else. Not since you."

"Then if I died, you'd sense me through my daughter, crave her...where does it end, huh? This fucked-up spell of Matches has got to end!"

"It ends when Moira ends. Believe me. Please. If anyone is playing a game here, it has been her."

"I will not be with you if you do not let me know everything."

"I let you know what actually matters."

"From your perspective, not mine!"

"Everything I do is for you. Please listen to me. Please do not go. You do not need to call upon Roman."

"Well, do this for me. Stay away from me until this is all finished. Until I am either dead or able to be alive without losing my memory…as that alone is probably thanks to this bitch you call your ex and not even Moira this entire time! Leave me be until I figure this out or I am buried. Leaving shit out is the last thing I need right now from *anybody*!"

She brushed the back of her sleeve across her cheeks, trying to rid the tears he did not deserve to see, as Roman appeared next to her, slightly behind her. His eyes, for once, showed shock at the extent of the tension between them. She looked to Roman with a pure expression of thank-you for showing up for her so quickly, seeing him nod in return, seeing him notice that she just wanted to go, and now. He looked at Daemon with a deep sense of worry for him this time, knowing he really must have messed up good, whatever the reason. Daemon gave him no satisfaction of even a second glance his way, keeping his full focus on Claura. He saw her unable to keep it together more and more by the second. Her body turned already to walk away from him as her broken voice barely got the words out through her pain.

"You motherfucker…"

There was absolutely zero humor. Shaking her head in disbelief, her emotions were beyond repairable right now.

Seeing her more hurt than furious made him pause in a way he hadn't had to experience since she awoke after going through childbirth with no child to hold. He watched Roman and her walk away from him, vanishing seconds later. Yet compared to the distance that was just in her eyes, it mattered none.

# Chapter 32

# Lasagna

Roman knew before they even left the realm that it was damn time he had some alone time with Claura. He knew Maya could help and was even anticipating her return, but he chose to take her elsewhere first. Never in a million years would he have figured he'd be taking her anywhere where Daemon's permission was not needed first. Something beyond sour had just gone down between them both, and he wasn't sure where to start, but his heart and mind were dead set on being there for her either way right now and simply starting somewhere. He decided it was damn time she got a real break, one she deserved, one from everything that has happened since she got on that plane per his request that day. Roman took her to his home, where he lived in only a few blocks from the hospital. He landed in his living room, holding her around the waist slightly to steady her as he knew she still was getting used to this despite her powers…that he could sense she didn't even want anymore.

# THE WINGED WITCH OF MATCHES

"I want to go back." She looked at him through tears. "I want to go back, Roman." She knew he would be able to see what she meant before she even got pregnant the second time.

"I hate being in the middle here, but what did he do? This time, I need to know," she asked it gently, backing away from her slightly.

"You aren't in the middle. Moira is."

"Ya, what's new."

"No," she said as she sat down on his sofa with full mental exhaustion on her face, looking up into his eyes and seeing him think about it a little more.

It took him all but three seconds before it sank in. She saw him cross his arms over his chest, swiping his hand over his jaw, looking away for a split moment as if to retrace his thoughts to just actually be sure with this.

"Motherfucker...I see now." He sat down next to her on the sofa, keeping some space between them. "How long ago?"

"Before I even existed," she answered.

"So you can't blame him so much then," he tried to say as gently as possible, seeing her breathing stagger in different rhythms to match her nerves.

"I blame the connection, this stupid connection that we all have to deal with, sensing our true Match through others first, and despite that...he fucked my mom, Roman!" She looked at him lowering his gaze and rubbing his forehead, his expression of not knowing where to begin. "They were together, and now he is joining me in killing her. That is fucked up!"

"I should have just brought you here to this home the first time. I am sorry, but I mean that. I left for a reason too, Claura. I got sick of it all too."

"Did Maya fuck your dad?" She watched him scoff at her question.

"No."

"Not that you know of. I feel like I can't trust him anymore that I can't trust what he says."

"He left it out because it simply does not matter at all to him anymore. I believe that, Claura. I could see it on his face now that I know what went down."

"I don't want to be with anybody until I don't have to die anymore, don't have to forget everything anymore. Even him."

"He won't be able to stay away from you forever, you know that."

"He would have had to if you and I never met! I am starting to see now why that may have been or a reason!"

"Claura, stop! Life can go in a dozen different directions no matter what you choose to do."

"Exactly, Roman! I would love to have it go in just a dozen different directions instead of the fucking fifty that is daily now!" She saw him stand up with her now, coming closer. "Stop! I don't even want any of you near me. I mean it. I need to figure this out, end it somehow, maybe just end me…huh? Let's just fucking do that!" She saw the instant seriousness enter his face, knowing she was starting to mourn the real trust she felt she had with Daemon and really feeling the hurt sink in now by her escalating and hyperventilating sobs.

"Claura, breathe."

"Enough with that!"

"Claura, fucking breathe!" He grabbed her wrists now, trying to be gentle with her, still moving her arms everywhere, attempting to escape his grasp.

"I see now. I see why Dayla died. Blessing in disguise not to have to be in this world I am apparently a part of. I don't want it! I don't fucking want it! I still want to just be with her, and it's so obvious now that that is never going to go away! Nobody in any realm is going to be able to help that, ever!" She felt him force her hysterical body into his arms now, noticing for the first time just how strong Roman actually was. "If she can't be there with me, I do not want to go back! Daemon is no longer enough." She felt him squeeze tighter, holding her close through her bawls. "You all have Aiyana now. None of you really need me. Please don't take me back!"

"Your son? What about him?"

"He is around three hundred years old and has not called out to Daemon once for help, as he apparently added that to the bargain, meaning he has been fine this entire time and will remain fine. He has been in one of the most powerful realms his entire life. I find it hard to believe he has not been able to reach out to me this entire time if he really wanted to. It made me think that perhaps he just wants to be left alone."

"You do not know that for sure."

"I do not care to know anything for sure anymore." She sniffled next to his ear, enjoying his closeness more than she expected she would. She wondered where it was coming from.

"I know the feeling." He leaned his face toward her head more, inhaling deeply, taking a moment longer to enjoy comforting her before pulling away. He sensed her sobs subsiding slightly.

"What do you mean?" She watched him wipe away a couple of her tears with his thumbs before turning around to walk away from her, grabbing a cigar box off the table and lighting one while slightly leaning on one hip.

"You are not the only one here who has lost trust in your Match, my dear." His tone made it obvious he had felt alone in the matter for some time now.

"Tell me."

"I think you have enough on your plate." She watched him get comfy in one of his chairs, leaning back, studying her for a long moment before looking away at the cigar in his hand, watching the smoke.

"Please distract me right now. Please. I am losing it after today's events."

"Maya will not explain to me why she could not just tell me about the spell she had to use on Daemon and Aiyana for so long. She will not tell me why I had to be left out for the entire time until you came along."

"I'm sure she has her reasons."

"Which, as her Match, I deserve to know."

"Perhaps to keep you here, where we would cross paths."

"How would she know that would even happen, huh?"

"No damn clue, Roman. I am tired of trying to figure things out."

"Then stop." His tone meant not just for today but for as long as she damn well pleased.

"I have to try."

"You are burning yourself out."

"I simply want Moira dead before I can move on with everything else."

"What if you can never truly end her? Hmm?"

"Aiyana seems dead set on it."

"Good for her."

"I sense tension."

"My ignorance toward Tronan caused her…trauma."

"No, it did not. You acted the way every father does. It's pretty shitty of them to make you feel bad for it."

"Tell them that."

"Gladly."

"So you do want to go back?"

"Nice try." She watched him lean his head in his hand now, really thinking over it all for her.

"I will never make you go back, Claura. Never. You can stay here in my home for as long as you want, just like I intended for it the first time."

"Why did Tronan have to even be there?" She looked down at her hands with aggravation.

"It was not supposed to be him. There was another guard hired."

"Hired?"

"Yes. Until I could visit…and hopefully—"

"Hopefully?"

"In time, call you mine," he said calmly, honestly.

"I am such a fool for not seeing that back then. I am sorry."

"There's that sorry again." He gave her a reassuring smile.

"I am serious. I am sorry." She looked into his eyes, steady. She saw his complete confidence in returning the gesture, his face holding absolutely no inhibition when it came to reading her.

"I sensed Maya through you."

He watched her look away, silently laughing with her eyes as she looked around the room more now.

"Don't doubt it."

"And then I sensed you through Maya." He eyed her with a soft intensity.

"What does that mean?" She was still not looking at him again.

"You already know."

"Please do not. I beg of you."

"He had you first. But I found you first. What do you think that says, huh?"

"Roman, I cannot handle this whirlwind anymore. Please do not say this shit!" She stood up as if needing space from him too now. "I love how smart you are, but this is too much. You need someone who is smarter and who can keep up with you. That is not me, despite what you may believe."

"I am missing something."

"Get in line."

"I don't do lines."

"Well, if you truly believe what you are saying, you've already been in one…in line behind two others you have always detested."

"Listen. To. Me." He saw her turn to face him now. "In this lifetime, who was first in line?" He saw the realization behind her eyes despite her lips not wanting to admit it. "And you keep forgetting about him more and more with each reincarnation, right?"

"Please…"

"Right?"

"Damn you," she whispered between them, looking away and then back to him. "Don't you get burned out always needing to figure everything out as well?"

"When it comes to us, there is something I am missing."

"Perhaps his ex that was in that realm is the cause of such, as she likes to steal memories that belong to you and never return them until she deems necessary."

"Sounds like they still kind of belong together, if you ask me."

"It was not fair of him to keep something like that from me, necessary or not."

"I agree."

"You were Moira too once."

"And wish I could erase every memory. Perhaps I have not been able to for the simple fact of not needing to hide that from you like he has done. It is obvious he has something to hide when it comes to his time with her. Or maybe it is just because he truly does hate her too."

"Still does not completely add up. And I feel like any conversation with him about it now will not truly put my mind at a hundred percent ease, despite how much I wish it so. Do you think he will stay there, in that realm where Devalia is?"

"Don't really give a shit."

"Sad to say, Roman, for some reason, I don't either."

"I know. I can see it. Despite it just starting."

"I hate this."

"We will go see Conroy together, just the two of us. Just let me know when you are ready."

"Now."

"No. You are exhausted. That dose they gave you was meant for people five times your size. I can still smell it lingering in your system. You need to sleep that off."

"I want to see him real soon. I want answers."

"Oh, so do I. He better be worth the trip, higher realm or not." He heard her slightly laugh at his words, completely unscared of his tone about it. She saw him reach out to gently pull her head close to place a kiss on her forehead before gesturing toward the stairway. "Pick a room. Get some sleep. Come down when ready."

"Are you going to stay here or go home to Maya?" She saw his fingers move slower now at her question as he reached for another cigar, his brow creasing.

"What do you want me to do, Claura?"

"I will not tell you what to do." She watched him stand straight, facing her, lighting it. The vanilla aroma of it was beyond soothing for some random reason. His face looked very pleased with her response. It was as if it truly humbled him.

"I needed a break too," he finally said, sounding calm and distant.

Turning to head into his nearby office now, she watched as he walked around his desk to sit in his chair. He heard him in her head to just tell her to go get some rest. She obeyed with gratitude, heading upstairs with legs that still felt heavy, walking into the first room that had a bed in it, not caring to be picky. She did not care to get under the covers. It was just pure pleasure in resting her body atop the mattress, the pillow feeling perfect beneath her cheek, being surprised yet beyond thankful for the feeling of just being so damn comfortable here in this room right now, in his home with him. She fell asleep in less than a minute even after everything she had been dealt today—yet again.

*****

Roman felt him trying to break through into the earth realm and land near his home, intentionally making it difficult for him out of spite and for just a bit of self-amusement. Knowing that this was his own home, he had the ability to do so despite being less powerful than Daemon. He felt him try to appear in the living room, only for Roman, at the last second, made him appear outside the front door. He knew he needed his permission to even enter across his threshold upon his first time entering. It was one thing of the realm world he appreciated, how every being had this power over another despite who they were dealing with. He could not shake the feeling that Claura and himself were coming toward the end of something, and he was more than agreeable to it. What was eating at his brain more was why they were aligned now more than ever in the situation.

He took his time leaving his office to open the front door, seeing Daemon on edge more than he wanted to have to deal with right now. The peace and quiet that had been coming from being here, with Claura upstairs resting, was bringing him a feeling of comfort he was not ready to let go of for anybody.

"Daemon."

"Roman."

"She is resting."

"I just need one minute."

"Then try reaching her in her dreams 'cause you're not coming in."

"She is able to block me."

"Good. Now go home to Devalia. I can smell her on you." He saw his temper rise in response.

"She matters not."

"Really? Seems she has brought you back to your roots with just one visit."

"I have let that life go, Roman."

"Save your lies. You can't change who you really are, Soldier." He was pleased with the surprise on Daemon's face at how much he actually knew about him, about what realm he really came from. "Your temper that you keep under control for Claura will still always be there, lingering under the surface. She deserves someone who can actually stay in control."

"Are you implying something here, Roman?" He watched Roman step outside with him now, closing the front door behind him and making Daemon have to back up.

"You and Tronan have never been good for her. Not completely. And due to the actions of you both, you are proving it to her. She is smarter than both of you combined, even with this curse of losing her memories. So wake up and realize that after this little Moira secret you decided to keep from her, you've lost her trust. And do you know what happens when you lose the trust of someone like her, Daemon?"

"She needs to hear me out."

"You lose her."

"She simply does not understand."

"She is tired of this, and you are not giving her the break she deserves."

"And you are bringing her back here, to where all those terrible things happened to her that are still more fresh in her mind, in this place?"

"This is what she knows. To her, this is familiar, and I admire your efforts with her library realm and all that, but this Claura, in this reincarnation, you have failed to know how to do what is best for her."

"I have done nothing but try to help her."

"Really? Because you've done nothing but keep her distracted from what is really going to help her. How long did you think you'd have had until she found out, huh? Killing her mommy would have really gotten you off the hook with that sealed truth, ay?"

"Moira deserves to die. She has done nothing but come between me and everything that matters to me, and for way too fucking long now, I may add!"

"Claura is not a killer! You are! You come from that kind of world. She does not. You have been trying to get her to do this *for you*!"

"I have been trying to end this bullshit!"

"You have been yearning to use Claura's powers for your own selfish reasons, and you fucking know it. I am taking her to see Conroy myself, and you won't get to see her again until she literally asks it of me. Do *you* understand?"

"I fucking dare you."

"Unless her not going to his realm to speak to him has somehow been to your benefit too here, hmm? And it's really quite the coincidence here, Daemon, that of all the people to be your ex, it's a woman who can take away other people's memories."

"I never asked her to do such a thing to Claura. Never."

"Look at it from her perspective."

"She has to believe me."

"She is in no frame of mind to trust you. She doesn't even want to go back, for *anyone* right now, even your damn son that you apparently have together. And she does not mean for just a while. She was in hysterics and suicidal when I arrived here with her, you understand? And you caused that. She is mourning you already. You just have yet to see it."

"I cannot lose her."

"Then use your fucking head. Elsewhere!" Roman snapped, turning around to open the door and walk back inside, slamming it shut in his face.

He felt the rumble through the ground, slightly shaking the entire house even as Daemon left, making Roman pause, wondering if it woke her up. He heard no such noise from upstairs and figured she was still needing to sleep off the dose those assholes gave her. In a way, he was appreciative of how it let her sleep through this. He did not want her to have to deal with Daemon again so soon. The bastard was selfish, the depths of it coming to the surface here even more than Roman thought possible. He suddenly just wanted to take Claura somewhere where she could really feel at peace, really feel okay. He debated how to help her in some way before they realm jumped again, thinking it was probably best she had a simple human-like outing before they went on their little adventure, just wanting to help her in a way that would make up for her being tossed into such a world that was due to his choices in the first place. He owed her that much. He headed slowly and quietly upstairs to check on her, knowing he had yet to even see her with his own eyes again since their last conversation despite being able to hear her steady breathing from downstairs for the past ten hours.

He leaned on the doorframe, arms crossed over his chest, watching her curled up on her side. Her breathing was so shallow it was almost silent, her chest barely rising over and over again. She looked so peaceful—serene even. A quick moment of wishing he had the dream ability like Daemon and Tronan took place, the desire to know what was going on in that head of hers, only to be immediately replaced with giving her more respect than they both had been able to—the respect she deserved and the respect to be left alone. He turned to walk away and suddenly heard her whisper it, turning to see she was still in her sleep. He was unsure of how to react to his name being said on her lips while she was sleeping so peacefully in his home. The subconscious gesture made his brain need answers even more now about how Claura and he were connected somehow. His literal soul was starting to itch for the answer, and the feeling was only getting stronger lately. He looked forward to seeing Conroy just as much as she did now. So help him if this higher realm person did not have the answers they needed, for he was unsure of where they could possibly go next for help. He took a deep breath, glancing at her one more time before turning around to head back downstairs to check online for places he could take her, knowing he needed to do this for her first.

*****

Claura woke to the smell of something delicious lingering from downstairs. She inhaled and smiled, sensing it may be one of her favorites, knowing the scent well. She chose to take a few more minutes to just lay there with her eyes still closed, enjoying the comfort of the bed—the peace and quiet here. Who knew that a place still in the city could be so not noisy? Roman was truly lucky to be able to have a home like this. She suddenly wondered if he used any of his abilities to block out the noise on his property on purpose, as it's what she would have done from day one after signing the mortgage paper for sure—if she knew she had powers, of course. She saw where her thoughts were taking her again and not wanting any part of it. And not just yet. Claura truly felt done with the other realms she had been to. She did not want to go back. After everything she had found—family, love, a place to call her own realm—somehow, it still all felt like it was just not good enough compared to being here with Roman.

This felt right.

This felt normal.

She opened her eyes and looked around at the room now, wondering what time it was. She felt him sense that she was awake from a distance, also feeling him kind of ask permission from her first to speak to her yet in her mind, not wanting to bug her at all until she was ready. She answered by starting first, feeling his small smile of relief that he did not ask too much.

*What are you making? Smells so good! And what time is it?*

*Lasagna. You've slept for seventeen hours.* He felt her inwardly feel sorry about it, laughing at her for needing to feel that way. *Perfect timing, really. Come down and eat, and then I want to show you something. If you want to get out of the house that is.*

Okay.

She felt him smile at her simple answer. He sensed as well that he did not want to get into things just yet—just let things damn well just be for a change. She forced her body from the perfect bed, taking a moment to do a full circle, admiring the room. Seeing a gorgeous antique mirror on the wall, she stepped closer, seeing herself up close, actually liking how she looked so rested for a change, uncaring of her messy hair and disheveled clothes in comparison. She thought about fixing herself up and using her powers and then decided against it. Just something about not needing to worry about any of that while here with Roman made it easy to not even bother worrying about how she looked. The man had watched her go through labor. Surely, today was still a step up from that. She simply used her powers for a toothbrush and some paste in the bathroom, reaching to use his own brush for her hair, and aimed to head downstairs, seeing him through the layout of the house as she headed off the last step toward the kitchen. She took a real look around now, feeling so at ease compared to her prior mood upon arrival. Her thoughts led her to feel like she needed to say sorry to him, literally starting to mouth it, followed by him shaking his head no as he licked some sauce off his finger before speaking.

"Don't apologize, please."

"I am just embarrassed," she said, rubbing her tired eyes while yawning.

"You are not the one who should be feeling embarrassed, love." His tone implied more than he wanted to give away, yet knowing it was inevitable, the topic was to come up in time anyway.

"He came already, didn't he?" Her face showed how uncomfortable it made her, followed by her shock at being uncomfortable about anything that had to do with Daemon. "I am really done with him, aren't I? Simply because he connects to everything that has to do with that kind of life, not even so much…him." She looked like she wanted to cry at how her emotions were just ten steps ahead of her here. "One realm jump, one situation, and I am falling out of love with him." *And I hate it.*

"He will need more time," Roman said gently, looking aggravated still at the drama it may cause in the meantime, for them both. Seeing her think it over, her thoughts led to Maya in all this, wanting to care about his Match situation as well. She watched him shake his head no again as if it was just not necessary to talk about her. "She is fine with her...time."

"Just respecting your wishes, perhaps."

"All too well...for a Match." She saw the frustration and question about it in his eyes.

"I see."

"Makes one of us." He inhaled deeply. "How much do you want?"

"That smells so good, and I am so hungry, so *a lot*." She watched him smile again as he added another bit to her plate.

"Table, or just eat here?" He gestured that the stool along the island was good enough for her if it was for him.

"Lasagna has always been one of my favorites," she admitted.

"Me too."

She watched him sit down next to her along the large island. She glanced at his strong hands and forearms for a quick second, admiring how good he actually looked—a dark cobalt blue dress shirt with black slacks, looking like he had just got home from the office or was getting ready to head in.

"You know, most people just live in tees and sweats in their own home."

"Not me. Never cared to be underdressed."

"Why is that?"

"Got called into the office a lot at random times. It just got easier to not have to change. Besides, if you get the right ones, they can be just as comfy as scrubs and...sweats. I got tired of wearing the same thing all the time, being in the hospital and on-call so much. I simply missed normal clothes, and no one questioned me, not once." He gave her a small wink before taking another big bite.

"I recall you wandering in at random hours for me. I thank you for that, Roman. Dearly."

"Just doing my job."

"Really?" She was half-smirking at him, seeing him think it over before looking back into her eyes. She took a moment to smile over her messy hair and still half-awake visage.

"Of course, I looked forward to knowing you needed me. You know that, Claura. I won't hold things back from you. That is just pointless to me."

"It ruins everything."

"That it does."

"It feels like they are lying to you, or may as well be."

"Agree." He looked at her sternly now while chewing, wanting her to know he was really appreciative of her words at the moment. It was clear on his face that even someone like Roman just needed someone to listen and understand him, really understand him, from time to time.

"Being over there, know what it did the most, it seems?"

"What is that, love?"

"Everything that happened took me farther and farther away from you."

"I know."

"You were my main comfort zone right from the start of our first appointment together, and then when I left you to go to Romania, it was like instantly things just kept separating us."

"I know."

"And then I couldn't stop it, the whirlwind of events. And in the back of my mind, no matter what was happening, all I wanted was to know that you were still around despite not always having the time or right moment to show it." She saw him finish chewing and take a good look up into her eyes, pausing at her words, thinking it over, and seeing her eyes stay dry for a change as if the words were helping her feel better and not cause more emotion for once.

"I know."

"That is just it, you know…already. Every damn time, don't you?"

"I try my hardest, which is why I am taking us, without anyone tagging along, to see Conroy soon. But first, we need a day."

"A day?"

"Uh-huh. I have made plans for us if you want to. If you want to stay in, that is fine too."

"What plans?" she asked softly, pushing her plate toward him again, smiling with her eyes at her need for him to get her a refill. He lightly laughed and got up to appease her appetite more.

"Well, your realm was like Venice, so I thought maybe a boat ride on the canal here would be nice. I can see it in your mind that you like to be on the water."

"Ya, I do, and I don't even know why." She scoffed at her memory again, or lack of it.

"No idea?"

"Nope."

"Well, it'll come. In time." He felt her energy stiffen at his words, at her worry for if she'd even have time—even have a future.

"You have lived this long, over and over apparently. You will find a way, Claura. Something tells me you are too smart not to."

"I just wish I could do it on my own. I feel weak for needing help from someone I have never met before."

"Conroy will help you, somehow. I will help you. Let's just start there, okay? You have time to still figure it out. Besides, I like knowing it is just you and me going. Somehow, it feels more right these turn of events."

"Why do you think that is, these turn of events?" She took a small bite as if the topic was making her stomach nervous now.

"You know, it bothers me to say this to you more than it does to even Maya."

"Say what?"

"That I do not know."

"Why would that bother you more?"

"For some reason, you feel more important to me. And I need to know why."

"I do not want to come between you and her."

"How can you when it feels like you came before her anyway." He sighed as he said it, looking at her not at all like it was her fault but instead just annoyed that he could not figure everything out yet.

"Can we back burner this, please? My brain is starting to… again…"

"Our boat ride is in thirty minutes. Walk isn't far. Did you want to shower first?"

"Do I stink?" She slowly sniffed her upper arm, seeing him smile gently at the action.

"No, you do not stink. But—"

"But what?"

"That realm stench is still on your clothes."

"So I stink, just say it."

"Fine, you smell. Go wash. I'll wait."

He laughed as he leaned toward her to kiss her forehead, placing his hand on her upper outer thigh as he did so before letting go and getting back to his food. The action felt so normal.

"I love your home." She saw him get more intense at her first two words before relaxing again before she even finished her sentence.

"I love you in it. Finally." He looked dead into her eyes, making no effort to hide anything from her. He saw a dozen different emotions going on behind her eyes, her mouth choosing to voice none. "You full?" He gently reached for her plate before standing to put their dishes in the sink.

"Ya. I'm full."

She watched him move around his own home with new ease she could relate to, feeling lost in the moment, inwardly thinking that ya, she was full—full of a feeling of comfort and peace around this man. She did not even realize until that moment that she was constantly feeling more intense—thus draining—energy from the brothers the entire time they had both been entwined in her life. She was inwardly thankful that Roman was here to be that safe space to fall back into once again. She realized in that moment it was something she would never be able to live without. He brought that security to her from their very first moment of looking at each other in his office at the hospital. Tronan took it away and replaced it with what he had to offer for security, then Daemon, and now she could finally get back to where she felt like she actually belonged. The security she felt around Roman was never meant to be replaced by anyone else in the first place. She took a deep breath, feeling unsure of how much of her thoughts he was seeing, deciding to just let it be and headed upstairs. She let the silence stretch between them as she left the room to get ready.

# Chapter 33

## 3 Bowling Balls

It was summertime on good old earth realm, and Claura felt so grateful to enjoy a late afternoon where scary loopholes under bridges didn't exist. Not that she knew of anyway.

"No bridges. Promise."

Roman saw her thoughts easily, strolling behind her, hands in his trench coat pockets. He enjoyed just being back home with her, looking around at the sites, keeping an eye on their surroundings while enjoying watching her just be happy. It really amazed him actually that Daemon didn't think to do this for her, for how smart the man was. Selfishness really did make one blind, no matter where you came from. He felt bad for him. For once, he really did. Losing someone like Claura, despite any future efforts he was planning to still get her back, was not meant to be an easy task. Even though Daemon still had yet to see how resolved she was in her decision, Roman knew it was practically cemented in stone by the look on her face alone. Her heart had been torn in too many different directions and done so in such a short amount of time. Despite all that magic could do for good in different worlds, whatever magic was doing when it came to Claura, it was simply causing her heart to break. And she deserved better. She deserved normal. She deserved to be happy and away from any realm that took that happiness from her. She just wanted her daughter, and no amount of magic or love or the perfect realm was going to fill that hole inside her. Daemon was a damn fool to not see that about her, to not see her for who she really was in this lifetime.

"Roman, is that it? It's gorgeous." He stepped closer to her and followed her pointing finger, loving how her face moved closer to his when she had to turn to see his expression.

"Think so." He checked his watch. "Yup. It is."

He placed his hand on the small of her back to suggest they get moving. He enjoyed watching her have a jump in her step that she deserved as she neared the dock, his taller strides keeping up with her easily. He was grateful for the line of only five other people, even if the boat was a larger one, as he just wanted this to be relaxing for her. He saw her look at him with an inquiry as to where to sit. He pointed toward the front, seeing the comfortable seating along the bow. He wanted to claim it before other people did. He took off his jacket and sat down along the left side, relaxing back into the seat, one leg up while the other foot remained planted, his left arm over the side. He looked out over the water, enjoying the sights from this view, thinking over how it felt not strange at all to be sharing this without Maya and instead with Claura.

He should be feeling guilty.

He wasn't.

Thinking over it for a minute, knowing he would always love her, but things just weren't the same anymore after their 150-year ordeal apart. He never imagined that a child between them would bring them apart instead of together, feeling like there was a piece missing about that as well still. It most likely had to do with her being much less talkative this time around in their relationship. Other than the sex, it just wasn't the same. He hated to admit to himself that he was mourning Maya already, just like Claura was doing now with

Daemon. His heart was no longer in it. His heart was starting to feel at home elsewhere.

Turning to see what she was doing, she saw her play with a small child who was intent on demonstrating the proper use of their toy as if it were the most serious thing in the world. She saw the smile it brought to her face, loving the look of her being so engulfed in the moment. If anyone deserved time with a child, it was her. He hated not being able to save her daughter. He hated not being able to do a damn thing despite all his knowledge and all the technology now. He knew before her that day just what was happening in her womb, getting ready to have to tell her, his heart broke…and then broke again as he watched her face while telling her. He wondered if that was the moment he truly fell for her, the same way her thoughts in the kitchen earlier made it obvious she just may be falling for him as well. Despite their feelings, the situation still needed to make more sense. He simply knew deep down that he did not want to make the same mistakes with Claura that he had with Maya, as falling so fast for someone always held consequences of some kind. Even if they took decades, even centuries, to show, the truth appeared all on its own in good time.

Claura looked up at him as the child ran away back to their parents suddenly, as apparently, she got bored to them already, laughing at herself slightly over it. And the sight of him in the warmth of the sunset, top buttons undone on his bright, deep blue dress shirt, the light casting the perfect shadows along his jaw and facial features, her breath caught. She watched him sitting there looking out into the sights, playing with a toothpick between his lips, lost in deep thought yet looking relaxed. Damn. She never looked at him the way she was looking at him now. Just damn.

Without looking at her, he tapped his fingers on the open spot in front of him on the seat between his legs, scooches up straighter for her, and just waited. It was as if it was the most natural thing in the world for her to curl up in front of him right now, acting like an actual couple. She stood up to walk toward him, just staring down at him for a moment, waiting for him to look up at her. The expression of love and uncertainty on his face let her know he was having the same new and confusing feelings here.

"I can at least hold you, Claura. What harm comes from that?"

"A lot. Been told that before." She leaned on one hip more, looking down at him like she was sad she was pausing with this. Nothing about Roman made her feel like he would hurt her, harm her.

"I will never be like them," he said, watching her just stare down at him, her whole face showing that she was unsure of what to say. "I will never touch you the way they have." His tone made it very clear he was not happy with them, all three.

Jayson. Tronan. Then Daemon.

Knowing his comment could be taken two ways by her, letting her face answer for him. Hurt across her features appeared first at the memories she held, followed by the realization that maybe he meant he was planning to never touch her in that way at all.

"They never deserved to touch you. Not once. Not when it was all possibly due to some magic spell behind it instead of something real." He saw her pause still, making no effort to say more. He let her make her decision despite how long it took. She looked uncertain and even nervous, but she moved her hand in that small way that said, "Fine, move over."

Curling up against him, her back against his chest, as she put both her feet up next to his left leg, realizing her body against his was a better fit than she expected to have this feel like.

"I just need your body heat. Not you," she admitted playfully, feeling his chest move against her backside as he laughed, loving the sound of it. How it just felt more genuine coming from his body behind her compared to all the others. It took a few minutes, but eventually, she leaned her head back against him too, relaxing into him more, enjoying the sights with him as the boat picked a steady pace atop the water now. Noticing how he hadn't bothered to move at all for some time as if not wanting to take away from her efforts to get comfortable against him. Truly, he felt at ease behind her, his breathing steady, the rhythm of his heart making her melt into the moment really. She felt his chin nuzzle atop her head now and again, depending on where he was looking around at the moment, and felt him place a kiss on the top of her hair from time to time as well, which she absolutely loved but would not dare say so—not out loud. The silence between them went on for the majority of the ride, and it had nothing to do with the fact that they could communicate telepathically between them. The simplicity of being surrounded by other normal humans, not beings with too many powers, added a semblance of easiness to the outing. It was refreshing. Sometimes, coming back to just whatever felt like home, really home, was what was actually refreshing.

It was what would actually help.

*****

Roman opened the door for her, loving the smell of her hair close to his face as she brushed by him, seeing her aim for the kitchen first. Leftovers were clearly on her mind. "I see I made the recipe right this time." He smiled as he shut the door and removed his coat, kicking his shoes off before strolling after her.

"No doubt."

She reached for the heavy pan in the fridge, having difficulty with its weight and almost dropping it. Roman used his speed ability to catch up to her, grabbing it gently and lifting it to place atop the island with ridiculous ease. He saw her frown out of the corner of his eye.

"You seem stronger lately."

"It is a pan of lasagna." He lightly laughed at her seriousness with this.

"To me, it feels like three bowling balls."

"I like cheese. On top of more cheese. Sprinkled with extra… cheese." He grinned at her gently.

"I'm serious."

"Me too." He touched her nose quickly with his fingertip while giving that crooked half-smile he did, walking around her to grab her a plate. His fingers brushed the side of her waist as he did so, the look on his face making it hard for her to tell if he did it consciously or not.

"He could tell while he visited earlier, couldn't he?"

"Who's that?" He made it obvious he preferred a different topic.

"He sensed your increased strength. I find it hard to believe you kept him outside during his visit."

"Perhaps he is just finally coming to his senses."

"Why do you say that?" He watched him sigh as he put her plate in the microwave now. He gently pressed the buttons slowly as if his brain was elsewhere completely already.

"Daemon has a temper that he has been hiding from you. He comes from a realm that has been literally titled Battlegrounds by some others in nearby realms. And I can see it in your memories during your little visit to meet Devalia that his true colors showed."

"Her first hit from him, it made him feel like a stranger to me." She watched him nod solemnly as if he hated her having to be there while they were doing that and not so much what went on between the other two. "I never saw it in him with how he acted with me."

"I fear that you are the only time in his entire existence he has had any control. But it does not excuse his born nature that will never stop lingering beneath the surface."

"Why would that be fearful and not a good thing?"

"Because you can only hide who you truly are for so long. Who knows when or how it would have come out of him later down the road."

"I really feel like it never would have been directed at me."

"You do not know that for sure."

"He would never hurt me like that, Roman. Why the hell is he so okay with hurting her like that?"

"Because that is his true nature."

"A woman beater? Seriously!"

"He is what we call a myriad soldier. Myriad, not in the number or quantity of beings like him, but how every being in and from such realm has the willpower, magic, and strength of a thousand soldiers in each and every one of them. His realm is like Sparta, pretty much. As for her, you worry needlessly. Her kind does not feel pain hardly.

It is why they are…rough. And with Daemon's true nature, she simply is able to handle him. I am not saying he is a damn monster, just…unpredictable is their thing. I do not know how he controlled himself with you, but he did find a way. I give him credit there."

"Do you know why he hates her so much? What happened?"

"I do not. As much as I hate that he will be back at least once more, it does give you time to ask him yourself." He saw her squirm on the stool, looking anxious with her thoughts, the beeping on the microwave breaking the silence. "Eat. At the table this time." He walked around her with the plate toward the adjoining dining room.

"You not hungry?"

"Maybe later." She took the chair next to her, enjoying watching her sit at the end as if the place at the table was meant for her all along. "So what would you like to do for the rest of the evening?"

"Her grave." He avoided his gaze, just in case he thought it silly for some reason.

"Flowers first?" He saw her shy and uncertain expression face him now, her lips slightly smiling while trying to hold her food in her mouth.

"Uh-huh." Tears swam through her smile, the mixed emotions on her face getting the best of him again. "That sounds perfect."

"Just ask, Claura." His tone was low and serious. It clearly meant for her to just say it, whatever it was, about absolutely anything she needed or wanted.

"Thank you."

She meant it back and not just for some pretty petals. Her fingers came up to rub her temple, letting her hand intentionally hide her face as she started to cry while letting thoughts creep in about her daughter. "One picture of her smiling with her eyes open, that would have been enough…beyond helpful. Just one, ya know." She stared into the distance. She lowered her hand now, noticing it shaking. She let her tears fall onto her food as she took another bite.

"Were you able to get her a decent gravestone?" She already knew the answer. She had already seen it for himself, visiting the spot right after she got on the plane that day. He watched her shake her head no, seeing her thoughts that she got one that was good enough due to that being all she could afford. "Why don't we go get her a new and better one then? Hmmm?"

"It won't make a difference."

"Yes, it will." It meant it was more for her.

"I do not know what to have engraved on it."

"Loving daughter. Simplicity always works."

"I have no choice since I did not get to know her, now, did I?"

"You got to be her first home. You felt her move in your belly for months first. She got to feel the comfort of being close to you in that way for a while in what was her beginning. Her life was short, but she knew nothing but warmth and love from being inside you while growing. She was no place safer. She knew no safer place for her entire short existence."

"Thank you, but that's not good enough."

"I know, sweetheart." He reached out to wipe her tears from her cheeks as he leaned forward toward her. "Would another day just be here before we go, do you good? Do you want that?"

"Yes and no." He looked sorry for being confused. "You decide. I am truly fine either way."

"I think it may be best to get this little trip over with for both of us. After we get her, *and* you, some flowers."

"I have actually never been given flowers before. Not once."

"Would me doing that for you make you uncomfortable?"

"I do not know. But I am not worried about it, either way."

"It matters to me. Please take this seriously."

"It's just flowers, Roman."

"How would you know if you've never been given them?"

"Go smoke a cigar."

"Answer me."

"I do not have an answer! Why is this so important to you?"

"Because your reaction to me matters. Your reaction to everything and anything I cannot turn my focus from. It just fucking matters, Claura."

"Have you ever bought other patients flowers, huh?" She saw him laugh at her in disbelief, not hurt in the slightest at her piss-poor jab.

"They only wish."

"Oh ya? How many wished?"

"Stop this. I care about nobody from that place. Nobody."

"Who curbed your appetite from time to time, Roman? What special lady got to experience you in that way during your time here away from Maya?"

"Why are you doing this?"

"Hiding something?"

"Ahh, I see. Should have seen this coming. Thanks to all them assholes you've had to deal with, here we go with trust issues." Watching him get up to walk away from her now.

"I do not have a trust issue with you, Roman!"

"Then why are you saying this to me right now?"

She saw him turn as he shouted it back, walking back toward her.

"Because it is unfamiliar territory with how much *I do* trust you!" She wiped her wet cheek with the back of her sleeve, hating seeing him more than any of the others get heated with her. It hurt more for whatever reason despite her being the one pressing here. All she wanted to do was be held by him again. "I am scared! Something inside of me is telling me that you are my last chance! My last chance before truly giving up, and you are not even fully available! Do you have any idea how foolish that makes me feel!" She watched him stand there with his hands on his hips, looking angry at so many things happening behind his eyes as he glared back at her.

"Did you not hear me earlier? Believe me earlier?"

"With what?"

"When I said you are not getting between me and anyone. That, for some reason, it feels like you came first, despite who I am so-called Matched with now in some way. Do you remember?"

"Yes."

"Good. Don't make me repeat it again."

"This is not fair."

"No, trust that I am *also* getting beyond fed up with it. And at the same time, I want you to stop worrying about it. Stop even thinking about it at all."

"Okay. So just keep being okay with acting like a fool for you while you remain in control toward me completely. That is actually okay with someone as smart as you?"

"You simply see me being in control. You have no idea what I am constantly fighting to keep you from seeing in my head."

"Really? That is how you are trying to help me after everything! Literally admitting you are keeping things from me too! Fuck you, Roman." She walked past him toward the door. She hated that she could not control the words coming out of her mouth. He heard her fighting with the handle, sinking in what he did. "Unlock the damn door! Please!"

"I don't do runaways, darling. We are going to finish this conversation, and we are going to do it now." He remained where he was standing, his back to her, hearing her pulse increase.

"I need space."

"You being here is the space you need. From them. From the other realms. I am not the one you need space from. Do not lie to yourself in this, please." He turned to see her facing the floor, her palms up on the door leaning against it.

"You are going to turn me into a fool, just like they have done. It is only a matter of time."

"Do you know why I cannot get you out of my damn head, Claura? Even when I *was* with Maya?"

"Don't say that. You two are still Matched. You have to be, Roman. Why else would it not work on you and Maya that day I spoke that spell on the balcony to unbind me to Tronan? To unbind Daemon from Aiyana! Why would it not just work on all of us!" She saw him contemplate, yet seeing him still not care. He truly looked lost over Maya, but that was not enough for her. Claura needed him to be absolutely sure as well here that this was not a one-way thing by any means. "Because you two are still meant for one another, Roman!" She hated saying the words. Something inside her made it hard to even leave her lips.

"No, I don't think we are. The space between us has been too cozy for her. I do not trust that. And I care more about figuring out *why* that is than fixing things with her. I no longer trust her. Just like you no longer trust Daemon. This Match thing we all got to deal with, as far as I am concerned, can go fuck itself. I will choose who I want to be with, not some fucking predestined spell."

"Why then?"

"Because you are the smartest, sexiest, and most alluring woman I have ever known, whether you see that or not. Now get your ass back over here, calm the fuck down, and watch a movie on the couch with me." He saw her pause before turning to face him. "I mean it, Claura. I am done with this realm bullshit, done with this ability to have these all and mighty powers bullshit, fucking done." He swiped his hands outward, standing as determined as ever. "Because none of that shit means anything to me if it keeps taking you away from me. If it keeps taking away the one, *I choose* my damn self."

"I can't believe you just said that." She faced him now, wiping her wet cheeks with the back of her sleeve.

"No bullshit with me, sweetheart. I mean it."

"Okay, well…popcorn?"

"Extra butter will have to do." He aimed toward the kitchen, seeing the resolve in her face to no longer want to leave good enough for him for the time being.

\*\*\*\*\*

Claura could not stop laughing at their chosen movie. They debated for a good ten minutes before meeting in the middle, settling on *Murder Mystery 2* on Netflix. He watched her curled up on the other end of his couch, eating popcorn, giggling away. She saw him content with just listening to her, not laughing half as much.

"This isn't funny to you?" she finally asked him, looking worried at being the only one doing more than smiling here.

"It is. I am simply enjoying your little-girl giggles just as much, is all."

"Want me to stop laughing? Is that it? I am laughing too much like that person that talks too much during a movie almost, aren't I?"

"You can talk or laugh all you want, sweetheart. It does not bother me."

# THE WINGED WITCH OF MATCHES

"What does bother you, Roman?" She nudged his foot with her toe, enjoying the sight of him looking so comfy on the couch with her, his feet up, making his legs stretch toward her, leaning back on the other end. She reached for more popcorn in her lap, glancing at the TV again as she waited for his answer.

"We already went over this." He looked at her seriously, shoving more popcorn into his mouth as well. "Please don't try to leave again," he said with love but like he meant it.

"Where am I to go?" She smiled with her mouth only, the heartbreak over what happened in the other realms still deep behind her eyes.

"I meant what I said earlier, Claura."

"You said a lot of things."

"I love seeing you in my home."

"What if that changes? Hmm?"

"Why would it change?"

"Because so many things won't stop changing around me. Perhaps I am cursed in that way."

"With me, they won't. I can assure you."

"Assure away, please."

"Okay, well…Tronan was a false tie. Daemon was a liar who, despite how much he loved you, was still okay with using you. I have no reason to use you, and there is no spell between us. There is nothing fake going on here, and there never will be. I am quite done with fake, my dear."

"Maya feels fake to you now?" She watched him nod. "I never in a million years would have seen that coming."

"Me either. There has been a distance between us ever since she came back around, despite the distance we had already had to deal with beforehand. It is simply not the same anymore. The sex is great…but there is nothing else there for me anymore with her. I have tried to keep it going, but it just feels foolish."

"So you are still having sex, at least?" She looked away from him, not wanting him to see how much the answer was important to her now.

"It is over, Claura." He got up to set the bowl on the table before walking into the kitchen. She heard him ask her from the other room. "Beer? Wine? Water? Bourbon?"

"Water. And, Roman?"

"Hmm?" She heard him close the cupboard, the sound of a glass hitting the marble countertop next.

"If she was not truly dead for those decades apart from you, how did she survive her heat cycle without you?" She felt his energy instantly pause with whatever he was doing in the other room. She heard his feet move slower now as he rounded the corner of the wall to stand there and look at her with the biggest question on his face, contemplating on a whole new level even for him.

"How did I miss that?"

"Another spell, maybe? Devalia somehow being paid in some form to mess with you too. Who knows?" She adjusted on the end of the sofa now, getting comfy as she turned to be able to face him more. "Ask her." She saw his face darken about having a reason to see her with this new insight. "You loved her for so long, Roman. Just talk to her about it."

"Seems we have both been Matched to a liar." His feet moved backward slowly as if still in deep thought over it all, backing into the kitchen out of sight again. "You have our drinks. Where are you going?" She heard him grab two other glasses and, with all drinks in tow, a large glass bottle now included, come walking back in and sit on the couch next to her again.

"What is that?"

"Grey Goose."

"Really?"

"Really."

"Can I handle a drunk, Roman?" She raised her eyebrows at him, actually looking slightly worried. "Is she really worth getting trashed over right now? I mean, you have already admitted to it being over from your end, anyway although I hope you aren't just saying that to please my presence here. That would make me really disappointed in you, Roman." She watched his serious-yet-taken-aback expression follow his first swig, looking at her more intently. "I am enjoying this time with you. Please don't ruin it. She has had so much time with you while you were together…so you say it's over. I am just getting started." Her soft-spoken words had him setting his glass down after a long, long pause between their stares. "Despite you saying I came first somehow, we have no proof of that. Maybe this will be the only lifetime I will get to know you and be next to you. Please don't waste it."

Her voice was so low and so tender, the feminine undertone making her words sound like the most humble music to his ears. Never in his life had he expected to hear her say that. The all-powerful Claura was letting her walls down with him, completely and so easily. It was a comfort he was not familiar with, a comfort he did not know how to wrap his head around.

Claura watched as he got up and headed toward the kitchen, taking the bottle with him. She heard the fridge open and close again, watching him walk back into the living room, this time not stopping where his butt had been originally planted. With pure, gentle ease, he reached for her and picked her up, pulling her to his end of the couch and placing her against the front of him just like they had curled up on the boat together earlier. He reached for the blanket underneath the sofa, spreading it out over them, his hands on her sides, pulling her up and even closer against his chest before settling in behind her. She felt his face move close to hers.

"Forgive me," he said, sounding genuine and calmer even.

He placed a kiss on her cheek before reaching for the remote on the table, the action causing her back to press against him more before he leaned back again. He watched his strong fingers press Play. She took a few minutes to get used to the feeling again before resting fully in the warmth of his body behind her.

"You forgot my popcorn refill." She felt him laugh in response.

"Use your powers."

"It's weird in a way, like what if I accidentally make plastic popcorn or something?"

"Just try."

"I honestly don't know the spell, even for that."

"Can blast people off their feet, sending them a hundred yards or more, but can't make some damn popcorn?"

"Do you think my powers could have saved my baby?"

She felt him tense behind her, yet he only paused for a short moment before answering.

"I would not have risked it," he admitted.

"Ya…" She felt him kiss the top of her head. "So that is why you did not try, with the powers you already knew you had while I was pregnant?"

"Powers are not all they are cracked up to be. So many realms look down on earth. All I see is a place with less problems, despite what the human world thinks. A human's shorter lifespan alone makes for less…trouble."

"Maybe it is just my family. Perhaps other places with different people would have made it worth it. Different circumstances. Other realms, perhaps. Other lifetimes even." She scoffed lightly to herself, brushing her hair behind her ear absentmindedly.

"Those circumstances brought you back around to me."

"So losing my daughter that started this whole thing—"

"No. Her death had nothing to do with what would have still been my efforts to keep you around. You know this, Claura. I have never hidden this fact from you, despite me not making it more clear either due to all that has happened."

"Ya, I do…"

"Then why are you saying this?"

"Lingering untrust…perhaps." She felt him take a deep breath behind her.

"I am sorry so much has happened to you. None of it was ever my intention."

"I got to know where I am really from. I think that is all I would have liked to be shown, honestly. Nothing else."

"That is what you deserved. Not all the other bullshit."

"Do you regret becoming like them, not being fully human anymore?"

"Used to, but I've come to terms with it. It has its perks. I just do not care to use them so much anymore. Something doesn't feel right when I am in another realm. Just always feels like I am in the wrong place. Then when I thought I lost my Match and daughter, I just kind of gave up."

"And still feel like it just isn't what it should be, even with them back?"

"Yes, and that is not going to change." She saw the question in her mind, her obvious need for more reassurance still.

"Are you really reading my thoughts while simultaneously having a conversation with me?"

"Hard not to. Your head is right in front of me. And you have not yet learned, or been reminded of how, to put a mind block up that well." He saw her small smile, reaching to brush her hair behind her other ear before following her gaze and looking back at the tv. "Stop worrying, please. And watch this damn movie with me," he whispered close to her ear, his tone trying to be playful.

He reached for the remote again that he placed atop her stomach on top of the blanket, rewinding the movie for them both. The feeling of his fingers brushing her abdomen felt more natural than any previous touches from others. The same went for the feeling she was having while encased in his arms. They were love, Tronan and Daemon, they really were. But Roman was love and genuine comfort. It was a genuine feeling of just being home. She enjoyed the feeling of no rising heat cycle at just his touch. It was nice not to feel controlled by something that was completely hormonal. It scared her slightly, making her wonder if she was really right for him and him for her with it not happening. Yet, on the opposite side of the same coin, it mattered not. Twenty minutes into watching the movie again, she was already unable to keep her eyes open, falling fast asleep to the sensation of his strong heart beating against her small back, his steady, low breathing close to her ears. She heard him whisper to her to just go to sleep while he finished the movie. She loved the feeling of him keeping so close while as well keeping his hands to himself as she let sleep take her over fully.

# Chapter 34

# Hulk Juice

The silence of the house with Claura sound asleep in his arms was coming to an end. Roman did not know how he figured it out, but he could feel Daemon returning yet again, and it was clear that landing outside the front door was not on his mind this time. Roman simply waited, using a quick spell to keep her sound asleep, one that would block out all noise around her. He was willing to be the only one with their night ruined here. He watched as Daemon appeared in the dark interior of the living room, nothing but the moonlight and a couple of lights still on in the kitchen, making it possible to see the whole downstairs. His entire energy was one of pure jealousy and fury, Daemon's eyes lethal like a predator about to pounce as he took in the sight before him.

"And this loophole came from?" Roman asked, as usual, putting his mind before emotions.

He chose to break the tension first, for some reason uncaring of any buttons he may press despite Daemon eyeing him like he would kill him this very night.

"Her dreams. And seeing how she is feeling so beyond comfortable in your arms, consider yourself done, Roman."

"So you lie to her in reality and manipulate her in her dreams to get your way. Truly unafraid to sink yourself deeper here, aren't you?"

"She is mine. She will always be mine. She will forgive me for this in time. And in the meantime, if you take this further with her, I will kill you."

"Must be exhausting always having to return to being a killer to get your way."

"I am not the only one manipulating her here."

"So you admit it. And I do not need to play such games with her, Daemon. Your ways, along with your games, despite how much you try to hide that that is what you are doing...have literally pushed her into my arms." He gave zero smirk—full truth.

"Neither of you know what truly happened. It is not my fault her memory has gotten worse with each lifetime. You do not understand how difficult it has made things for both of us. I have been trying to help her, and in keeping bullshit from her from past lifetimes that *no longer* matters...I am doing such for her."

"It has gotten to that point for her that she no longer gives a shit. Keep ignoring that, and you are simply continuing to ignore her. And ignoring her is the last fucking thing I will ever do."

"Bring her home so I can speak to her, please."

"I will never force her to go back there. She has to want it for herself. She sees such a place as your home, not hers."

"I am begging you, for once, Roman."

"You know she will speak to you again eventually, Daemon. Why is it so hard for you to just leave her alone for a while?"

"I can't breathe. I literally can't even breathe right with her gone."

"You've had practice. Figure it out. Again."

"This may be my last life with her due to her own wishes that I am respecting despite it tearing me apart inside. Please do not take that away from me."

"That's funny."

"How the hell is that funny?"

"Few hours ago, she asked me to spend what may be her last life with her. Not you."

"I find that hard to believe."

"Well, when she is ready to talk to you, just ask her yourself. She has a question for you anyway. I am curious myself."

"What is it?"

"How you kept in control for her compared to Devalia. Would you have actually been able to stay that way forever for her, truly, Daemon? Or was that what was useful for the times you had a break from her in between her reincarnations? You had time to get back to your roots before having to suppress it again for her once she was reborn again. And this last time, it built until it boiled over ridiculously easy at just one visit with Devalia due to you having to remain with my daughter for so long."

"When I kill you, your brain is going first."

"So I see." He watched Daemon just wait for him to clarify more. "I understand, Daemon. I actually do. After so many lifetimes of seeing her die and get reborn and die again, of course, things would change for you in the middle of all of that. And that is exactly what is happening now. You need to accept how this is now changing her as well, permanently."

"I was trying to make this fair for the both of us. You must see that as well. I know I have messed up with her this time more than usual. It is because I have been unable to fucking focus right since she told me she does not want to try to fix her reincarnation spell anymore. You have no idea what that has done to me!"

"Well, unless you can come up with a better solution for her, you need to just stay the hell out of her way. Leave her be."

"I cannot be without her. I have been trying to find a way despite her wishes. I have been trying to figure out how to really save her."

# THE WINGED WITCH OF MATCHES

"Wake up! You already have, over and over again! So find a way to fucking deal with it, as this is the most important time to do that for her! Whether you are truly Matched to her or not, I will not let you ruin this for her. She will find a way, and you will not be allowed in the fucking way."

"True Match or not, seriously? Your hopes are a bit high there, Roman."

"Are they?" He swiped his hand over her body in front of him, still on the sofa, as if to say, "You sure?" "Because she has been nothing but happy and relaxed while here with me. Meanwhile with you, she's been nothing but stressed about something over and over again."

"What are you saying?"

"Your time is done. Go home."

"My home is in your fucking arms!"

"For as long as she damn well pleases."

Roman watched as Daemon tried to reach for control, clearly wanting to kill him even more now, followed by watching him fail in a matter of five seconds. Roman moved faster, surprising himself but welcoming the change as he moved out from behind Claura in a way that left her sleeping peacefully. He remained completely oblivious to any surrounding noise still, grateful he had already taken the time for such a spell with what was about to go down literally feet from her. He grabbed Daemon around the throat, lifting him in the air to slam his entire body back down atop the glass coffee table. The noise shattering through the quiet of the home was enough for neighbors to hear. Roman inwardly wished he would have taken a moment to place a spell around his entire home and not just Claura. The last thing he needed was the cops showing up, wasting the time of two omnipotent beings from an entirely different world. This type of situation needed to be done in a completely different realm. He debated it in his mind while reading the shock on Daemon's face at his newfound strength of being able to hold even him down, only to dismiss any idea of leaving Claura right now. He came here to be with her. He refused to leave for anybody, even this asshole. Despite how Daemon felt about her, his ass was still trying to control her choices for his own damn benefit.

"I always knew there was a deeper reason why I hated you two, and Claura needing to be in the middle to show me is my last goddamn straw with the both of you," Roman growled, deflecting his hits with ease, still feeling the sting yet enjoying that that's all it was now from any contact from Daemon—just a damn sting. He lifted him and shoved him into the wall, getting one good hit from him in return before grabbing him again to toss him across the room into the far wall, seeing Daemon pause for once before attempting anything back, staring him down as he straightened himself.

"Hulk juice for dinner, there Roman? Where the fuck is this coming from?"

"No idea."

"You do not know, of all people, how you are suddenly stronger than even me now?"

"Nope. And not going to question it as long as it helps me keep you the fuck out of my life. Our life." Intending for that to hit a serious button.

"You really think she is yours now, don't you?" He saw Daemon step closer.

*Since before she even met you and your brother. Since she walked into my office and looked up at me that day with her growing belly, dealing with a pregnancy all alone and heartbroken. Only for your worlds to come into her life and break her heart even more.* "I let her decide. She came to me. Unlike men like you, assholes, I do not need a bonding bullshit spell. I do not need a heat cycle to make her want me to touch her. Some of us men out there do it the old-fashioned way without bullshit magic."

"*We* have a goddamn son together. You are literally messing with the mother of my own goddamn child!"

"In her mind, she grieves Dayla, not your son. If you are unable to see things from her perspective, then it is clear I always gave you too much credit, which, trust me, will never happen again."

"I find it hard to believe she doesn't even care about our own son."

"She does not remember! She remembers her stillborn daughter, you fucking fool! You are not seeing how much you are combining

Claura's lifetimes together each time she comes back to you when, in her mind, she remembers only what she knows now!" He walked closer to him now, pointing his finger, fear of this soldier before him forever completely gone. "With each reincarnation, you have lost your touch in doing what is right for her. *Nobody* should have to do what she does just to remain alive. You are a selfish bastard who does not deserve her. You should be willing to let her go by now, especially when *now* that is what she actually fucking wants from you. It is at that point, Daemon, Match or not, she is done with you, with all of it. And unlike you, I will not force her to do this to herself anymore."

"There has to be a way. If you yourself really care about her, you would help me in this!"

"Go home."

"Roman, listen to me!"

"Fucking leave!" He swiped his hand, using his more intense powers to send Daemon to an in-between of two realms that were far, far away, enjoying knowing it would take him some time to figure out where he actually was and how to get the hell out, even with his supernatural myriad soldier abilities. He took a moment to glance at her, still sleeping, seeing her eyes had remained closed during the whole ordeal, wondering how long it'd take Daemon to enter her dreams again. He wondered why her block was down from him now in that way compared to before. He hated the fact that maybe she did miss him and needed to talk to him eventually in person still yet knowing he wasn't one to judge when he still had to finish things with Maya. He tried to wrap his head around how much more important Claura was to him compared to Maya in just a matter of a couple of days alone with her. It was as if his very being had been waiting to just have some privacy with her for so much longer than he could wrap his head around.

He headed into the kitchen to wash Daemon's blood off his hands, enjoying the sight really. He looked at his clothes, knowing he needed to change and fix the living room before she woke. He did not like to have to keep her under a sleeping spell without her permission first. He needed to correct his actions somehow despite being grateful she was not at all in the middle of Daemon's second little visit. Already deciding in his head, he would make a call to have Dayla's gravestone taken care of, saving her the trouble of picking such a thing out…twice. The late hour mattered not. People everywhere were happy to be owed a favor by a doctor.

As much as he wanted to curl up behind her again and get some sleep, he knew there was really no way in hell he was going to be able to shut his brain off now enough to get some shut-eye, and he already knew she would sense his tension next to her and wake up due to it. Despite her not caring to use her own witch powers, however strong they actually were, her intuition was clearly not something to be underestimated. He inwardly hoped for zero more visitors for some time, yet another side to him now looking forward to it. He wondered to himself where the hell his new strength had come from, wishing he had taken Claura more seriously sooner. He knew he had felt slightly different lately but had no idea how much change had actually taken place within him until he needed to use it on Daemon. He inwardly hoped this better not be due to Maya again, for whatever reason, feeling a bit shocked at the fact that he now was able to hold both the supposedly stronger, more omnipotent brothers by their necks with ease. If this new level of power and strength came from Maya, deep down, he did not want it. He wondered if this was a way, or a trick of some sort, for her to get him to come back.

Roman finished up some emails and bills in his office, seeing the sun rising through the windows and hearing her breathing change in the other room as she woke. He had been slowly letting her come out of the sleeping spell over the past couple of hours, just needing some time to himself to think things over and calm down. He was unsure of how the conversation would go with her once she knew what took place, as it was obvious he was hell-bent against keeping things from her. He would not risk losing her. He was not going to be a fool so easily. He sensed her stirring and feeling strange about being alone on the cushions and got up to walk over to her, leaning down on his heels before her.

"Would you like some coffee?"

"Sure. Creamer?"

"Uh-huh." He got up to make a cup for her. He knew she saw the still lingering tension all over his face.

"What is wrong?" She leaned up on one elbow to be able to see him better as he walked around the wall and out of sight. "Roman!"

"How was your sleep?" He got at her dreams already by his tone alone.

"Different," she answered warily. "How was yours?"

"Different."

"Goddamn it. He visited you too, again, didn't he?"

"Do not worry about it. I said he would need more time to come to his senses with this. That is all that is happening."

"Way to leave a lot out."

"He is able to enter my home by manipulating you in your dreams to let him in. Please tell me why you would allow that?"

"It was not here in this house we are in. I was letting him come in to talk to me in my office, in my realm, in my dream. That is where I was. I feel stupid now for not seeing it. He has already been invited into my office, so of course, he does not need permission to enter. It was hazy."

"So he tricked you."

"Seems so. How would that still work?"

"I assume just a yes in your mind to let him cross through the door was good enough for him to make use of it."

"What did he do, Roman? What happened?" She got up to stand next to him in the kitchen now, glancing at the sink, seeing the blood drops still along the sides of it. "Please tell me…no…oh no…" She reached for his hands, looking him over.

"It's his. Not mine." He looked at her with the obvious question he had been trying to figure out since it happened. "I do not know how I am now stronger, but I am."

"Okay. Good." She looked unsure yet relieved.

"Really? That makes you happy that I am the stronger one now?"

"Well, kind of…" She looked at him with worry.

"Well, it is probably from Maya, meaning if it's borrowed strength from one of her silly spells like she loaned me to hold Tronan that day on the balcony, I do not want it. What I do want is to know why you let your block down with him in your dreams."

"Do not look at me like that, please! He simply would not let up, so I caved to simply get the conversation over with."

"And how did it go?"

"It didn't even last long. As soon as he sensed exactly where I was and what I was doing in real time…his jealousy took over, and I guess when he left, it was here to see you instead."

"Don't ever leave that door open for him again. I mean it."

"What if it doesn't matter anymore anyway, whether I make that mistake again or not, as you are stronger than him now? Is this really a worry now?"

"Having more strength does not mean I want to still put up with the bastard."

"Same. Now give me my damn coffee. It is too early for this shit." She swore under her breath as she lifted her cup and headed toward the dining room to sit. Seeing him slowly walking toward her to sit down as well.

"Do you mean that, Claura? Really mean that? I need you to be sure."

"How can I be sure, Roman? Please tell me how to be sure, and I will gladly do it. Since my actions while here with you have not meant as much as I thought apparently if you need to ask that." She watched him scoff at her words. "I am not trying to be funny. This is not easy for me. I have every right to talk to Daemon if I want to, just like you still need to have a chat with Maya as well, anyway… eventually. I guess at least I had the courage to do it sooner rather than later."

"Doing it in a dream does not count."

"Sure about that?"

"Very sure. But you are not ready, which is why I wish you would have not let him in, in any form."

"He would not let me wake up! I tried reaching for you."

"I see. I have to tell you something. Daemon would not let you wake up in your little dream with him, but in real life, put a sleeping spell on you to sleep through the whole ordeal."

# THE WINGED WITCH OF MATCHES

"So you both are crossing lines with me today. Great."

"He did it for himself. I did it for you."

"Explain."

"He wants you back for selfish reasons. I want you to not have to deal with him and enjoy a damn night's sleep. Particularly in my arms, undisturbed."

"Well, in that case, it seems we will have to try again."

"So you want one more day here?"

"No, Roman. I want the rest of my life here."

"The note from Conroy, forget about that? He is looking forward to seeing you as well."

"I have a feeling he has waited a long time, so what is a little more waiting going to hurt?"

"Promise me something?"

"What's that?"

"Keep your damn block up tonight."

"Okay."

"And another thing…"

"Hmm?"

"Don't ever use it on me."

"Don't give me a reason to. Besides, I don't think I can anymore." He clearly meant his powers might have improved in other areas now too.

"We shall see. If he tries again, I will see if I can simply join you."

"What happened to face things to the literal face?"

"I guess you have to meet selfish cowards where they are comfortable sometimes."

"You know, I do not want to hate him so much. I really don't. It just has been nearly impossible to be on the same page with him during this…lifetime…I guess."

"I know. And all that does is prove even more how much he doesn't deserve you."

"For a while, it really felt like he did. I am mourning that more than him, you know. It's like he can read my soul while simultaneously disagreeing with my heart. It's just so…confusing."

"I can relate, sweetheart. More than you know." He watched her swirl her fingers on the edges of her now-empty cup. "I have something to show you."

"Flower time?"

"Flower time."

*****

Roman watched her walk closer to the new and shiny gravestone. It doubled in size compared to the previous one, the carving into it more detailed and intricate. His whole intention was to not have to see her cry while picking out a new one, but at least seeing this one brought out happy tears in a way—women, always crying.

"I caught that."

Claura turned to see him return a smile. He pulled a tissue out of his coat pocket for her, watching her small, shaking hands take it from his grasp before turning back around to face her baby girl's grave. He stepped closer behind her, placing his hands on her hips and leaning down to place the side of his face against her cheek.

"Despite you being apart from her right now, she is still so lucky to have you as a mom," he whispered it close to her skin.

"This is why I am unafraid to have this be my last life."

"I know."

"It is so far-fetched. I have never been to church, but there has to be a place for her little soul. Somewhere where she can live out a life, at least once."

"There is love. Something so precious can't just disappear as if it has never been. I believe there has to be something. I mean that." She felt her place her smaller hands over his now, the small action making him just want to be there for her more. No matter what she asked.

"You would have been a good dad." She decided to let her walls down again, showing him that she believed his earlier words about his efforts and that he would have remained in her life despite her losing her child or not.

"Makes me so happy to know that you believe me, Claura."

"With you, it is so opposite to them."

"How so?"

"Believing them made me a fool. Not believing you, that makes me a fool."

"As much as I hate everything that happened, at the end of the day, it is simply their nature. The realm they come from shapes them in these other worlds that the humans here do not even know exist. I could tell that you were more like me before you even hopped on that plane. That you were the type of person who even with powers and abilities and all that, somehow you were still over it."

"Why is that so? What are we missing in all of this, Roman?"

"I plan to figure that out for us. Believe me." He squeezed her from behind, feeling her melt into him before slowly letting go. "I will give you a moment. Take your time." He felt her reach for his hand before he completely broke contact, looking up into his handsome face.

"Thank you," she said softly, watching him nod gently in return, staring into her eyes for a minute, raising her hand to place a kiss on it before stepping forward to place one on her forehead as well before walking away.

*****

Roman could see the resolve in her eyes of just wanting to go back home already after her visit to her late daughter. It added a feeling to his insides. He sensed he missed her in a way that she was coming back home with him. It felt so natural, as if it had somehow taken place before this turn of events.

Somewhere.

Somehow.

"I am going to enjoy a hot shower. Maybe just a movie again when I come back down?" she asked, turning to watch him entering the doorway behind her.

"Sure," he said, looking distant yet content, the look confusing to her.

"Sure? Am I getting boring for you? Graveyard then couch again already…I'd understand." He failed at a smirk his way, it being clear in her eyes that her troubled thoughts were still lingering.

"Well, we could do other things."

"Like what?" He saw him turn his back slightly to her as he hung their coats up. Some of his back-burner thoughts came through at that moment despite his efforts to hide them. He sensed her not knowing how to react—feeling her get nervous next to him.

"I am happy just holding you, Claura."

"Why does it scare me more with you?"

"Because it will be more real with me." He eyed her as he finished taking his shoes off, standing close to her now, making her have to look up to read his eyes. "I do not need a heat cycle. I do not need any spells or magic. It will simply be more real with me. That is what scares you. You were drawn to the others due to something else playing at hand. With me, that won't be so."

"I should want that."

"Should?" He took one step closer, making her have to lift her eyes more to keep looking up at him.

"No…I meant…" She looked annoyed with herself now.

"What did you mean?" He stepped even closer to her, his face full of concern, of wanting an answer.

"I need time to wrap my head around this." Her tone was impatient, agitated, and worried.

"Around what, exactly?"

"Everything! Everything that keeps changing so fast, Roman!"

"Like I said before, take a damn break from overthinking so much. That is what you are here for. That is why you are here, with me, right now."

"Originally here with you for a break, not here with you to be with you. I am so confused. I cannot make the same mistakes with you. It is different with you, and I cannot understand why!"

"Damn right, it is. I am not selfish. I am not fake. I love you, Claura. I have for some time, and it has been damn hard watching circumstances keep taking you further and further away from even getting to spend some damn time with you. And I love you the way a damn man should, without magic."

"I do not know what the right way is, magic or not. Every time I fall in love, it's only inevitable that I fall back out! I am scared to fall for you because I am more scared to fall out of love with you, Roman. What if another bullshit situation takes even you from me after everything still!"

"You do not know real love. Not yet. Because I am going to take all the damn time I please with you in more ways than one. I am going to be the one to show you what you deserve." He saw her look sad and still confused, with happy tears behind her eyes all the same. "Stop. You worry needlessly with if you are good enough for me. I have already made that clear. Just you being here in my home fucking completes me." He watched her remain quiet, looking startled yet comforted at the same time, her eyes continually averting from his intense ones.

"I think I have loved you since the first time I met you that day in your office for my first appointment. Do you remember?"

"I know. And of course, I remember. I haven't been able to get you out of my head since."

They stared at each other for a moment, letting the silence of the house encompass them once again. His eyes watched her glance quickly over his upper body before back into his face. "Sweetheart, no." He saw the confusion in her eyes, seeing her fear of not being wanted by him even with what he was telling her. "Unlike them, I will always have control with you. Go do what you need to do. I'll wait down here." He glanced at her hips quickly as he walked past her to go back into his office. He was able to keep it in his mind, and his mind only now, exactly what he wanted to be doing with them underneath his hands—underneath him.

*****

Tronan and Aiyana decided to make a little visit themselves after seeing Maya. The look of loss, confusion, and heartache all over her mother's face as she went to see her about these shield spells made her realize that she would have to give her mother the pleasure of feeling like a mom with her finally for another day. It was clear that anything but pleasure was written across her face as they appeared outside, seeing her sitting alone on the outdoor porch.

"Mom?" She sounded concerned.

"Yes, dear." She took a deep inhale as if to center herself before looking into Aiyana's face—both of their faces. Despite not being around her much, Aiyana already knew there was something deeply wrong due to the lack of at least an attempted fake smile from her mother, as she so often did, no matter how dire the circumstances were.

"What is wrong?" She watched her turn away from her now, staring into the woods to her left, looking angry and lost.

She instantly knew this was serious, as her own mother cared not to even speak of her growing physical changes yet again. Aiyana had grown to be about seventeen years now in just the past couple of days, and for her to not say a single word about it, that alone was immensely surprising to Tronan and herself.

"It is between me and your father. Please do not intercede in this."

"Can I help at all?"

"I am afraid not." She watched Tronan step closer now. She was willing to make eye contact with him for a moment before looking away again. She heard the obvious question in his mind before it left his lips.

"Where is Roman?"

"Away."

"Away?"

"Yes! Away!" She looked like she wanted to cry.

"Have you two not spent enough time apart already due to me?" Aiyana said carefully, being taken aback by the look on her mother's face, expecting it to be appreciative of her trying to help, not the opposite. She was hiding something. "Mama, you look beyond distraught about something. Just talk to him. He is your Match. He will understand."

"So young you are. So much to learn still of things outside the books."

"Shall I visit him?" She chose to ignore her hurtful words.

"Them." She heard them question with a "huh" in sync before her. "Roman is with Claura. Has been for a few days now."

"And that is bad, why?" Aiyana asked.

"He cares not at all to speak with me anymore. Just as she cares not to speak with Daemon at all right now." She watched them both look at one another. Seeing it creep in, it was clear they had missed out on a lot happening while keeping to themselves in their own home.

"That can't be completely true. All issues can be fixed. Somehow," Aiyana pushed.

"That so? Kill Moira yet?" Maya said quickly, feeling Tronan's displeased reaction to her tone as if she was daring her own damn daughter to just go do it already. She watched him nudge Aiyana as if they needed to leave and just let her mother be right now. It was obvious this conversation was only going to get more sour.

"I was simply giving Claura the chance to do it first, as she has a child in the mix."

"You are my child. You were in the mix. That counts for enough."

"What are you truly saying here, Mom?"

"That Claura wants nothing to do with this anymore, and her decision is rubbing off onto Roman."

"I am so goddamn confused," Tronan implied, rubbing his hand over his face, looking away from them both for a second. She sensed him reaching for Daemon in his mind, wanting answers, causing his frustration to increase with whatever private response he got.

"I need to speak with Dad anyway. We will go see them."

"You are wasting your time."

"How do you know? Have you even tried to go see him?"

"I just know."

"Your lack of answers is starting to push both of us away, dear Mother."

"I simply saw this day coming a long time ago, dear daughter."

"What does that mean?!"

"You will see. Soon enough."

"Wow. After so long of wanting to have conversations with my own mother, it turns out I kind of waited with high hopes for nothing, now, didn't I?"

"Tell him I already said—"

"Tell him yourself!" Aiyana snapped, turning to walk away from her now, her gait full of agitation.

She saw Tronan not give her another glance, still busy with whatever was happening in his mind with Daemon. She knew full well that Daemon and herself completely brought this upon themselves. She hated knowing she was too much of a coward, to be honest with Aiyana, fearing what the look on her face would be more than she realized now that the moment had come to tell her the truth of what she did.

# Chapter 35

# Reassuring Mission Complete

Claura could hear the commotion as soon as she opened the shower door, wondering how the hell she could not hear it sooner with her advanced witch hearing now. She wondered if Roman had done it on purpose, not to want her to worry and just enjoy herself and let him deal with whatever was happening downstairs. She felt her nose moving before even telling it to, instantly being able to tell who their latest visitors were by their scents. Tronan was an easy one for noneasy reasons. Aiyana's voice no longer sounded so young, yet she was surprised at herself for not really caring to see how different she looked anymore. She was truly so beyond done with a realm world full of magical bullshit and fake love bonds. They did not feel like real family to her. Roman did, and only Roman.

She took her time getting dressed the old-fashioned way, letting father and daughter have time to get it out of their system, hearing

Aiyana's own mother's name be brought up more than once during their arguing. One comment about Roman being a bad father for some reason made her skin burn, her head hot, and her temper rise despite her efforts to leave it between them. Roman had wanted nothing but to get to know her and help her and had already apologized, only for Aiyana to still look at him with hatred, which was a little too extreme for Claura's patience level anymore. She saw it in his memories on the boat, between their moments of perfect silence, sharing more between them of what happened while apart. Roman did not deserve this, and for Maya to act lately in a way that would even risk losing Roman, she could not help but think that this daughter of theirs was way too comfortable with putting the blame on the wrong parent here.

Something was missing.

Again.

And she was over it.

Now hearing both of them shout at Roman, two against one in his own home, her control left her with pleasure. Her nerves literally itched to defend him just like they had when she sent Tronan flying that day, and itched even more than when she had felt like she needed to defend Daemon a time or two. Roman was just more important and had been this entire damn time.

They all turned to see Claura turn the corner at the top of the stairs, eyeing them all back with a sense of abandonment, making it linger in the air instantly that she was never going to care to be a part of their world again, family or not, especially with what she just heard come out of Aiyana's mouth, making it clear the drama was always going to be present one way or another.

"What was that, Aiyana?" She looked at her with surprise and disappointment.

"He heard me," Aiyana said, a little too much confidence in her tone for Claura's liking.

"Oh yes, as did I," Claura said, reaching the bottom of the stairs, coming closer to her first with haste, her anger making Aiyana lift her hand while stepping back a little, more so to give her power access in stretching out from her palm than out of fear of Claura. Claura simply did a small gesture with her raised hand, making the power and purple lights in her palm turn to literally smoke, as if a candle had just been blown out. She watched her face turn into shock and wonder and a little bit of anger as she looked back to her cousin again, still coming toward her.

"What did you do?" Aiyana said, looking more than annoyed.

"With me, dear cousin, we do things the old-fashioned way." She stepped closer to her now to smack her a good one. "Shame, that new face is so pretty." She saw Roman step up to take care of Tronan's obvious response, shoving him back along the wall with his mind alone. "Stop making your own damn father, who loves you unconditionally, feel like shit for acting like any father would! Your issue is with Moira, not him, and it's time to wrap your pretty little head around that like an actual adult!"

"Fuck you! I can't believe you just hit me! And how the hell did you literally erase my powers!" She looked at her hand, trying again, nothing. "I need them to protect myself, Claura!"

"Use your head. That is how you protect yourself. You think you are safe now, with your powers and being protected by him and his brother, hmm?" She gestured toward Tronan with a raw annoyance. "Tronan is a dangerous man. Your love for him will not change that. And his brother is even more so."

"How are you two doing this? Roman is the least powerful of us all." Aiyana turned between her father and Tronan, shock and question in her eyes. "Dad!"

"It's new. And hopefully…permanent," Claura stated with impatience while eyeing the two love birds closely. She saw the confusion and worry in their expressions.

"Claura, please. We want to help. What is going on here?" Tronan asked gently, trying to calm everyone down. Grateful, his words, along with his tone, made Roman let him have use of his body again. He slowly eased away from the wall to stand beside Aiyana again, feeling concerned for her even more so now with this new information.

"Aren't you two supposed to be on some honeymoon? This doesn't even concern you both!" Claura snapped, looking at her cousin as if the more annoyed she looked the more it just fed her own annoyance in the matter.

"My mother is acting suicidal!" Aiyana shouted.

"I know the feeling!"

Claura stepped closer again, making Tronan look to Roman with help, already accepting of the changed circumstances here with their increased abilities for whatever reason. She was clearly used to being the lesser, stronger one his whole life anyway, already from his not-chosen soldier brother.

"Please tell me what Daemon did, Claura. Please," Tronan asked. He saw just the mention of his brother's name bring pain and fury to her eyes. He did not miss at all the look of her no longer really needing him, and that really surprised him. This was truly a turn of events he did not see coming between Daemon and Claura, for they had been Matches lifetimes over, and no matter what happened between them, they never truly separated—not until she was to be reincarnated again to keep breathing and to keep even existing.

"He fucked my mom. Kept it from me instead of just being honest for whatever reason. Thought it was okay to use my powers to end her so I'd never find out. And he is from a realm where it's normal for him when I am not around and reincarnated again yet to act like a wifebeater with his ex, who, by the way, steals and keeps your memories from you. Not to mention, she is still absolutely in love with him. Just the look on her face alone proved it. He chooses what he wants me to remember every time I am reborn. The trust is gone, and it's not coming back."

There was silence from everyone other than the sound of Claura shifting in stressed-out circles, hands on hips, before heading into the kitchen to open the fridge. Roman knew full well she deserved to get drunk if she damn well pleased. He was planning on it anyway to happen at least once after everything.

"Okay, well…and my parents here?" Aiyana swiped her hand out as if to say "WTF."

"She will not stop keeping things from me. I fear our bond is not pure, just like Tronan and Claura's was. After all this time, after having you, going through everything with you…it has separated us somehow for good, apparently."

"Will you not try?" She looked up at her father with sorrow.

"I have. It does not matter how much you love someone, Aiyana, when the trust isn't there…nothing else really is. Nothing that matters. Please believe me."

"I do. There is something she will not tell me as well."

"So you know my frustration."

"So how does that boil down to you both being here together?" Tronan stepped forward now, still keeping a distance to make it clear it would be useless to him to give Roman a reason to slam him back up against the wall, hearing Claura come back into the room in a hurry behind them, sitting down on the sofa—Roman on her left, lovebirds to her right, Grey Goose and its lovely thud upon the table in the middle before her.

"Alcoholic now?" Aiyana sounded unafraid to test sarcasm so soon again.

"Only when you're around." Claura eyed her before pouring one. "Dear cousin, would you like some? Hmmm?" She looked at Tronan as he scoffed, smirking. "What?"

"She cannot handle it," he answered, wrapping his arm around her waist, looking at her like he loved her for such a silly fault alone. *My champagne girl.* She winked at her as he spoke it to her in her mind, finding her returning glare amusing before she looked at Claura again.

"Why is that bad? That shit is awful."

"Well, now I know what to shove down your throat next time you bring too much attitude into our home." She smiled while gesturing "cheers" before swallowing. She saw Tronan's surprised look as he faced Roman, followed by him trying to hide it. She saw it still needed to sink in for Aiyana. The "our" gave it completely away.

"I hope you both know what you are doing," Tronan said. "For if your powers fade"—looking to Claura and then back to Roman more intently—"I am sorry to say I cannot help you."

"I look forward to his blood a second time," Roman said casually.

He saw Tronan's expression of shock, letting him have a few bits of what happened through their mind link alone. He watched him need to take a moment to absorb what this could mean for his own brother and what this was truly doing to him.

"You truly do not know how this came about, how you both are stronger than all of us now, even my brother?" Tronan finally asked after a long pause between all of them.

"No clue," Roman answered him.

"Sorry, little cousin. Seems like you're not the most powerful witch anymore," Claura said, winking at her, pouring another swig.

"Well, I'll follow in my mommy's footsteps here and throw this one out there…Moira dead yet?" She crossed her arms, leaning on one hip, staring at Claura on the sofa below her.

"She hardly makes herself known, and look at you!" She lifted her hand as if to clarify her sexy little curves before them all now. "She clearly does not care to keep you cursed anymore." Her tone and gestures made it obvious two good swigs were enough to get her own party started before them. "So I am going to put Conroy first—"

"We are," Roman corrected her.

"*We* are…going to go chat with him first. Tomorrow?" She looked at Roman with amusement behind her question.

"Depends on how hungover you are now, sweetheart." He smiled, knowing he was already in for some trouble and in dire need of more control for tonight.

"We will go." Tronan gestured for Aiyana and him to leave, pulling her closer.

"Just one, cuz?" She shook her glass at her, wanting to see the torture on her face.

"Save me the bottle. So next time I visit, I can smash it over your head."

"Or save it for Mommy, who is clearly keeping something from the both of you." Her semi-drunk and fully self-amused tone clearly meant to try to trigger something.

"Okay, let's go."

Tronan forced her feet to move a little faster. He sensed his little firecracker getting ready to be lit, feeling her turn to face Roman at the last second before they faded back into their own home way over in Romania. He was kind of nice knowing she was on the same planet, at least of all the realms, of all the places Tronan could take her, as Roman's face showed he was pleased about that small fact in particular despite his differences with his own daughter right now.

"Dad?" She watched him look from Claura to her, standing as still as stone across the room, arms crossed over his chest as he remained deep in thought about something as usual. His eyes alone told her to just go ahead. "Forgive me?" She watched him just read her face for a long time, unblinking. He looked lethal in his own fatherly and supernatural way.

"We'll see." A smile barely reached his eyes. As much as he loved her, her young, obnoxious enthusiasm to make sure her own point was beyond heard in someone else's home he was not too impressed with. He watched them fade a moment later, feeling their energy fully gone not long after, watching Claura pour yet another one already.

"I visited my dead daughter's grave today. This has nothing to do with them, any of them. This"—raising her glass slightly toward him—"is for Dayla darling."

"Dayla darling?" He smiled. "Yes, that would have caught on fast with her, wouldn't it?" He watched her pour more, her eyes already looking doozy. "At this rate, you will be puking within the hour." He reached to help her not fill her glass so much, easily getting the bottle from her grasp. He saw her sigh with displeasure but letting him have his way as he returned it to the fridge for her.

"I saw it in your mind, Roman, that you were okay with me getting drunk just once."

"Just slow down. I am not taking your happy hour away from you."

"Happy hour…yes…" She smiled, looking slightly dizzy already.

"What about it?"

"When you came to Romania to see me, seeing you in that bar, it was right after I heard Moira speak to me for the very first time in my head. Know what she said to me?"

"Do tell."

"She asked me if I wanted to know who my real Match is in all of this."

"And you took her seriously?"

"Never. Her voice irritates me too much."

"Can relate."

"Are you sure, dear Roman, you want to be with someone who is the literal daughter of someone like her? I must remind you of her in certain ways."

"Why do you keep doing this?"

"Because I need to feel close to you, and being constantly reassured by you does that for me. Since you have yet to want to be closer to me in other ways, ya know…like put your hands on me. Really on me." She stood now to walk toward the kitchen after him, almost falling over, feeling him suddenly appear to steady her. "Ahh, now that's better." She smiled up at his face, looking completely fine with him, and him only, being this close to her.

"It does not matter to me at all who your parents are. Understand?"

"Who are your parents? Hmm?" She saw him get slightly agitated. "And that day, in the car, you still have not answered me."

"About what?"

"How old you really are."

"Does it matter?"

"Yes."

"Why?"

"It just does." She saw him pause, up nice and close, still holding her upright. She took advantage of the moment, looking over his face and his ridiculously handsome features. The man was a walking model with light brown eyes and dark brown hair, his features a cross between Italian and German. "But it's okay, you don't have to tell me, as I think Daemon lied about my age anyway. I don't know how I know. I just do. So...you see, I can't give you an answer back anyway."

"I do not care to discuss a past that will not serve us now. It is meaningless. Clinging to the past has brought nothing but trouble, trauma, and heartache. I only want to move forward, Claura. And I only care to do it with you."

"Your answers are always so damn good. You know that?"

"So reassuring mission complete, again?"

"For now."

"Good."

"Guess what?" She leaned in closer to his face.

"Hmm?" His hands had to squeeze tighter to balance her as she shifted in his arms. He watched her tap her temple with amusement in her eyes.

"To reassure you, my latest love...my little witch block is up."

"From everyone but me, I hope." He watched her nod, already looking tired, hearing her belly grumble. "Chinese? Great place down the street that delivers."

"Perfect." She felt him lift her up completely with just one arm, placing her back onto the couch to get comfy, taking a moment to kneel down before her between her knees. He held her head with his hands, fingers splayed gently through her hair, pulling her face close to his. He watched her smile at his need to pause. It was obvious she was not going to tell him no, especially with his handsome face so close to hers.

"I am only going to do this because I know I will be able to stop."

"Oh, how reassuring." She tried to sound funny through her already husky voice. She watched him shake his head no that, that was clearly not what he meant. He pulled her lips to his, creating the most gentle and sentimental contact between them. It literally made her forget to take a breath in the middle of the moment that he gladly let drag on. No one had ever been this gentle with her—ever. She had no idea the softest of kisses could still be so damn thorough.

"Please keep going." She felt him start to pull away and hated it.

"No."

"Roman, really! My lady parts are literally already vibrating." She took in one deep inhale of agitation as if she was annoyed with her body, not meaning to be funny at all.

"The answer, sweetheart, is no." He watched her lower her face, her hair falling around it enough to hide her expression, next to her getting up to move away from him and wobbly walk into the kitchen. Grey Goose on her brain. Permission was not needed. He followed her to lean his hip against the counter, taking the bottle from her. He saw her start to mouth a protest before realizing he was simply pouring it for her. He saw her look of "sorry" and then "thank you" across her face, unrealizing what biting the tip of her finger did to him as she watched it pour. Her face was all relaxed, and her eyes were slightly glossy, making her look sexy and seductive without even trying.

"Why not, Roman?" she asked in a low voice, sounding sad about it really.

"I will have you when you are not inebriated."

"How long are you planning…"

"I am not worried about it."

"I am." *Because this may be my last lifetime, I don't want to waste it, not with someone like you before me, right now, willing to share it.*

"Then stop," he said gently. "There are a million ways to love you and reassure you without needing to jump right to that."

"Last thing we are is jumping here, and you know it. We've known one another for quite some time now, despite finally actually spending time together."

"My dear, please stop pushing this. I get you are used to men who hardly show you other forms of love first, but I am different. I am willing to do better. In the long run, is that not what you want?"

"My last life may not be that long…how much of a long run will we even have together is what is scaring me. Meanwhile, you get to keep living as you are, for much longer, and it'll be without me."

"All the more reason to not rush anything to only risk ruining it. I have done so before and regretted it. It took something away from me that I will not have taken away from me when it comes to you."

"What are you saying?"

"You don't get the beginning back with someone, Claura. Forgive me for just not wanting to truly fuck it up with you, and only you in particular."

"Who are you referring to, Maya? Another?"

"Definitely Maya. Another reason I am actually glad it is over. The more I look back on everything, the more I see red flags right from the start."

"Such as?"

"I do not want to talk about her. Not this. Not right now. I want to enjoy my evening with you. Your presence alone is enough to bring me peace and help me feel like myself again, which is something I had not realized was fading with her until you came here with me. I am tired of feeling blind to so many things just by being with her. To be honest, other than our physical chemistry, it is starting to feel like a game."

"I can relate."

He gestured for her to go into his office. "Menu is already on an open tab on my computer. Can order as much as you want. I prefer having enough for leftovers." He handed her glass to her. He kept a close eye on her as she walked around the corner of the island, glancing at it slightly. He watched her pause and glare at it, yet with a small amount of fear on her face. "What is it?"

"If I hadn't slipped that night in your home, almost hitting my head on the corner of the island back in Romania, Tronan may not have shown himself before you arrived. And maybe none of this would have ever happened."

"I fear it still would have somehow." He saw her anger about it on her face, and she clearly agreed with him. "Claura, look at me." He pulled her back close to him. "It is all over. You accomplished so much. You need to be proud of yourself, not look back on all of it with regret. You broke the curse upon my daughter and that library realm you created alone."

"I do not miss it. And I should. Allie alone deserved a goodbye from me. I wonder if, in past lives, I got sick of everything as quickly as I did this time. I really just still want to remember more about me than anything. I must have left more information for just me to find somewhere."

"You already know enough about yourself. I already know enough about you to last me lifetimes over. Lifetimes where I would never keep things from you." He held her face between his hands again. "So stop," he whispered so close to her lips.

"I am sorry. There is just so much that keeps popping into my head still. I want it to stop, I really do."

"Then grab your drink, go order some food for us...as I like everything on the menu, and come curl up with me. Undisturbed this time. Okay?"

"Okay."

"And one more thing that I never thought I would say."

"What's that?"

"Thank you for smacking my daughter." He loved the sound of her instant laugh and the way her head fell back while she did so. From her buzz or not, the sight made his eyes finally light up the same way in return. It made him realize that he never actually heard her truly laugh before now. He was already inwardly determined to make it happen more often. "You are so beautiful, Claura." He pulled her close for a soft kiss again as her laughing started to subside, feeling her go from giggles to moans against his mouth, feeling it make something within him rise to the surface. His hands were already reaching down to cradle her ass to pick her up and set her on the center of the large island before him. Her eyes looked surprised, yet her hands were not shy to take advantage of the opportunity. Roman loved the feeling of her inner thighs tight against his sides as if needing him to stay in place and just keep doing what he was doing. Feeling her hands pulling him closer, her mouth got slightly more aggressive, her sounds getting harder to resist by the second. He leaned toward her while cradling the back of her head with one hand, forcing her to lay back on the marble underneath him. His other hand felt wherever he pleased, retracing this moment in his mind more times than he could count. He lifted her shirt, trying to have some discipline not to just rip it off, feeling her soft skin under his palm. He loved the sight of her lifting her sexy midriff toward him, clearly wanting him to just keep going.

"You will let me know if my strength..."

"Not worried about it," she said quickly, sounding almost agitated over it before forcing his mouth back to hers.

"I am serious, Claura. I'd rather not have you at all than do what they did. They have had time to learn their strengths and limits yet still fail. I have not."

"I will simply let you know, Roman. Stop worrying, just like you keep telling me to do."

"This is different, and you know it."

"Agree. You are stronger." She felt his hands slow down, not liking it one bit. "Just like I am."

"I do not want you to have to use your powers to handle being with me for any reason."

"I will tell you. Please." Her voice begged him to just keep going.

"I do not think you will," he said, sounding stern while his eyes proved he hated having to say it, looking worried as he searched her face. He watched her looking hurt now and hating it. "And you should not have to."

"And you are not willing to try, at least?" She watched the frustration and resolve on his face be her answer. She lets her head fall back, closing her eyes, swearing to herself. "Your level of control is ridiculous." He covered her face with her forearm, taking in a few deep breaths to calm herself. She felt him lift her shirt with both hands to place a kiss atop her middle, right above her belly button, loving the feeling of his strong hands on her sides as he did it. The way he held her was so purely Roman, and she loved every second of it, every little movement he did. "I don't have it in me much longer...even if you do. You treat me like you will always be there for me. Well, right now, I need this. A woman has needs too, you know. And I think since realizing I am an actual witch, it has somehow made it stronger, for whatever damn reason."

"You think I don't? I have thought about this for so goddamn long."

"Then why…" She suddenly felt his mouth go lower, her pants ripped from her body, her shirt disappearing next with his mind alone, to be left in her bra and little lace undies atop the counter before him. She felt him shift his body to move lower, only to come closer again to place his arms underneath her to lift her ass back up a little more on the surface before returning to his original position.

"My level of control is not ridiculous, but your climax is about to be." It tested her reaction to a soft suck over her pink lace, enjoying how easily she slightly jumped under his touch more than expected. "Relax for me, sweetheart." She sensed him looking at her face for a moment while he went back to just his hands exploring more. Claura just enjoyed the sensations of being before him like this finally, hearing him unable to hold in a low manly growl from his throat as his eyes took in the sight before him. He saw her hips slightly writhing already, and he had hardly even touched her yet. He watched her lean up just enough to unclasp her bra in a hurry and toss it aside before lying back down, in clear waiting for whatever he wanted to do with her. She felt his hands get slightly more intense now, knowing if he got rough, it would bring back memories yet also knowing Roman would stop for her. He was able to be in control. That helped her relax more than he knew, even if she wasn't showing it physically.

"I am. Trust me." She felt his arms cradle her hips, his fingers reaching slightly under her lower back, perfectly holding her in place for what she was anticipating more than she realized now that the moment was here. His mouth was so warm, his tongue so gentle, his movements so in sync with her rising waves. She was almost embarrassed by how easily she was starting to feel it so soon. She felt him laugh in her mind about worrying about him making her cum only once. It brought her relief yet nervous with anticipation.

"Apparently, I am more sensitive in this lifetime," she admitted, feeling his mouth get more aggressive as if to intentionally stop her from thinking and just start enjoying. His hands slightly moved her hips with the rhythm of his mouth, doing it in such a way that it was making her rising waves linger and linger, building ever slower and slower. The man knew what he was damn doing, literally forcing her own climax to not just build but build at whatever pace he pleased. "Oh my god...how the fuck are you doing that!"

She took a moment to lift her gaze. The sight of him pleasing her body below made it all even more intense. She suddenly felt it build to a point where her legs were starting to shake, coming so close to a climax, only for him to move slightly off her clitoris and give nearby areas attention.

"Roman!"

"I already said I'd take my time with you how I damn please." He stood up slightly to be able to reach his hands higher on her body again, playing with her soft skin, wrapping her up into his arms to pull her closer. "And I meant it, beautiful."

He forced her mouth to his yet again. He felt her body quiver beneath him, just needing release already. He heard her softly begging for him to just keep going. He looked into her eyes, meaning to make this a moment he would have for forever. He held her semi-upright with his arm, hand clasped in her hair, forcing her to keep looking into his face while his other hand slid lower. He felt her do that jump again as his fingers slid inside while his thumb worked her clit. He felt the pulsing from her muscles slowly increase, letting it build, watching her face closely, knowing precisely the exact moment when she would start to really climax. She felt him move his hand away while his other one lowered her back down onto her back. He saw her expression of frustration mixed with passion, looking at him like she had truly given up on something, and everything was completely in his control now, whether he remained in literal control or not. He lowered his upper body between her thighs again and placed his arms and hands to cradle her hips while his mouth went back to making what was still a building orgasm for her finally boil over. Her cries, literal cries, at finally being able to really climax, had him reaching for control he never had to fight for before. Roman had every good intention of giving her a release and not taking it further, not tonight, not yet. But the sight of her right now in his grasp, laying like this before him—damn him.

He kept his mouth on her until the waves were long over, lingering with pleasure before slowly working his way back up her body. "OMG...I can't breathe. I can't open my eyes."

He saw her try to smile. Her breathing was still labored. She wrapped her arms around his head and neck, feeling her shaking thighs try to squeeze his sides as he leaned over her. She felt him kiss her neck, pulling her closer to him, his arms wrapped around her smaller body, forcing her backside off the counter.

"Climax whisperer?" she said it close to his ear, unable to even get the words out loud just yet. She felt his body shake lightly as he laughed, his face still enveloped in the crook of her neck, inhaling her scent. The sound of his warm laughter was so close that it was warming her insides. "I have truly never felt anyone do that." She felt him take in one more deep inhale close to her skin before moving his head above her again to look down into her eyes.

"Heat cycles do not guarantee skills."

"Roman, you just gave me the best climax of my...lifetime." She saw him smile in return at her wording.

"We shall have to make up for all the ones I have missed then."

"How do we know you missed them?"

"Good Lord, please don't tell me this situation is something that repeats itself. I am not sure I could handle that."

"I feel like you'd be worth it."

"I would not want that for you."

"Know why it's been you all along...really?"

"Hmm?"

"If it's what's best for me, you are willing to give me up."

"Last thing I will be with you is selfish."

"I know. This whole time I was with them, you remained still, waiting for me to come to you on my own. Not any other way."

"I will have you no other way."

"Please don't let me get sucked back into that world. Please."

"Well, if it happens, we go together."

"Let's finally go see Conroy together tomorrow. I have no doubt you can for sure realm jump us there now with your increased powers."

# THE WINGED WITCH OF MATCHES

"I do not want you to get your hopes up. We do not know what he is like, what he knows, how he can help. Please don't put too much faith in this person, okay? Whatever happens, we can remain here. That is good enough for me."

"Do you even want to go still?"

"Yes."

"Why?"

"I do not know. It just feels like we should. And just us two, for whatever reason."

"Okay."

"Okay." He was still atop her, loving the feeling of her this close in his arms. She took a moment to just look at her, feeling her small, slim fingers caress through his hair. She read her eyes, gently kissing her lips, admiring the relaxed and sated look on her face. She saw it in her eyes that she wanted to return the favor. "In due time, my love. Because"—glancing at his office computer—"I am ready to curl up with you, have some food, and just be."

She watched her gently nod. Her eyes said so much as his hands explored for a few more moments before lifting her to carry her to his office chair himself. He sat down with her placed on top of his lap, watching her enjoying adding items to their order, leaning back and relaxing behind her. He enjoyed the feel and sight of her sexy little bottom on his lap. He slightly smirked at her food choices.

"What?"

"Oh, nothing." He sounded beyond relaxed, leaning back into his chair behind her a little more.

"Do you want something else other than..." She watched him casually shake his head no.

"You just added my three favorite things first."

"Hmm...well, you have good taste then."

"As do you." His deep tone suggested recent moments, making her blush appear instantly in the light from the screen. Hearing her clear her throat.

"Shall I add dessert, or is that going to just be me again?" She turned to wink at him quickly, choosing to ignore her own blush still across her cheeks as she took in his expression and returned her eyes to the screen.

"We'll see." His one hand squeezed her hip. He watched her make her last click on the mouse with enthusiasm, as if she was still just enjoying being back to doing normal human things, whether small or not, whether a real witch or not.

"Be here in thirty minutes." She turned to eye him. "Dessert first?" She was half-smiling and half-serious. "Not going to lie, Roman. That felt pretty amazing." Her tone sounded nervous yet more than ready at the same time.

"I know what you are doing," he said softly, eyeing her closely. He looked at her like she was the only real peace he had known for a long time now—a very long time.

"Oh ya?" She watched him gently nod as he leaned forward to gently grasp her sides more, turning her whole frame to face him. He placed her legs over the sides of the chair, enjoying the sight of her straddling him with her thighs out to the side, admiring how perfect her curves were from any angle.

"Can you really blame me?" she said it low, loving his look of complete longing and satisfaction as his eyes followed where his hands explored.

"No." He was still focused on feeling her body, her curves, her soft skin before him. He was taking his sweet time. His tone was full of intention, understanding, and acceptance, all bundled into that one little word. He looked completely confident in himself other than not knowing where to begin with her, so many possibilities all leading to her perfectly climaxing before him again. He wanted it to be truly underneath him this time, yet knowing he meant to keep his word.

"You will make me beg, won't you?" He looked down at him, sounding annoyed slightly, seeing his eyes jump to her with a sliver of concern atop the already lingering passion.

"No. Not exactly."

"Your short answers are making you sound like her. I need more from you, Roman, and it's not my fault. I just do. You are not the only one who is different here." She watched him get more focused on her words as he looked into her eyes, slowly leaning forward to wrap his arms around her, squeezing her ribs and back with obvious entitlement.

"Promise me something, sweetheart." He saw her lean her head to the side slightly as if to say, "What?" Her eyes looked sorry yet not sorry. "In *our* home, never bring her into our conversations again. Understand?"

"Just being honest."

"And I love that. Just like I love you." He forced her lips close to his. "Not her. You." His grip got slightly stronger. "Now lean back onto my damn desk, make your fine ass comfortable, as I prefer my dessert first. Always." It sank in for Claura how he needed only ten minutes tops last time to do what he did, the anxiousness building at what he was about to do with thirty.

Use the link in front of book or scan the given QR code for the entire series, as well as other titles. Available on Amazon.

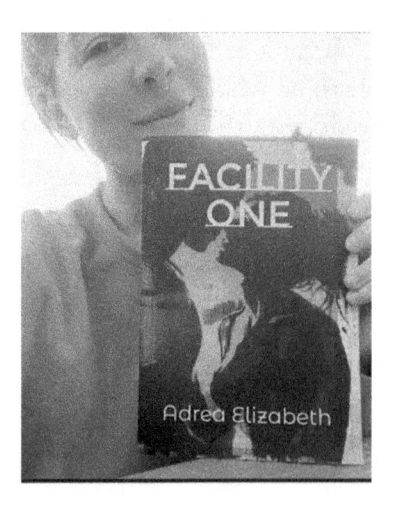

The author

Instagram
@simply_adrea

# About the Author

Adrea Elizabeth is not an author who started writing on a whim. Her reasoning behind it is a personal one. She was suffering from severe postpartum depression. She was pretty far from okay, and to put it quite simply, she was thinking of ending her life. She already suffered from depression and bipolar. She had dealt with severe suicidal mood swings at least twice a year since she was a very young teen, and the only way to truly get through it was to sleep it off—to shut out the world, get away from people and stimuli, and just sleep. But once she became a mama, that was not an option anymore. She could no longer just enjoy a dark room until she felt okay again. And she got really scared, terrified even, because postpartum wasn't going to be just a day or two deal like depression was.

She knew that this was going to stick with her for *months*. So she thought about it, she prayed, and she came up with the idea to try to write a book. She needed something that was going to keep her mind busy, to pull her away from what postpartum was putting in her head, something that was going to keep her busy for a long time.

So she decided, why not try to write a book? So she did. The intention was two hundred pages, just to see if she could do it, with zero intention to show anyone or publish it—just something for her, in the privacy of her own home, to keep her busy, to help her feel just "okay." And it worked. Before she knew it, two hundred pages were five hundred, then parts 2 and 3, and so on. She wrote this entire series in about ten months, and every day that she typed away, she felt better. And now she more than feels better. She feels proud—truly proud of all her books. And because of that, she is happy to share them with others now. She dedicates her series to all the mamas out there who may be suffering from postpartum depression and to know that they have it in them to do exactly what she did, which is to find their own way to tell "postpartum" to go fuck itself.